Praise for

MADWOMAN
UPSTAIRS

"For those who like their Brontë with a side of wry, turn to the hilarious *The Madwoman Upstairs*. . . . Sam's self-conscious quips are LOL hilarious and do Ms. Brontë proud."

—*USA Today*

"[A] piquant paean to the Brontë sisters."

—*The New York Times Book Review*

"Part mystery, part picaresque, Catherine Lowell's *The Madwoman Upstairs* is a smartly conceived first novel."

—*Elle*

"An enigmatic father's legacy sets the scene for gothic intrigue involving the last descendant of the Brontë sisters in Catherine Lowell's irresistibly clever Oxford debut, *The Madwoman Upstairs*."

—*Vogue*

"A smart, clever, and properly gothic novel. . . . Deftly, Lowell combines a rollicking treasure hunt with a wickedly dark story."

—*Star-Tribune* (Minneapolis)

"An entertaining and ultimately sweet story."

—*Kirkus Reviews*

"Lowell has hit it out of the ballpark with this novel."

—*RT Book Reviews*

"An enjoyable academic romp that successfully combines romance and intrigue."

—*Publishers Weekly*

"An engaging literary mystery filled with juicy speculation about the life of the Brontës—a delightful reminder that how we read fiction matters."

—*Stanford Magazine*

"Lowell crafts a first novel that is as enthralling as it is heartbreaking. Brontë aficionados and fans of Sloane Crosley's *The Clasp* will love this title."

—*Library Journal* (starred review)

"A thriller tailor-made for English majors. . . . Lowell is an intelligent writer who bears watching."

—*Booklist*

"Catherine Lowell's terrific first novel is a mystery, a love story, and a very dark comedy with the Brontës, of all people, playing a role back there in the shadows. The book is about the traces that literature and our ancestors leave in us, and it is about memory as a token of love."

—Charles Baxter, author of *There's Something I Want You to Do* and *The Feast of Love*

"*The Madwoman Upstairs* had me hooked well into the wee hours; this book is absolutely addictive. Set in the most romantic parts of Britain, the story takes us on a clever present-day romp through the literary universe of the enigmatic Brontës and drills deeply into all their dangerous secrets. Catherine Lowell has such a unique, inspired turn of phrase that you'll find yourself laughing out loud even as she lures you deeper and deeper into this delicious mystery that is destined to become the page-turner of the year."

—Anne Fortier, author of *Juliet*

"Catherine Lowell's debut is a smart and funny literary mystery set among the dreaming spires of Oxford University. Lowell's deft handling of her quirky characters and unpredictable plot twists make *The Madwoman Upstairs* a charming and memorable read."

—Deborah Harkness, author of *A Discovery of Witches*

"Smart and surprising and fiercely funny. Catherine Lowell is a thrillingly original talent."

—Jennifer duBois, author of *Cartwheel*

THE MADWOMAN UPSTAIRS

A NOVEL

CATHERINE LOWELL

TOUCHSTONE

NEW YORK   LONDON   TORONTO   SYDNEY   NEW DELHI

Touchstone
An Imprint of Simon & Schuster, Inc.
1230 Avenue of the Americas
New York, NY 10020

First Touchstone trade paperback edition November 2016

TOUCHSTONE and colophon are registered trademarks of Simon & Schuster, Inc.

For information about special discounts for bulk purchases,
please contact Simon & Schuster Special Sales at 1-866-506-1949
or business@simonandschuster.com.

The Simon & Schuster Speakers Bureau can bring authors to your live event.
For more information or to book an event contact the Simon & Schuster Speakers Bureau
at 1-866-248-3049 or visit our website at www.simonspeakers.com.

Interior design by Maura Fadden Rosenthal

Manufactured in the United States of America

1   3   5   7   9   10   8   6   4   2

The Library of Congress has cataloged the hardcover edition as follows:

Lowell, Catherine, 1989–
The madwoman upstairs : a novel / Catherine Lowell.
pages cm.
1. Brontë family—Fiction. 2. Family secrets—Fiction. I. Title.
PS3612.O887M34 2016
813'.6—dc23
2015026688

ISBN 978-1-5011-2421-1
ISBN 978-1-5011-2630-7 (pbk)
ISBN 978-1-5011-2422-8 (ebook)

To my beautiful parents

THE MADWOMAN UPSTAIRS

CHAPTER 1

The night I arrived at Oxford, I learned that my dorm room was built in 1361 and had originally been used to quarantine victims of the plague. The college porter seemed genuinely apologetic as he led me up the five flights of stairs to my tower. He was a nervous man—short and mouthy, with teeth like a nurse shark—who admitted through a brittle accent that Old College was over-enrolled this year, and that the deans had been forced to find space for students wherever they could. This tower was an annex to Old College. Many tragic and important people had lived here before me, apparently: had I heard of Timothy the Terrible? Sir Michael "the Madman" Morehouse? I shook my head and said that I was sorry—I was American.

The porter, Marvin, dropped my bags inside. The stairs had left him breathing heavily, and a thin line of sweat appeared in the crease on his forehead. He was not making direct eye contact with me, I noticed. I wasn't sure if this was due to sheepishness over the condition of my room or because he had nearly choked over my last name when I first introduced myself and hadn't quite recovered.

I made a quick inspection of the room. Whoever had quarantined the plague victims had done a thorough job. The walls were covered in peeling red paint that gave the chamber the look of a giant, bloodshot eye. In the corner was a boarded-up fireplace and a horrible painting of a woman, who, by the look of it, was halfway through drowning.

"Well, Miss Whipple," Marvin said with forced optimism. Fuzzy, uneven scruff covered the lower half of his face like a failing garden. "Will you be happy here?"

I didn't know what to say. This was not a dorm room; this was the sort of place people dumped you when they secretly thought you were insane.

"Very happy, thank you," I said. "That woman in the painting— who is she?"

He looked past me. "The Governess. Beautiful, isn't she?"

"May we get rid of her, please?"

Marvin's eyes widened as though I had suggested castration. "Pardon?"

"She reminds me of someone," I explained.

"Miss Whipple, she is part of the tour."

I said, "Ah," not understanding the reference, and we suffered a small moment of silence. I could tell he wanted to leave—his upper lip was twitching like a small, impatient alarm. I didn't blame him. I wanted to leave too. After one last look around, he reminded me about the meet-and-greet tea in the quad tomorrow, gave me a hasty good night, and closed the door.

With Marvin gone, I was alone with *The Governess*. Something, surely, was not quite right. From the two nights I had spent in college during interviews last December, I knew that everyone else's rooms would not reek of feet and damp meat. Some had windows. The room in which I had stayed even had friendly blue walls. So friendly, in fact, that during those two nights, my room was the watering hole for all the English literature candidates. We sat on my bed and looked at the pale blue walls and bonded over the fact that applying to Old College was one of the more miserable things we would ever have to do. I felt at home in that cozy blue room—at least, up until Shelly from Portsmouth asked me whether I was really a Whipple, and did that mean I had an automatic advantage over the rest of them?

My cheeks burned. Shelly from Portsmouth was a leggy red-head whose arms were covered with mysterious moles. At the time, I said, "Of course not." Insulted, I had also added a "Good night, I'm a little tired." But the next morning, I wondered if Shelly from Portsmouth hadn't been right. It was clear from the moment I walked into my interview that Dr. Margaret King from the Old College English department wanted nothing more than to interrogate me about my family. I was impressed that she managed to restrain herself for as long as she did. She was a pinched woman whose crooked flamingo legs ended in two pointy black shoes. There was a girlish smear of lip gloss on her lips and front tooth, and she smelled of artificial water-melon. Her interview questions had pertained to Aphra Behn, about whom I knew very little, but judging from the sort of novels scattered around the room—*Belinda, Love in Excess, Emma*—I assumed that she was a woman, a writer, and dead. I launched us into a discussion about proto-feminism and offered a borderline insightful comment about male hegemony, but it wasn't enough. The pointy shoes started to tap.

"And, of course," I said, "Behn's work paved the road for the Brontës."

It may not have been true, of course, but it didn't matter. The name Brontë was like a drumroll. The pointy shoes stopped tapping and one of the flamingo legs crossed over the other, freeing the right foot to wag.

She had found her excuse to launch a series of questions at me—all of which I had been asked before, all of which I knew how to answer well. *How did the lives of the Brontës affect the vitality of their writing? Yes, that's very true, Miss Whipple, interesting insight. How did Emily Brontë revolutionize the modern conception of the novel? Yes, that she did—right, right.* The interrogation began to acquire a more personal nature: *I gather you've read the press surrounding the Brontës, especially about their surviving family? Oh goodness, Tristan Whipple was your* father? *Well, I admit I did wonder whether he might be a relative. . . . If you don't mind my asking, were you two close? Ah, I see. A fascinating man, your father.*

Then, as it always happened, Dr. Margaret King became Maggie again, a schoolgirl ogling her literary heroes. The Brontës pulled their age-reversing magic trick and there she was, a wide-eyed teenager who wanted nothing more than to traipse over the brooding English moors like Catherine and Heathcliff. I nodded and smiled and prostituted my ancestors until, together, we'd exhausted every nuance of *Jane Eyre. But what does the wedding veil* mean*, Miss Whipple? Oh, goodness, how clever! Is that what your father thought too? Oh, I'm being so insensitive—forgive me, dear.*

I usually became a "darling" at this point in the conversation, but "dear" was okay too. Whenever I became a dear, I fell mute. A dear couldn't explain what she really thought about her relatives.

When King stood up at the end of the interview, I did too. Even in heels, she was several inches shorter than I was. She smiled, but timidly, like a brainy child who's forgotten how to make a friend.

"Well, Samantha," she finished brightly, "are all Americans this tall?"

"Just the tall ones," I said.

I headed for the door. She called after me, "May I ask—do you also write?"

I fumbled for an apology and told her that no, the talent in my family had unfortunately been squandered in the last century and a half. My father had been the exception, not the rule. She walked toward me, hard heels clanking on hard tiled floor. I thought she might like to say something else, but she just opened the door and tilted her head to the left, just like my mother used to do when I did something right. But it wasn't I who had impressed her. As my sneakers plodded back down the polished hallway, I once again tipped my hat to my three dead female ancestors. Even in the grave they managed to exert the power I could not.

The cell phone on my lap gave an aggressive buzz, alerting me to three new e-mails. Apparently, my tower had wireless internet, but no windows. The first message explained that the meet-and-greet tea party would begin at 10:30 a.m. in the quadrangle, and no one was to walk on the grass, if you please. The second e-mail provided me an excuse not to attend: my professor—a Dr. James Timothy Orville III—had arranged a preliminary meeting tomorrow morning to discuss the objectives and requirements of our tutorial and to supply me with a list of important deadlines, which I would be left to peruse at my own convenience. He signed his note *O*.

The last e-mail was from B. Howard from the trusts and estates division of the British National Bank. The blood drained from my face. B. Howard had already called once this evening, after I landed at Heathrow. Ours had been a brief conversation, in which she informed me that now that I was at Oxford it was time to discuss my late father's somewhat confusing will. *I know that this must be painful for you, Miss Whipple,* she told me over the phone, *and I gather you have only just arrived in England this evening—yes, Customs will be straight ahead, surely; just follow the signs—but as you know, this is a sensitive matter and now that you will be at Oxford it must be discussed in a timely fashion. Can you still hear me, Miss Whipple? Miss Whipple?*

At the time, I explained that I was in a terrible rush and that I would call her later. Really, I had just been sitting by the baggage claim carousel, chewing on a soggy British sandwich. The thought of discussing my father's will turned my heart inside out, in the way of all unhealed despair. I had a vague and unpleasant idea of what was in that will, and it was not something I wanted to discuss—not with Marvin, not with Maggie the Mortician, and not with B. Howard of the British National Bank.

I walked to my bed. Beneath my feet, the old floorboards creaked and cracked like old bones. On the rectangle of wall directly underneath *The Governess*, I noticed a series of scratches and carvings, etched deeply into the stone. There were gouges and stick figures and what appeared to be several Roman numerals. I was half expecting to find the name Byron, but the only legible letters were the initials *J.H.E.*

I took a seat. My gaze rested upon *The Governess.* For several moments, the woman in the painting and I stared at each other in unpleasant recognition. She was clutching something in her hand—a folder? A book? The Bible? Behind her was a half-submerged mast, on which sat a bird, dark and large, wings flecked with foam. In its beak was a gold bracelet. The bird was staring at the Governess, but the Governess was staring straight at me. She had bright eyes, thin features, and the expression of a caged animal. I remembered her well. I had read about her, once upon a time—or, at least, I had read about someone very much like her. *It is in vain to say human beings ought to be satisfied with tranquillity,* she once told me from within the pages of an old, terrible book. *They must have action, and if they cannot find it, they will make it.*

I couldn't look at her any longer. I switched off the lamp on the nightstand and fell into darkness.

Sunshine has a way of softening the recollection of the previous evening. But when I walked outside in the morning, the sun was nowhere to be found. The sky was a dull shade of concrete.

I had dressed in three layers of black for my first meeting with James Timothy Orville III. In his e-mail last night, he had introduced himself as a research fellow in nineteenth-century British literature. I sincerely hoped his interests extended to the twentieth century as well, because I had made clear in my personal statement that I had a well-developed vendetta against the Victorian era. If James Timothy Orville III turned out to be a George Eliot enthusiast, then I might have to quit here and now. There would be no switching professors and there would be no switching courses. Old College was unique (and famous) for its rigidity. Whereas other Oxford colleges offered classes and seminars in addition to tutorials, Old College students suffered one hour-long session each week, alone with a single tutor. The hope was that the intensity of the relationship would trump any diversity of instruction. What it really meant was that my entire education and mental health rested in the hands of one person.

I walked around the perimeter of campus, making sure to steer clear of the lawns. (I had once read that the last student who walked on the Old College lawn was chased off by a porter wielding a stick.) I found the exit gate, which, as Marvin had explained last night, was not the same as the entry gate, and please don't confuse the two. Several members of the college staff were transporting tablecloths inside the quadrangle. The meet-and-greet tea, I presumed. I was relieved that I didn't have to go. Orientations only highlighted my dissimilarity to other people my age. My father had homeschooled me for as long as he was alive, which meant that I had spent the first fifteen years of my life living in a pleasant anachronism. His idea of a Friday night was to fill up the paddling pool on the front lawn, stir up a margarita, and read me Shelley until it grew dark. He disliked Shelley—it was actually my mother's middle name—and Dad would read every verse with dripping sarcasm. *O! lift me as a wave, a leaf, a cloud! I fall upon the thorns of life! I BLEED!* It was the sort of joke only the two of us found funny. I couldn't remember why we needed the paddling pool.

Twenty-eight Broad Street, the meeting point suggested by James Timothy Orville III, turned out to be an underground pub. Near the entryway were two pots of skeletal flowers and a life-size statue of Hereward the Wake, who was holding his own head on a stake. I walked through the second set of doors and stumbled directly into the bar, which jutted out of the side of the room like a bad tooth.

There was a lone bartender, a wild-eyed redhead with lips the color of undercooked beef. She was drying dishes with a rag.

"Excuse me, is this The Three Little Pigs?" I asked.

She looked me over, unimpressed, and handed me a menu. The top read, *The Three Pigs' Heads*, and I congratulated myself on arriving twenty seconds early. I noted a number of boozing patrons: a squawking couple guzzling Irish coffee, a woman who appeared to be counting her teeth with her tongue, and a double-chinned man with a barking, pterodactyl laugh. I searched the room for the withering old man with a well-trimmed gray mustache and a suitably gold monocle who could possibly have the name James Timothy Orville III.

My eyes alighted on a figure in the far corner of the room. He was sitting down, with one hand resting on the table in front of him, one in his lap. At first, I thought he was one of Hereward the Wake's friends—stuffed, almost lifelike. But when I squinted and peered into his corner, I saw the slow rise and fall of his chest. I stared at him, and he stared at me, and as he stared at me his eyes narrowed, and as I stared at him I began to panic because it occurred to me that this non-old, non-gray, non-ugly man might be James Timothy Orville III.

There was a raucous burst of laughter from one of the nearby tables, where a woman with a big scream of a hat was pushing a Kleenex up her sleeve. My professor—God, was that really him?— watched as I crashed into a nearby table leg. He looked like a safari animal attempting to be incognito.

I stopped in front of him. There was a moment of silence. He had a noble, expansive forehead that made me want to write calligraphy on it. When I didn't move, he said:

"Well? Have a seat."

I dropped into a chair. He was young—couldn't have been over thirty—and seemed tightly bound in his clean, pressed suit.

He said: "I am James Orville."

I didn't have a chance to respond because a gray-haired waiter emerged from behind us and paused in front of me. He seemed to be waiting for me to order, so I said, "Just a steamed milk, please."

"A what?" he said. His eyes were vague and cloudy, and I had a feeling that the sixties may have been a blur for him.

"Steamed milk?" I repeated.

The waiter turned to my professor, whose gaze had not left mine. "Two fish and chips and a pint, Hugh," he said.

Hugh left and the two of us sat in silence. Orville stared at me, and for the first time, I realized how difficult it is to stare at two eyes at the same time. I wondered how I had ever done it before. He reached into his briefcase and pulled out a slender blue file that he dropped on the table without looking at. His expression was impassive. Somewhere, I just knew, he must have a slew of illegitimate children, all named Bartholomew.

"Well," he said, and he smiled—almost. "Tell me about yourself."

I gave a nervous laugh. "No, thank you."

"That wasn't a question."

"I'd rather not discuss me if that's okay," I said. "How are you?"

He blinked. I moved my left leg on top of my right, then back again. It seemed unfair that he should be so young, and that I should be even younger. He did not respond, and as a result, neither Orville nor I said anything for several moments.

"What would you like to know?" I asked, finally, even though I already knew. Orville, like Maggie the Mortician, would want to talk about my last name. He would want to discuss my father. He would want to discuss the fire, the estate, the legend. He would want to know what Emily Brontë ate for breakfast on the morning of December 5, what erotic poems Anne wrote in her spare time, what Charlotte secretly had tattooed on her bottom. It was my own personal curse, being related to the three most famous dead women in all of England.

I swallowed and said, at last, "I was born in Boston."

His expression didn't change. He had picked his acne as a kid; there was a small chain of scars above his right eye.

"I'm an only child," I continued.

Silence.

I took a breath. "I went to a small boarding school in Vermont, which you probably haven't heard of, because it really is very small, and I haven't been to Europe much, unless you count Paris, because that's where my ex-mother lives. Excuse me, ex-wife. I mean, my father's ex-wife. My mom. I don't get a chance to visit her much, because, like I said, I live in Vermont. I mean, Boston, but I said that already. I—"

"Miss Whipple," interrupted Orville.

"Yes."

"Can we get on with it?"

I said, "Pardon?"

"I am your tutor, not your therapist," he said, somewhat bored. "Please take care to remember that in the future."

I said, "Sorry."

"Never apologize."

"Sorry."

"Tell me about your *academic* self," he continued. "I would like to know what interests you, besides run-on sentences. Why did you come to Oxford?"

"Everyone's got to be somewhere."

"Is that supposed to be funny?"

"I don't know, was it?"

I gave an awkward laugh, which fell flat. I envied people who could talk to important people like normal humans. I had never been particularly smooth. Orville's face was expressionless in the pale light.

I said, "I came here to study English literature."

"And why was that?"

"I like books."

"You *like* books."

"I'm good at reading?"

"I did not ask whether you are literate. I asked why you are study-ing English literature. What do you imagine it will provide you?"

"Unemployment?"

"I beg your pardon?"

"Joke," I said. "Joke."

My cheeks were burning. Suddenly, he leaned forward across the table, resting his entire weight on his forearms. He looked like a sur-geon who, in the midst of a routine operation to find someone's soul, had discovered it just wasn't there.

He was frowning. "What is the *purpose* of literature to you?"

He might have been asking me if I believed in God.

"English is the study of what makes us human," I said. It was a phrase I had learned from standardized tests.

"Human biology is the study of what makes us human," he said. "Try again."

"English is the study of civilization."

"History is the study of civilization," he corrected.

"English is the study of art."

"Art is the study of art."

I let out a flush of air. "English tells us stories."

"If you can't think of anything intelligent to say, don't say anything at all."

I shut my mouth. Orville leaned back in his chair. The waiter named Hugh returned and dumped two plates in front of us. On each one was a fish that looked like it had died tragically by drown-ing in its own fat. The scent was something savage—salty and prehis-toric, wrought from an age in which people still ate each other. Hugh shoved a pint of ale on the table in a final act of punctuation.

Orville unfolded his napkin in his lap. He had a strong chin and thin lips that cut across it in a straight line. Right now, they were pursed to the point of invisibility. He did not seem like the sort of person who would frequent dimly lit pubs before noon. The entire place reeked of ale and centuries of smutty assignations.

"Perhaps we can try going about this a different way," he said. "What sort of authors do you admire?"

I said, "Name a few and I'll tell you if I like them."

He raised his eyebrows, and I wondered if I had been rude. He severed the head of his fish with one thwack of his fork.

"Milton," he said. "Do you like John Milton."

"No."

"Chaucer?"

"No."

"Thoreau?"

"Oh, please."

There was a bit of a pause. Orville seemed to be considering whether I was, in fact, a criminal. He took a small, well-proportioned bite.

"T. S. Eliot?" he said. "Jane Austen?"

"No, and no-but-nice-try."

"Coleridge, Keats, Wordsworth?"

"No, sort of, and no."

He paused. "Brontë?"

I paused. I had been right. Orville did, in fact, want to discuss my relatives. How could he not? We stared at each other in a moment of mutual understanding. He knew who I was; I knew that he knew; he knew that I knew that he knew.

I crossed my arms in a way that felt childish even to me. "That depends. Which Brontë?"

"Charlotte."

"Hah."

"Is that a no?"

I didn't respond. The name Brontë had, predictably, changed everything. He was still frowning, but it was now a curious frown. From across the room, the man with the pterodactyl laugh let rip another roar.

"Can you appreciate no authors?" Orville asked.

"I appreciate them," I said. "I just don't like them."

"Why?"

"Personal reasons."

"Which are?"

"I thought you weren't my therapist."

Orville placed his napkin back on the table. He almost smiled. Almost. The trajectory of the academic year was now spanning out in front of me, and it looked like one blackened stream of intellectual dictatorship. The more time Orville and I spent together, the more I would become one of those pale-faced vampire children in films who emerge only to say something unsettlingly prophetic in a half whisper.

"Won't you tell me a little about yourself now?" I asked.

He raised an eyebrow again. I half hoped he would say nothing, or snap at me. But to my surprise, he became quite friendly.

"What would you like to know?" he said. "I was born in London to two academics, matriculated at Cambridge when I was fifteen, graduated when I was eighteen, earned a graduate degree in the States, and for the past eight years have been a fellow at Old College, where my research focuses on the structural and grammatical integrity of texts, and contends that a perfect novel is proof of authorial invisibility."

I said, "That sounds riveting."

"I dislike still water and raw fish, never exercise except in the early morning, and find *A Separate Peace* to be one of the most singularly moving works of the twentieth century."

I nodded. I had a feeling that he had given this autobiography many times before, and to many students. I wondered how many he had taught, exactly, and how many of them had at some point been undone by his hellish beauty.

"You attended Cambridge at fifteen?" I clarified.

"Yes."

"What—you couldn't get in any earlier?"

He took another bite of fish. "Why don't you tell me what you hope to study this year."

I answered, "Postmodernism."

"That is a very small swath of literature."

"With a great overall concept: books don't have answers because life has no meaning."

His eyes flicked from one side of my face to the other, as though he were skimming an empty book.

I continued, "For example, have you ever read *White Noise*? It's—"

"Yes, I've read it."

"Sorry."

"Stop apologizing," he said. "Do you honestly believe that life has no meaning?"

I said, "Is that a problem?"

"How old are you?"

"Twenty."

A small silence. He leaned forward; instinctively, I leaned back. I thought he was about to question why a first-year was twenty years old instead of eighteen, but all he said was:

"I imagine you think you are very complicated."

"Meh."

"Excuse me?"

I didn't respond.

"You have misread *White Noise*—and, I wager, all of postmodernism," he said, dabbing his mouth once with his napkin. "What appears to be a lack of meaning is in fact an example of authorial craft. DeLillo illustrates the inability to communicate through a *medium* of communication; he asserts that the world is too complex to understand in language that is unusually *simple*. He demonstrates significance precisely through a *lack* of overt significance. I imagine you cannot find its 'meaning' because you lack the passion to try."

Passion. There it was, my least favorite word. It was the elusive—yes, meaningless—term people used when they wanted to believe they were more human than other humans.

The lamp nearby sputtered, leaving Orville's face shrouded in a half light. I was silent. He reached for the blue file in front of us—my application?—and flipped through it like it was one of those picture books that tells a story if you run through the pages fast enough.

"Our meeting times will be on Thursday, from half eight to half nine in the morning," he said. "By next week, you will have read the *Old College Book of Disciplinary Procedures*, which you will find in the post in a few days. You will also have prepared an analysis of Robert Browning's 'Porphyria's Lover.' The highest mark any late assignment will receive is fifty percent. If you do not complete the reading, do not bother coming to see me."

I nodded. "Sir?"

"What."

"Browning was not a postmodernist."

"I never said he was."

He tossed me my academic file and told me to have a nice day.

CHAPTER 2

My father and I had only discussed my inheritance once. I remember it well. I was fourteen. My mother had walked out on us a year earlier, and the only other woman in my life was Rebecca, my math tutor, who came on Wednesdays and Sundays. This particular Thursday, my father and I were sitting in the Heights. That's what he called his library, which he had modeled after Heathcliff's bedroom in *Wuthering Heights*. It was his personal sanctuary, and as such, it was filled with mountains of crap: excess gravy boats, turtleneck sweaters, spare copies of *The Republic*, and a Hemingway voodoo doll. Hanging from the one visible window ledge was a collection of upside-down dried roses. Dad said that each one represented one of his early rejection letters from major publishing houses. To me, they just looked like unlucky parachuters.

That morning, we were having breakfast on the carpet. He generally used the mornings to explain something he thought I should know: the evils of adverbs, the benefits of cremation, the legal ways to avoid taxes. At the time, he was forty-one, six foot six, and drinking whiskey in his coffee. I was five foot eleven and impossible.

"Sammy," he had said.

"Dad."

"I'm going to die someday."

"Pass the syrup."

There was a plate of home-cooked pancakes on the floor with us.

I remember because Dad had left them on the stove too long, and the bottoms were dotted with charred circles, big and brown like the spots on a cow. He handed me Vermont's finest.

"When you're older, you'll inherit the Warnings of Experience," he said.

"The Warnings of Experience?" I clarified.

"Correct."

"Why when I'm older?"

I should have asked him, *Why the Warnings of Experience?* but when you're young, you never think to question the absurd.

All he said was "Fourteen is an ugly number."

And that, right there, had been the extent of our conversation. I asked him not to talk like that anymore, because losing my father was an old and very terrible nightmare of mine. With my mother living in Paris at the time, designing wedding dresses, my dad was all I had left. And he was great. He had soft, sloppy hair, and all that hair complemented an out-of-shape writer's body, just fit enough to be able to lift me up when we hugged. He had square glasses and only two wisdom teeth, a bald spot on his right calf, and eyes like an eagle. He was great in the ways that only dead fathers can ever truly be great.

As far as I knew, no other living person was familiar with the Warnings of Experience. I wanted to keep it that way. The outside world had long suspected my father's family of hiding something, and the constant media attention was growing tiresome. Historians liked to point to the fact that an enormous number of Brontë "artifacts" had gone missing over the years, or were otherwise unaccounted for: the girls' old mugs, paintings, notes, sketches, letters, and a few early novel drafts. Somehow they had been "lost." Where else could they be, people said, but with my father? Dad was the only living relation of Patrick Brontë, the father of the illustrious Brontë siblings, who outlived all of his children (and wife) and, legend had it, had preserved the Brontës' most precious belongings for posterity. One of Patrick's siblings gave birth to one of my great-several-times-over-grandfathers, whose spawn ultimately ended up producing my lovable and rather eccentric dad.

Public speculation about the Missing Brontë Estate had reached an all-time high in the last twenty years. Its mystery incited a dangerous curiosity within the strangely large world of Brontë fanatics, who had all likely read the novels as children and loved them for the rest of their lives. These people were far too easy to convince that since the Brontës were Romantic and Passionate people they had something Romantic (and more importantly, Lucrative) hidden in their past. Journalists did nothing but feed the flames. Headlines grew more and more sensational (*10 Mind-Blowing Reasons Charlotte Brontë Was Secretly Loaded*) until the rumors began infecting the minds of normal people, people who had never even heard of the Brontës before. Instead of believing that my father was hoarding old mugs and sketches, the average uninformed gossip columnist was quick to believe that Tristan Whipple was hiding gold mines, ruby rings, and Gutenberg Bibles. The Brontës themselves became somewhat irrelevant.

All of this taught me only two things: First, when you're one of the last Brontës, you unwillingly inherit an extraordinarily large and peculiar fan base. Second, when you are a handsome and reclusive single father, you inherit an even larger and more peculiar fan base. As a child, I had always found my father's fame perfectly normal, like one of those standard life facts you learn at five years old: the sky is blue, the sun sets in the west, fathers are always in the news. But the media attention drove my poor dad crazy. He started refusing interviews, and avoided public appearances when possible. His novels became even more cryptic. He locked himself in his study for hours on end. He started to leave strange trinkets all over the house, so that in case any reporters did break and enter someday, they would find lots of confusing story material. To the outside world, I'm sure my father was a madman.

The irony was that in all those years, I never saw him whip out any hidden Brontë memorabilia. There were no mugs and there were no ruby rings and there were no gold mines. My father cared only for the novels themselves—*Agnes Grey*, *The Tenant of Wildfell Hall*, *Jane Eyre*, *Wuthering Heights*, *Shirley*, and *Villette*—which, last time I checked, were still in the public domain. Dad spent his entire life studying these books, picking them apart and analyzing them word by word. He was in awe of them, the kind of awe most people reserve for dark and mysterious women. *These novels are alive and all other books are dead,* he would say. *Do you understand?* He used to give me lessons on them, reading from his worn copies as he made incomprehensible margin notes. I'm sure he knew something the rest of the world did not. But when I'd ask him what it was, all he'd say was: *Sammy, I'm just trying to teach you how to read.*

For a time after his death, the Brontës became my true love too—but only briefly, and only by default. I figured that if deconstructing the Brontë novels had been my father's life project, I would finish his work. Perhaps there *was* something important that I had been missing, and perhaps it was my job as Last Heir to figure it out. From age fifteen to age fifteen and a half, I spent an inordinate amount of time researching the Brontës, re-creating their lives, trying to know them the way my father had—as relatives. I pored over the few history books in my father's library that had survived the fire; I wrote poems and stories in a morbid Brontë style; I developed imaginary friends in the form of Anne, Charlotte, Emily, and even Branwell, the drunk brother. I suppose I thought it might, in a way, bring my father back to life.

It all came to nothing. To this day, I still did not understand what made my father so impassioned on the subject of his three long-lost cousins, or what he might be looking for. Now, I was cursed with all the knowledge I had acquired about them. I felt like an Olympic athlete who hadn't worked out in years and was stuck with the muscle-turned-to-fat around her shoulders. I still knew Charlotte, Emily, and Anne like no one should ever know anyone. I knew their shoe sizes and their height; I knew their stupid little secrets; I knew what they fought about and what they laughed about; I knew about the mole on Emily's right foot. Love always came with scars, and this was mine: the knowledge that the friends I knew best were those I had never actually met.

It wasn't until boarding school that I studied the Brontës in an academic context. Starting high school at sixteen years old meant that I was two to three years older than all my classmates. I had fought to be placed with the rising junior class, but when my mother enrolled me, she explained to the administration that my father's homeschooling experiment had been an "unmitigated disaster," and recommended that I start with the freshmen so I could recover from all the academic damage that had been unfairly inflicted upon me.

My hope was that my first formal English class on the Brontës would help me understand my relatives better—or at least shed some light on what my father had spent his life trying to figure out. But I was disappointed. Mr. Martin's class was the first time that I saw how the rest of the world knew the Brontës: not as moles and shoe sizes but as dramatic Hollywood films, badly made PowerPoint presentations in class, dolls for little girls. They were everything *but* human beings.

Mr. Martin boiled down each sister's character so that they lost all taste, flavor, and flair. We learned that Charlotte was the eldest, the most famous, and the ringleader of the family. Four foot eleven. Strong, opinionated, admirable. The entrepreneur. A real nineteenth-century ballbuster. *Jane Eyre* was her brainchild. Mr. Martin didn't bother mentioning that it was the sort of novel you adored as a child and then misunderstood for the rest of your life.

The second sister, we learned, was Emily—intensely passionate, wild, and imaginative. She was the action figurine with windswept black hair, a heaving bosom, and a petticoat drenched from her wild traipses across the stormy English moors. Her greatest work and only novel was *Wuthering Heights*, considered the most romantic book ever written by those who had never read it carefully.

And then there was Anne. Quiet, forgotten Anne. The last Brontë. The youngest. The failed social reformer. Meek. Moralizing. Sweet. Author of the most boring book, *Agnes Grey*, the one that never made it to SparkNotes. She was the Brontë who had been overshadowed by her infinitely more talented sisters. In other words, the Loser.

I approached Mr. Martin one day after class to complain about his complete misunderstanding of my family. He had a heart-shaped face with a fuzzy beard and stubby fingers resembling baby pickles. On his desk were the plastic bags that he put over his head when it rained.

"I don't think you're being fair to Annie," I said to him.

"She speaks!" he said with a kind smile. "I thought you had taken a vow of silence."

I shook my head. "I think you're wrong about Annie."

When he smiled, thick creases gouged his cheeks, like Earth's fault lines. He cocked his head to the side. "Annie?"

"Her friends called her Annie."

"And how do you know that?"

"My dad told me."

His smile faded at the mention of my father. The look on his face said, *I don't know what to say. Help me.* I knew the expression well. I saw it on the face of every fourteen-year-old girl in my dorm. No one knew what to say about my father's death, so no one came near me.

"You're not explaining Anne the way my father used to," I told Mr. Martin. "You're making her boring."

He sat down and gestured that I should do the same. I ignored him.

"Did your father tell you quite a lot about Anne?" he asked.

I frowned. "Are you a reporter?"

"Goodness, of course not."

He was silent then, and uncomfortable. I wondered if he read the newspapers. If the rumors were true, could it be that the largest literary inheritance in recent history would fall into the hands of a teenager?

I took a breath. "Do you know anything about the Warnings of Experience?"

"The what?"

"The Warnings of Experience. Please tell me what it means."

He looked sympathetic, as though I was a lost, poor, friendless child—for the first time, a true Brontë.

"Samantha, would you like to sit down and talk?" he said.

I meant to say, "I'd rather not," but it came out "I'd rather rot." I left the room.

It was in those first few months of high school that I began to realize something rather awful, something that I would skillfully repress for years. Every member of the press believed that my father had left me something tangible—a Brontë treasure. Everyone was wrong. What I had was the Warnings of Experience. And the Warnings of Experience, I had come to believe, was not an object. It was just another one of my father's esoteric lessons. Perhaps reporters would have figured this out had they ever seen the whiskey in Dad's coffee and the veins in his eyes. I was the only one who had seen the Great Tristan Whipple sprawled out on the couch like a beached starfish. I knew—deep down, I knew—that his parting gift to me was a warning not to become like him. There was a reason B. Howard of the British National Bank could not understand his will, and there was a reason I didn't much want to discuss it. It was because, I suspected, there was actually nothing there.

In retrospect, I should have returned Mr. Martin's smiles and attempt at friendship. He was simply doing his job, which was to introduce kids to literature. But at the time, there was nothing I hated more than his lectures about *Wuthering Heights*. *It's a book of raging contradictions,* he used to say. *Nature versus civilization, heaven versus hell, love versus violence.* Supposedly, he was teaching us how to do "close reading." We were not doing "close reading." Close reading was when my father analyzed chapter headings for two hours. I once told Mr. Martin that he was missing the point of the book; Mr. Martin said that the point of the book was that we were never able to understand it fully. It was a markedly different way of thinking than Dad's, and I found the transition between the two terribly disorienting. In the end, there was only one thing that came out of my cumulative education: a whole lot of white noise.

On Thursday morning, I made my first trip to the Old College Faculty Wing. It was a miniature castle at the heart of campus, in the middle of a wide, lake-size lawn. I recognized the building immediately from posters, postcards, and BBC dramas. It was giant and rectangular, studded with stone turrets and four looming gargoyles, all of which appeared to be frothing at the mouth. This, right here, was the defining building of Oxford, associated with so many scandals throughout the years that it now accounted for fifteen percent of tourism in England.

The concept of a faculty wing was an unusual one at Oxford; in most of its colleges, professors worked and lived alongside their students in the residential quarters. Such was the case at Old College until 1811, when the faculty took over this old manor. I took the back route to avoid today's tour groups. The walk wasn't nearly as scenic, thanks to all the weeds, and as I neared the rear of the Faculty Wing, I happened upon a small, abandoned freshwater well. It was old and ugly. I hadn't noticed it the last time I was there. It reminded me of the portable toilet I had once spied behind Buckingham Palace. Perhaps it had been Photoshopped out of all the postcards.

In a few minutes, I reached the front of the building and found the entrance. The solemn stone walls were scarred and battered, as if by too many catapult wounds. Inside, the foyer was wide and dark, like an elegant prison, and smelled of old honey and rum. There were two stuffed bison heads above the doorway and an old urn at the center of the room, out of which several denuded branches emerged like antlers.

Orville's office was on the third floor of the West Wing, as he had explained in his last e-mail. I climbed a glorious staircase the width of a yacht, and there it was, unavoidable—the English department, visible to all passersby thanks to the giant banner that read, in Latin: *From One Example Learn All.* I walked down a deserted, umbilical corridor. It was lined with closed doors, labeled with surnames: Milton, Norris, Northington. Then, Orville. The door was closed, with a sign on the outside: *Tute in Session: Kindly Leave.* I took a seat on one of the rickety chairs nearby and waited. A sheen of sweat ripened over my body.

Soon, the door to Orville's office swung open and a wild-eyed student erupted, sobbing and furious. Her boots made angry taps as she stormed down the corridor, hair bouncing behind her. I stayed put until the noise of her heels grew soft and then disappeared. I smoothed my palms over my jeans and entered Orville's dimly lit room, which smelled as though an animal had just been smoked. The curtains were bloodred and drawn. This was not an office. It was a small library, two stories high, with thin ladders and impractical balconies and an expensive ceiling featuring a gaggle of naked Greeks. It was the sort of library you'd marry a man for.

Orville was sitting in an orange chair by the fireplace, not smiling. I saw a small stack of papers on the table in front of him, as well as a tea set and a pocket-size *Magna Carta.* I approached slowly.

"Welcome to your first tutorial," he said. His five o'clock shadow was gone, and in its place was ruthlessly scrubbed skin.

"Thank you."

He motioned toward the tray on the table. "Coffee or tea?"

"Do you have any hot chocolate?"

"This isn't a restaurant."

"Sorry."

"Sit," he said. "No, not there. Farther away, please. Yes, that's right. You will sit over there; I will sit here."

I moved away from the chair next to him and took a seat on the opposite couch.

"Nice office," I said.

"Yes, it is, isn't it?" he said. "It was a battle to secure this one. It has the finest views of the gardens—do you see? Ah, the curtains are drawn."

I said, "Are all these books yours?"

"Of course they're all mine." His chin tilted up; he might have been speaking about his children.

"What did you do to the girl who just left?" I asked.

"Eliza did not complete *Ulysses*. I take my tutorials very seriously. If you do not feel as though you are emotionally equipped to perform, please leave now."

I said, "I'll be fine."

"Very well," he said. "Let's get on with it. Please tell me about 'Porphyria's Lover.' "

"Sure," I said. "It was pretty bad."

"Pardon?"

"I thought it was a terrible poem. Really awful."

He blinked. "Try to be more articulate, please."

I waited. He waited. I crossed my legs. What did he want? I was an essayist, not a public speaker. If he wanted to know my opinion, he should have read the twenty-two hours of thought I had already poured onto the page in front of him.

"Bad," I said. "It was a bad poem. Did you read my essay?"

Orville regarded me for a moment, then reached for the paper in front of him. He held my essay between his thumb and forefinger, like a dish towel. "You mean this?"

He tossed it to me. It landed with a small splat on my side of the table, like he was belching out the last of his lunch. There were no double check marks written on it, like there always had been for me in high school. Now, red scribbles bled into the page. I picked it up. The first comment in the right-hand margin read, *This is a pathetic sentence.*

"Read me your opening paragraph," he instructed.

"I can't," I said. "You've crossed out most of it."

"Read what's left."

My breathing was shallow. I was supposed to be good at this, I reminded myself. Hadn't I applied to Oxford as a literature major? Rational, methodical, systematic pieces of analysis were my forte. The heat gathered in my cheeks and it occurred to me that years from now, when I was old and bedridden with some twenty-first-century plague, I would feel grateful that I was not in this office.

I cleared my throat and read my own writing aloud: " 'Robert Browning's "Porphyria's Lover" appears to be a poem about beauty.' "

I stopped. Orville had begun gently stroking the wood of his arm-rest like it was the snout of a giant, drooling pet tiger.

I looked back at the page and continued: " 'However, beauty in the poem proves to be as illusory as the narrator's sanity.' Should I go on?"

"Please don't."

"What's wrong?"

"Is your writing always so flat and uninteresting?"

"Only when I don't like the subject matter."

"Everyone dislikes that which they cannot understand." Before I could respond, he said, "Why don't you tell me what you were trying to argue. I couldn't read past page seven."

My cheeks flamed. My feel-good, every-opinion-is-valid high school had not prepared me for a one-on-one tutorial. High school had taught me that classrooms were a safe space where every opinion was right. It was an environment in which Ophelia could be compared to both Dido and the hooker from *Pretty Woman* and no one would object. Once upon a time, I used to be comfortable with confrontation, but that had been a long time ago, when my father was still my sole tutor. Now, I felt rusty, like a cheerleader trying to squeeze back into her uniform after gaining a hundred and forty-five pounds.

I cleared my throat. "All I mean is that for a poem about the preservation of beauty, the poem itself isn't beautiful."

"What do you mean, the poem isn't beautiful?"

"It's about a man who strangles his lover with her own hair," I said.

"And you don't find that beautiful."

"Do *you*?"

Orville stood up and walked to the fireplace, so that his back was toward me. I imagined he was contemplating what a waste of a Brontë I was.

"What about the exquisitely sensual way in which he kills her?" he said. "He wraps a strand of her own hair around her neck, treating her body as a work of art—a temple of aesthetic pleasure. Her beauty is so ephemeral that the only way to preserve its perfection is, paradoxically, to destroy it. You have overlooked the poem's nuances."

"What nuances?" I said. "The poem is not subtle at all. It's written in blunt, simple, stupid words. The speaker is a madman and a murderer and a lunatic. He doesn't even say that the woman he kills is attractive. You're imagining a beauty that does not exist." For good measure, I added, "Sir."

He turned back to face me. "Do you honestly believe that beauty cannot exist in something that does not appear to be beautiful?"

No, I thought to myself. *Yes. No.* I decided not to answer the question. I said, "You're changing the definition of 'beautiful.'"

"You're forgetting the subjective nature of beauty."

"You're wrong to think that beauty is subjective."

"Isn't it?"

"No," I said. "People know what's beautiful, and Browning gets that. He is making a fool out of you."

"Me?" Orville said.

"Yes. You. The poem is ugly and Browning knew it. The point was to see how many delusional academics he could trick into thinking it was worth analyzing."

There—right there. Both of Orville's eyebrows raised at the same time.

"And for that matter," I continued, "if you believe what you say, then you shouldn't find fault with this stunning piece of poetry I provided for you." I tossed my essay back at him. "You are simply unable to see the inner beauty in my deplorable lack of passion."

There was a small pause. Orville almost smiled. "Do you take me for a fool, Samantha?"

"Do you really want me to answer that question?" I blurted.

He stopped. My cheeks flamed. "Well," he said, "now we're getting somewhere."

With that, we began the tutorial in earnest. The next hour passed in a state of intense discomfort. Orville told me that my sentences were bland, and had I ever read something called a stylebook? I informed him that I was merely exercising artistic license. He explained that my inverted commas were used incorrectly and that, anyway, I should really have a look at the *Oxford English Dictionary*. I told him that I didn't know what an inverted comma was and that he should take this argument up with my muse. He seemed terribly content, as though he knew no finer pleasure than arguing over line breaks and semicolons and adverbs. I wondered what the women in his life thought of that.

I did manage to learn a few things over the course of the morning. First, overusing the word *and* betrayed my limited understanding of elegant writing; second, some people actually did know what the word *heteronormative* meant; third, my sarcasm was not helpful, thank you very much. I learned that only Americans refer to their tutors as professors; at Oxford they were generally dons or fellows, so I should kindly note that. I thought I might relax into the rhythm of the tutorial, given enough time, but my posture was stiff from beginning to end. Orville was terrifyingly articulate. Had his entire vocabulary been limited to twelve words, I'm sure he would have found a way to include *discursive*.

"There is one thing I am curious about," he said, as we neared what was either the end of the tutorial or the end of time. I considered mentioning that he had just ended his last thought with a preposition, but thought better of it.

"If we might," he said, "I'd like to return to your accusation that the narrator of this poem is a madman."

I glanced at his grandfather clock, which was broken. "We only have three minutes left," I guessed.

He didn't move. "So speak quickly."

I did my best to summon my thoughts out of their tortured stupor. "The narrator is a madman. What is there to debate? That's why it's juvenile to call this a great piece of art. People have a bad habit of assuming that anything insane is automatically profound. Ergo."

"Ergo what?"

I frowned. "Ergo, that's it."

"You cannot say 'ergo' without something following it."

My face grew red. It was one of my grammatical inaccuracies that my father must have found too amusing to correct.

I said, "Ergo, authors uniformly assume madness is deep. They're wrong. Sometimes, insane people aren't tortured artists. Sometimes, insane people are just insane."

Orville frowned. "Consider the afflictions that drive sane men into madness: love, money, blood, power. The condition of insanity is but an exaggeration of the very qualities that make one human. Wouldn't you say that madness, therefore, is but a magnification of reality?"

"No, I would not say that."

"Have you never been in love?"

I blinked. "What?"

"You. In love."

"I don't think you're allowed to ask me that."

His expression did not change. "I ask only because the memory of being in love will help you understand this poem."

"Understand what? What it means to want to kill someone?"

"Precisely. Passion can take even the most rational men in directions they would not anticipate. Think of what Browning has done to elucidate this point: He has given a murderer a rational voice. He has channeled madness into an intrinsically organized, structured art form. He is encouraging you, Samantha Whipple, to recognize sanity within the insane. If you cannot appreciate madness, then you cannot appreciate great art."

I said, "I'm sure the woman being strangled had a hard time appreciating this man's art."

"She's a fictional woman."

"That's what they all say."

I waited. Orville glanced at his watch. "Very well, Samantha—we will continue this conversation another time. You may leave."

He stood and walked to his teapot on the opposite side of the room. I stayed where I was. We didn't say anything. I picked up my violated essay and shoved it into my bag.

"Have *you* ever been in love?" I asked.

Orville looked back at me and let out a bark of a laugh. "I'm a great deal older than you are."

"I mean, properly in love," I clarified. "The kind of love you strangle people over."

The dishes gave a clank. I couldn't tell whether that meant yes or no. I imagined a horde of secret lady admirers falling all over him, one by one, getting caught in the spokes of his bike as he moved around the city.

"You probably just haven't met the right girl yet," I said, giving a sweet smile. "When you meet someone you really want to kill, I bet you'll know."

He brought a fresh cup of tea back to the center of the room and set it down on the table. He was a very tall man and the teacup was miniature in comparison.

"Do you have somewhere to be?" he asked.

I blinked. With the lesson over, a switch seemed to have turned off in his mind, ending our relationship for the time being. He sat down and unfolded the newspaper in front of him. I was unused to sudden coolness in teachers. My father had always been the same person in and out of the classroom. After a day of lessons, he'd take me down to the grocery store and we'd count the lobsters in the tanks. Orville was silent, and I couldn't help but think that all I had done was rent him for the hour.

I slung my bag over my shoulder, and slipped out of the room unnoticed.

CHAPTER 3

A few weeks later, when I was en route to my first dinner in the Great Dining Hall, I discovered that I had made the front page of the *Hornbeam*, Old College's student newspaper.

LAST LIVING BRONTË DESCENDANT
ARRIVES AT OLD COLLEGE

It was printed in heavy, self-righteous black ink. The paper had infected all of the Old College arcades, and now, discarded copies were flying in the brisk wind like English tumbleweeds. There I was, on the cover page of every paper—too tall, with straight, American teeth. Brown hair, brown eyes, no makeup. The author of the article, an H. Pierpont, must have found my high school yearbook photo floating around the internet. I looked a lot like myself and a little like a man. I snatched a copy off the ground and read:

> *The only surviving descendant of the family of Patrick Brontë (father of the illustrious Brontë trio) is Miss Samantha E. Whipple, a first-year English Literature candidate at Old College, and the orphaned daughter of the late Tristan Whipple (best-selling author of* Convenient Fiction, Tortillas on a Mantel, *and* This Is a Book!). *According to Sir John Booker, former Cambridge University don and present curator of the Brontë Parsonage and Museum, Miss Whipple is heiress to the Vast Brontë Estate.*

A small squeeze of breath escaped me, as though I had developed a slow leak. I silently welcomed Pierpont to my shit list. I was not an *orphan*, thank you very much. I did have a mother, even if we didn't speak often, and she was a real live mother—red-cheeked and frizzy-haired. And where, exactly, had he dug up "the Vast Brontë Estate"?

"Oi!"

I looked around. The voice came from behind me. In my anger, I had marched to the front steps without seeing the queue that had begun to form. I apologized to no one in particular and fell into line. In their black capes, my classmates reminded me of very small children, or very old men. Everyone else seemed to know to wear college dress robes. It was raining, so I had worn a yellow poncho.

Once I was in line, my eyes fell upon a girl with dyed blonde hair who was standing directly in front of me. She had also missed the dress robe memo, and was wearing a shirt advertising *Thor the Hammer*. The guy next to her was a tall redhead sporting a brave attempt at facial hair. I could tell the two of them would be dating soon; her body was leaning toward his and he seemed ready to inhale her.

"I hear she's loaded," the girl was saying with a bat of her eyes. She had a copy of the *Hornbeam* clutched in her hands.

"I'm reading her dad's books for my next tutorial," said the boy.

"They're a bit overrated, yeah?"

"Do you know how he died?"

"Wasn't it an accident?"

"He was a drunk."

"Oh, was he?"

"I'm Thomas."

"Ellen."

They shook hands. Samantha Whipple, having served her purpose as Conversation Filler, became irrelevant.

I glanced down once again at the *Hornbeam*, which was wilting from the sweat on my fingers. *The Vast Brontë Estate*. I hadn't heard the phrase in years. It was a term coined many years ago by a well-known Cambridge professor, Sir John Booker, when he penned a hostile and inane op-ed of the same name. At least, "inane" was how my father described it. Sir John had accused Dad of hoarding an enormous wealth of primary sources, denying the academic world the joy of their analysis. I remembered the article mostly through my father's reaction to it. The morning after the piece appeared in the London *Times*, I recalled coming downstairs to find him frying bacon, something he only did when he was angry. Dad was actually a vegetarian, but he enjoyed the way bacon self-destructed in the pan by stewing in its own grease—like all liars, cowards, and idiots, he used to say. When I approached him, Dad turned, brandished his spatula at me, and explained that Sir John was a perfect example of a man who a) didn't know how to read and b) didn't know how to think. I remember nodding and adjusting the bow on his apron. We both had an unspoken understanding of what was coming: a slew of inquiries from reporters, fans, and critics, and yet another departure from the makeshift privacy we had slowly built together. As the years passed, all I came to know of Sir John was that he was "the son and heir of a mongrel bitch," to quote my father—and, I suppose, *King Lear*.

I glanced down at my phone. No new messages. Earlier this evening, I had finally summoned up the courage to call B. Howard, hoping that she and I might be able to square away everything on the phone and never need to talk again. Her voice had been crisp and surgeon-like as she explained that she was sorry, but an in-person meeting was necessary, and as soon as possible.

"Your father's will was exceptionally confusing," she explained in a way that let me know she had already spent far too much time thinking about it.

"Haven't you had five years to go through it?"

"That's not quite enough time."

I told her that I would have to get back to her regarding a meeting date, as I had a large volume of homework, thanks to my tyrannical professor, who belonged in an evil German fairy tale. Now, however, as I looked down at the *Hornbeam*, I wished we had set up an appointment and met already. Blanche Howard would have told me what I already suspected—that my father had left me nothing—and then I could have gone to the press and kindly explained what should never have required outside confirmation: I was nobody.

A small breath of wind hit my shins, the only part of my body not covered by my yellow power-poncho. Thor the Hammer and her new boyfriend were laughing about something as the rain fell quietly around us. Her giggle sounded like a bottle of champagne popping. The line began to move. I envied Thor for such seamless flirting. It was as if she had taken some special class that I had missed in high school, where you learn how to be social. What had I been doing all those years, anyway? I scooted closer to my soggy, chattering classmates, aware of the acute loneliness you feel when surrounded by so many other people. The line moved quickly, and soon I dropped the *Hornbeam* on the ground, leaving it to crumple into the puddles.

At dinner, I sat next to a Swedish third-year who looked like an underwear model. Thick neck, small waist, jutting jaw. He had a watered-down face, pale like the inside of someone's arm. This is how our conversation went:

"I haven't seen you before," he said. The accent was strong.

I said, " 'To be omnipotent but friendless is to reign.' "

"What?"

"Shelley," I said.

He extended a hand sideways. "Hans."

"No, Percy Shelley," I said, taking his hand. "Said that quote. Sorry."

"All right, yeah."

"I'm English."

"You sound American."

"I study English."

"Ah," he said. "I'm math."

I hated meeting people. Being homeschooled for a decade had not granted me social graces. My father never corrected the expressions I had learned incorrectly, because he thought miscommunication was funny, and as a result, I went to high school thinking that it was *trivilous* instead of *frivolous*, *exasperate* instead of *exacerbate*. I lived in a world in which people still said "jolly." I spent high school saying things like "if urged."

I glanced around. The Great Dining Hall was four hundred and seventy-two years old, begun by Old College Master John Stuart VIII during his second year in office. The stone was blackened and it looked like the building had been smoking the same cigar for centuries and had dribbled ash all over itself. Tonight, the six long tables inside the hall were bathed in a sickly, yellow light, and students crammed around them like too many animals at a trough. The only empty tables, reserved for faculty, were at the front of the room, facing horizontally.

On all the walls around us were paintings of English kings and Old College presidents, whose portraits filled up every bit of space like uneven, mismatched graves. The collection looked like a Tetris game that Michelangelo had started as a kid and, frustrated, left spackled onto the wall. The table I chose faced the north wall, which meant that Richard III was glaring down at me, a chicken leg in his hand. I glanced at the sour men in the portraits next to him, and couldn't help but feel that we had walked into a loud argument between them that had suddenly been silenced.

Across from me were two girls, one of whom had a name that I believe began with an *A*, and the other of whom had a field of study that was abbreviated *PPE*. PPE had introduced herself as Marissa, though it might have been Melissa. Melinda. Abigail. Horace? Hans, meanwhile, gave me a quick debriefing regarding his life. I learned that he liked Chinese rum, had three middle names (all beginning with *E*), and ended more than one thought with a loud grunt. His father was English, his mother was in the bottled-water business, and all of their friends were undertakers.

"Where do you live in college?" he asked.

"In a tower."

"Hah."

"It has no windows and it smells like venison."

He paused, and the smile faded. "You mean *the* tower? You live in the *tower*?"

I nodded.

"You're the Brontë then."

Again, I nodded.

He gave a slow smile. "No one's lived there in years. The tower, I mean. People call it the Tower of Extinction."

"Because people die in there?"

"No, because you're so isolated that you never procreate."

"I see."

"*I* could visit you if you wanted."

"What?"

"What?"

We stopped talking because the room had fallen silent. The faculty had arrived. I looked behind me to find a solemn procession of middle-aged men and women. One woman—short and squat—was leading the way inside. She looked like a Geraldine, or perhaps a Thomasina, and all in all resembled a bathrobed granny. It took several minutes for all of them to reach the front tables. When they did, I noticed that half the seats were empty. Had the faculty caught the plague? The squat professor, Geraldine, gave a toast in Latin, and then we began to eat.

"Why do they look so serious?" I asked Hans.

"You are looking at the most brilliant minds in the Western world."

"They don't look very friendly."

"Anyone who teaches here has fought his way to the top. The entire process is rather vulgar. Don't think this is a pleasant group of people."

I squinted back at the tables. In a room filled with bland black gowns, the empty seats stood out like missing teeth.

"There appear to be quite a few people gone," I said. "Were they all killed off?"

He followed my gaze. "Eating in hall is a privilege. Sometimes people lose that privilege."

It sounded like a phrase he had repeated several times before. I wondered how many times he had been scolded as a child.

"What'd they do?" I said. "Walk on the lawns?"

No response. I wasn't sure if he'd heard me. Surely the Greatest Minds in the Western World were exempt from mortal punishments? I noticed that my own professor was conspicuously absent. I thought of the *Old College Book of Disciplinary Procedures*, a thick green volume I had found tucked inside my mailbox a week ago, and which, according to the letter attached to it, I was "encouraged to examine" before term began. Nowhere had I found any restrictions regarding eating in the dining hall, an observation I shared with Hans.

He laughed. "You actually read the whole rulebook?"

"No."

I had tried to make it all the way through, but I failed. For one thing, half of it was still in Olde English. For another, the print was comically small, as if the author had been concerned that two hundred pages weren't quite enough to squeeze in all the creative and arbitrary punishments available to students and professors. According to the rules I *did* read (and remembered), students who jumped the queue were to be sent back to their dorms immediately; professors and students were supposed to sit a prescribed distance away from each other at all times; professors and students were never to spend more than an hour alone under any circumstances. Most crimes, I noticed, ended in "timely expulsion." It seemed to me that the college had dealt with a number of infractions in the past and was now trying to send a clear message to its lawyers: "See? We tried."

Hans and I fell into a patch of silence. He was very good-looking (did I mention?), and as a result, I found it difficult to think of something to say. Politics? Religion? Witty banter? What did good-looking people talk about, anyway? Somewhere during the second course, he broke the silence for me. He was a student of mathematics, he explained, but his true passion was writing. I told him I hated writing; he didn't ask me why. I learned that he worked three jobs and cooked twice a week, and that, if I wanted, I could visit him in the Porters' Lodge (affectionately called the Plodge), where he worked part-time. There was no central heating there, however, and the place had small holes in the roof, and in the snow it was impossible to walk there, so I should dress warmly and be prepared. I nodded. This is what I was learning about Old College: it was miserable and perfect. Everyone had a morbid fascination with its obsolete customs, even—and most particularly—those who pretended to hate them.

Near the end of dinner, Hans said: "I notice that you keep looking at him."

"Who?"

"James Orville."

I gave a start. "What? Where? He's here?"

"No." He pointed up toward the wall. "Dr. Orville."

"What?" I squinted to make out the portrait above us. "I thought that was Richard III."

Hans laughed. "Close."

I stared up at the half-eaten chicken leg caught between the man's hands. "Orville's a little young to have his own portrait, don't you think?" I asked.

"He won the International Arts and Literature Prize at twenty."

"I don't know what that is."

"It's a big fucking deal."

"As big as being a king of England?"

He shrugged. "A matter of opinion."

"I don't understand," I said. "Orville gets a spot on the wall, but not at the dinner table?"

He hesitated. "Something like that."

Pudding arrived but I couldn't seem to eat. I was much too aware that Richard III—Orville?—was watching me. His gaze was steady. He looked like he couldn't decide whether he wanted to be a good ruler, or Caligula. I'm sure that to a more experienced observer, the answer would have been obvious. For now, I wished he would wipe that cheeky grin off his face.

<hr>

It happened several nights later.

I was returning to my tower from the library when I discovered a small package leaning against my door, like a sultry actress from the 1940s. It was wrapped in an old copy of the *Hornbeam*. As I approached, it seemed to breathe, *Where have you been, baby?*

I thought it must be a belated birthday gift from my mother, but then again, she had already bought me something, hadn't she? Fluffy slippers—the impractical kind. I picked up the delivery. No scotch tape. Someone must have wrapped it in a hurry. There was a message scrawled in thick black marker across the top.

Here.

I took the package inside, to the refrigerated air inside my room. I set it down on the desk. *Here.* Was that *Here you go, dear*, or was that *Here, fool, it's yours*? No address. No return address. The sender must have lived within Old College walls. I ripped through newspaper wrapping, then let out a small shriek.

It was a book—one I recognized immediately. Not because of the title, *Agnes Grey*, but because of the ink stain above the *Anne* in *Anne Brontë*, which appeared just below the faded portrait of the young woman on the cover. This book—this ugly, jam-stained book—was an emblem of my childhood. It was Turkish coffee and burned pancakes. It was Shelley in the paddling pool, and the shadows of friends I once knew, conjured out of a dank, dusty literary graveyard. This book had belonged to my father.

My mind drew a breathless blank. *Agnes Grey*. Here, in my lap. What? No. There was no single creature who could have delivered this to my doorstep. My father's library had burned down many years ago. This was an elaborate, twisted trick. No one could have known what this book meant to me, or how my father and I had read it together, long ago. I sat down. All I could see was the Governess, whose eyes seemed suddenly bright.

I did the only thing I could do. I grabbed my phone, dialed, and let it ring once, twice, seven times.

"*Claude, c'est toi?*"

My mother's voice was smooth and light. It belonged bottled up and stored inside her wine cabinet. There was a party bustling in the background. I heard dishes and laughter and friendly epithets. I imagined all of France was gathered around my mother to eat cheese in a city that was sparkling like a thousand opals.

"Hi," I said.

"Alice?"

"Samantha."

Another pause. I knew she was surprised. She was the one who usually called me, on the first of every month, like an invoice.

Someone let out a loud laugh in the background; then Mom said, "*Sammy! Bonsoir!*"

"Yes, *hola*," I said. "Did you send me something in the mail?"

"Say it again?"

"Mail. Did you send something?"

"I hope they fit!"

"I mean a book."

"A book?"

"You didn't ever steal anything out of Dad's library, did you?"

There was a long pause. "I'm going to have to change phones, will you hold?"

I held. I held for a long time.

"I'm back," came the voice on the other line.

I took a breath. "Did you ever steal anything out of Dad's library, before it burned down?"

"What kind of a question is that?"

"Please," I said. "I have to know."

"No, I did not." She sounded wounded, and I felt a strange, detached triumph, as though *Agnes Grey* arriving had been a fortuitous way of enacting punishment for her lengthy and inexcusable absences. There was a distant clatter of dishes in the background.

"Tell me what's going on," she said. When I didn't answer, she prodded, "Sammy?"

"Please don't call me that. It makes me feel like a sheep."

"A what?"

"A sheep."

"Listen, darling—"

"Baaaaa."

There was a pause, and I knew she was pressing her lips together, like she always used to. "Tell me what's wrong. Are you all right?"

I glanced back at *Agnes Grey*. "I'm hallucinating."

"I'm switching rooms again so I can hear you."

"You don't have to do that. I should go."

"Samantha?"

"It's fine."

"I—"

"Talk soon."

I hung up.

I flipped open *Agnes Grey*, the brilliant little devil. I might have been looking at a perfectly preserved corpse. Yes, it was my father's copy. Instead of underlining key sentences, or elegant phrases, Dad wrote things like *Here!* and *There!* and *Bah!* I read the opening paragraph:

> *All true histories contain instruction; though, in some, the treasure may be hard to find, and when found, so trivial in quantity that the dry, shrivelled kernel scarcely compensates for the trouble of cracking the nut.*

God, I had forgotten how much I hated this novel. I made a desperate glance back at *The Governess*, which was hanging on my wall, watching me like a spy. *Help me,* I thought. But she was preoccupied with sinking. Once a governess, always a governess. She was holding a book in her hand too—was *Agnes Grey* drowning her, also? I looked at the book in my palm and wondered if this could possibly be my inheritance. Was my father's much-debated estate really just a 1997 Penguin edition of a novel that had been sitting on bookshelves for a century?

My breathing grew quick and shallow. I felt like an amnesia patient whose memory has suddenly been restored, to her great displeasure. All the facts I once knew about the Brontës were coming back to me in a lethal avalanche. The Brontës' ghosts were rising out of the unquiet earth; I could almost hear them demanding why I had left them alone for so long. I stared at *Agnes Grey* and I began to remember things I wished I could forget: the madwoman in the attic,

Grace Poole, the parsonage fire, Thorp Green. Yes, yes, Thorp Green. Hell, I hadn't thought of that place in years.

I pulled out my phone for the second time that evening. Blanche Howard had warned me that discussing my inheritance was a matter of great urgency, but I hadn't anticipated that a book would appear at my doorstep if I didn't act fast enough. I had no other choice: it was time to arrange a meeting with the British National Bank.

CHAPTER 4

Agnes Grey is, without question, the most boring book ever written. It tells the story of an impossibly meek nineteenth-century governess (Agnes) who describes what it is like being an impossibly meek nineteenth-century governess for over two hundred pages. The plot is famously dull—a badly disguised autobiography of Anne Brontë's own less-than-riveting early twenties. Agnes, the daughter of respectable yet poor parents, becomes a governess at a manor suspiciously similar to the one where Anne Brontë herself worked. There, Agnes meets a slew of well-dressed villains: materialistic, frivolous, and rife with satirical potential. But Agnes—and by association, Anne—never offers the sort of biting social commentary that would have upgraded *Agnes Grey* to *Pride and Prejudice*. Reading the book leaves only a sense of gasping emptiness, and the disappointing feeling that Anne Brontë missed her opportunity to be truly great. The novel is about a woman who isn't allowed to speak her mind, and was written by a woman who also wasn't allowed to speak her mind. It was handcuffed right from the get-go.

Critics at the time found little fault with it. Agnes was everything a young lady ought to be: moral, weak, waify. Unlike the other Brontë novels, *Agnes Grey* met with relatively little contempt. "It is infinitely more agreeable" than Emily Brontë's *Wuthering Heights*, read one review, leaving "no painful impression on the mind—some may think no impression at all." Poor Anne. I used to fancy myself as something of her reincarnation, caught in the similarly oppressive shadow of older, illustrious writers. "A queer little thing" was what Charlotte called her youngest sister. George Smith, the Brontës' publisher, called Anne a "gentle, quiet, rather subdued person." Her manner, he said, was "curiously expressive of a wish for protection and encouragement, a kind of constant appeal which invited sympathy."

I was eight or nine when my father first sat me down with *Agnes Grey*. Dad viewed the Brontë books as private diaries the rest of the world didn't understand. We started with *Agnes Grey* because it was the most "coded" of the Brontë novels, as he put it. Then we moved onto *Wuthering Heights* because it was the most "literal," and after that came *Jane Eyre* because it was the most "unfair." Then, and only then, my father said, would we take a look at *The Tenant of Wildfell Hall* because understanding it required first reading the other three. *Are you ready?* he used to ask me. *Are you ready for them?* My father wasn't a certified teacher and he didn't have much of a syllabus. He himself never received a college degree, which I assumed was out of genuine disinterest—Dad loathed modern education and its feel-good teaching methods. In his mind, all teachers should use a combination of the Socratic method and basic training. He did try to create some semblance of a classroom, however. We used the rectangular kitchen table as our desk, a baguette as our pointer. If I received less than eighty-five percent on any of his oral examinations, he made me go outside and play soccer.

Under Dad's philosophy, books were not shape-shifting constructions of a reader's imagination. Novels, he said, offered the specific clues, maps, and guidelines necessary for their own evaluation. By *clues*, he did not mean metaphors and he did not mean symbolism. He meant actual clues. To him, every book was its own treasure map. A good novel, he said, left the close reader with a useful souvenir. All you needed to do was learn to see what was right under your nose. (This, I remember, was a refrain he enjoyed repeating.)

I remember our lessons on *Agnes Grey*. My father explained that the only parts of the book worth reading were the chapter headings.

"Recite them to me," he said.

I asked, "Why?"

"Read them out loud. You'll see."

We were at our kitchen table. I flipped open the book to the table of contents. Someone (likely me) had spilled something red and sticky on the opposite page. Ketchup? I read the chapter titles out loud. "'Chapter One: The Parsonage. Chapter Two: First Lesson in the Art of Instruction. Chapter Three: A Few More Lessons.'"

"You get the idea," Dad interrupted.

"No, I don't," I said.

"Lessons. Do you understand?"

"Sorry, what?"

"They're lessons."

"What are?"

"Exactly. Are we on the same page?"

"Metaphorically?"

"Literally."

"What?"

"Excellent."

The discussion went on like this for the rest of the day. *"A few more lessons."* Get it, Sam, get it? *Why would she write that?*

Now, years later, I thought I understood. What appeared to be meekness and agreeableness on Anne's part was deliberate subversion. Her protagonist held the post of governess, one of the least powerful positions a woman could occupy in the nineteenth century. And yet, Anne's novel immortalizes Agnes, giving a loud, persistent, and permanent voice to one of the most inconsequential figures in history. Almost one hundred and seventy years later, Agnes is one of the only governesses left who is barking orders—and, by extension, so is Anne. *"First Lessons,"* *"A Few More Lessons."* She is the ageless teacher, and we, the readers, are her eternal students. Here is her first lesson, on page one:

> *All true histories contain instruction; though, in some, the treasure may be hard to find, and when found, so trivial in quantity, that the dry, shrivelled kernel scarcely compensates for the trouble of cracking the nut. Whether this be the case with my history or not, I am hardly competent to judge. I sometimes think it might prove useful to some, and entertaining to others; but the world may judge for itself.*

It is a curious opening paragraph, which is perhaps why my father wrote in the margin: *CURIOUS*. Anne begins a piece of fiction by calling it a "true" history. I wouldn't normally conflate Agnes's words with Anne's, but this was one of the most poorly masked autobiographies I had ever read. Agnes's "true" history is, in many ways, Anne's. The author is hiding behind her protagonist, desperate to blurt out something important, but unable to expose her true self. The only thing she can do is ask her readers to read her novel carefully, so we gain the "instruction" that will help us discover the "hard to find" treasure. What has Anne hidden inside the text? Did my father know, or was that what he was trying to decipher, alone in his study? Anne, like all good teachers, must have known that a discovery was valuable only if you figured it out on your own.

Her novel ended with the cruelest joke: *And now I think I have said sufficient.*

Hah.

James Orville wrote me an e-mail the following week. It always surprised me to think of him using technology. It was the same surprise I would have felt upon seeing Odysseus whip out Google Maps.

To: "Samantha J. Whipple" swhipple@old.ox.ac.uk
From: "James Timothy Orville" jorville@old.ox.ac.uk
Subject: Necessary Improvements

Dear Samantha,

I did not enjoy your essay on *Paradise Lost.* My recurring concern is the way in which you craft your sentences. Have you ever taken a course in creative writing? I think it might help ease the banality of your prose.
All best,
O.

From: "Samantha J. Whipple" swhipple@old.ox.ac.uk
To: "James Timothy Orville" jorville@old.ox.ac.uk
Subject: RE: Necessary Improvements

Dear O,

I'm sorry you dislike the way I write sentences. Have you considered that it might be because you're not reading them aloud, in a Russian accent? Usually I find that helps.

I have done creative writing before. I greatly dislike it.
Best,
Samantha

To: "Samantha J. Whipple" swhipple@old.ox.ac.uk
From: "James Timothy Orville" jorville@old.ox.ac.uk
Subject: RE: RE: Necessary Improvements

It surprises me that you dislike writing, given your family history. In addition to next week's assignment, I would like you to read the writing the Brontës penned as small children—you will locate it in the library under "Brontë Juvenilia." Have you read *The Chronicles of Angria*? Or *The Tales of Gondal*? I think you will discover that reading stream of consciousness will help ease your inner critic.

I couldn't think of a nonhostile response, so I chose not to respond at all. There was only one reason my "inner critic" was so well nourished: James Orville. Nothing squashes creativity quite like a frowning British man. And yes, I had read the Brontës' juvenilia, thank you. All of it. The Brontë siblings began writing as very small children, before they even developed the full vocabulary to express their thoughts. As a child, I had read those stories cover to cover, over and over again. I did not have any brothers or sisters, and as a result, I would dream myself into the Brontës' darkened living room and pretend that I was there, too, on those stormy evenings, in the middle of all the chaos and all the tantrums as the Brontë siblings wrote their very first stories.

In my mind, I would always be sitting next to Anne on the east side of the dining room table. Emily would be to my right. There would be blank parchment in front of us, because whenever you walked into the Brontë home, there was always blank parchment in front of you. Occasionally, Branwell or Charlotte would stand up by the fireplace to recite their latest masterpieces. I had never liked Branwell. He was confident, swaggering, bigmouthed, and incurably in love with himself—the kind of person who would never have been nice in high school. He was a young man in a world that existed to benefit young men. Twelve-year-old Charlotte would be small, compact, and quarrelsome, like a Viking child. The two of them would often act out the latest adventures from Angria, the imaginary world they had created together, one inhabited by swashbuckling adventurers and plagued by the political intrigue of the rakish Lord Northangerland. Emily, Anne, and I—seated at the table, glassy-eyed—would watch patiently as the latest drama unfolded.

I knew why Orville wanted me to read *The Chronicles of Angria*. Charlotte and Branwell's prose was wild, passionate, and unencumbered. This was imagination in its purest form, perfectly transcribed from two young, uncorrupted brains. Historians later discovered *The*

Chronicles of Angria and concluded that Charlotte and Branwell's imaginary world was a sweet, playful, grammatically terrifying yet overall beautiful expression of childhood. Orville, I'm sure, would agree. I saw it quite a different way. Anyone who had spent time in that darkened living room with the girls and me would have seen how earnestly Anne and Emily would have loathed the writing of their two self-righteous siblings. Anyone who paid attention would know that Anne and Emily disappeared every night after midnight to develop their *own* imaginary land. Under the covers of Emily's bed, they would exchange the daily news from Gondal, a glorious world of dueling dragons, ruined castles, haunted buildings, fainting heroines, underground passageways, crypts, catacombs, labyrinths, omens, villains, curses, and magic. The imaginary kingdom of Gondal became Emily's pride and joy, more so than any of her future poetry—more so even than *Wuthering Heights.* It took months before Branwell and Charlotte found out about it. When they did, that's when all the problems began.

Despite what historians (or Orville) might say on the subject, I knew that Angria and Gondal were not innocent fantasies. Each was an empire wrought of competition, whose outlandishness existed solely to vanquish the other. It was Charlotte and Branwell versus Emily and Anne. Whose fantasy world was better? Who had the best-developed characters, the most vivacious and fantastical plots? It was a war between imaginations, and it lasted far longer than any of the siblings could have anticipated. Angria and Gondal set the foundation for the central, unspoken conflict of the Brontë lives: which Brontë was the best?

At first glance, the answer was Branwell—that is, until he reached his twenties and drowned his talent in alcohol. The next-best bet was Emily, but she soon detached herself from real life, preferring her imaginary worlds to this one. That left just Charlotte and Anne. The Viking versus the Nobody. Who would be the greater success? Which one—Anne or Charlotte—would write their family into immortality? Could a small, timid child ever go up against the Great Charlotte? The competition between Anne and Charlotte was the silent struggle of their lives, and their best-kept secret.

I explained all of this to my mother once, but I stopped when I realized how deeply my intimate friendship with my father's dead family frightened her. She had come to live with me soon after the funeral, in the non-charred half of the house, and assumed I was going mad, just like my father. She said, "Imaginary friends are not good, Samantha, not good at all." I was beginning to sound too much like my dad, I suppose, and Mom hated every part of him she found in me. She viewed Dad as something radioactive that had exploded and left little pieces of himself lodged in the people around him. As the body closest to him, I had borne the brunt of the toxic aftermath. To be fair, her worries weren't entirely unfounded. I used to pace around my father's destroyed library in small circles for hours, like one of those crazed tigers at the zoo that only knows one path. The only thing that had survived the fire was the handwritten sign over the library door, which now read: *If you're careful enough, nothing good or bad will ever.* Apparently, the fire had singed off the "happen to you."

During those few months, I began writing. "Creative writing," as Orville might call it. Every night, I wrote a new story and recited it to my mother. The plot would always involve me in the Brontë living room, talking to Emily about plants, dogs, or the rakish Lord North-angerland. Mom would clap after I read her my stories, then ask me if I was sure I didn't want to be a doctor. I understood her concern. My stories were not very good. They didn't have much of a story line, and, in the way of all serious fiction, they ended with the untimely deaths of everyone.

Mom grew worried. The more I wrote, the more I imagined she thought I'd go on to drink myself to death and set the house on fire.

I resented her lack of trust. Occasionally I would walk around with deliberate facial tics, just to keep her on her toes. In retrospect, I should have been more sympathetic. Mom was, after all, only thirty-seven at the time. There were days when I'd find her sitting at the edge of the paddling pool, jeans rolled up, filling the air with old songs by The Carpenters. I didn't realize how terribly sad she was, because at the time Terribly Sad was something only I had ownership over.

One evening, I was sitting in her bathtub, and she was brushing her teeth in an ankle-length cotton nightgown and gray socks. "We've Only Just Begun" was playing in the background. It was the most morbid love song I knew, the kind that played at funerals during slideshows and made you thankful to be alive but deeply conscious that Karen Carpenter was anorexic and had died of a heart attack at thirty-two. I was in the middle of reading her my latest story, "Life Is Pain, Mother." She interrupted me before I even hit the climax:

"Just stop. Please, stop." She flung a bit of toothpaste against the mirror.

"I—"

"Stop! Goddammit, do you hear me?" she snapped. "You sound like a human grenade."

We didn't speak of it ever again. Soon, I went to boarding school. She went to France. One of us was looking to grow up quicker; the other was looking to stay young.

I stopped writing after that. I feigned outrage at my mother, yet I was secretly relieved. I knew, deep down, that I had no talent. It was the same way guests at weddings secretly knew the couple would be divorced within a year. I was incapable of writing anything non-autobiographical. No matter what I tried, the protagonist ended up being a tall brunette who secretly longed to be outside her own skin. Even when the main character was short and blonde, she was actually tall and brunette. I had read Nabokov and I had read Milton and

I marveled at their ability to create characters that bore no resemblance to their own selves whatsoever. Were they geniuses in a world of losers? Or were there glimmers of themselves in even their most outlandish fictional creations? My father used to say that all protagonists were versions of the author who wrote them—even if it meant the author had to acknowledge a side of himself that he did not know existed. It just required courage.

My lack of literary talent was more a tragedy than a disappointment. The real problem was this: my father was in the grave, and I could do nothing to write him out of it. I had no sweeping statements to make about loss, or life, or their inextricable link. His death was not beautiful, and I couldn't pretend it was. At the same time I knew that, untreated by art, his death would go unacknowledged. It would be flat, useless, real, and forgotten. And if there was anything I disliked, it was waste. I began to dislike every author who ever lived. Hemingway, Keats, Pinter, Shakespeare, Wordsworth, Tolstoy. Rumi, Euripides, Roth, Poe, García Márquez. Homer too, because *The Odyssey* was so long, and so good. These were writers who could take life's biggest disasters and turn them into something beautiful and universal. They could repurpose abandonment and morph it into an enduring form of connection.

More than anything, I began to resent women writers. Burney, Austen, Browning, Shelley, Eliot, Woolf. Brontë, Brontë, and Brontë. I began to resent Emily, Anne, and Charlotte—my old friends—with a terrifying passion. They were not only talented; they were brave, a trait I admired more than anything but couldn't seem to possess. The world that raised these women hadn't allowed them to write, yet they had spun fiery novels in spite of all the odds. Meanwhile, I was failing with the odds tipped in my favor. Here I was, living out Virginia Woolf's wildest feminist fantasy. I was in a room of my own. The world was no longer saying, *Write? What's the good of your writing?* but was instead saying, *Write if you choose; it makes no difference to me.*

And yet I couldn't produce anything of value. Now that I could say anything I wanted, I had nothing to contribute. I was unable to take advantage of the intellectual emancipation for which my own ancestors had struggled so fearlessly. I had taken the freedom Virginia Woolf and Charlotte Brontë and Mary Wollstonecraft had sent me, and thrown it right back at them.

For that, I knew I would never be forgiven.

I met Blanche Howard of the British National Bank on a cold Saturday in November, in a grimy café that looked like something bombed out of the Second World War. Blanche (pronounced *Blahnche*) introduced herself and we had a polite conversation about England's cloud cover. Did I know that we were in for a dire winter? Her face was as pale as a shark's belly.

We sat down, and Blanche placed an old, faded shoebox on the table in front of us. The corners were sealed shut with orange packing tape. I stared at the box and the box stared back at me. My heart began to pound and I thought for a moment that it might come ripping out of my chest. Could this be my inheritance? No—surely not.

Blanche ordered coffee. She had the translucent look of a middle-school boy.

"Forgive me for asking," she said abruptly. "But did your father *know* he was going to die?"

I said, "I don't think anyone plans on dying like that."

"No, of course not," she said without a blink of remorse. Her voice was brittle and high-pitched, just as it had been on the phone. It was what baby plants would sound like if they could talk.

"I ask because he came to England only a month before he died," she said. "He visited Oxford, and then he visited our bank. He explained that he wanted us to deliver his estate directly to you, but only once you were here, at Oxford. He handwrote his will. Did you know that? It was almost impossible to decipher. Would you like to see it?"

"Not really."

"I have a copy with me."

Before I could protest, she reached into her purse and pulled out a sheet of laminated paper, which she held up for my inspection. I took it from her. Yes, yes, it was Dad's illegible handwriting. His *f*'s looked like lazy treble clefs; his lowercase *a*'s were topless. Every bit of blank space on the page had been used and abused. The whole thing looked like a splat of black spaghetti. I caught my name here and there, but it was impossible to string together complete sentences. I glanced at Blanche.

She took a breath, then let it out. "You see my problem."

"I see your problem."

"I'm not sure whether he was trying to write poetry, or a will," she said. "Perhaps they were the same to him? He gave us very few concrete statements. What we have managed to glean—and mind you, this required a not uncomplicated effort—is that if anything were to happen to him, he wanted you to receive this inheritance, but *only* if you were studying at Old College. How did he know that you would be at Oxford? And why, Samantha, did he suspect he would not be alive to give this to you himself?"

I didn't answer. I couldn't decide if it was a necessary question, or just personal interest at this point. I hadn't the faintest idea why Dad assumed I would study at Oxford. I also didn't know he visited it before he died.

The coffee arrived but Blanche didn't drink any. She just held the cup in both hands and blew on it.

"Well?" she pressed.

"I don't know," I said. "He always used to say that Old College was the last place where you could still read the writing on the walls."

"What does that mean?"

"I have no idea."

Blanche let out a breath. "Your father was a secretive man, I gather."

"He made a career out of it."

She took an exaggeratedly petite sip from her cup. I put down my father's will and adjusted my scarf around my neck, like a noose. I recalled many conversations he and I had had about college. Once, we had been sitting in his den, one of us eating cottage cheese and the other drinking whiskey, when he fixed me with his watery stare, told me to sit down (I was already sitting), and explained that traditional English schooling was the last beacon of hope in a world undone by soft American institutions. *A brain only reaches its true potential through conflict,* he said, *the same way courage only finds its wings through necessity*. He would have loathed the boarding school my mother had chosen for me. Blanston Academy only produced fragile, sensitive powder puffs like—I feared—me.

I turned back to Blanche. "It was the only school he ever did mention to me. I guess it was always at the back of my mind."

"Did he ever attend Oxford?"

"He didn't go to college."

"But he must have at least been familiar with the colleges."

I shrugged. "Maybe."

She took a notepad out of her purse, along with a plastic bag half filled with small chocolates.

"Do you see the signature at the bottom of the page?" she said. "Yes, that's right—there. Your father had a witness present when he signed his will, as he ought to have done. It was a Miss"—she reached for her glasses and peered down at her notes—"a Ms. Rebecca Smith. Your . . . ?"

I frowned. "Former math tutor."

"Ah," she said. "Former math tutor."

She scribbled something on her notepad. Rebecca Smith was a

name I hadn't heard in years, and I didn't welcome it. That name brought me back to an old and smelly place.

Blanche seemed to be waiting for an explanation, so I said, "Rebecca came on Wednesdays and Sundays."

"I see," she said. "Rebecca Smith is no longer at the address your father lists, nor does any Rebecca Smith ever seem to have lived there. Do you know where Rebecca Smith is at the moment?"

"She's dead."

Blanche raised her eyebrows. "How dead?"

"Pretty dead."

She frowned. "I'm sorry." She waited a respectable moment of silence before asking: "Is it difficult for you to talk about her?"

I let my silence speak for itself. My father simply adored Rebecca.

Blanche carefully selected a chocolate from the bag in front of her. Her thumb and forefinger looked like escargot snatchers—the small, pewter kind that came in fancy restaurants. She offered me one but I shook my head. She popped one like Advil.

"In case you're wondering, this is what he left you," she said, pointing at the shoebox.

I swallowed. "Yes, I wondered."

"Before you open it, I'd like to ask you something else."

"Go for it."

"If you read the will carefully—or at all—you'll notice that your father went to great, repetitive lengths to make sure that the contents of this box would remain private, and that it would be delivered to you in person. He didn't want you to *stumble* upon it, do you see? At the very end, he scribbled one final note—look here—a footnote he seemed to have penned in a great hurry."

I followed her gaze to the will. She was right. There was a slanted scribble on the right-hand side of the page. It looked like an addition an editor might make upon discovering a missing sentence.

"I can't make it out," I said.

"I believe it says, 'And keep it all away from John.'" Blanche looked up. "Does that mean anything to you?"

"John Booker?" I asked.

Her eyes brightened. "You know him? Who is he?"

"He used to teach at Cambridge. Now, he runs the Brontë Museum, at the Brontës' old home."

"I will assume that he and your father did not get on well."

"Take you me for a sponge?"

"Pardon?"

"That's what Dad always used to say when Sir John came up in conversation."

She paused. "I see."

"He liked to call him a 'huge hill of flesh.'"

Blanche blinked, then pushed her glasses to the edge of her nose. She wrote down something that was probably unnecessary.

"Did he ever try to contact you after your father's death?" she asked.

"Sir John? Many times."

"And?"

"I ignored him."

Blanche's eyes widened and didn't go back to normal. I looked away, feeling strangely ashamed. Then, without another word, Blanche put a palm on the shoebox and slowly slid it across the table. I thought I saw a note of relief cross her face. The problem was now mine, not hers.

I was silent for a long time. I must have looked as agitated as I felt, because she sounded almost sympathetic when she said: "Why don't you take a deep breath? This is only a box."

"That's what Pandora thought."

"You look like you might be expecting a body."

"Maybe. My dad spent his life resuscitating the dead."

"Are you quite all right? You look ill."

"I'm fine. This is just mourning sickness."

She frowned. "You're expecting a child?"

"I meant actual mourning sickness. You know, like getting sick from mourning?"

Blanche pursed her lips and for a moment she looked like a squid. I imagined what it would be like to come home to her every night, to boiled potatoes, three green beans, and a piece of cod, all arranged in an isosceles triangle on her plate. I envied her, in a way. This was her day job. She would return home and think nothing more about any of this. I took a deep breath and then let it out.

"Thank you," I said. My voice cracked. "You've been kind. I'll open this now."

To my surprise, when I lifted the box, it was light as a coin. Was it empty? I used my keys to tear through the tape. It sounded like I was ripping into flesh. There was only one item inside: an old, tattered red bookmark. It had silver sequins and a small, glittery string coming out of the bottom. On it were the words *Much Madness Is Divinest Sense*, right underneath an unflattering picture of Emily Dickinson, who looked as though she had just accidentally stapled herself and was trying to appear cheery anyway. It was a relic of my childhood that I had not seen in years.

Blanche peered over the table, and her thin lips turned into a frown. "What does it mean?"

I said, "Oh, hell."

"I beg your pardon?"

"His-and-hers bookmarks."

She said, "Sorry?"

"Twins. He had the other."

"I don't understand."

It grew difficult to speak. "Dad used to mark important passages in books I hadn't read, then hide the books around the house for me as small surprises. I would find the book and his bookmark inside and know that it was a present from him."

Blanche seemed alarmed, like I had announced an air raid. Her breath was coming quickly. "Your father went to all this effort to leave you a bookmark?"

I glanced at the old shoebox. I felt a painful constriction in my chest. My voice came out soft, and low. "I think he knew no one else would understand it."

"Do *you* understand it?"

"Oh, hell."

I felt ill. Really—very ill. Someone seemed to have punched a hole through my torso all of a sudden, and the rest of my body was flapping around the gap.

"Are you sure he didn't leave me any money?" I said, looking up. "Like, cash money?"

"Quite certain," said Blanche. "He was very much in debt. And—that is—he seems to have lost quite a bit in the divorce."

"Yes, my mother is comfortable," I said. "Did he, by chance, leave me any books? *Agnes Grey*, perhaps?"

"As I said—just the box."

"*Nothing* else?"

Here, Blanche looked apologetic. "Even if he *did* own something else, I'm afraid your legal claim to it would be questionable, since nothing else was ever referenced in his will. This box—this bookmark—is all you have from him. I'm sorry, Samantha."

I moved the bookmark between my fingers, watching Emily Dickinson go in and out of focus. I considered going to the newspapers and revealing the truth—that the Brontë estate had actually been manufactured in China—but I thought better of it. Reporters would only think I was hiding something.

Blanche said, "You look terrible. What is it?"

"Do you mind if I leave?"

"Pardon?"

"I mean, are we done here?"

"You look as though you've seen a ghost."

"I'll just go. Thank you for your time." I gave Blanche the will and packed my things. When I stood up, I crashed into the chair behind me.

"Sorry about my manners," I said. "I was raised in America. By wolves. And my father."

"Samantha—"

I collided with a man in a top hat and then escaped the café into a world where everything was the color of cardboard.

Christmas Day, 2006. It was snowing. The tree was decorated with homemade ornaments, once edible and now stale. My mother had stormed out of the house exactly ten days ago, almost to the hour. The damage she had inflicted upon the kitchen door was still visible. Her exit was dramatic. I remembered her high, strained voice; I remember the echoes of myself sobbing hysterically, saying desperate and lonely things that I didn't care to think of anymore. Mom hugged me so tight that it hurt, and then she was gone.

My father tried to explain their separation to me, but I already knew what had gone wrong. My father married my mother when she was a very young person—a very young person who would probably not have married him had she known him better. She did not understand that Tristan Whipple came with booze, books, Brontës, and weeks of unexplained absence when he mysteriously fled to England. She did not know on her wedding day that her husband would leave her. Not physically, of course. I think he just forgot she was in the house sometimes.

As I said, it was Christmas Day, 2006. My father had invited a guest over and it was not my mother. It was Rebecca Smith, my new tutor, fresh off the boat from England. She did not like traveling by airplane because it frightened her. This struck me as strange, because she was a teacher of math and used the word *literally* three times in a sentence. She thought that everything in life—homework, emotions, bath temperatures—could be solved with an algorithm. She once explained a bad relationship to me through a graph. The y-axis was intensity of emotion; the x-axis was time spent away from each other. She was brilliant, Dad had to explain.

He had known Rebecca for many years. They had met in England, when Dad was a young man. She was fifteen years his senior. Somehow, he had convinced her to become my overqualified algebra tutor. She was a visiting professor at Harvard and surely did not need part-time work, but my father must have been very persuasive, because for the next year and a half, she came over on Wednesdays and Sundays to teach me how to think of life as a giant graph. She was lovely, accomplished, and amusing, and my father liked lovely, accomplished, and amusing people. Rebecca enjoyed my father because they both liked cabbage and they agreed that true civilization had ended after the Peloponnesian War. *Literally.*

I remembered when we first met.

"My name is Rebecca," she told me. Her voice was glossy.

I asked, "Like the book?"

"Like the name."

"Do you know the book *Rebecca*?"

"No."

"It's about a woman named—"

"Rebecca?"

"Oh, so you've read it?"

She hadn't responded, and that had been the end of the conversation.

I did not know why Rebecca Smith felt the need to be there on Christmas morning, 2006. It was a cold, brittle day. My father had hidden my present underneath the tree. The gift was the size of a small piano, and it had been there for two days, draped in a pink bedsheet. Dad told me not to touch anything underneath because the present was radioactive and might implode. I had been counting down the days until the grand reveal. If he was going to divorce my mother, then it was only fair that I should receive a massive, ostentatious gift from him, like some sort of worker's compensation. I wished I didn't have to open it in front of Rebecca. She would misinterpret the gift as a gesture of kindness, when really it was an attempt at an apology.

The three of us sat in a triangle by the gingerbread-decorated tree, awkwardly. I was on the floor by the presents, my father was on the couch, and Rebecca was in the chair by the fireplace, arms thin and folded, with an expectant expression on her narrow face. Inwardly, I compared her to my mother, and found that my mother was lacking. Rebecca might have been much older but she had a stately beauty. She was handsome, not pretty.

When my father gave me the go-ahead to open my gift, I tore off the sheet in one large magician swoop. To my surprise, there was nothing there. I saw only a pile of plastic chairs, the kind you find in cafeterias for pint-size kids. Was this a twisted joke? I looked at Dad, close to tears. But he was grinning. He motioned to the floor. I peered under the wilderness of chairs. Underneath the closest one was a small, solitary envelope. I opened it. Inside, I found Emily Dickinson's face. My father had given me a bookmark.

I started crying in earnest. I would have been inconsolable had Dad not rushed over to me, eyes lit up. He said, *Dammit, Samantha, don't you get it?* He tried to explain. This bookmark was a clue that would lead me to my real present. If I followed the hunt correctly, I would find a matching bookmark. If I failed, the present would be lost.

"Courage," he said. "It requires courage to find it."

Rebecca was sitting on the chair, ignored and confused, eyes wide like a cod's. This made me feel pleasantly exclusionary, and I cheered up. I read the text on the bookmark over and over again. *Much Madness Is Divinest Sense.*

Immediately, I quitted the room in favor of my father's library, aka the Heights. I knew it was where he kept all of his Emily Dickinson poetry. The Heights was perpetually dark but I used the pale light from the shut window to fish through his lowest bookshelf, which contained all the books he liked the most: *Daniel Deronda*, *The Epic of Gilgamesh*, *Portrait of a Lady*. There—I found it. *The Greatest Works of Emily Dickinson.* To my surprise, the two hundred and seventeenth page had been dog-eared. On the page, one passage had been highlighted in bright orange:

> Exultation is the going
> Of an inland soul to sea,—
> Past the houses, past the headlands,
> Into deep eternity!
>
> Bred as we, among the mountains,
> Can the sailor understand
> The divine intoxication
> Of the first league out from land?

I had never read this poem before, but I gleaned its meaning easily enough—or at least the meaning I knew it would have for my father. We had a basement in our home that he referred to as "Deep Eternity." (*I'm heading to Eternity,* my father would sometimes say when he went off in search of spare batteries.) I reread the Emily Dickinson poem. *Can the sailor understand . . . ?*

I darted from the room and ran to the basement, passing a bemused Rebecca and a beaming father. Deep Eternity was a home for all of our dead electronics and broken bikes. There was a chalkboard on the far wall, and today, there was one sentence written on it. *It was a bright and cold day in April, and the clocks were striking thirteen.* George Orwell.

And then, slowly, I realized what my father was doing. He had constructed a treasure hunt for me, built out of literature. The game lasted well into the afternoon. Most of his clues were the opening lines of novels, none of which had ever been meant literally:

> *Through the fence, between the curling flower spaces, I could see them hitting.*

> *The sun shone, having no alternative, on the nothing new.*

> *In the beginning, sometimes I left messages in the street.*

This last one led me out to the sanitary sewer in the middle of the street. My father had marked it with a giant masking-tape *X*. Rebecca, bored, had retired to take a nap, so it was just me and Dad— the way it should have been. I picked up the heavy metal lid. Did my father expect me to climb in? *Courage,* he had said. I would need courage. I descended the small, damp ladder, and there, to my great surprise, was a giant Dean & DeLuca bag, in which my father had hidden a shoebox containing *The Wizard of Oz.* My Christmas present. It was a wonderfully ornate early edition. Inside, my father had lodged his own Emily Dickinson bookmark. Twins.

It remains, to this day, the finest present my father ever gave me— and finer than that was the pride on his face when I returned to the house, clutching my prize. I devoured *The Wizard of Oz* that very day, if only because I wanted to be lost somewhere, and a book seemed like a good place. I loved Dorothy more than any protagonist I had ever known. She longed for something so deeply that it came true. (This level of imagination, Dad said, was the greatest and most elusive of life skills.) That day, I fell back in love with my father. His bookmark was my entry into a world—*his* world—the one that he used to escape life, pain, divorce. Here was my escape too. He was helping me, in his own way.

Recalling Christmas of 2006 made it all the more cruel that seven years later, I would be sitting in my lonely Oxford tower with Dad's bookmark in my lap—just with no Dad. If I knew my father well, this bookmark was a clue. The clue would lead to another clue, and another clue after that, and then maybe this time I would find the Warnings of Experience. But this game was meant to be played indoors, in a closed system—a backyard, or maybe even a library— not across an entire country. I had no idea where to start. And couldn't he have explained this all in a letter? I put the bookmark down on my desk, right next to *Agnes Grey*, and sat back in my seat.

For the third time that evening, I found myself dwelling on Rebecca Smith. It surprised me to learn that my father had chosen her to witness the signing of his will since a year and a half after Rebecca became my tutor, my father politely asked her to leave. He had never told me why. It bothered me to think that they secretly kept in touch. Couldn't he have asked a lawyer to be a witness? Or my mother? It was a stupid choice on his part. Rebecca had died only months after my father did. The papers said that it was a boating accident, off the coast of Scotland. To this day, her remains were lying at the bottom of the sea, along with all the gold rings she kept around her middle finger, and along with everything my father had ever told her. Down with her, I suppose, went my first clue.

CHAPTER 5

The weeks passed and as my preoccupation with *Agnes Grey* and my bookmark grew, I developed an equally pressing concern. As it got colder, all I seemed to be doing was growing stupider. Every tutorial I suffered with Orville invariably turned into a verbal lynching. Our syllabus implied that I was studying critical theory and the masterpieces of the Western canon. What I was actually learning was the agony of speechlessness, and the exhaustion of contemplating my own idiocy.

"But what does it *mean?*" Orville would ask. He liked to sit in his chair—the stuffed, lumpy, cancerous piece of orange leather by the fireplace—and ask me the same question over and over again, until my temples throbbed and the only thing left in this world was his sick grin and meterstick. The sick grin, I imagined, was a construction of my too-easily-terrified imagination; the meterstick was something Orville kept in his right hand so that he could thwack the coffee table for additional punctuation.

This particular morning, we were having an impromptu pop quiz on "An Essay on Criticism." Orville had handed me the text the moment I arrived. Now, twenty minutes later, here I was, sweating dramatically.

"You're still not telling me anything, Samantha," he said pleasantly. I had a volume called *English Masterpieces* in my lap, which I had come to know as *Hell: Volume I.* In it was everything that I hated:

"The Rape of the Lock," "The Wasteland," blurry pictures of Wordsworth, and four thousand and seventy two footnotes.

Orville asked, "What is 'An Essay on Criticism' about?"

I said, "Criticism."

"Are you being sarcastic?"

"That depends. Was I right?"

Orville's gaze was steady. His shirt was fitted, and through his
sleeves, his biceps appeared to be flexing and unflexing on their own.
It was fascinating and disgusting at the same time. My palms were
damp and leaving perspiration marks on the book's pages. I imagine I
had the sweaty sheen of a woman in labor.

He said, "Let's try again. What is this essay *about*?"

"It talks about the role of poetry and critics."

Thwack.

I jumped. The meterstick made an empty, twiggy sound against
the wooden table. He appeared at ease, as though he had been slashing unruly furniture his entire life.

"An essay does not *talk*," he said. "Tell me something less juvenile."

I said, "It's about poetry in the modern era."

"Tell me something less vague."

"Modern era meaning post-Reformation."

"Tell me something less incorrect."

I blinked. Orville's jaw was twitching. In all the lessons I had had
with my father, I had never felt so powerless. Had I had any backbone
myself, I might have—

Thwack.

I jumped back to attention. "Sorry."

Finally, Orville put the meterstick down. "Oh, for God's sake, Samantha, if you keep apologizing, I am going to have to lower your marks."

He reached for his tea. There was a worn, tortured look to his face
when he concentrated, and I was disgusted to find myself attracted to
it. Intelligence carried a handsome degree of authority.

Orville leaned back in his chair, in a gesture I recognized. I knew what was coming next: his favorite question, and my least. Sure enough, he motioned toward "An Essay on Criticism" and asked, "Does this piece of writing strike you as reliable?"

I restrained a desire to hit something. Teachers had been asking that question for years and it made me batty. Questioning the reliability of a narrator was an attempt to prove that every novel written— every verb, every comma—existed solely for the sake of subversion. There was no such thing as face value; there were only authorial biases and self-constructed identities.

Orville looked pleased. I was beginning to believe that he enjoyed nothing more than watching me froth at the mouth and implode.

I answered, "Yes, it is reliable."

"Wrong," he said. "How can it be reliable? The essay deliberately exemplifies that which it admonishes. Pope offers specific advice for writers and then ignores each of his own instructions."

"Sure."

"He deplores the use of metaphors, and then proceeds to liken 'expression' to an unchanging sun, 'false eloquence' to a prismatic glass, and words to leaves. Alexander Pope," he concluded, "is a fool."

"I—"

"I'm not finished," he said. "Crucially, it is Pope who engineers this contradiction. He is a master masked as a fool masked as a master. Do you see? Alexander Pope," he concluded, "is a genius."

"Make up your mind."

"No, *you* must make up your mind," he said. "Pope's essay demands that the reader be the final critic. He is teaching you that the best student will question his opinion."

I waited for the *thwack*, but it didn't come. The bubble of silence was disarming, as though an orchestra had missed its cue. We waited, lingering in the swollen pause.

I cleared my throat. "May I speak?"

He looked kind—almost. "Please."

"Pope is just pretending to solicit another's opinion. Anyone as young or as cocky as a twenty-three-year-old genius is only feigning modesty."

Orville raised an eyebrow.

I continued, "He wrote this poem for the one purpose of showing how much smarter he was than everyone else. You said it yourself. He engineered it. He's a pompous ass masked as a modest man masked as a pompous ass."

I wanted a meterstick, too, just so I could hit something for the hell of it. Instead, I swallowed and tried to maintain eye contact with Orville. There was another silence, longer this time. For a moment, we sat staring at each other, so deliberately frozen that we could have been posing for a hidden portraitist.

"Tell me," Orville said, smiling, "why does a twenty-three-year-old protégé, as you say, elicit such a violent reaction from you?"

"I'm not being violent."

"Look down."

I did. I had the first page of "An Essay on Criticism" clenched in between my thumb and forefingers. It was crumpled in my grip and the page had wilted, like the damaged wing of a dove. I took the book off my lap and gingerly placed it on the table.

"I don't like Alexander Pope," I explained.

"Some say that hate is only unachieved love."

"Whoever said that obviously never hated anyone before."

I caught his eyes then and, as usual, looked away. His jaw was strong and square, like it had been forged out of steel.

I thought the conversation might be over, but he said, "There must be one author who arouses your less aggressive passions."

Passion. There was that word again. I sat back in my chair, trying to think of authors I halfway liked. But Orville's face had induced a temporary amnesia, and every author I knew promptly evaporated from my mind. The only name I could think of was Julius Caesar.

I said, finally: "Frederick Douglass."

Orville's eyebrow curved upward again—slowly, this time, with expert precision. "Frederick Douglass, the former American slave and abolitionist?"

"Yes."

"Any reason?"

Yes, I had a reason. No, I did not want to share.

I said, "I find him . . . poignant."

Orville leaned forward to scribble something on a sheet of paper. He was so large that his limbs seemed to spill out of the mouth of the chair; his knees buckled, his pant legs hiked upward, his elbows jutted over the armrests. The image made me wonder what a young man was doing in such an old chair, and why, out of all the careers James Orville III could have chosen—espionage, torture, psychological warfare—he had picked a profession that cooped him up in a fourteenth-century literary prison, with books as his companions and quivering students as his lunch.

"Very well, Samantha," he said, finishing a quick note to himself. He stood up and, after a brief search through a nearby shelf, pulled down a book. In a moment, he handed it to me. "As you wish. Frederick Douglass. Let's begin."

"Now?"

"I expect you can discuss him very well, if you are so passionate about him."

I blinked. Wasn't the tutorial over? Besides, I had lied. Frederick Douglass was not my favorite author. He was my father's. Dad always said that Douglass's *Narrative* was one of the two finest pieces of literature he could recall. The other was *Anne of Green Gables*, which he said grasped shockingly real-world themes. (Like the narrator, Dad had always been terribly concerned with whether or not *Anne* should be spelled with an *e. Tricky things, names, aren't they?* he had once said to me.)

"Tell me why you like this book, Samantha," Orville said, smiling.

I gave a grunt and picked up *Narrative*. I flipped to the scene my father found most interesting. It was the moment in which Frederick Douglass described a brutal slave master, Mr. Gore. I put my thumb on the page and handed the open book to Orville. At the end of a long and gory account of their dealings, this is what Douglass had to say:

> *. . . and thus the guilty perpetrator of one of the bloodiest and most foul murders goes un-whipped of justice, and uncensured by the community in which he lives. Mr. Gore lived in St. Michael's, Talbot county, Maryland, when I left there; and if he is still alive, he probably lives there now. . . .*

Orville read the passage and looked up, unimpressed.

I explained: "Douglass is telling the truth. Not spiritual truth, or metaphorical truth. *Literal* truth. Douglass is not so subtly asking his readers to hunt down this man and kill him. He might as well have given us Mr. Gore's street address, apartment number, and morning schedule."

I could almost feel my father's ghost erupting in the corner of the room, egging me on. *Yes, yes,* he would say, *that's very good!* Yet Orville had a frown on his face. He interlaced his hands on his lap.

"Do you think that Douglass is a reliable narrator?" he asked.

Something twitched in my face. I wondered if Orville knew he slowly was driving me to apoplexy.

I said, "Now may not be the right time, sir, but I really hate that question."

He ignored me. "Answer it."

"No, I mean, I *really* hate it."

"Answer."

"Yes," I said. "Frederick Douglass is reliable. If you can't trust a diary, how can you trust any author who has ever lived?"

"You can't," Orville answered. He handed me the book. "Which is why the life of an author should not inform the evaluation of a book.

We must treat this text as any other work of fiction. Turn to page seventy-one."

"No."

"Pardon?"

"Sorry."

I cracked open the book. Page seventy-one. I looked down. In my old copy back home, this was the scene on top of which I had doodled a dragon.

"Tell me what's happening," Orville said.

I glanced at the page. "Frederick Douglass is fighting his master."

"He's not just *fighting* his master," Orville said. "He is engaging in one of the most epic battles in any slave narrative. The fight lasts for a full two hours, or didn't you notice?"

I didn't respond.

"Two full hours, Samantha," he repeated. "Do you find nothing suspicious about that?"

"No. The man was ripped."

"The man was lying." He stood up, one hand in his pants pocket, one hand behind his back. "Have you ever fought with someone, Samantha—really, physically fought?"

"Have *you*?"

"Few people can stand more than a few minutes of full exertion. Douglass, the narrator, exaggerates the struggle so the gravity of his situation becomes more apparent. It is the most basic concept of fiction, which you continually fail to understand. This is not a fistfight; this is the universal battle between oppressor and oppressed. It is the turning point in a slave's fight for freedom. There is no way Douglass could have made us viscerally feel this moment's significance without first turning it into fiction. You need to look at a book as an artistic entity, not a self-serving diary. He is not one slave. He is every slave who has ever existed. This is not *literal* truth, but *emotional* truth."

He had walked toward my couch and was now standing over me. I could smell the tuna on his breath.

I said, trying to stay calm, "I don't think you and I understand literature the same way, sir."

"Yes, I can see that."

"You think that good nonfiction is, in fact, fiction. I think that all good fiction is actually nonfiction."

He frowned. "Did your father teach you that?"

"It's part of what he called 'tangible truth.'"

A pause. Orville's gaze bored down into the top of my head. A strange emotion seemed to be kneading its way through his normally inexpressive face. I knew what he was thinking: Did my father believe the Brontë novels were nonfiction? I didn't say anything.

"Very well," Orville said. "You may go."

He turned around and walked to the windows, where he brusquely threw open the curtains. An aggressive morning light tore into the room. I had never seen the room in natural light—only ever by the hellish glow from the fireplace—and it was grayer than I imagined it would be. It was like a vast ocean floor that had been drained of water, and now everyone could see how old and tired it really was. I started to pack up but stopped myself.

"Sir?" I said.

"What is it?"

"How much do you know about *Agnes Grey*?"

"Why do you ask?"

"Instead of reading Alexander Pope or Chaucer, how about we read Anne Brontë?" I said. "I would be curious to hear your analysis of her books."

There was a long silence. I didn't think I had asked a difficult question, but perhaps I was mistaken. For the first time, he looked awkward.

"Samantha, I—" He stopped himself. "That is—I would prefer not to discuss the Brontës with you."

"Why not? It's an academic project."

He didn't look convinced. "I cannot help you."

"Why not?" I said, and when he didn't respond, I added: "*Please?*"

I sounded more desperate than I had intended, and I wished I could reel my words back in. Our eyes met. My cheeks burned. I wondered if this was another one of the rules in the giant green *Old College Book of Disciplinary Procedures*: *Professors shall not help their students.* I turned away. I could feel Orville's eyes on me as I packed up. When I was finished, I walked to the door. My hands were shaking. I never asked for help, and people shouldn't be rejected on their first try.

"Do you know what I think?" I said, turning back around. "I think you're refusing me because I know a lot about the Brontës and you do not."

He stared at me with a calm, experienced expression. "Don't flatter yourself, Samantha."

We didn't say goodbye.

Someone at Old College was out to get me. This person's name was H. Pierpont, one of the *Hornbeam*'s most prolific and consistently irritating staff writers. If Pierpont's last two articles weren't bad enough ("Tower Welcomes New Occupant But Has Anyone Ever Seen Her?" and "Who's Afraid of the Big Bad Brontë?") I woke up on a chilly November morning to some more verbal vomit in the paper:

BRONTË LEGACY EXPOSED?
PARSONAGE CURATOR WRITES NEW BOOK

This latest article was about Sir John Booker, who had apparently turned his nasty op-ed from years ago into a nasty book. According to Pierpont, his forthcoming exposé promised to "unpack the literary legacy of the Brontës" and would be "interesting." I wished people would stop publishing their opinions on the Brontës. New books did nothing but feed an increasingly delusional public imagination. My fuller-than-usual in-box was already stuffed to the brim with unread inquiries from the press. I deleted them systematically, one by one, the way one might shred defunct checks.

I crumpled the flimsy page of the *Hornbeam* in my fist and tossed it into the bin in the corner of my room. So far, my attempts to figure out the identity of Pierpont had met with no success. The *Hornbeam*'s website had surprisingly little to say about its staff. For a student who so enjoyed meddling in my business, Pierpont revealed nothing about his—or her—identity.

Perhaps I had Pierpont and the *Hornbeam* to thank, but as the next few days passed, I couldn't help feeling that I was being watched. During meals, I would turn around to find the gaze of faceless, nameless students resting upon me; during my walks, joggers would sometimes do a double take. And more than once as I walked through the exaggeratedly carpeted Faculty Wing, I felt a sidelong look from a passing professor. Those eyes followed me down the hall and into Orville's office, where sometimes I imagined they still watched me from behind his closed doors. Had I done something *wrong*? Had I walked on the lawns, spoken out of turn, or used my spoon in a regrettable fashion? Had I violated page two hundred and eighty-four in the rulebook? Or was it simply suspicious that I was a young woman spending a great deal of time with Oxford's only aggressively attractive professor? For whatever reason, the entire Faculty Wing had become one giant, raised eyebrow.

It was around this same time, in late November, that I decided I could no longer look the Governess in the eye. It was too painful. I had tried to live in peace with her, but I had failed. She seemed to be screaming out to me—louder, then louder. Would I let her expire?

Well? Would I? She reminded me of Anne. She reminded me of Emily. She reminded me of Charlotte. If I wanted to get philosophical, she reminded me of myself. (I did not want to get philosophical.)

If the painting had had any other name, it wouldn't have bothered me so much. But the word *governess* brought up an image of a formerly pretty young woman clad in a black frock, staring down at the floor and contemplating which would kill her first: boredom, destitution, or insanity. Being a governess was one of the evils that my father had once outlined in his famous poem, "Being a Governess and Other Evils." He used to tell me that no matter how desperate I became in life (was this a likely scenario in his mind?), I should never become one. Once, when our mustached neighbor in Boston called to ask whether I might like to babysit his squealing, cherry-faced child, Dad threw a strange species of fit. He called the job the last legal form of slavery. I tried to explain to him that governesses hadn't existed for a hundred years, but he waved me aside and walked to his shelf. He pulled out *Emma* and read Jane Austen's description of governess Jane Fairfax: "With the fortitude of a devoted novitiate, [Jane] had resolved at one-and-twenty to complete the sacrifice, and retire from all the pleasures of life, of rational intercourse, equal society, peace and hope, to penance and mortification for ever."

"Ergo," my father had said.

Nineteenth-century governesses all looked exactly the same: pale, bitter, and vaguely suicidal, just like the woman in the painting that now rested on my wall. Equal to their employers in nature but not in station, they were stuck in an uncomfortable, friendless limbo. A state of drowning, so to speak. Theirs was a contemptible life, nourished by resentment from the staff, indifference on the part of the family, and the hilariously little sum of twenty to forty pounds a year. A governess represented an entire generation of educated, respectable women whose fathers had simply run out of cash. I suppose it struck too close to home for dear old Dad.

And yet, if my father had wanted to steer me away from the life of a governess, it appeared that he had failed. Here I was—lonely, clad in black, and living in my own little corner of Old College, where I spent my days pacing back and forth in my tower. I was pale and thin and unmarried. Orville was the master; I was his dependent. I was not quite a child and not quite an adult, not quite his friend yet not altogether a stranger. Either I was taking to English literature well, and had begun to find impossible parallels between unrelated things, or else my life was, in fact, becoming alarmingly Victorian.

To no one's surprise, governesses ended up comprising a large portion of lunatic asylum residents. Certainly Henry James had known this when he wrote *The Turn of the Screw*; certainly Charlotte Brontë knew this when she wrote *Jane Eyre*. There was a very thin line between a governess and madness, so much so that the thing being "governed" often became madness itself. The majority of governesses were left to die alone, go insane, or else write books about the happy ending they never had. Or, in the case of my relatives, all three. All the Brontë women had been governesses at some point, thanks to a lack of money or of a husband or of a brother who could hold down a job. Aside from painting, the only other ways an unmarried woman could earn a decent wage were by writing, acting, or prostitution (and sometimes the first and second were seen as synonymous with the third). Poor Anne had it the worst. In 1840, after two years with one family, she went straight off to a manor called Thorp Green, where she was governess to the Robinson children for the next five years. It was the most transformative period of her life, one that changed poor little Annie in more ways than she could possibly imagine.

There was nothing else to be done. I pulled my blue bedsheet off my bed. After giving it one giant shake, I draped it over *The Governess*. There it hung, edge grazing the floor, like a veil on a corpse bride.

CHAPTER 6

On Saturday morning, I awoke to a knock on my door. It was Marvin, my shark-toothed friend, who had introduced me to this decrepit home on my first day. To my surprise, there was an entire frat party's worth of tourists behind him.

I said, "Hello."

The crowd was thick and I found dozens of eyes staring at me like I was the reincarnated version of Bloody Mary.

Marvin smiled. "It's time for the tour."

He sounded perky. I had forgotten about the tour that visited my tower every weekend. Normally, I woke up early and left long before any tourists arrived, but this morning, it had slipped my mind. I hadn't cleaned today, and all of my dirty socks were still on the floor in what looked like a sacrificial half circle. There was an empty hummus tub on the desk, and my clothes from yesterday were piled on the back of the chair. The Governess still had a sheet over her terrible face.

I turned back to Marvin. "The tour is earlier than usual? Or did I just wake up late?"

"You woke up late."

I nodded. "It's hard, you see, not having windows."

Marvin came inside, and the pile of visitors followed him like a great spurt of toothpaste. Protectively, I crossed my arms. My feet were bare and exposed. The woman standing closest to me was several inches taller than I was, with a fanny pack that said: *I Heart*

Dromedaries. I made a point of not making eye contact with anyone, since most people in the room, I noticed, had cameras.

"Welcome to the tower," I heard Marvin saying. He enjoyed his job—I could tell. In his voice was the self-satisfied smugness of someone who, at long last, felt powerful. "This tower, as I mentioned earlier, has been the home of many famous inhabitants of Old College. It became something of a tradition for each one to leave something behind for posterity."

I maneuvered through the crowd, head down, picking up stray pieces of underwear. I ducked inside my wardrobe to change clothes. It was dark and splintery inside and barely large enough for me to lift my arms. I wiggled into a turtleneck and jeans, crashing against the side of the wardrobe more than once.

"Turn this way, please," I could hear Marvin saying, "and you can see the exact location where Sir Michael Morehouse's cat was buried alive in the wall. Do you see the discoloration of the brick, right about here?"

When I finished changing, I opened the wardrobe door and stepped outside. Immediately, there was a disorienting flash of light. I blinked—once, twice. Someone had taken a picture of me. An emergency response went off in my body. I looked to my right to find a squat, purple-shirted teenager holding a disposable camera to his face. I panicked. Quickly, I made my way to the opposite end of the room, eyes on the floor. The crowd was thick, and I stepped on more than one shoe. I needed to get out of there. I would not appear on the cover of another newspaper, thank you very much.

Marvin was speaking quickly and with more energy than before. "And over here—do you see? No, this way—is where a former student engraved his initials. If you look closer—"

There, I found my purse. I slipped on my shoes and slid toward the front door. I was shaking. With one last breath, I closed my tower door behind me and I fled down five flights of steps.

Once outside, I took a moment to collect myself. It was reasonably warm, to my surprise. I took a short walk around campus, trying to find comfort in my old, long-lost friend, the sun. I had only made it halfway around the path when I found myself near the Plodge, the small cabin near the entry gates, which was currently puffing smoke out of its chimney. This, I knew, was where Marvin worked. And if I remembered correctly, it was also where my Swedish model friend worked. I walked past the porter on duty (she gave me a small nod of recognition) and I found Hans sitting in the room off the right, heels kicked up on the table. He was blindingly blond.

When he saw me, his face cracked into a smile and he moved to an upright position.

"Well," he said. "This is unexpected."

I said, " 'If you do not expect the unexpected, you will not find it.' "

"What?"

"Heraclitus."

There was a painful silence, in which it occurred to me that I might never have a normal life.

"What I mean is, Heraclitus said that," I corrected.

"Ah."

"Sorry."

Then he smiled again. He had the distinctive look of a European tennis pro—an electric white athletic shirt, a slightly hooked nose, long spindly legs. His shirt seemed to trap the muscles in between his ribs. I fidgeted. I didn't date much, and I felt like a tourist in someone else's sexual fantasy.

I said, "I'm surprised you remember me."

He laughed. He must have thought I was joking, but when I remained silent, he said: "You're the Brontë."

"Do you mind if I stay awhile?"

He motioned to the seat across from him. He was smiling, but I noticed a degree of cautiousness in his face, as though I were a nervous seal.

He said, "We could also go out."

"Out where?"

"Out into the world," he said. "You've heard of it, yes?"

"Don't you have to work?"

"I'll close up early."

"You can do that?"

He grinned. "Are you impressed?"

He packed up his things. I watched him pull on a suede coat and he led me outside, into the warm sunlight. I didn't realize how desperate I was for a fun afternoon. Already, I was thinking about how I would remember it, years later.

He asked, "What do you want to do?"

"I don't know," I said. "I haven't been to Europe in a while."

"All right, sure."

We exited the Old College gates and began walking down High Street, which reeked of diesel and cigarettes. There were double-decker buses on the streets, filled with dour, flat-featured people and a few dogs that, pressed up against the windows, looked subaquatic. It was pleasant walking with Hans—like driving a shiny Maserati. I can't remember what we talked about. All I registered was that he tended to explain things one too many times and that with his accent, the way he pronounced "Google" sounded like he might kill someone.

"Well?" he said, finally.

"Well what?"

I looked up. We had stopped walking, and were standing right in front of the Oxford Theatre. Some of the letters had fallen off, and now it read OXFORD EATRE. I realized why Hans had stopped— the poster in front of us advertised the newest adaptation of *Jane Eyre*, which was set to hit theaters this weekend. Charlotte Brontë's beloved novel. I vaguely recalled that someone from the press—was it the *Daily Mail*? the *Paris Examiner*?—had e-mailed several times last week asking for the "Brontë take on the film; were you offended by all the sex?" I hadn't responded. A new adaptation of *Jane Eyre* came out every year, and every year, it was exactly the same. An unknown actress would play Jane, and she was usually prettier than she should have been. A very handsome, very brooding, very "ooh-la-la" man would play Mr. Rochester, and Judi Dench would play everyone else.

I made a noncommittal grunting noise and nudged Hans in the bicep to keep him moving. He didn't budge. He had stumbled across the family tombstone of his companion, and felt obligated to pay respects.

"Who's that supposed to be?" he asked. He pointed to the corner of the poster, at the blackened shadow of a woman right next to the last *e* in *Eyre*. The only visible part of her was her two red, wet eyes, and the outline of a gloomy face. She was looking straight at me. We faced off like two chess masters who were meeting again after years apart. I was silent for a long time. The madwoman.

"Can we keep moving?" I asked.

Hans looked at me curiously and kept walking. Then, quite suddenly, he veered down a small avenue.

"Where are we going?" I asked.

"I have an idea. Let's go to the Ashmolean."

I followed him. In about ten minutes, we arrived at a large, ornate structure with grandiose columns and the self-importance of a Wordsworth poem. A museum. There was a sign outside advertising the special exhibit: *Early Women Writers*. I turned to Hans with a grimace, but he seemed strangely excited at the prospect of a museum, like he hadn't used his brain in years and wanted to give it a go again.

I must have looked as unpleasant as I felt, because Hans said: "What's wrong?"

"I hate women."

"Pardon?"

"I meant writers."

He led the way inside. The foyer was a vast marble chamber that smelled like hot glue. The red-cheeked man at the door handed us each a pamphlet and told us not to miss the official opening of the exhibit in a few weeks, when Sir John Booker of the Brontë Parsonage would be doing a book signing, alongside some other notable speakers. I feigned disinterest and followed Hans upstairs, past the Pre-Raphaelite display, and past a statue of a headless Roman, until we arrived at the main attraction: *Early Women Writers*.

Judging from the brochure, the exhibit featured the sketches and notebooks of a handful of women: Mary Wollstonecraft, Frances Burney, Eliza Haywood, Mary Shelley, Jane Austen, and, of course, the Brontës. These were the ballsy "early adopters"—the women who became novelists long before it was cool. At the time they lived, a woman who ventured outside the domestic sphere ran the risk of pernicious public scrutiny. Yet all of these ladies gave the finger to everyone and did it anyway.

"Are you all right?" Hans asked.

"Yes," I lied. I was sweating profusely. I started walking quickly, head down. I felt like I was lost in Madame Tussaud's Chamber of Horrors. Rationally, I understood that the gallery was meant to glorify freedom of speech and gender equality. But all I could see was a tribute to suffering. The history of these particular writers was a history of censorship. Their work was defined not by what they wrote, but what they had been forced to cut out. Frances Burney—poor Fanny! Hers was the first gallery we visited. She burned all her writing at age fifteen, due to her family's scorn. And Jane Austen—dear Jane! I charged through her gallery so quickly that at one point Hans had to jog to keep up. After her death, her letters were painstakingly edited—entire pages ripped out—to the point where the Jane Austen we know today was not the woman who actually lived. I walked quicker and quicker. I felt a ringing in my ears. All the portraits on the walls stared down at us from their cages as if they were instead looking out the window of a strange asylum. I could not help feeling like someone was screaming very loudly, only from a great distance.

Which brought us to the Brontës. Their gallery was on the third floor, up another flight of stairs. The bright sign read, *A Life in Art: Charlotte, Emily, Anne*. I stood outside for a moment to calm myself down. There was a girl in the center of the room, who, judging by her suit and badge, was either an intern or a very new employee. She was speaking to two Indian tourists. We walked inside.

"She's young," I muttered to Hans, motioning toward the tour guide.

"She's hot," he said.

"What?"

"She's not," he corrected. "Not young."

She couldn't have been older than I was. Her hair was the color of saffron. There was a shy streak of crayon purple in her bangs.

"What most people don't realize is that it's possible to understand the Brontës solely in terms of their attention to visual art," she was saying. Her voice echoed around the hollow chamber.

Hans and I began to wander. My heart was still banging in my chest. I recognized most of the drawings here from the Brontë history books my father had owned. Hans pointed out various sketches the way he might have pointed to a breaching whale from the lido deck. I smiled and nodded each time, and he would look at me expectantly, as though storing my response for future reference. I hated seeing the sketches in frames. It was the same way I didn't like to see stuffed deer heads mounted on a wall.

"Pretty," I lied when we stopped in front of one of Charlotte's larger paintings. I didn't recognize this one. It depicted a prince leaning over a sleeping woman draped in elegant sheets.

"Would you mind not standing so close to the art?" said the

museum employee with the purple streak. She had come up behind me. The Indian couple had left.

"Sure," I said. I took a step away from the wall and said to Hans: "See how morbid this all is? It really gives a picture of what was going on in Charlotte's mind."

The girl cleared her throat. I turned around. She was right behind us.

She said, "This drawing is an exact copy of A. B. Clayton's painting *The Atheist Viewing the Dead Body of His Wife*."

Hans tilted his head to the side. "The Brontës copied someone else's work?"

"Naturally," the girl said. She had a squirrelly voice. "Copying existing prints was the way women learned to draw. No one expected them to become artists. Drawing was a use of time, like embroidery."

I blinked and didn't smile. "What was your name?"

"Amanda."

She was pretty. Stretchy pants. I looked between my two companions. I registered how objectively attractive Hans was. Big blue fish eyes. Trimmed, corn-blond hair. He looked like a well-dressed Visigoth. The two of them belonged together far more than Hans and I did.

He pointed to another painting on the wall. "Look at this one."

"Another copy," said Amanda.

Hans pointed to another one. "That one?"

"Copy."

"Those three over there?"

"Copy. Copy, copy." She smiled, revealing a gap between her two front teeth. "As I said, civilized ladies copied existing prints."

"What about uncivilized ladies?" I asked.

"I beg your pardon?"

"There are several known original Brontë paintings out there," I said.

"Very few, and they are quite dull," said Amanda. "But if it helps, what little visual creativity the girls had, they more than made up for with their writing. They learned how to paint pictures with words. Their books, you could argue, were translations of their paintings."

She was very young to be speaking in such assured, textbook sentences, and I wondered if she had recently written a graduate thesis. My breath grew short. I didn't like people insulting the Brontës' originality. That seemed like a job only I had the right to do. I also didn't like being interrupted with the facts. The Brontë world I had in my own mind was clean and tidy and didn't have a ton of room for the opinions of outsiders.

"I wager, then, that there are more than just a few original Brontës out there," I said. "Jane Eyre herself starts out copying prints, but develops into a creative artist. I'm sure Charlotte did the same."

"Perhaps."

I could feel my face growing heated, so I turned around and walked toward another side of the room. I stopped in front of a painting I had spied in the corner earlier—it was of an unattractive woman in her even more unattractive profile, which lacked dimension and resembled an Egyptian hieroglyphic. Bonnet strings encircled her neck like chains. I recognized this painting. I had seen it over and over and over again as a child, in my dad's books.

"Would you say this is a copy?" I asked Amanda, who had appeared behind me.

"No," she conceded. "That one is not."

"I didn't think so."

"Do you know who it is?" she asked, looking vaguely impressed.

"Ann Marshall," I said.

She gave me a gap-toothed smile, as if we were about to become great friends. "I see you know about Thorp Green."

I thought about responding that yes, I knew about Thorp Green, and no, I was not a savage, but I thought better of it. Instead, I took a small amble around the room, trying to calm myself. I was angry with Hans for bringing me here. It was as insensitive as bringing an alcoholic to a beer factory. He seemed far less curious about the exhibit than he was about my reaction to it. But in a moment, he came up behind me and rested his hand on the small of my back. Immediately, I felt calm; his skin must have had a sedative property to it. His voice was sweet when he whispered, "Let's go, yeah?" My heart gave a small contraction. I took a final peek around the gallery and pointed to one last painting on the way out, eyebrow raised.

Amanda answered my unasked question: "Copy."

We thanked her and left.

Hans and I went for ice cream at Moo-Moo's, then made an aimless circle around a deserted park. On the way home, we walked by the Oxford eatre, which, in addition to *Jane Eyre*, was also playing *The Grapes of Wrath: A British Musical Comedy*. When evening fell, we walked home. I felt proud. I was having fun. If anyone asked, which they wouldn't, I could tell them all the exciting, borderline romantic things I had done today.

"I think it's admirable that you're not giving people what they want," said Hans as we neared Old College. We were walking slowly.

"What does that mean?" I asked.

"It means you're not telling anyone what your father really left you. I assume you must have a reason, which I find loyal and charming."

"I really don't know how else to explain this to people. I don't have anything."

"Suit yourself," he said, smiling. "But let me congratulate you on becoming the icon of the decade. A beautiful orphan locked in a tower? Male imaginations around the country are running wild."

I made a face. "Have you ever been to my tower? It's really not that great."

"No, but I'd love to see it."

I gave a shaky laugh. The Old College gates were locked, so we entered through the side door, at the south side of campus. We passed the deer park and the pond. Hans told me to look at the stars, and I did. I didn't see any. I saw only a smear of clouds, as though someone had written something obscene across the sky and then tried to blot it out. When I turned back to find Hans smiling at me, I wondered if it hadn't been something of a trick.

We found ourselves on the backside of the Faculty Wing. I recognized the ugly freshwater well I had observed once before.

"Halford's Well," Hans said, answering my unasked question. "Named after an old student."

"What is it used for?"

He shrugged. "People dump their stuff in it sometimes. Old lecture notes, beer bottles. Rumor has it that once someone fell in and died once."

"Was it Halford?"

His answer was to take my hand in his. Nothing, I learned, brings you into the present quite like holding hands. The past seemed irrelevant; the future, unnecessary. I became aware of a new emotion pulsing through me—I think it was relief.

Hans turned to me. "Want to go upstairs?"

I blinked. The calm I was feeling quickly dissipated. I could see my tower in the distance, gleaming in the moonlight like a giant fang. I said, "No."

"What?"

"Sorry. I didn't understand the question."

He said, "Come upstairs."

"I live upstairs."

"That's why I asked."

"Where do you live, again?"

He smiled. "Your place is closer."

"No—I meant, where do you live in the world."

"London."

"Wow, London."

Conversation fizzled. There was nothing to do, it seemed, but go to my tower. The tone changed. We spoke in choppy, scripted statements. I can't remember what we said. We seemed to be reenacting a play. By the time we reached the fifth floor, I was panting. I fumbled for my keys, dropping them once before I managed to get the door open. I barely registered that it wasn't locked.

Inside, I half expected to find the tour group, ready to take some pictures of Bloody Mary's secret assignation. But the room was empty. It smelled vaguely of aftershave, and I wondered who was hiding in my wardrobe. Then I realized that the aftershave belonged to Hans. He had taken off his jacket and was standing right in front of the Governess, examining her watery struggle. He seemed most interested by the bird in the painting, the one carrying the bracelet in its beak. Had my bedsheet fallen off, or had Marvin done a dramatic unveiling? Either way, there it was—her awful face. And was it my imagination, or had the painting actually changed since the last time I saw it? The woman's frown seemed to have grown deeper, her condition more serious. She was drowning faster; she was about to get swept under. She wasn't looking directly at me anymore. She was looking past me. For the first time, she seemed to be trying to tell me something—something important.

Hans said, "She looks like you."

"Thank you?"

He made a swift tour of the rest of the room, picking up random objects and setting them back down in place like an appraiser.

"Who etched those initials?" he asked.

I followed his gaze. He was looking at the patch of defaced wall near my bed. *J.H.E.*

I just shrugged.

"There must be a lot of history here."

I fumbled with my boots until I managed to yank them off. My hands were clumsy and felt swollen. When I stood up, Hans was standing very close to me. There was a half smile on his face. I had the impression that he had done this many times before. He came closer and brushed a strand of cold hair away from my face. My lips, all of a sudden, felt very fat.

"You're a fraud, you know," he said, smiling.

"What?"

I looked down at his hands and gave a gasp. He had my father's *Agnes Grey* in his hands. For one horrible moment, I thought that he knew to whom that book had belonged.

"Pardon?" I said.

"You seem to care so little for your relatives. But you have all their books."

"Just the one," I said. My heart thumped loudly. I was sure he could see the blood pulsing through my face.

He brushed the bangs away from my eyes. "I think it's sweet."

"What's sweet?"

"You keep *Jane Eyre* on your pillow."

He leaned in for a kiss, but I stopped him. Frantic, I spun around. He was right. There, on the small, lone blue pillow on top of my sheets, was *Jane Eyre*. I froze in terror. It was my father's tea-stained copy, the size of a brick. The same *Jane Eyre* that should have burned in an ill-fated house fire five years ago. It stared up at me like a runaway child returning for more money.

My breathing was quick, panicked. Hans didn't seem to care, or else he seemed to like it, because he moved toward me and snaked his entire arm around my waist. We had a brief and incoherent conversation about me being pretty, or maybe about him being pretty. My cheeks flamed as he brushed his lips over my closed eyes. *Jane Eyre, Jane Eyre.* I was trembling. What was *Jane Eyre* doing here, and how had it gotten inside? *Agnes Grey* had at least had the dignity to wait outside. Hans started kissing my neck—no, no!—and then his lips found mine, again and again. My brain was working overtime and I let out small, strangled noises. Hans misinterpreted my reaction and kissed me with more fervor. He began a journey down my neck, then around my ear, and then back to my neck again, while all the time a voice seemed to be calling to me from somewhere else: *Jane, Jane!*

Finally, I broke away, shaking violently. Something was falling apart inside me, and it was not anything I wanted someone else to see. I told Hans good night. I don't remember much after that except for the look of hurt on his face, and the click of the door when he left. I sat at the edge of my bed, rocking myself slowly. This was what happened when you tried to date a Brontë, I recall thinking: a book always got in the way. I suppose I had a species of fit, because unconsciousness closed the scene.

Later—much later—I descended the five flights of stairs like Mad King George and stumbled into the evening air. If I stayed in my tower any longer I was sure my mind would slowly unravel and leak everywhere. Outside, the dewy courtyard looked like it was covered in cold sweat. I was right: the afternoon sun had been a cruel trick. A storm was on its way. The wind circled overhead like a hawk; the clouds were pregnant with rain. I had *Jane Eyre* firmly clutched in my hands as I walked. The asphalt was slippery and I caught myself from falling more than once.

I was left to devise a series of suspects who might have been responsible for tonight's cryptic and borderline illegal delivery. First—my mother. How was I so sure that she was still in France? I hadn't seen her in years. Perhaps she was really camped out in the Old College dungeon. But she would never have had access to my father's books, not after she stormed out of our lives, and especially since the library had *burned*. The second possibility was Rebecca, who was so very, very dead. The third option was Blanche from the National Bank. But she seemed equally as unlikely. A bank associate would hardly steal a client's family heirlooms and then give them back to her in secret. Lastly, I supposed, there was Sir John, the curator of the Brontë Parsonage, who by process of elimination seemed like the only option, since he was the only Family Nemesis I knew of. But I had never even met him, and how could he have come by a book that to anyone else in the world would mean nothing? It was not a valuable first edition. My father's copy of *Jane Eyre* had been purchased at a Barnes & Noble.

Desperately, I replayed the afternoon in my mind. There had been so much fluff to the day—Hans, the museum, Amanda—that I wished I had thought to focus on the one part of it that mattered: Marvin and his damn tour group. Had the culprit been the Russian? The amazon? Why had I kept my eyes fixated on the floor? And why hadn't he locked the door on his way out?

I was panting, and for a moment I imagined the book was too. This was not a novel. It was a force of nature. Here, in my hands, was the collective imagination of a million teenage girls. *Jane Eyre* was one of the most famous novels ever written. It was the book that put the Brontës on the map. It was the reason Charlotte Brontë became a celebrity who hobnobbed with Thackeray. It was the reason that women today secretly fantasized about mystery, danger, and brooding men. *Jane Eyre* was a twisted Cinderella story, about an emotionally brutalized child who grows up and finds a job as a governess in a dreary manor. She falls in love with the surly master of the house, Mr. Rochester, who conveniently forgets to tell her that he already has a wife, named Bertha, a thrashing madwoman who, by the way, he has locked up in his attic. Rochester asks Jane to marry him, but his insane wife's brother interrupts the wedding to tell Jane the inconvenient truth. Then, to make a long story short, the shit hits the fan.

The novel wasn't quite as horrible as *Agnes Grey*, but I found it no less threatening. Much like *Agnes Grey*, *Jane Eyre* was not fiction, and I didn't care what James Orville III had to say otherwise. Charlotte Brontë had merely changed the names of people and places from her own life. She sent Jane to the same miserable Christian boarding school that her sisters had attended; she modeled Jane's dead friend Helen Burns on their own dead sister, Maria; she modeled Mr. Rochester himself on Charlotte's tutor in Brussels, Mr. Constantin Héger. Of course, in reality, Héger had been a happily married man, and poor Charlotte pined for him for the rest of her life. There was no romantic ending for Charlotte, but that's where writing your own novel can be so useful.

The similarity between Jane's and Charlotte's lives did not end with characters. Halfway through *Jane Eyre*, Rochester almost burns in his bed, in an attempted murder masterminded by his mad, incarcerated wife. It had always sounded familiar because it *was* familiar. Branwell Brontë's bed caught fire, too, around the time Charlotte came out with *Jane Eyre*. In the book, it had been a lethal revenge plot. In real life, no one knew what had caused the fire, even to this day. Branwell's elbow? An unlucky gust of wind? A malicious trespasser? Near the end of *Jane Eyre*, Rochester's insane wife sets fire to Thornfield Hall by setting curtains aflame and dragging them through the house. Charlotte never allowed curtains in the house until she was thirty-nine years old, due to an all-consuming fear of fire. This, to me, did not seem coincidental.

If *Jane Eyre* was at all rooted in reality, then one enigma remained for me: the madwoman, Bertha. She was the cackle that haunted Thornfield Hall; she was the character whom Jane Austen would never have written. Her function in *Jane Eyre* had been the subject of debate since the 1960s, thanks to two books on the subject, *Wide Sargasso Sea* and *The Madwoman in the Attic*. It was now accepted that Bertha was a symbol of feminism one hundred years before feminism became trendy. Angry, powerful, and sexual, Bertha is the outer manifestation of every rebellious inclination Jane feels on the inside. Just as Bertha is trapped in an attic, Jane is locked in the confines of her dismal occupation, and the social and political limitations of her gender.

It was all a very tidy theory, but it didn't go far enough. Bertha was entirely unlike any other character the Brontës ever wrote. She was wild and foreign, so terribly out of place that I didn't trust that she came entirely from someone's imagination. If it were true that Charlotte had swiped many of the characters in *Jane Eyre* from real life—who, exactly, had been the model for the insane woman living in the attic?

Suddenly, I let out a small shriek. I had lost my balance—my arms flailed, and I landed in a heap on the grass. A sharp pain hit my ankle. I hollered and swore; the twist was bad. It was my right foot, the same foot I had broken years ago, when I had climbed the trellis of our home in Boston and fallen. I clutched my newly angered ankle as if I might strangle it back to its former self. I looked around for a sign of help. All I saw was the vague outline of Halford's Well and the Faculty Wing beyond, stern and unfeeling. I looked to my left and to my right and realized that I had been walking on the lawn.

Above me, the wind took aim. I should not have underestimated the weather. The black clouds looming overhead brought me back to a pre-modern era, when women still died of chills. The rain started to fall, strong and synchronized. It was too painful to stand, so I just sat there, like bait. I had *Jane Eyre* trapped underneath my coat. I secretly hoped it was bleeding in the rain, my father's margin notes leaking out like someone's last breath.

It was some time before I saw my first beacon of hope: a shadow emerging from the Faculty Wing. I stayed very still. Was it a faculty member? I sat up straight and gave a weak holler.

The figure stopped and turned. It had, I noted, a huge head.

"Who is there?" it roared. Baritone.

"The student Raskolnikov?"

He must have not heard me, because he said: "Speak!"

I tried again, but my voice was snatched by the wind. The shadow began moving toward me. Immediately, I recognized him. My heart sank. Orville. What was he doing here at this hour? Shouldn't he be at home, with a leggy girlfriend? His coat billowed behind him like a broken, flapping tent.

I tried to look chic, like one of those women who know how to arrange their limbs in front of the camera. But I was splayed over the lawn, drenched. I'm sure I looked like I belonged on a toilet.

Orville arrived and stood over me. A puff of white air escaped his mouth. The rain was pounding his hair onto his forehead. He didn't bother brushing the stray strands away from his eyes.

"Samantha," he said, expelling a breath.

I said, "Hi."

"What in God's name are you doing on the lawn?" His voice was sharp; he sounded like a human Weedwacker.

I looked around. "Ruminating?"

"Are you hurt?"

"No."

He stopped. "How badly?"

I pointed to my right ankle. "I can't move it."

He looked left and then right, as if waiting for the medic. Then he knelt to the ground, elbows resting on his knees. He glared at my foot like it might heal by intimidation. I felt as though I was back in 1820 with a pale pink frock and the last name Dashwood. Orville poked at my boot with a gloved index finger.

"Does that hurt?" he said. His features were stern.

"Yes."

"How about now?"

"You're doing the same thing."

"Now?"

"Really?"

Gingerly, he took my foot in one hand and removed my boot.

I squeaked, "Sir!"

My cold, socked foot flopped out of the shoe and gleamed in the muted lamplight like a dead fish. I had never felt so naked in my life. I willed myself away—back inside, back in Boston, anywhere but here. His hands were clammy and wet, and he was hurting me more than I cared to admit. He peeled off my sock—good God, the impropriety.

"Please," I said, wincing. "I'll be fine."

He didn't answer. He moved his fingers in slow circles around irrelevant parts of my foot.

In a moment he concluded: "Sprained."

We stared at each other. The rain continued to pound, like coarse salt.

"Thank you, doctor," I said.

He glanced at the dim outline of the Faculty Wing, then at the well. His frown was impressively unpleasant.

"Did you say that you saw anyone?" he asked.

"Sorry?"

He snapped, "Did you *see* anyone?"

"Just you. Why do you ask?"

"This is not the best place to be found. Come, I'll help you up."

He wrapped one of my arms around his neck and helped me to a standing position. Quickly, I removed my arm from around his neck, but he reached for it and slung it back over his shoulders.

I gave a surprised yelp. "What are you *doing*?"

His free arm wrapped around my waist. "I'll take you to the hospital."

"I don't need a hospital."

He reached for my knees and attempted to lift me but failed. I was nearly six feet tall and he was not quite as strong as he thought. He straightened back up and we stood, immobile, in an awkwardness so profound it seemed beyond the power of expression.

"Please," I said, "you don't need to do this. You'll only get back problems when you grow up."

He didn't answer.

My cheeks warmed. "I meant—when you get old."

Silence.

I corrected, "Older."

"Samantha," Orville said, and he let out a breath, "there will come a time when you will need to learn not to be scared shitless of me."

I shut up.

He helped me limp toward the entrance gate. My brain seemed crowded and swollen. The silence was loud and ugly, and in my mind, it stretched out for several years. Occasionally I found myself muttering, "Interesting."

At last, we exited the college. There were only a few cars splashing through the glassy puddles on High Street. We both saw the cab as it rounded the corner.

"*Taxi!*" Orville bellowed. The cab swerved, lurched, and screeched to a stop by the curb. We piled into the back, out of the rain. Orville told the driver, "Take me to the Radcliffe Hospital."

The man looked at us in the rearview mirror. "Is it a boy or a girl?"

Orville reached forward and slammed the plastic partition shut.

The hospital was a white Soviet-looking building by the freeway, whose inside still reeked of all the recycled breath from the afternoon. After depositing me on a chair in the deserted waiting room, Orville found the receptionist at the front desk, a thirty-something nurse with pinched lips and three piercings.

"She's taken a spill," I could hear him explain.

Someone was typing in the distance. The nurse, glancing my way, said, "Your daughter will be fine."

He said something I couldn't hear. I was clutching *Jane Eyre*, flipping through pages absently. Some of the ink had bled, but for the most part, my father's comments remained intact.

Orville returned a few moments later. I snapped the book shut.

"Have a seat," I said. "Dad."

He walked to the chair directly next to me, then changed his mind and sat farther away, with one chair between us. He reached for the *Herald Tribune* on the table near us and shook it open.

"You really didn't have to do this," I said. "This is not in your job description."

"You don't need to remind me," he said. "What in God's name were you doing out at this hour?"

"I was going to ask you the same question."

"I was finishing some work."

"I was taking a walk."

"In a storm?"

"I had a rough evening."

He stared at me. By itself, his face wasn't terribly handsome—there were crooks in strange places, and his eyebrows were much too large. But he had an impressively focused stare, unreadable and perfect.

I looked away. When I held my ankle still, the pain was dull, like a protest that was losing momentum. I examined it for several minutes in silence. When I glanced back up, I was surprised to discover that Orville's stare was still on me.

"Samantha," he said, "are you in some kind of trouble?"

I pretended not to have understood. "Sorry?"

He opened his mouth but closed it. He turned back to his paper. "Forget it."

I didn't look away. "May I ask you a personal question, sir?"

"No."

"Do you believe in ghosts?"

"No."

"Me neither."

A long pause. "Have you been visited by a ghost, Samantha?"

"That's just it. No."

He paused. "You'd *like* to be visited by a ghost."

"Yes, maybe. Don't you think it would make things simpler? At least I'd have a tangible problem."

"A ghost is tangible?"

"More tangible than nothing."

"What is it you're trying to tell me? Never mind, don't answer," he said. "I can't help you."

"I wasn't asking for your help."

"Perfect."

"Now that you mention it, will you help me?"

I tried to pin him with my best, sorrowful gaze, but he had veiled any emotion on his face.

"Please don't look at me like that," I said.

"How am I looking at you?"

"If there's anything I can't stand at times like this, it's apathy."

He turned back to his paper. "Whatever."

A tune erupted in the waiting room. "Somewhere Over the Rainbow." Someone had jazzed it up and slowed it down and now it sounded more like the theme song from *Titanic*. I found it incredibly depressing. Finally, I picked up *Jane Eyre* and tossed it into Orville's lap. I might as well have handed him a wet diaper. He put down his paper and stared at the book.

"Yes?" he said.

"Can you please take a look?"

He reached for it and examined the first few waterlogged pages. "Who wrote these margin notes?"

"My father."

At the mention of my father, Orville's interest seemed to grow. "Was he well in the head?"

"That does appear to be the million-dollar question, doesn't it?"

He read, " 'Roses are red, violets are blue, I see something, and you don't.' What did he mean?"

"You tell me."

"Was that note meant for you?"

"I'm not sure."

"Your father left you this book, though, yes?"

"I'm not sure who left it for me. I found this in my room today."

"I don't understand."

"Me neither."

There was a mix of confusion and surprise on Orville's face. I thought he might ask me a question, but although he opened his mouth he shut it, silent. After a moment, he handed the book back to me.

"I will wager a guess and assume that, like most women your age, this was your favorite novel growing up."

I said, "Not even close."

"No? I thought women loved *Jane Eyre*."

"I don't like the main character."

"Who?" he said. "Grace?"

I blinked. "Who's Grace?"

"Grace Poole."

I said, "She is the servant, not the main character."

"I see you haven't read the book very carefully."

I opened my mouth to respond, but I was interrupted by the sound of sharp heels coming down the hallway. Someone short and squat entered the lounge area. She was a middle-aged woman who had obviously been very pretty once. Now she sported a wide, gasping girth. In a green and gray peacoat and a feathered hat, she looked like a spotted mushroom. Orville muttered a low epithet under his breath. She waddled over. I recognized her; she was the woman who had led the faculty processional at my first dinner.

"Dr. Flannery," said Orville, without standing.

Her heels clacked on the linoleum floor. The popping sound bounced back and forth between the sterile walls. She didn't say hello, only glanced between the two of us. Her blush looked like she had instead smeared lipstick on her cheeks.

"A student?" was all she said, raising a brow. The lines on her face lifted in concert.

"How is your aunt?" he said.

"The morphine is doing its job." She turned to me. "What's your name?" Out came a nice little smile, one that did not reveal any of her teeth. "Tell me your name, please."

"Samantha." I couldn't stand up to shake her hand, so I gave her a small, childish wave.

"Yes, you're Miss Whipple," she said. "I've heard a bit about you. James, haven't we heard a bit about Miss Whipple?"

Orville stared at her silently. He was slowly rotating a pen between his fingers, like a baton, or some form of skewer.

"Miss Whipple rolled an ankle," said Orville.

Flannery made a noise that sounded like "aww" but it also might have been "aaah." She glanced back at me, tilting her head to the side in—was it sympathy? No, I don't think it was. I wondered if she carried around the *Old College Book of Disciplinary Procedures*, and whether she was about to whip it out of her pocket and smack me across the head with it. After all, I had been alone with a professor for almost an hour. Someone, somewhere, was probably gasping.

"Doing what?" she asked me in a let's-have-a-sleepover voice. "Nothing naughty, I trust?"

"I fell," I said.

"Where?"

"Enough," Orville interjected. "She's tired, Ellery."

"Ellery" was looking at me, not him. She really did have a nice face—girlish, bright. "Where were you, dear?"

"By Halford's Well," I said. "I think."

Flannery turned back to Orville. He put down the pen. I glanced between the two of them. Once again, I was missing something.

"You do know going near that well is *strictly* forbidden after hours," said Flannery.

"Ellery," Orville said in a warning tone. "She fell."

I felt my face redden. Flannery smiled, this time with teeth. They were crooked, like barbed wire. No wonder she hid them. Her face wasn't so pretty anymore.

"Do you know how Halford's Well got its name, Samantha?" she asked.

Suddenly Orville stood, so abruptly that it took Flannery and me by surprise. Flannery faltered, although she made an effort to conceal it.

"That's enough," he said.

Flannery stared back up at him with flattering confidence. She was like a dwarf who had been told to kill a giant and didn't know how, exactly, she was going to do it.

"Nasty things, rolled ankles," was all she said to me before she left. I heard her shoes rapping along the hallway to the door. When we were alone, Orville sat back down in his seat, breathing heavily through his nose.

"Sir?" I ventured.

But he just stared in front of him. Someone came to us with a clipboard. The doctor would see me now.

CHAPTER 7

On the afternoon of December thirteenth, I grabbed my crutches (my ankle was badly sprained) and made the trek to the Ashmolean Museum. Sir John Booker was scheduled to give an opening speech at the official launch of the *Early Women Writers* exhibit. Apparently, this was the fourteenth stop on his tour. I was attending only because I had decided it was time to finally meet him.

The lobby was packed, and a luminous banner read *Early Women Writers: Gala*. Milling between Greek statues and segments of Roman ruins were hordes of annoyingly normal-looking people. I was disappointed. I had wanted to find old women dressed in hippie uniforms and clutching small pugs. I always felt better about my preoccupation with the Brontës when I saw that other people had it worse than I did. But everyone else here seemed maddeningly average. The Brontës were just something they did on Saturday afternoons, like canasta. They were nothing but tourists in my sinking town.

I decided that my name for the day would be Elvira Erstwood. Whipple raised too many questions in this crowd. The woman at the door bought it and handed me my incorrect name tag. The art of pseudonyms was something I had learned from my father, who had learned it from the Brontës, I suppose. Dad used to have backstories figured out months in advance. Snodgrass D. Diddleworm (his pseudonym for going shopping) was a thirty-three-year-old personal shopper from eastern Kansas; Echo Woodraine (his gym alias) was

a shy poet raised in Lithuania, with a killer backhand. Dad was the
name he used when he couldn't figure out what else to be.

I headed straight for the buffet table, which was located between
the disembodied marble heads of Theodotus and Sotades, the
Obscene Greek. I recognized some Old College faculty members:
Man-with-Nice-Office was here, and so was Earl the Cubist, who
at the moment was straightening his Snap-On Emergency Bow
Tie with one hand and eating an unripe strawberry with the other.
Orville was here too—I spotted him immediately. He was in a black
suit, talking to a woman who was wearing peach stockings and a
short gray dress. The look of lust on her face irritated me. I was
beginning to resent all the women Orville had ever known, down to
his grocer. As I watched the two of them together, I imagined what
it would be like if I were with him instead—perhaps at a cocktail
party in a black-and-white movie, telling women with long cigarette
holders what a fine bridge player he was.

"You're standing so far away," interrupted someone behind me. It
was a tall man with graying hair and a dictator mustache. His breath
was fantastically unappealing.

I looked around and said, "From?"

"I'm Jerome." He extended a hand; I took it. His skin was damp.

"I'm Elvira."

"No, you're Samantha Whipple."

I didn't answer.

"I recognize you from the papers," he explained. "I was wondering whether you would come. We're all curious to hear your thoughts
on Sir John's book." He motioned toward a table in the back, where I
could see stacks of shiny hardcovers glittering like snake eyes.

I cleared my throat. "What brings you here?"

He shrugged. "The women."

"Charlotte, Emily, or Anne?"

"No, thin brunettes, such as yourself."

He wasn't smiling. He took a sip from his drink. Before I could respond, he explained, "I teach at the Sorbonne. I am giving a lecture upstairs on Eliza Haywood at four this afternoon. I also play the violin and express myself with extraordinary emotion. Would you object to a drink this evening?"

A voice came from behind me. "Hello, Jerome."

I turned around. It was Orville, who was standing with one hand in his pocket, the other holding a Perrier. I didn't even know he had seen me walk in. The Dictator and my professor shook hands.

"Samantha, this is Oren Smith," said Orville.

I frowned. "Oren Smith."

Orville explained, "He writes for the *Paris Examiner*."

Ah, Oren Smith.

"Sorry for deleting all of your e-mails," I said.

"Shall we meet later?" he asked.

I couldn't respond, thankfully, because Orville led me away by the right crutch, all the way to the second buffet table. Someone had spilled water on the tray of crackers and they looked like swollen sponges.

"You're welcome," Orville said.

"For what?" I asked. "You've ruined my night of wild animal passion."

"Take a scone."

"That's dim sum."

He took one from the platter and held it out for me until I took it.

"How do you know him?" I asked.

"I met him at a lecture I gave in Paris once."

I told him that I was also going to Paris. I meant to say "soon," but instead I said "someday." We entered a vast, bottomless silence. I scrambled for better conversation topics. This all would have been far less stressful in the movie version of our lives. The long silences would have been edited out. Orville and I did not say anything else, and I followed him to the third row of the seating area, where the chairs were white, plastic, and wobbly.

Our options were limited: we could either sit by the man with a cotton-ball beard and excellent Santa potential, or next to the woman who had taken off her hiking boots and was cooling her toes on the tiled floor.

"Which one?" I asked Orville, motioning between the two.

He turned back around as though he hadn't realized I was still there. "Oh, are we sitting together?"

My face reddened. Perhaps I had been wrong to assume that some sort of bond had formed between us since the hospital. I looked around, helpless, like a show poodle.

Orville let out a breath and said, "Very well, have a seat."

He chose to sit next to Santa, who reeked aggressively of curry. Orville helped set my crutches on the floor. There was, I realized, a copy of Sir John's book underneath every seat. I picked mine up and gave a loud yelp. Orville, startled, turned to me.

"Is he shitting me?" I said.

"I beg your pardon?"

I flashed him the title: *The Vast Brontë Estate*.

"Have you read this?" I said.

"No."

"It's about the Vast Brontë Estate."

"I gathered."

"Christ," I said. "I hate the Vast Brontë Estate."

"Is there anything you don't dislike?"

"Do you know this man—Sir John Booker?"

He said, "The academic community is rather small."

I opened the book to find a full page of reviews. The *New York Times* gushed, "Rich with rare primary sources, *The Vast Brontë Estate* is a remarkable triumph." Some other presumably important person had called it "abundantly fearless" and "quite human," with "elements of mirth."

I flipped through the book, breathing heavily. It was not, as I had feared, another essay about my family. Nor was there much text at all. I seemed to have stumbled upon a picture book. Sir John had cataloged everything the Brontës had ever owned, each with a photograph and a brief caption. On page three was a watercolor by Emily; on page one hundred and three was Anne's first rhyming couplet. No analysis, no description. The pages continued, a never-ending sea of photographs:

"The Daffodil"
A poem written at the age of sixteen by Anne Brontë
Donated by the Floss family in 1892

Notebook with a reddish hue
Used by Emily Brontë in 1842
Donated by Unknown

I didn't see any "abundant fearlessness." The book was comprehensive, careful, and chronological, but it was dull. I felt a note of relief, and then a small sense of triumph. The book was as dead as its subject matter. I flipped farther and farther until suddenly, halfway through, I landed upon a blank page. I frowned. In place of a photograph was a big, empty white space. Above it was a bit of text:

Sketch of fern
Painted by Anne Brontë at Thorp Green in August 1840
MISSING

And then—

Believed to be in the possession of the Whipple family

I let out a small, punctured wheeze. Slander? Libel? Lawsuit? I looked up from the book, to my left and to my right, thinking for a moment that everyone must be watching me. But the guests were carrying on as they should have, oblivious. I looked down and flipped through the next pages. I saw more and more blank boxes, proliferating like baby rats:

Day dress
Worn at Thorp Green by Anne Brontë in September 1842
MISSING
Believed to be in the possession of the Whipple family

My cheeks flamed. Every single missing artifact was attributed to us. What kind of personal vendetta was this? I flipped through more and more pages, furious. They were all lies. My family did not own "sketch of fern," as riveting as it sounded. Nor did we have "mug decorated with birds," or "painting of woman wearing ring." Sir John had published the Vast Brontë Lie. My breathing became labored, agitated. If I was angry, it was only because anger is a good cover for complete terror. I was being attacked for a reason I could not fathom, by someone I had never met, and by someone who also happened to be far more powerful than I was. I glanced at Orville, hoping he might be able to see my overheated face and wide gecko eyes and leap to my rescue. But he was examining something underneath his fingernail and couldn't be bothered. I replaced the book on the floor and tried to kick it farther under my seat. I don't think I had ever felt quite so alone.

In a moment, a tiny Chihuahua of a woman with forcefully blonde hair took the makeshift stage in front of us. Her cheeks were taut and shiny, like the skin of an apple. She gave Sir John an obsequious introduction. I didn't know he had attended Cambridge, Oxford, and then Cambridge again; nor did I know that he had published a total of seven books on the Enlightenment, which seemed unnecessary. He had been knighted for his cumulative body of work, including his "significant contributions to the study and theory of literature," and had received several other awards that sounded equally severe and important. The more I listened, the more hopeless I felt. There would be no contradicting someone of his caliber. The great reward given to intelligent people is that they can invent all the rules and equate any dissent with stupidity. The lady onstage went on to list so many accolades that I imagined them all stacked on top of each other like pancakes. No one could fill Sir John's shoes, not even he.

At last, the Chihuahua stopped talking and Sir John took the floor. I crossed my arms, almost instinctively. There he was: the Son and Heir of a Mongrel Bitch. I could almost hear Dad's bacon frying in the pan as he muttered insults under his breath. Sir John was nothing like I had imagined. I had pictured a corpulent blond who looked like Nero. On the contrary, the man in front of me was thin, old, and tall—surprisingly handsome—with long hair the color of trampled snow. He had pulled most of it back with a hair tie and let it flop behind him like a beaver tail.

He walked to the podium with a slow stride. I had never seen an old man loom quite so tall. I sank back down into my seat. He had clearly been very attractive as a young man, and was neither as visually grotesque nor as interpersonally awkward as I would have hoped.

I turned to Orville and whispered, "How do you know him, again?"

"He's very famous."

"How famous?"

"It's time to be quiet."

I shut my mouth. Despite the raucous applause, Sir John did not look happy. In fact, he looked strangely irritated. His intellect must have impressed everyone but himself.

"Thank you for the introduction," he said. "It is a pleasure to be here."

He didn't sound pleased at all. He had a clenched accent and spoke as though his jaw had been cemented shut at some point during his adolescence. I wondered briefly if his teeth were fused. We watched as he tried to adjust the microphone to fit his height. When it didn't work, he wrenched it out of its socket. The speakers made a ferocious shriek.

"This afternoon," he said, "I'd like to talk to you about the genesis of this book, and the proper relationship between textual criticism and authorial intent."

I leaned over again and tapped Orville on the shoulder. I whispered, "Sir?"

"It's time to be quiet," he repeated.

"What's textual criticism?"

"You don't know?"

"Is it when you insult people using bits of text?"

Orville ignored my comment—I assumed I had been incorrect—and returned his focus to the stage. There was something familiar about Old Man Booker that I couldn't quite place—the ghost of someone I knew, perhaps, lurking behind his features. Maybe my father had introduced us after all, once upon a time.

"As many of you know, the subject of authorial intent has been at the center of academic debates for decades," said Sir John in a bored drawl. "There are those who would argue that our interpretation of a text should not be influenced by external factors, such as biographical information about the author, historical circumstances, or even words the author may have written to encourage a certain perception of his or her work. These people contend that the intention of the author is not only unimportant but entirely irrelevant, and that the only clues of value in literary criticism are the words on the printed page."

He gave a dramatic and well-timed pause.

"These people," he said, "are incorrect. So incorrect, I might add, that to espouse this philosophy is to surrender logic and regress to a savage, primitive time."

I could feel audience members around me shuffle in their seats. A few people whispered to each other excitedly, as if Sir John Booker had just proposed the end of worldwide oppression. I glanced at Orville for an explanation, but to my surprise, he looked livid. I had never seen him show this much emotion before, but there it was. He was watching Sir John as if the man were a literary terrorist. I didn't understand. Had Orville somehow been insulted? I guess I wasn't used to textual criticism.

"When we read a work of fiction," Sir John continued, "we enter into an implicit contract, one requiring us to infer, to our best ability, the author's desired message. One might then ask: How are we to find out with certainty what a writer wanted to convey, if that writer is now dead? The least imperfect method we have is to look for evidence in the earliest versions of an author's work. If we can identify any incremental additions and omissions between drafts, we can begin to remove errors in the dissemination of an author's message. In my own study of the Brontës' writing, I have come across ample evidence of self-censorship in their first, second, and third drafts of their novels, indicated by a few large, illegible sections that were entirely scratched out. What can this allow us to infer? Can we suppose that the novels' original intent was to expose something the authors later decided to conceal?"

There was an air pocket of silence, which I'm sure he calculated for effect. It was the result, perhaps, of being in front of a classroom for most of his life. Sir John stared directly at the audience. Directly at me, I thought.

"A second method to arrive at an author's true intent—which I have practiced for years—involves looking beyond the earliest drafts of a text, or anything the author wrote, for that matter, and finding instead the influences that shaped the author's most mundane daily life. Clothing. Paintings. Yes, even dishware. We cannot separate the Brontës from their lives on the moors any more than we can extricate Jane from Charlotte, Agnes from Anne, or Cathy from Emily. The censorship we find in their writing is nowhere to be found in their unpublished, unscripted 'doodles,' sketches, and in some cases, letters. What did they exclude from their novels, and is it possible to piece together those omissions by carefully examining their revelatory old possessions?"

The word *doodle* was wonderful in a British accent, but no one else seemed to notice. I wasn't making it up this time—Sir John did look at me, albeit briefly. I tensed.

"In my book, the one you see in front of you, you will not find a series of objects," he said. "You will find a true portrait of three of our most enigmatic authors, one that helps us unlock the riches inside their most cryptic novels. Thank you, and good afternoon."

And with that, he gathered his notes and walked off the stage. The speech was over. It had barely lasted three minutes. The audience indulged Sir John with hefty applause until his lanky old-man body had left the stage. He did not look happy or proud; rather, his expression had the implacable apathy of a Byzantine portrait. I thought, perhaps, that he might be hiding something.

In any case, I believed I had found the source of disagreement between Sir John and my father, or at least one of them. For the most part, Dad fell in the camp of the "incorrect" people—the ones who believed in the sanctity of a text and judged a novel only on the words on the page. Dad, though, had a somewhat mutated version of this theory. To him, books were living, breathing things. Once a book left the brain of the author, it took on a life of its own, and served as the only liaison between the reader and the author. If you read carefully, the book could tell you all sorts of secrets—sometimes about its characters, and sometimes about its creator. Sir John was studying the Brontës' lives for clues about their texts; my dad used the texts, and only the texts, to arrive at the truth about the Brontës.

I turned to say something to Orville but stopped myself. His cheeks were bone white and his jaw was twitching, ever so slightly. He was straightening the cuff of his sleeve, over and over.

I said, "You look angry."

Orville said, "This was a preposterous discussion."

"Do you want to talk about it?"

"No." He turned to me, face flushed. "Has it ever occurred to you that I might dislike the Brontës as much as you do?"

My brows lifted. No, the thought had not occurred to me. I sat back in my seat, silent. Orville turned his gaze back to the spot that Sir John had just vacated, his lips arranged in a hard, thin line. Then, without saying another word, he got up and left.

Sir John was standing to the right of Adonis's half-naked statue when I approached him after the book signing and reception. I had waited until the crowd around him had thinned and scattered. One of his arms was dangling limply at his side; the other was clutching his opposite elbow as though containing a leaking wound. His cheeks looked like sunken battleships. There was no passion in his expression—just cool, collected anger. I wondered if he were secretly a Calvinist.

I was at an automatic disadvantage on crutches. By the time I hobbled near him, I was panting. He seemed to know exactly who I was. Perhaps he had taken one look at the crutches and the sweat pouring off my face and knew that I had to be my father's daughter, trying to span a great, great distance between two people in the hardest way possible.

I introduced myself. "Samantha Whipple."

He fixed his dark eyes full upon me. There was an unceremonious directness to his face that I recognized from somewhere—where?

"You look like your father," he said, impassive. "Same veins in your eyes."

Up close, I could see the fragile wrinkles around Sir John's brow, left over from years of frowning. I waited; he waited. Both of us, I imagined, were expecting my father to materialize as a ghost in between us.

I said, "How are you?"

"Let's step outside."

It was late afternoon, and the sky was an even shade of white. Sir John walked in the detached way of someone who was accustomed to having students trail behind him. His body was frail and seemed much older up close than it had from a distance. When we reached the steps of the Ashmolean, he stopped, turned, and looked my way. I'd never thought I would fear a man's brain more than I feared Orville's, but here was a man whose intellect was even sharper—sharper because I was not yet sure of its full scope, and everything looming and unde-fined seemed terrifying.

Dad used to tell me that Sir John's main faults included not know-ing how to read, and not knowing how to think. He credited him with being the least imaginative man he knew. I wondered, now, if Dad had been wrong. Sir John was unfortunately the more respect-able scholar of the two of them. Dad wrote the occasional "academic" article here and there, but he had never bothered to go to college and had spent the majority of his time reading and writing fiction in his hovel of a study. Sir John, meanwhile, had spent his career accumu-lating academic degrees, developing well-articulated theories with the support of the oldest and most prestigious institutions in the world.

Sir John turned to me. "I tried to contact you, over the years."

"I know."

"You did not respond."

"I know."

My breath quickened. I would have liked to tell him that I'd been rude mostly out of sheer awkwardness, not spite, but I couldn't bring myself to speak. He must have been expecting some kind of adult who was used to handling conflict. I couldn't even look him in the eye. I was aware of inexperience clinging to me like a strange film on my skin. I felt guilty and embarrassed, and I did not want to be here.

He glared at me coolly. "Do you know who Patrick Brontë is, Miss Whipple?"

The question took me by surprise. I said, "Of course."

Patrick Brontë, the father of the Brontë sisters, received so little attention from the public that people tended to forget he even existed. He outlived all of his children, reaching the ripe old age of eighty-four. No one gave him much thought. It's uncanny, the way old men have a habit of becoming invisible even when they're the only ones left in the room.

"I imagine you do," said Sir John. "Patrick Brontë was a secluded writer, diseased by selfishness and the delusions of his own fame, whose literary pretensions prevented him from confronting his staggering mediocrity."

I swallowed. "Sure."

"He homeschooled the Brontë children, denying them both proper education and any friends, and as a result he turned them into social pariahs. When all of his offspring eventually died, it was he who helped resurrect them, fabricating a myth around their lives, and engineering their immortality. He saved all of their notes, their journals and books, locking them away or distributing them to select relatives. Patrick Brontë, in other words, was in the business of making and propagating mysteries. Does this sound familiar to you?"

The heat rose to my cheeks. "I don't answer rhetorical questions, sir."

Sir John's stare intensified. His eyes were cold, bright blue gems.

I added, "Maybe Patrick Brontë was just a private person."

"Or maybe he was an exceptional businessman."

"I don't understand."

"I have been tracking Patrick Brontë's possessions for years," he said, "using old letters and biographies to piece together what once existed in the Brontë estate. And this book still only includes half of what I believe there was. The majority of the Brontë possessions were passed down through Patrick Brontë's side of the family—which, as you know, led to your father—and now, I suppose, *you*. Patrick Brontë left the general public the banal half of the Brontë estate: the spoons and the plants and the scribbles. What he kept tightly wound within the family were the artifacts that he thought were most personal, and therefore the most valuable."

"Monetarily valuable?"

My cheeks reddened. Maybe *monetarily* was not a word. Sir John glanced at his watch and let out a slow breath. Students were not supposed to waste his time.

"Did your father ever tell you how we met?" he asked, impatient. His voice was sharp and did not belong to the old body he inhabited.

"No, he did not."

"Many years ago, I made a discovery that changed my life. I was conducting a research project on Elizabeth Gaskell at the time. You know Mrs. Gaskell, of course?"

"Yes."

"The Brontës' contemporary and Charlotte's biographer."

"Right."

"I had spent months identifying her surviving descendants. My research brought me to a Mr. Edward Elmes, a barrister in London, who was the great-grandson of Gaskell's second cousin. I paid Edward a visit. Can you imagine what I found hanging in his living room?"

"Was it Elizabeth Gaskell?" I asked.

"It was an original Anne Brontë watercolor, resting above the fireplace. You can only imagine my astonishment. I had studied the Brontë art for years, and yet here was a drawing I had never seen before. It was informal and half-finished—not signed and presumably not anything Anne ever intended to show to anyone. Edward Elmes clearly did not know what it was or what it was worth. I was stunned. At the time, I had assumed all the remaining Brontë artifacts had been discovered. I wrote to your father and introduced myself, explaining that I had found something of great importance regarding his family. I assumed that two men of above-average intelligence would work together amicably, and do this discovery justice."

A pause. He was growing angry—I could tell by the way his upper lip twitched.

"A few weeks later, Tristan flew to England," he said. "The watercolor was on my desk when he arrived."

"You stole it from the poor old man?"

He ignored me. "When your father arrived, I presented my discovery. I shared my theories, and explained why those particular brushstrokes must be Anne's. I believe your father agreed."

He cracked a knuckle. It was very un-English.

"And?" I prodded.

"We had a brief conversation, and then your father fell silent. All he did was listen. He stood, then sat, then stood. He walked to the table. He walked away from the table. He asked for a drink, which he did not consume. Then he walked out of my office and I never saw him again. He refused to acknowledge any of my future attempts at communication. I have never met anyone as offensive or as off-putting as your father in my life."

"You sound like my mother."

"What he did not realize, of course, was that his silence achieved the exact opposite of what he anticipated. Our meeting convinced me that there must be a world of Brontë artifacts that the surviving family had painstakingly hidden from the public. As the days and weeks passed, I found that I could think of nothing else. Within a month, I had taken a leave of absence and begun a new search, tracking every letter written by the Brontës, their friends, their families, their extended families, their descended families. I was astonished by the references I found in the letters—mentions of a gold brooch given to Anne by her late mother, an ivory quill Branwell used to write, a draft of a second unfinished novel written by Charlotte. Did you know Charlotte had another unfinished novel? Where is it, Samantha?"

"I have no idea," I said. "If I might ask, what are you hoping those objects will bring you? I'm not sure how much you'll be able to glean from a quill."

"A deeper understanding of their novels, of course."

"Of course."

His eyes narrowed. "Anne's undiscovered watercolor helps explain, to some degree, why all the Brontë protagonists were painters and not writers. The easel was the Brontës' first outlet for their creativity, allowing them to express what they may not have been able to put into print. This painting tells us that when the Brontës painted from their own imaginations, they kept it to themselves."

"Sure."

He gave me a cool smile. "You're feigning disinterest but I can see that you will think of nothing else for days."

"No."

"No?" He gave me the condescending look that you might use upon a small, pouting child.

"My father wouldn't have cared for some old quills or sketches," I said, breathing quickly. "He cared about two things in life: the novels, and that I learned how to read them. You and he were searching for different things."

"I see you do not know your father as well as you think you do."

It was a low blow, only because it was actually one of my deepest fears. I was blushing and I'm sure Sir John could tell. His cool, practiced glare wouldn't leave my face. He was the seasoned killer whale, waiting for the young penguin to slip on the ice and fall into his jaws.

"You know, I think you glossed over some parts of your story," I said. "Like what you really said to my dad to make him walk out."

"Your father felt threatened," he said simply. "I had the power to expose the private world he had built around his family."

"In your search for these 'missing artifacts,' then, did you actually find anything?"

Here, his smile finally fell. He cleared his throat. "Very little."

"I see," I said. "Is that the 'very little' that's in your book?"

Sir John's eyes flashed. "Don't be smart."

"I never know what people mean when they say that."

He stood up straighter. For a moment, I thought he might reach for a pair of spotless white gloves and strike me. "Had your father worked with me, we could have found everything."

"It's hard, though, to find imaginary things."

"Watch your tongue."

I shut up. I knew I was being reckless, but I couldn't let Sir John be right. It was a cheap trick to speak ill of a man who was not alive to defend himself. We were silent for a few moments, during which Sir John turned to look out at the horizon. He was shaking his head slightly, as if couldn't fathom the number of idiots born in America. I wondered if he had any kids himself. The answer must have been no. Fathers tend to know when tempers are born of anger, and when they are born of fear.

"I should get going," I said. "It's getting late."

It wasn't getting late.

"You should learn to trust me," he said, wrapping his scarf a bit tighter around his neck. "There is no other soul alive who knows more about your relatives than I do. I imagine I can solve more than a few mysteries for you."

I paused. "What does that mean?"

He looked my way. "Are you sure there isn't something you'd like to tell me?"

"No."

"Nothing you'd like to get off your chest?"

I paused. I thought back to the copy of *Jane Eyre* in my bedroom. An unpleasant suspicion resurfaced. This man was, unfortunately, one of the last living threads connecting me to my father. Could Sir John be the person who had left me his books? No. And yet . . . he looked so classically suspicious, just standing there, that I was quite sure I had found the culprit.

I said, "Out of curiosity, why do you ask?"

Sir John didn't say anything, and in that one lack of response, it seemed likely—beyond all probable doubt—that he was a key suspect in the delivery of both *Agnes Grey* and *Jane Eyre*. I stared at him with narrowed eyes and waited, hoping I might receive my answer via osmosis.

"I see," I said.

"You see what?"

"Is it *you*?"

"Pardon?"

I came out with it: "Why are books being delivered to my doorstep?"

His face changed. For the first time, he looked surprised. I had my answer before he even opened his mouth: no, no—he didn't know anything. I was wrong. He knew nothing, the same way I knew nothing. We waited in silence. Oops.

"You are receiving *books*, Miss Whipple?"

I faltered. "No. Yes. That is—just a few."

"I don't understand."

"*Jane Eyre*. *Agnes Grey*. The usual."

Sir John asked, "The *original* manuscripts?"

"No. The Penguin editions."

He frowned. "Did they belong to your father?"

I didn't respond, which, of course, was all the answer he needed. This was not going as planned. I could feel the power draining out of me. There was a sudden fire in Sir John's cold eyes that startled me. No wonder my father hadn't liked him.

"Well now," he said. "I'm glad you told me. Who left them for you?"

I waited. "*You* did?"

For the first time today, he was flushed. I watched him pull out a pen and business card from his pocket, and scratch something down.

"I would like to see these books," he said. "You must tell me when the next one arrives. Here is my personal e-mail."

"There won't be another book."

He scoffed. "No one would think to give someone *Jane Eyre* and *Agnes Grey* and exclude *Wuthering Heights*. They're a set. And when the next book arrives, I imagine that you will need my help to figure out what they all mean."

"I can read on my own, thank you very much."

"Your father apparently thought otherwise."

My cheeks reddened. Sir John gave me an unkind smile.

"Don't you feel foolish?" I said, in what I hoped was a jab. "Going on a treasure hunt at your age?"

He didn't answer. Instead, he handed me his business card. I shut my mouth because deep down, I knew that he was right. I did need help. There were two planes of understanding in this world; he was on the highest, and I was on the lowest. This, I suppose, was the problem with office hours: students were allowed to appreciate the brain in front of them, but at the end of the day, they were never granted full access to it. It was the welfare state of intelligence.

As a farewell, Sir John extended a hand. I took it, and he pressed a cold, loose handshake onto my fingers. Somewhere, I knew, I had felt that handshake before.

That weekend, I read Sir John's awful little book, cover to cover. As I had anticipated, I had never seen a single one of his so-called missing artifacts floating around my father's house in Boston. After ten years of hunting for relics, was this the best a knight could do? Despite his stated motive of better understanding the Brontës, I had a feeling that this entire book was a personal grudge first disguised then sanctioned by academia.

There was one particular part of his book, however, that piqued my interest. All of the Brontë objects that my father supposedly owned had been painted, written, worn, or used by Anne during her stint at Thorp Green. On paper, Thorp Green was simply the name of the estate where Anne Brontë had spent five years working as a governess. In reality, it represented the most turbulent and transformative period of Anne's life. She had left the parsonage as a normal woman, and returned home five years later as a disgruntled writer. That same year, she, Emily, and Charlotte began their literary careers in earnest. Coincidence? Not likely. Something happened at Thorp Green to inspire three of the most important novels of their time.

That Sunday, I stepped inside the Old College Library. It consisted of dimly lit corridors and small study rooms lined with old books. I found the one I was looking for—*The Big Book of Brontës*—and took it with me to the Catherine Howard Room. There was only one other student inside. He had *Irrepressible Boils of the Sixteenth Century* in front of him but was gazing into the distance, immobile, as though something was happening to his spleen and he couldn't quite decide what it was. I took a seat. All I could hear was the mysterious sounds of a toilet flushing—mysterious because I had never once found a restroom in this building. I opened *The Big Book of Brontës*. If

I remembered correctly, chapter ten would be dedicated to the Thorp Green Years: 1840–1845.

For better or for worse, thanks to my months of infatuated study as a teenager, Thorp Green was as real to me as anything I knew in this world. I could still see the old plants I had envisioned in the dusty foyer; I could hear the doors opening onto the toes of eavesdropping servants. I knew Thorp Green's inhabitants like my own friends. Mr. Robinson, the head of the house, would have been a portly, bad-breathed ex-crook with a pinky ring and a closely cropped mustache. His name was Edmund but he would really look like Vinny from Staten Island. His wife, Lydia, would have been a frail creature with eyes like a bat's who believed most things were très middle-class. The two of them—Edmund and the bat—would have four, angular-faced children.

What the world knew was this: Anne Brontë arrived in May of 1840. She left in 1845, leaving an unsettling radio silence in between. The only thing anyone knew was that the entire experience left Anne "sick of mankind and their disgusting ways." One hypothesis for What Happened At Thorp Green was easy to find in history books, and it concerned Branwell Brontë. In 1842, Anne persuaded her employers to hire her brother as an art teacher to young Edmund Robinson. (Really, I had a feeling that Anne just wanted to rein in her brother's sexual carte blanche—and what better way to induce celibacy than to become a male governess?) The results of Anne's act of charity were catastrophic. Branwell quickly set his eyes upon Mrs. Robinson—twenty years his senior, and the wife of mafia-man Edmund. One thing led to another, and before long, Branwell Brontë initiated a nineteenth-century version of *The Graduate*.

It was high scandal. Mrs. Robinson was the wife of a wealthy landowner; Branwell was a blossoming alcoholic with a dead-end job, massive debt, and no friends. The affair ruined the promise of a smooth career for his poor sister; Anne was now forced to confront, as she put it, the "very unpleasant and undreamt of experience of human nature." In 1845, Edmund Robinson discovered the affair, kicked Branwell out of the house, and threatened to shoot him. The lovesick puppy returned home, flopped on his bed, and eventually drank himself to death at the ripe age of thirty-one.

At least, that's how the story went. If it were true, it must have indeed been upsetting for Anne. But was one badly thought-through affair enough to account for her complete transformation? There was nothing extraordinary about this particular seduction except that it involved an older woman, and the whole affair was très middle class. Anne would have witnessed Branwell's womanizing too often to be shocked. No, something else must have been going on in the shadows of that manor—something that would drive a shy nineteenth-century woman to sacrifice her good name and write not only one but two novels.

Here, I turned to the world of the servants. Thorp Green had an entire soap opera's worth of maids, butlers, cooks, cleaners, and gardeners. There was one member of the staff whom I found unusually intriguing: Ann Marshall, with whom Anne Brontë became reasonably close. Ann was the personal maid and confidante of Mrs. Robinson, and a strange, reclusive person. Much like Anne Brontë, she had arrived as a wide-eyed girl in her twenties, years before. By the time she died, alone, in 1847, Ann Marshall was a frail spinster who never spoke more than two words at one time to anyone. What accounted for the dramatic change? And what was it about Thorp Green that took in young women, then spat them out as pale versions of their former selves?

I picked up the book in front of me and did a quick search for Ann Marshall's portrait. Relegated to a tertiary character in the Brontë lives, she usually only made it into the footnotes. And yet, she was the only servant whom Anne Brontë had ever taken the trouble to paint. I found her portrait on page four hundred and twenty. She was plain and aging, with turned-down lips and a rounded nose the size of a small umbrella. She was wearing an ugly brown frock and an old bonnet. It was the same portrait I had seen in the Ashmolean. I stared at her sour face, as I had so often done before.

My lip curled. Ann Marshall was the spitting image of Grace Poole, my least favorite character from *Jane Eyre* (and, apparently, Orville's favorite). "There she sat," Jane Eyre remarked of Grace, "staid and taciturn-looking, as usual, in her brown stuff gown, her check apron, white handkerchief, and cap." In *Jane Eyre*, Grace Poole was the personal caretaker of the madwoman and the bearer of a terrible household secret. I would have wagered anything that Ann Marshall's story was similar. And Anne's?

At this thought, I closed the book, feeling a resentment that I hadn't felt in years. There was no denying the parallels between Anne Brontë's time at Thorp Green and Jane Eyre's time at Thornfield Hall. *Jane Eyre* told the story of a lonely woman who becomes a governess at a lonely manor, uncovers a horrible mystery, and then runs away without telling anyone what really happened to her. If it sounded like Anne Brontë's life, it was because it *was* Anne Brontë's life.

It left me with one nagging question. How, exactly, had Charlotte Brontë gotten away with stealing her sister's story?

CHAPTER 8

The week of Christmas brought in the biggest storm of the season. The papers—the real papers, not the *Hornbeam*—had already speculated that it would be the worst we'd seen all year, so bundle up and stay safe, advised the perky notice in the *Telegraph*. I didn't read much else about it because reading the newspaper was a thing I no longer did. All it did was remind me of all the unread e-mails I had from English journalists inquiring about Sir John's new book. *Is it true? Would you care to comment? Would you be open to an interview? Would you kindly respond?*

I didn't think much of the approaching storm until Thursday evening, when Marvin asked if I needed candles. I was checking my mailbox (the "pidge") in the Plodge, and he was packing up for the holidays. Hilary term wouldn't begin for another month.

"Candles?" I asked. "Why would I need candles?"

"In case there is a power outage," he said. In his mud-colored bowler hat and matching trench coat, he looked as if he were going out for a walk in the 1920s.

"Does that happen a lot around here?" I asked.

He gave a shrug of a smile. "Your tower isn't known for its electricity."

"It's not known for its central heating, either."

Marvin looked somewhat sheepish. He held out the candles, like I had instead said, "Checkmate," and he was handing me his king.

I still carried residual anger toward him, and I believe he was aware of it. I had come here several times in the last month, demanding to see the list of people who had been inside my tower the day that *Jane Eyre* appeared on my desk. But Marvin insisted it was out of his power and outside the university's privacy policy to divulge names. I decided that he and I were no longer friends.

"No," I told Marvin, finally. "No candles."

"You'd prefer the dark?"

I let out a violent sneeze before I left, and said: "I hate the dark. I just dislike fire more."

By Christmas Eve I was in bed with a bad fever. My head seemed to have gained twenty pounds, and I half expected it to sway and plunge to the ground like a wounded bull. All I could do was lie back in bed and listen as the thuggish wind pounded on my roof.

Everyone I knew was home for the holidays. I had considered going to Boston for Christmas, but since my old house was now inhabited by two men named Schwartz, I would have had to stay with my old friend Sven the Tennis Pro. My mother had tried to insist that I spend the week with her in Paris, but that seemed like an even lonelier option. The more time we spent together, the more we would have to acknowledge how little we had in common. Besides, I would be visiting her at the end of January and that seemed like enough.

Now, of course, I wished I had somewhere to go. It was the one time of year when it was impossible not to compare yourself to fat, happy families. I hadn't seen anyone in three days and I was so alone that being alone had lost its meaning entirely. Three-dimensional people seemed to be a thing of a distant and cartoonish past. I began to talk to myself. Normally, at first, then abnormally. I re-created conversations I'd had—with my mother, with my father, with my old friend Sally, who ate with her hands. I invented conversations that never happened, sometimes with the Governess and

sometimes with James Timothy Orville III. I was becoming somewhat unhinged.

Time passed slowly, like an old horse wandering through the
Moors, trying to find a quiet place to die. At some point in the
evening—was it nine? ten?—I left my tower to brush my teeth.
Thanks to the flooding caused by the storm, the bathroom on the
ground floor of the tower was out of commission. I would have to
use the restroom in the main building, which meant a long (and cold)
walk down a connecting corridor. It was a dimly lit hallway, punc-
tuated with custodial closets and the occasional grotesque carving on
the walls. I walked slowly at first. I was wearing a coat and my oversize *I Love Lucy* pajamas. The shirt was ripped at the neck and hung
off one shoulder like a dislocated joint. A primordial death draft
seeped out from the building's pores, and I wrapped my coat tighter
around myself. I don't think even my father could have imagined a
place more removed from the stir of society—a perfect misanthrope's
heaven.

Suddenly, when I was halfway down the corridor, the lights went
out, silently and cleanly. I stopped. I tried not to panic. I waited for
my eyes to adjust but they did not. In the black void, I reached out
a hand and grasped for something—anything. I found nothing. My
arm was suspended in soupy shadows. I pulled out the mini flashlight
on my key chain, but its light was weak. Slowly, I turned and tried to
retrace my steps to the tower. I found the wall—yes?—and the door
that had been marked *Esphestus.* The air was wolfishly cold.

I felt very uneasy. An imagination left alone in the dark can be a
terrible thing. The sound of raindrops now echoed like footsteps in
the shallow night. Was there someone else in this corridor with me?
I paused, and listened. For the first time since I arrived at Oxford, I
wasn't quite as alone as I wanted to be.

"Hello?" I called.

No response. In a moment, my toes collided with the damp,

clammy stone of my tower's staircase. I let out a breath of relief, and started climbing. Five flights of stairs were still hard on my barely recovered ankle, and it took me twice as long as I wanted. I was panting when I arrived at my landing. The air was spiked with an unusual odor—clover? I hesitated only for a moment, then reached for my doorknob. I stopped. No, I was right—it was most definitely clover. A scent I recognized from long ago. I turned around. I wrinkled my nose and took another sniff. Perhaps my temporary blindness had heightened my sense of smell. Or else—

I blinked. "Hello?"

No sound, no movement—only the silent shifting of air, the slow trickle of heat along my forehead, and the distinct sense that if eyes could glow red, there would be two of them, staring at me from across the dark expanse.

I stopped where I was. "Who's there?"

No response.

My breathing was labored. I took a step forward and reached out my arm. After a few strides, my fingers gently collided with the opposite wall. I let out a breath, embarrassed. It had been nothing. I took a few steps back toward my door and let my mini flashlight shine its frail beam on the doorknob.

And that's when I saw it. Lying on the doormat, like a sleeping tiger, was *Wuthering Heights*.

I whirled around, too late. "Who's there?"

Suddenly, a great many things happened all at once: a swath of cloth swept past my right side; I let out a healthy scream; a gust of wind slammed against the side of the tower; a figure hurtled toward the stairs. In the weak beam of my key chain flashlight, I caught only one image: a white hand gripping at the handrail. I shrieked and backed up—unfortunately, right to the edge of the staircase, where I lost my footing. I let out a loud cry. My ankle gave way, and I found myself splayed out on the stairs. I clutched the handrail and tried to pull myself up. The uneven clacking of my visitor's footsteps had grown soft. Whoever it was was already halfway down the tower.

I stayed where I was, paralyzed by fear. We all have visions of bravery, but it often materializes only after the moment has passed. I wish I could say that I ran after the intruder and hunted him down, but instead I lay there, sprawled against the stairs, loath to make any noise at all. I was conscious of nothing but the cold stone beneath the palm of my hand and the searing pain in my reinjured foot. I touched the spot on my arm where the intruder had brushed past me.

After a few minutes, I felt well enough to stand. The real danger must have been gone because I was already beginning to imagine how I would tell the story to someone else. I brought myself to my feet and picked up the book from the doormat. *Wuthering Heights.* Of all the horrors! I flashed a pathetic light on the words *Tristan Whipple, his book*, which were etched on the cover in permanent red ink. The only other proof I needed of its origin was on the first blank page, where the outline of a human hand appeared. We had traced that hand, a long time ago, he and I. It was my eleven-year-old palm, my scraggly middle-school fingers.

I walked into my room and immediately tossed the book into the corner of the room, where I had discarded *Agnes Grey* and *Jane Eyre.* In the darkness, I imagined the three of them were tiny, grinning grinches. Emily Brontë's voice came unannounced into my head: *What else could it be that made me pass such a terrible night? I don't remember another that I can at all compare with it since I was capable of suffering.*

I stared into that blackened corner like I would stare at my own epitaph. Wasn't this the way it had always been? Just me and the Brontës, trying to see each other across an eternal void.

A half hour later, I was standing outside the Faculty Wing. The rain had abated, but the wind was something vicious, and it slapped against my face like a fish out of water. It was stupid of me to come here. I was not well. I should have been in bed. But the idea of being alone with *Wuthering Heights* was dreadful. My tower was not big enough for the two of us.

Really, I just wanted to see Orville. I recognized that it was Christmas Eve, and that he was likely home with his secret girlfriend and all of his illegitimate children, whom I imagined would be swarming around his ankles like bastard puppies. Yet despite the hour, it wasn't long before the front door of the Faculty Wing swung open. Two professors were on their way home. They were laughing. The man was holding a paper package in one hand and what appeared to be a centerpiece of a table in the other. Of course, I had forgotten. The faculty and staff who remained in Oxford for the holidays were always invited to their own Christmas banquet.

I recognized one of the professors as Flannery, the woman I had met at the hospital. She was wearing purple tonight, an unflattering shade the color of a bruise. Her companion was a withered old gentleman with a hooked nose and three moles arranged in a Bermuda Triangle on his lower left cheek. Both of them looked startled to find me there, but Flannery in particular seemed shocked—shocked, and then pleased. She was looking at me as though she had finally found proof supporting an old and elaborate theory.

"I'd like to see Professor Orville," I said.

Flannery was standing in the doorway. "What do you need, dear? It's a holiday."

I glanced at the door behind them, which was slowly beginning to creak shut. I hurried: "Something's happened, and I've come for help."

"Goodness, what is it?" said the man. He had a kind smile; I liked him. He looked like the sort of person who had gone by "lad" as a child. "You can talk to one of us, I'm sure."

"Thank you," I said, glancing between them. He and Flannery must have been a couple—he took her hand and she let him hold it. I looked away.

I said, "I'd prefer to talk to Orville."

"*Dr.* Orville," corrected Flannery. I looked back at her and then at the door, which had gently closed. She had a strange look on her face. "There is a resident dean in each college throughout the holidays," she said, repositioning her purse on her shoulder. "Surely you can talk to Dean Sidney?"

"I tried," I lied. "He's not there at the moment."

Flannery wasn't smiling. "Dean Sidney," she said slowly, "is a she."

I didn't respond. I had never met Dean Sidney.

"Why don't you go back home," she said, ending the conversation in a way that suggested she had many more things she could have said on the subject, were it not Christmas. The man tipped his hat and told me to mind the weather. Flannery smiled and followed him along the path. I wrapped my arms around my chest and said, "Yes, yes, very well." They took a right, and I took a left, but only briefly. As soon as they were out of sight, I doubled back. The door had not closed all the way, I noticed, and quietly I crept inside.

The electricity was out here, too, and the candelabras were lit. I hated the look of raw flame. It was unstable and manic. I walked quickly up the staircase. The light grew dimmer. I credited instinct with taking me toward Orville's room like a moth to a spiderweb. I let one hand graze the wall. I ran my fingers over the nameplates like I would read Braille. Milton, Norris, Northington. The last door, Orville's, was locked. I shouldn't have been surprised that he was gone.

Silently, I pressed my head against the cool wood, easing the heat around my temples. I felt ill—truly ill. I heard the thumping of my own heart as it beat through my ears. There was a terrible ache in my head, and for the first time in my life, I had so little strength that I could hardly stand. I pressed my back against the door and let myself sink to the ground. I decided to wait—just a moment—for the ache to go away.

It is past midnight and Anne Brontë is holding a candle. She is wandering around the upper corridor of Thorp Green, the one that leads nowhere and smells like cabbage. It is storming outside, and the wind is shrieking through the walls. Anne cautiously rounds the corner. She has heard Bessie tell the other servants there are rumors of a woman who roams these halls—a woman who is as large as an ox and taller than the master. Anne can hear this strange woman laughing at night, and she is determined to catch her. She holds the candle firmly in her hand and creeps down the corridor. Every night, she hopes to find something shocking, and every night, she finds nothing but her own reflection in the windows.

Suddenly, the upstairs hallway fades in front of her. How strange, *Anne thinks. It doesn't seem to be Thorp Green anymore, but a different house entirely, one with new, hardwood floors and ugly bright red curtains that have clearly been chosen out of a catalogue by a man. A girl steps into the hall. Why is she wearing pajamas? Her hair is dark and wild, and she has the bemused look of someone who has just awakened. The unease on the girl's face grows. Her eyes are wide and she is coughing. There is, Anne realizes, smoke everywhere. Then, in a moment, the girl is bellowing. She runs down the hall, but she can only move in slow motion. That's when all the men in uniform start pouring in—where have they come from, anyway? Whose nightmare is this? Someone tugs the girl around the waist and yanks her down the stairs, across the hall, out of the house—there is a great rushing sound by her ears. Anne is no longer on the outside, she is the girl, she is the one screaming—and why is she screaming? And more important, why are there so many people on such a narrow old street? The noise softens, settles, and dies. Anne is sitting on the sidewalk, and there is a uniformed man with big feet talking to her, and the sun is rising over the rooftops.*

"Samantha."

"Harrumph."

"Samantha."

I opened my eyes. At first, I saw only a reddish glow.

"Is this hell?" I murmured.

"To you, perhaps."

My eyes adjusted. I was inside Orville's office, lying on his leather sofa. He was sitting in the opposite chair, legs crossed, reading the paper. He was wearing a maroon sweater and glasses that reflected the dying flames from the fireplace. I wondered how many years had passed since I had sat down against his door, or whether we had always been like this, he and I, and my life before I knew him had all been an elaborate fiction.

I said, "What are you doing here?"

"I might ask you the same question," he said, shaking the paper once. "I returned from the banquet to find you sprawled on my doorstep like a Greek tragedy."

I squinted. "Was I asleep?"

"You were thrashing."

I let out a wheeze. "I'm a little ill."

I tried to stand, but was seized by dizziness. The horror of my nightmare came over me. I collapsed back down on the sofa. I was trembling. I hadn't dreamt like that in years. My limbs tingled, defeated.

"What time is it?" I asked.

"Ten minutes to two."

"In the *morning*?"

Orville didn't answer.

I said, "How long have you been sitting there?"

"Long enough."

I squinted at him, then at the fire. It was emitting soft orange sparks into cold air. I pulled the blanket over me—why did I have a blanket?—and tried to map out what had transpired. If I had, in fact, passed out on the floor of the hallway, then Orville must have moved me. My coat was hanging on a nearby chair; my boots were drying by the fireplace. Had Orville taken them off? God, what a thought.

The electricity must have come back on; one of the lamps in the corner of the room was bleeding a muted yellow. I pointed to the middle of the table, where a defrosting brick was wrapped in cellophane.

"What's that?"

He glanced at it. "Cake. Interested?"

I wasn't exactly hungry, but Orville stood and walked across the room. His legs seemed exceptionally long from my vantage point—he reminded me of one of those circus men who walk on stilts, with billowing balloon pants. I rested my head against the plump, swollen back of the sofa. The next time I looked up, Orville was standing over me, two glasses in his hand. When I didn't take one from him, he put mine down on the table.

"What is it?" I asked.

"Cognac."

I stared at it.

He waited. "Don't you drink?"

"Of course," I lied.

It was a strange sight, watching a faculty member take a drink. It reminded me that professors must have real lives—lives in which they wore boxers and occasionally cooked, lives in which they sometimes played tennis, sometimes slept with women, and sometimes just sat watching television, like the average peasant.

It was a minute before I could bring myself to take the cognac in my hands. I put my nose deep down inside the glass, then retracted it immediately. The stench was something awful. Perhaps I was more exhausted than I realized, but for a moment I thought I could make out my father's face on the surface, warped and vague. I put the glass back down. I didn't need it. People evaporated in alcohol, the way people evaporated in dreams.

I looked up and gave a small start. Orville, I realized, was watching me closely.

"Do you think about him often?" he said. The fire was dying and in the dim light, his eyes looked like two dots drawn by Sharpie.

I didn't answer.

"How old were you when it happened?" he asked.

"When what happened?"

A pause.

I cleared my throat. "I had just turned fifteen."

"How very terrible it must have been for you, Samantha."

His voice was low and gentle. I frowned and wondered, not for the first time in my life, if I talked in my sleep. We stared at each other for only a moment longer before he reached forward and unwrapped the frozen cake. He set his knife against it and gave it a good thwack. A piece fell to the table like a sledgehammer. He slapped a cold slice onto my open hand.

I held on to the cake gingerly. Orville was still inspecting me. I wasn't used to receiving his nonacademic attention. I brushed the hair away from my face. I felt the sudden need to prove that I could, in fact, be good-looking, if you looked hard enough.

"Sir," I said, "what's the punishment for breaking into someone's room?"

"Expulsion."

"Is it?"

"Are you considering breaking into a room?"

Another pause. The fire dimmed of its own accord. In the half-light, Orville's face looked incomplete, like someone had been too intimidated to finish his portrait.

"Someone left me another book," I said. "*Wuthering Heights*."

I thought I saw a note of alarm cross his expression, but he killed it swiftly.

"Your father's?"

I nodded. He frowned. A conversation about the Brontës was not one he wanted to have, it seemed. We lingered in a silence that seemed purely decorative. Then he stood up and walked to his bookshelf. I thought he must have forgotten about me, but he returned with an old, black book. It was *Wuthering Heights*.

I looked up at him. "Yes, I see you have it too."

"At one point, it was my favorite book."

"That's probably why we'll never be friends."

For the first time since I had known him, Orville came to sit next to me. The couch shifted with his weight. We were very close to each other and I wondered if he was breaking all the college's rules in one go.

"This was my father's copy," he said, flipping to the scribbled note on the title page. "See here? 'Dear James, love, Dad.'"

"Thoughtful."

Orville was so close that I could feel the warmth radiating from him. My face was next to his left shoulder and I wanted nothing more than to melt against him. I recalled the intense calm I had once felt when Hans took my hand in his, and I wanted to ask Orville to do the same. Instead, I said:

"Sir, may we please study the Brontës together?"

"No."

"I know you think it's a personal problem and that you're not my therapist. But really, this whole issue is entirely academic. I need your professional help. Someone is leaving me very famous novels, ones that my father spent his entire life trying to deconstruct. All I have is some messy old research, with no guidelines."

Orville said, "People have been studying these books for over a century. What did your father possibly expect to find? A missing chapter?"

"I don't know."

"Then please don't ask me to become involved."

"Please, sir. It will be just like regular tutorials, except useful."

Orville stood up and returned to his seat across the table. He sat at the edge of his chair and began packing up the defrosted cake, slowly, as though he were wrapping a delicate present. I pulled the blanket over my torso and stared into the fireplace. It popped and spat out flames like small arguments.

"Do you know the last image I have of him?" I asked.

A pause—then: "Who."

"My father."

No answer.

"He was trying to hang a painting on the wall," I said.

"You don't have to talk about this."

"It was a heavy painting," I said. "Framed. It was late. He was hammering, and it was so loud that I couldn't fall asleep. I went downstairs, and there he was, just standing there—the nail between his index and middle finger, the hammer in the other hand—looking down at himself as though his pants had dropped and he couldn't remember how to pull them back up."

Orville repeated, "Samantha. You don't have to talk about this."

I ignored him. "He had been drinking, and was swaying by this time. He lifted the nail to the wall and when he swung, he missed. I'm sure he hit himself on the fingers, but he didn't react. It was unfair. He was unfair. I started to yell at him to leave the painting alone and go to bed. I told him to stop breathing through his mouth like that. I was screaming because I had never seen him so imperfect. He waved his hammer as a response and smashed it into the wall. He started laughing; then he started singing. 'Bye, bye, Miss American Pie.' I went back upstairs and stuffed two earplugs in my ears and put a pillow over my head."

I stopped just then. I let out a breath.

Softly, Orville said: "And?"

"And, that's it."

We were silent. When I looked at him, he looked away. True, I was leaving out a couple of bits, like the actual fire. But that was where the memory grew holes, and the journalists had filled me in. Wasn't it curious, said the *New Yorker*, that the enigmatic Tristan Whipple should die in the same way Branwell Brontë *nearly* died— in the same way that *Jane Eyre*'s Mr. Edward Rochester had *nearly* died? It was almost as if Tristan Whipple had lived out an old destiny. In the hands of an exceptional poet, perhaps the incident could have been turned into something lasting and artistic. Wasn't it ironic, then, that the one author who could have done it justice was my father? I stopped reading the papers when I was sixteen.

I let out a breath. "By now, it's fiction. It's like it never even happened."

Orville didn't move. "Of course it happened."

"No," I said, standing up. "No. You'd be pretty surprised at how much it didn't happen. Where should I put my glass?"

All of a sudden it felt wrong to be there. I felt like a fraud. I had just described the last hours of my closest companion, and yet my eyes were dry. I was always one step away from raw emotion. Dad used to tell me that to tell a good story, you needed courage. Courage to fully become someone else, even if—and especially if—that person was a more vulnerable version of yourself. I was not a courageous person. I wasn't even crying.

I put down my glass. "I might try to forget this conversation."

"As you wish."

"Will you forget it too?"

He didn't respond. I walked over and slipped on my boots.

"Samantha, shall I walk you home?"

He looked so concerned that I had a hard time believing he was the same person who liked to strut around this room with a meter-stick. I shook my head and let out a cough that seemed to rattle all the bones in my chest. I gathered my things to leave, but I stopped at the door.

"Sir," I began, "in *Wuthering Heights*, someone breaks into Lockwood's room in the middle of the night. Do you remember?"

He said, "I remember."

"Lockwood realizes that it is, in fact, a ghost. A ghost so real to him that it becomes a physical reality."

"Yes. And?"

I waited. "Well?" I said—I practically gulped. "Do you think it's possible?"

I realized I didn't want to hear his answer, though. So I pulled my coat around me. Orville took a step forward. I didn't look him in the eye; instead, I thanked him for the cake and quitted the room. I heard him wishing me a merry Christmas as the door shut behind me.

Reading *Wuthering Heights* had always made me wonder whether Emily Brontë had done drugs. It was not always clear, even to her, where her imaginary world stopped and where reality began. For a woman who spent her entire life secluded on a desolate English wasteland, Emily Brontë had a curiously nuanced grasp of the world, much more developed than some of her more worldly literary counterparts.

She was my father's favorite Brontë. Emily, like him, had been a singularly antisocial creature who loathed publicity, had almost no friends, and ritually burned most of her writing. It was she who invented the family pseudonyms, happily hiding behind the name Ellis Bell like it was a giant plant. Emily stayed on the moors for most of her life, refused any form of medical treatment when she grew ill with tuberculosis, and died at the age of thirty.

Wuthering Heights was her one, beloved baby. It received very little praise when it was published in 1847, and Emily died the following year under the impression that it was a failure. The book was a weird, sick, twisted creature that brought to life a slew of unappealing characters. There were family trees as complicated as the Russian monarchy, plagued by an avalanche of similar names: Hareton, Heathcliff, Hindley. There was a plot, I guess, but it was grounded somewhere between the natural and the supernatural, heaven and hell, this world and Emily Brontë's dream world.

I had read *Wuthering Heights* several times and seen all the movie adaptations, from old black-and-white movies with too much wind and not enough dialogue to artistic French films saturated with awkward sex and visible chest hair. The image of Cathy and Heathcliff roaming about the cruel Yorkshire moors was about as famous as that of the *Titanic* sinking. No one seemed to doubt that this novel was one of the most passionate, romantic love stories in English literature. And yet, there is very little romance between Heathcliff and Cathy. Heathcliff is a beast, not a human. "He's a fierce, pitiless, wolfish man," says Cathy, who could also be describing herself. There are some moments of picturesque melodrama, but the love story is weak at best. Cathy and Heathcliff do not evolve together; they just *are*. Nelly Dean gives the best description of the pair: *Heathcliff gnashed at me, and foamed like a mad dog, and gathered [Cathy] to him with greedy jealousy. I did not feel as if I were in the company of a creature of my own species.* They both end up miserable, then dead.

The idea that this book was a great love story was Emily Brontë's little magic trick. She had always been a believer in grand dreams, and what better way to demonstrate the power of the imagination than to engineer a book that encouraged—no, required—her readers to imagine? The real romance between Heathcliff and Cathy has been invented by millions of eager readers. We must assume they love each other, even when some of the facts don't add up. And thanks to our significant efforts, their "love" feels as real as if Emily had spelled the whole thing out. Emily succeeded in doing what my father had always wanted to do: she made people use their imaginations.

Wuthering Heights was the second-to-last book my father and I read together in full. I was fourteen. He and I were sitting in our backyard, legs draped into our paddling pool. The water was orange because it had been there for three and a half years. I asked Dad if we'd get polio; he told me that I had already been vaccinated, maybe. He had been reading *Wuthering Heights* aloud to me over a series of days. Every day I would listen while watching our bare feet through the orange water. We looked like test subjects in a lab for radioactive waste.

Once we finished the book, Dad asked me what I thought of it. I said it was full of contradictions. *Contradictions* was my favorite word at the time, along with *flocculate*. Emily invented a brutal world that bred sin and immorality, yet revealed it through a narrator blinded by British politeness and manners. She created one of the most enduring loves in English literature, yet suggested that such a love could never survive. She demonstrated that those who live in the past are doomed never to escape it, yet she trapped the reader in stories of a violent, turbulent past. It was, I thought, a pretty good analysis for a teenager.

My father just splashed his foot once in the water without smiling. I could tell that he didn't agree with me. I tried to tell him about similes, but he interrupted to say that I was overanalyzing. I told him all about dichotomies and juxtapositions, but he said not to mention those insidious words again—did I want to have to go play soccer? *Dichotomy* was his least favorite word, right after *twinkle*.

I learned that day that my father cared about one scene, and one scene only: the Scene with the Hand. It was one of the first moments in the text. The narrator, who has been emotionally brutalized by Heathcliff's less-than-amiable hospitality, has a dream about a noisy branch outside his window. Dad reread the passage to me for added emphasis:

> *"I must stop it, nevertheless!" I muttered, knocking my knuckles through the glass, and stretching an arm out to seize the importunate branch: instead of which, my fingers closed on the fingers of a little, ice-cold hand! The intense horror of nightmare came over me; I tried to draw back my arm, but the hand clung to it, and a most melancholy voice sobbed, "Let me in—let me in!"*

When he finished reading, he said, "A little out of place, wouldn't you say?"

"What do you mean?"

"This is clunky, amateur writing."

"It's a dream," I said. "Lockwood is having a nightmare."

"Is it really? This passage does not fit in with the rest of the book. You have to wonder why it is here at all."

I said, "Maybe Emily was just a bad writer."

"She was a very talented writer."

"Maybe because it was her first novel, and she didn't know what she was doing."

Dad frowned. He was angry. There was a sickly, manic gleam in his eye, and I knew he would soon begin to gesticulate wildly. I wanted to stop the lesson, but I stayed put.

"Try again," he said.

"I don't know," I said. "Maybe it's not a dream and she thinks that ghosts are real."

"Better. Go with that."

"Go with what?"

"You'd be amazed to discover all the tangible things that can come out of dreams."

"Like drool?"

"Perhaps this is too advanced for you, after all," he snapped. "You're just not ready."

With that, the lesson was over. We didn't speak for days. I knew why he was upset. Dad thought I wasn't learning quickly enough. He didn't understand why, after all his efforts, I couldn't think the way he did. I was too conventional. Too calm, too sedate, and too much like my mother. He knew that I would read a book and think of it only as a book rather than as a part of myself—something that I could live and breathe. As hard as he tried, my beautiful, bizarre father could not teach me to be creative.

Then, of course, he died, not even a full two months later. I never did find out what made the Scene with the Hand so fascinating to him. All I could do was mull over the words he had underlined. *Let me in—let me in!*

I wanted to scream the exact same words back to him.

A few days before New Year's, I received a knock at my door. Another tour group, I supposed. Or was it another book?

I said, "Who's there?"

The voice was loud: "Open the door, Samantha."

"Professor?"

"Open the door."

I did as I was told. There, to my great surprise, was Orville. There was not a speck of snow or rain on his coat. I wondered if he had arrived by chopper. There was a suitcase in one hand and a small plastic bag in the other. He was panting.

"Do you mean to tell me that you climb all those stairs each day?" he said. I didn't answer. He entered and looked around. The chipping red paint from the wall glowed like drying blood. My wet, translucent bedsheets were drying on the fireplace mantel. We looked like we were standing inside a sickroom from the Civil War.

Orville cleared his throat. "Nice place."

I was shocked to discover him here. It was like seeing the pope visit a radioactive wasteland. I offered him a seat on my naked mattress, but he didn't take it. Instead, he passed me the plastic bag. I didn't look inside.

"Why are you here?" I asked. "On a Sunday?"

"It's Monday."

"Oh." I frowned. "Did I miss our tutorial? Have you come to scold me?"

"We have no tutorials for the next three weeks, until term begins again."

I said, "I didn't know that."

"Yes, you did. I sent you an e-mail."

"I don't read e-mails anymore."

"Which is why I figured I should come to talk to you in person."

"Yes, sir."

To my surprise, he snapped at me. "Stop calling me 'sir,' Samantha. I never asked you to call me that."

I paused. "What do I call you?"

"Dr. Orville."

"Can I call you by your name?"

"Which name?"

"James."

"No."

I shrugged. "That's fine. You don't look like a James, anyway."

"What do I look like?"

"Irving."

"Don't call me Irving."

I glanced at the Governess as if for moral support. She looked more hostile than usual today, as though she was preparing to shoot Orville from the hip and was just waiting for him to step within range. I noticed that his facial hair had grown in the last few days. The lower half of his chin looked like someone had shaded it in with a pencil.

I motioned to his suitcase. "Where are you going?"

"North for a week."

"I see."

"I handled myself badly the other night," he said. "I came to apologize."

I feigned indifference. "Sorry, what are we talking about?"

"You asked for an education," he said. "I should have given it to you."

"I don't understand."

"You are right," he said, ignoring me. "I do, in fact, know quite a bit about the Brontës. Perhaps more than your average person. Perhaps more than your average don. It may be somewhat cruel of me to deny you my expertise."

I raised an eyebrow. "Do you know as much as John Booker?"

He didn't answer the question. "All of this said, it is only fair you know that the Brontës bring up somewhat painful memories for me." He motioned toward the bag in my hands. "Here. Open it."

I did as I was told. There, inside, was *Wuthering Heights*. I was trying to remember a time when I looked down and that infernal book was not there. There was Cathy, right on the cover, clutching Heathcliff's bare, hairy chest. Heathcliff looked like James Dean. I recognized this book. It was James Orville's personal copy. The note from his father appeared on the first page. *Dear James, love, Dad.* For a moment, I couldn't speak.

"You can read out of this one if your copy is filled with as many margin notes as appear in *Jane Eyre*," he said. "We will do this in private. And you are not to mention it to anyone."

"Who would I tell?"

"Then we have an agreement?"

I nodded. He was standing very close to me. He smelled of chamomile and aftershave.

He glanced at his watch. "Read the book in its entirety and prepare an essay on the use of windows."

"Why windows?"

"Is it not obvious?"

"No."

"I will send you an e-mail with additional reading tonight," he said. "I expect you to complete it by the time I return."

I croaked, "Thank you. Really, thank you. I—"

"This visit?" he interrupted, holding up his index finger and stirring the air with it. "Never happened."

"Okay."

"And the tutorial we will have? It also will never have happened."

"Right."

He looked me over once, then gave a quick nod. He dusted off his scarf and made to leave but was arrested, quite suddenly, upon noticing the Governess. She looked good at the moment—the muted light flattered her solemn features.

"That painting. Where did you get it?"

I shrugged.

He said, "Answer."

"It came with the tower."

Orville looked between us, like he had just discovered my twin.

He and the Governess stared at each other in a vast recognition. He cleared his throat, and in a moment, his face readjusted back into its usual expression of apathy. He didn't answer me—just wrapped his scarf around his neck like nothing had happened.

He said, "She looks like you, that's all."

I pressed my lips together. "That's the second time a man has said that to me."

"Is it?" he said. He turned toward me. He was terribly attractive, and I couldn't seem to look at him directly. "Samantha, will you promise me to be careful?"

"Pardon?"

"Careful. You."

I gorilla-pounded my chest as an affirmation. Orville didn't understand what I was doing and I didn't either. Then he walked over to the door and closed it behind him. With him gone, I glanced back at the painting. She was different, yet again. Blame the lighting, the fatigue—anything—but the Governess, I was quite sure, had just blinked.

CHAPTER 9

Dear Samantha,

This is Sir John Booker from the Brontë Parsonage. How are you? I hope you passed a pleasant holiday.

I must say I am very disappointed. I would have expected your mother—if not your father—to have raised you with more manners. I have now left you three voice mails and have yet to hear back from you. As a father myself, I feel it appropriate to give you some advice. At some point in your life, you will have to gain the courage to face your problems instead of shutting them away with you.

Please have the courtesy to call me back immediately. I am curious to know whether your father's books are still arriving at your doorstep, and how I might be of help.

Yours,
John

Two weeks later, Orville and I agreed to meet at eight in the evening for our Tutorial That Never Happened. He chose an underground bar with a name too avant-garde to actually pronounce. Apparently, he had gone to great lengths to find somewhere where no one would ever see us.

It took me some time to find Agatha Street, which was a darkened artery in a sullen, residential part of town. Narrow, skeletal houses were stacked neatly against each other, pressed together as if to keep warm. I walked along, counting the numbers on the door. Number 11, the address of said avant-garde lounge, turned out to be an old door lurking incognito amid a wall of decaying brick. We were supposed to meet outside and Orville was late. I leaned against the wall and waited. A woman with grocery bags scuttled past, babushka'd tightly in a coat and scarf.

My cell buzzed. It was an unfamiliar number. I said, "Hello?"

"Is this Samantha?"

I frowned. No one ever called me. "Is this Mom?"

"This is James."

"James."

"Orville the Third."

"The reception is terrible."

I didn't know James Orville had my number, or a cell phone.

"I am at a crêpe stand," he said. He didn't finish his thought, because he had started rattling French in a rusty, sandpaper accent, presumably to someone else. When he resumed our conversation, he said, "Where are you?"

"On the street corner," I said. "Picking up men."

"Listen, I'm running late," he said. There was some sort of noise in the background—a truck, maybe, or a street cleaner. "I stopped for a bite. Are you hungry?"

"Not very."

He swore.

"What?" I said.

"Nothing—it's hot."

"What kind did you get?"

"*Jambon et fromage.*"

I said, "Ham and cheese."

"I was using the French."

"I was using the English."

A gust of wind slammed against the phone. He said, "I won't keep you waiting much longer."

I said, "Take your time—it's really exciting over here."

But he had already hung up. I was smiling, and then I stopped. It was always disconcerting to see people standing on the sidewalk, grinning to themselves. Then again, there was no one around to watch me. The streets had emptied rapidly. The wind stopped and started intermittently, like bad traffic. I pulled my jacket around my chest and raised the collar so that it armored the lower half of my face from the cold. This was the position my father called *turtling*. It was what my mother used to call *You're going to get acne*.

In ten minutes, a large figure appeared in the distance, wearing . . . a cape? Orville had left his wool coat unbuttoned and it flapped in the breeze behind him, Zorro style. When he arrived, he was taking the final bites of his crêpe. I was unused to seeing him in civilian attire. Tonight, he was wearing a leather jacket under his coat, Ray-Bans on top of his head, and a look that said, *I'm here, baby, let's go surfing*.

I nodded toward the remains of his *jambon et fromage*. "Smells good."

"Did you want some?"

"No."

He stood in front of number 11 and placed his palm in the center of the door, like it might be a magic portal that opened only for genies.

"I didn't know you spoke French," I said.

"*'Sous le pont Mirabeau coule la Seine. Et nos amour, faut-il qu'il m'en souvienne, la joie venait toujours après la peine.'*"

His accent really was atrocious—brittle, like a tin of stale cashews.

I said, "If you could stop, that would be great."

"You don't like poetry?"

"I don't like French, either."

Orville knocked on the door in front of us and stood back with his hands in his pockets. There was an abnormal calm about him this evening. Perhaps something had, in fact, changed between us since Christmas. Were we becoming low-level friends?

The door opened. The man on the other side was round in every way, with dewy pigeon eyes and a mop of dandelion-blond hair, which fell over his eyes like a wedding veil. He checked our identification and led us inside, down a small, rusty corridor and into a dramatically darkened salon.

Orville led us past the bar, which sparkled like a collection of pipe organs. The bartender was a woman with a plunging neckline and big, flat fish-lips. At the bar was a pack of men in multicolored ties, and dancing alone in the middle of the room was a softly swaying woman in green.

Orville found a quiet back table and removed his coat. He looked around. "Well?"

"This is definitely weird."

We slid into our seats, and Orville ordered us each a drink from a woman whose legs were so long that all I could really see was her plaid kilt, right in front of my face. When she left, Orville asked, "How did you like the reading for this week?"

"Which one?" I asked. "'*Wuthering Heights* Is a Freudian Sex Drama,' or 'Emily Brontë: An Analysis of Premodern Lesbianism'?"

"Both."

I said, "I thought they were a disgrace to academia."

"Because they were about sex?"

My eyes flew open. I didn't know James Orville III used that word. I tried to find something appropriately clever to say, but couldn't. Orville was testing me. I could feel it. My lips twitched but no sound emerged. Somewhere in my mind, Samantha Whipple was being terribly witty. It was a shame no one could hear her.

"I'd like to talk to you about your essay," said Orville.

"Sure."

"It was . . . different."

"That's for sure."

He didn't answer, and I thought he might be thinking of how best to fire me from school. I had written this essay at four in the morning, when I had given the finger to thinking up a legitimate argument. Orville had asked me to analyze the use of windows in a novel that had nothing to do with windows. I decided to argue that windows were not windows at all; they were all that separated the savage moorland from the civilized home, Thrushcross Grange from Wuthering Heights, even Cathy from her own self-constructed identities. Windows were the barrier between this world and the next, a barrier as ill-defined as the boundary between the reader and the text itself. It was a bullshit parade, and I was the proud mayor. I used the phrases *Jungian realism* and *linear archetypes*, and congratulated myself on achieving a level of douchebaggery I had previously only witnessed in shampoo commercials for men.

I cleared my throat. "What did you think of it, sir?"

Orville looked at me long and hard. In this lighting, his eyes were the size and shape of two olives.

He said, "It was one of the finest papers I've ever read by a student."

I blinked. He had a strange, sadistic smile on his face. I felt like a courtier who was finally receiving the full attention of the king, only to discover it was Henry VIII. The drinks arrived. Mine was green.

"I gather that you do not like what you wrote," he said.

"It was idiotic," I said. "Any fool can find obscure patterns in a novel, fabricate an intention behind it, and then trick people into believing it's relevant. I call that intellectual narcissism."

"I call it creativity," Orville said. "The purpose of literature is to teach you how to *think*, not how to be practical. Learning to discover the connective tissue between seemingly unrelated events is the only way we are equipped to understand patterns in the real world. And I did not give you this assignment on a whim. The world has analyzed window symbolism for decades."

"I did not know that."

He nodded with an "as I expected" expression. I pressed my lips together and drew the green glass toward me. Here was the first compliment Orville had ever given me. Part of me wanted to accept it—frame it, mount it on my wall the way some people did dead animals—but it didn't seem right, not when I was convinced of my own foolishness. I peered down at my drink and took a swallow. There was ginger and pear and an unrecognizable alcohol.

"Do you like it?" Orville asked, pointing to my glass.

"No. Can we trade?"

Orville passed me his drink. It was bronze and it tasted like it might have been scotch in its first life.

I said, "I hope you don't have mono."

"Do you have *Wuthering Heights* with you?" he said. "I'd like to begin."

I nodded and removed both books from my bag—my father's copy, and Orville's father's copy. I placed them on the table between us, feeling uncommonly vulnerable. It was as though I were actually handing him my kidney: it wasn't particularly pretty, and I didn't quite understand what it did, but it was personal and it was mine. I watched Orville's movements very closely. He wrapped his fingers around the spine of my father's book and pulled it toward him with a deep sigh. There was a look of torment on his face that made me furious. Why should the Brontës bring up more painful memories for him than they did for me? He was commandeering my claim to being tragic and misunderstood.

I carefully inched closer to him and told him we should start with the Scene with the Hand, since it was really the centerpiece of the book, wouldn't he agree? Orville waved me away and found the page himself, like a man who has thought through all of the text's nuances already, thank you very much. I felt a surge of protectiveness. What if he had a distorted image of this book in his mind? What if he imagined Cathy with long hair? Goodness, the thought.

I cleared my throat. "Can you tell me what this scene means to you? My father was preoccupied with it."

Orville must not have understood how desperately I wanted an answer, because he was contemplating something quietly on his own. I felt very alone.

After a considerable silence, he mused: "A beautiful scene."

"Oh?"

"It is a fine presentation of a lover's anguish," he said. "Heathcliff, moved by despair, imagines his deceased love everywhere he goes. An imagination infected by pain can take you to terrible places, Samantha. Here, the effort of resuscitating Cathy has left Heathcliff half in the real world, half in the next, forever tortured."

I had been expecting something a bit more original. I waited a respectable amount of time before saying, "Want to know what I think?"

"Naturally."

"I think the scene just means that a woman appeared at the window."

"I beg your pardon?"

"How do you know that someone didn't appear outside the Brontë parsonage, and Emily decided to put it in a book?"

Orville blinked. "Because we are academics, not fools."

I said, "Will you please stop overestimating my stupidity? The scene is entirely out of place otherwise. It's poorly written and doesn't fit with the rest of the book. You have to wonder why Emily thought to include it at all. It's probably because this actually happened to her."

"Please do not attach literal value to a scene whose weight is purely emotional," said Orville. "How would *you* feel if your sister appeared up at your window after years of being dead?"

I stopped abruptly. I repeated, "*Sister*?"

"Certainly."

I stared at him in blank horror.

"Heathcliff and Cathy," he clarified. "They are siblings."

"No. What?"

"Well," Orville corrected, "*half* siblings."

My eyes widened. I was silent for several moments, searching for the right words to express my shock. I felt like a cartoon rodent who had flung himself off a cliff only to be suspended over the abyss.

"Oh, for heaven's sake, Samantha," said Orville. "Read closely. Are we really expected to believe that the respectable Mr. Earnshaw pulls a scrawny, wild-eyed boy off of the polluted London streets, then raises him as his own child—all out of the goodness of his heart? The only explanation is that Earnshaw secretly fathered Heathcliff."

I looked away, and around the room. It was as though I had just glanced down only to find that I'd been naked all this time. The entire novel took on a new, grotesque hue. Of *course* Cathy and Heathcliff were half siblings. They tattled, they fought, they skipped into the moors hand in hand, and they never had sex. Their devotion to each other never evolved from childlike affection. What had Cathy once proclaimed? *I am Heathcliff, and Heathcliff is me.* I guess she was telling the truth.

I glanced at Orville in defeat. It was incredible, the ease with which other people's ridiculous ideas always struck me as true. I looked around again. Everything seemed flatter, all of a sudden. There was no more mystery in the lighting, no more romance.

"So that's it?" I said. "The greatest love story of all time is an advanced case of incest?"

Orville said, "Relax, Samantha. It's only a story."

"Nothing is ever just a story," I said. "Not in a world where windows can be seen as a portal to another world. Does this mean that Emily Brontë was secretly in love with her brother?"

Orville took a long, exhausted breath. "Let's not regress, shall we?"

"But it *could* have happened, couldn't it?" I said, growing animated. "Emily's whole life was a muddle between her fantasy life and her real life. Who's to say that she didn't appear at Branwell Brontë's window one night? Who's to say the two of them didn't have a very close personal relationship? What if this was the grand secret my father wanted to share with me?"

"Samantha, please—"

"After all, Cathy was a nutcase, and Emily Brontë was a nutcase; Heathcliff was unstable and so was Branwell. Emily wrote something grotesque and incestuous—maybe it was a reflection of her own life."

"Please stop saying incorrect things."

"You don't believe it's possible? It wouldn't be the first time the Brontës put their lives into their books."

"You cannot evaluate a novel based on the life of an author."

"Oh? Do you remember how, in *Jane Eyre*, the madwoman sets Rochester's bed aflame and he almost dies? Branwell also supposedly set his own bed on fire. Coincidence?"

"Branwell's near death was not the result of an attack by a madwoman."

"How are you so sure? He lived in a house with three destitute sisters whom he could have saved had he ever gotten a real job. Are you telling me that you don't think at least one of them wanted him dead?"

Orville regarded me for a moment. "You treat your relatives with extraordinary contempt."

"I have a right to," I said. "They split apart my family."

"They split apart mine, too, and you don't see me vilifying them."

I paused. The words seemed to have slipped out of his mouth without permission.

"Another drink?" he said.

"I haven't finished my first."

He turned to flag down the lanky waitress, but she had disappeared. He turned back to me.

"Where were we?" he asked.

"You were about to spill some dark secrets."

"Your problem, Samantha, is that you are trying too hard to find a grand meaning in these novels. Usually, meaning tends to find *you*, in the middle of the night, and when you least expect it."

"You mean like a murderer?"

"I mean like Cathy Linton's ghost," he said. "Emily Brontë's two eldest sisters—Maria and Elizabeth—died of tuberculosis as children, when Emily, Anne, and Charlotte were still very young. If there is any autobiographical inspiration for this scene in *Wuthering Heights*, then that is it. Have deceased family members and loved ones ever appeared to you in a dream, and felt as real to you as they did in real life? Love, like good fiction, can create reality from nothing. That, Samantha, is the 'purpose' of this scene, if you must have one. If a real woman did appear at the window, it would only be because Cathy's ghost is as real to Heathcliff as anything in the physical world."

I pressed my lips together. "I see we've come back to Frederick Douglass. You believe this scene represents mere emotional truth, while I—correctly—believe that it's literally the truth."

"Sometimes you need emotional truth to create literal truth."

I swirled my drink around and stared into it. "One day, you and I will schedule a two-hour fistfight, and I will show you that it can happen."

"I look forward to it," he said.

When he grinned, Orville looked like a wolf. He took his glass in his hand, realized it was empty, and returned it to the table with a smack.

I studied him carefully. "I have a question for you," I said after a pause.

"Go ahead."

"Do you know anything about the Warnings of Experience?"

A pause. "The what?"

"The Warnings of Experience. Do you know what that is?"

He frowned. "No."

I couldn't tell if I was disappointed or relieved. I said, "All right."

"Why do you ask?" he said.

"My father. That's what he said I was to inherit. The Warnings of Experience."

Orville didn't say anything for a long time. The room was dark and his eyes were lost to me. I held my own empty glass in my hands, looking down at the way it scattered the muted blue and red lights above us. I waited patiently for a response.

"Thank you, Samantha," Orville said finally, "for trusting me with that information."

I shrugged. "I just hoped you'd know what it meant."

He let out a long breath. I was about to return our attention to *Wuthering Heights* when he said, quite abruptly:

"I'm tired of thinking about this," he said. "Aren't you?"

I blinked. "I'm always tired of thinking about this."

"Good."

"Does that mean we're leaving?"

He glanced at his watch. "We'll have another round," he said.

Kilt Woman reappeared and to my great shock, James Timothy Orville III ordered two more drinks.

It turned out to be one of the finest evenings I ever spent. I ordered a plate of chocolate-covered hazelnuts that tasted vaguely of burnt fish; Orville ordered something covered in coconut that also tasted vaguely of burnt fish. I told him about my days as a disillusioned teenage writer; he told me that he once climbed mountains and dreamt of owning lions. Neither one of us looked at our watches. We both must have felt that it was a lovely thing to be the two of us, sitting in a darkened speakeasy.

The conversation turned from lions to Hemingway to organic food to our parents. I learned that Orville's mother had switched from academia to law when she and his father had divorced, and was now a powerful barrister in London, where she had taken a semipermanent new boyfriend and owned a plant named George. I spoke about my father, but only briefly. I explained our little games, and the stupid plans he and I used to make for the future.

"He promised me that on his fiftieth birthday, he'd take me to see Oscar's grave," I said.

"Who is Oscar?" Orville asked.

"Wilde."

"Ah," he said. "I didn't know you two were on a first-name basis."

"I used to be terribly in love with him."

"You know, he preferred men."

"Yes, and he is also dead. No one is perfect."

He laughed, and the noise startled me so much that I looked away.

"I would imagine you with someone more like F. Scott Fitzgerald," he said.

"Too young, too pretty."

"Jack London?"

"Out of my league."

He smiled. "You don't do yourself enough credit."

My cheeks brightened and I turned my attention to my drink. I took a manly gulp. Had I received another compliment? I wasn't sure. To everyone else there, I'm sure Orville and I looked like a couple, maybe from a moody Edward Hopper painting. I was aware of the impossibility of any relationship between Orville and myself, but perhaps that was why I couldn't stop imagining it. I felt safe knowing nothing could ever happen between us. The truth was that I had no idea what to do with men, and Orville would never have to know.

"Did you ever make it to Oscar's grave?" he asked.

"Dad never made it to fifty."

"Ah—I'm sorry."

"He and I always said we'd meet up there someday. You know, like people do at the end of foreign films? He would come from the south side, I would come from the north, and some birds would start flying."

"We should go."

"Home?"

"No, to the grave. Père Lachaise is a beautiful cemetery. You should see it."

I shrugged. "Or, I'll just write about it. He would have thought that was the same thing."

"Do you even write?"

"No. Are you going to get another drink?"

Orville gave me a long, searching glance before he turned away to flag down the waitress yet again. He ordered some beer. When he looked back, he said: "You know, I suppose I always fancied Agatha Christie."

"Funny," I said, downing the rest of my drink in one final gulp. "I would have pictured you as a Woolf man."

Pint number two arrived. Pint number one hadn't been very good; no wonder my father preferred whiskey.

"I didn't know you were allowed to drink with your students," I said.

It was around midnight, and I was holding an empty pint glass. I was drunk. Drunk? Drunk. It wasn't that great of a feeling. I felt like that protagonist in my dreams, the one who always tried to run but could never seem to move her legs fast enough.

Orville shrugged. "I'm not allowed to do a lot of things with my students."

"I know. I flipped through section C of the rulebook. It's long."

He let out a bark of laughter. "You may be the only student who has ever read that. I applaud you."

"Did you know that if you and I were having a tutorial, and I was to remove an article of clothing, you are required to submit yourself to the lawful verdict of your peers and the law of the land?"

"That sounds right, yes."

"Did you also know that any student who is found to have misappropriated property from a professor's office will have his own possessions seized, including, but not limited to, his lands and castles?"

"The rulebook is several hundred years old."

"So what happens if you and I get caught right now?"

"Execution."

"Guillotine?"

"Pistol."

I laughed. I found that I was swaying slightly. "I don't understand why the college has such irrelevant laws."

"Oh, I wouldn't call them irrelevant," Orville said, leaning back in his seat. "Some of the specifics are outdated, but at heart, the code of law exists to uphold the sanctity of an education, honor the respect due to fellow students, and maintain the propriety of the tutor-student relationship."

I raised an eyebrow. I didn't call attention to the fact that this tutor and this student were currently slurping beer at a bar, because English teachers were supposed to be good at reading between the lines. Orville's words sounded like the college's PR pitch. Thanks to some reading on the subject, I happened to know that the school had gotten into its fair share of trouble over the last few centuries. According to *Torrid Happenings of the Eighteenth and Nineteenth Centuries*, a book I had discovered in the library, the college had been home to all sorts of affairs, thefts, attempted murders, and would-be coups. What surprised me was not the nature of the infractions, but the glee with which they seemed to have been committed. Getting away with illegal things seemed as if it might have informally been the college's most respected sport.

I drummed my fingers on the table. "Have *you* ever done anything wrong, sir?"

Orville, who must have been thinking of something else, looked up. "Hmm?"

"Have you ever violated the rules?"

"In what way?"

"I read somewhere that Old College has seen quite a few trysts in the last few decades."

Orville's eyes jumped to life. My cheeks immediately reddened. I hadn't meant to say it—or, at least, I hadn't meant for it to sound the way it did. I had intended my question and my statement to be two independent thoughts. A harsh silence fell over both of us, and I wished I could jump under the table. My words lingered between us like a slow-motion bullet.

All he said was "I don't think you realize how serious a question that is, Samantha."

The mood collapsed swiftly and cleanly. Orville did not seem angry—just silent. He must have been remembering why he spent most of his time with people his own age. He motioned for the check, and when the waitress gave it to him, he covered up the price with half of his palm. Once he was done paying, we stood up. I followed him to the door.

I cleared my throat. "You know, that tutorial was not terribly help-ful," I said, in an effort to lighten the mood. "I guess I'll have to wait for meaning to come find me in the middle of the night, with a bludgeon."

He didn't respond. It was cold outside, probably, but my beer blanket was thick and my torso felt warm and alive.

Orville drew his coat around him. "I'll walk you home, Samantha."

"Don't. What if someone sees you?"

"It's past midnight."

"Yes, but a man's reputation once lost is lost forever."

I smiled but Orville didn't react. We walked down the long street in silence. I couldn't tell whether I had said something wrong, or whether I had said something true.

At the next block, he changed his mind and waved down a cab with one solid raise of his right arm.

"Thank you for the drinks," I said.

"Please, don't mention it."

"Don't worry, I won't."

The cab pulled up in front of us silently. I was expecting a hug, or perhaps a smile, but Orville and I said goodbye in the most stilted way possible: he gave what might have been a bow, and I saluted him. After a small lingering glance, we each disappeared into the night.

Dear Sir John,

Thank you for your letter. I would have reached out sooner, but I've actually received help already with the books. Did you know Heathcliff and Cathy were half siblings? I know, I know—of all the rotten tricks.

I would, however, rather enjoy visiting the parsonage. My father once told me that I'd find him there, someday. Can we arrange a weekend visit?

Also, sometime would you tell me about being knighted? It all sounds very interesting.

Best,

Samantha

CHAPTER 10

The Fire took place on a calm, noiseless evening, sometime past midnight.

The year was likely 1847, possibly 1846. No one knew the exact date. The four Brontë siblings were home with their father at the parsonage, all together again. Charlotte had recently spent two years in Brussels, taking lessons from (and falling in love with) a handsome married man named Constantin Héger. She had fled, heartbroken, upon the realization that her professor would never return her love. At that same time, Anne and Branwell had recently come home—wide-eyed and traumatized—from their mysterious ordeal at Thorp Green. No one, not even Emily, knew the true reason for their hasty return.

It was a picturesque reunion, at least from a distance. Biographers lovingly recall this period as the most prolific of the Brontë lives. It was the time when Charlotte discovered (and soon published) Emily's secret poetry stash, and the year the three sisters began writing their most famous novels. But something was very wrong. Each sibling had returned home with only bits and pieces of the person who had left. Charlotte had lost her confidence, Anne had lost her sweetness, and Branwell had lost his talent, his sobriety, his dignity, his sense of humor, his coat, his house keys, and all of his friends. Instead of writing playful juvenilia, the family began writing with a manic need, the way people do when they have too much to say and not enough time. In 1846, Charlotte wrote her worst novel, *The Professor*, a badly disguised version of her experience in Brussels. Emily wrote a novel about twisted families who lived on the moors and descended into insanity and depression. Anne, meanwhile, was busy working on a Top-Secret Manuscript that she refused to share with anyone.

Of all her siblings, Anne was the one who had experienced the most radical transformation. Rather than the civilized, even-tempered young girl who had left years before, she was now impatient, unpredictable, and deathly silent on the subject of what had happened to her at Thorp Green. She had grown determined and fierce. Emily, I'm sure, would have found the character transformation very fetching and would have encouraged Anne to dress in britches and start brandishing a sword. Charlotte would have been less pleased. How had it come to pass that Annie—small, scrawny, baby-faced Annie— was now her equal?

Charlotte must have been able to hear Anne through the thin wall, scratching her quill across old parchment late into the night. Competitiveness would have surged like a poison through Charlotte's veins. For the first time in her life, she would be desperate to read the writing of her insignificant little sister. Could Anne's novel possibly be better than *The Professor*? It was a question of no little importance. There was room for only one star in the family. And wasn't it Charlotte's right to be remembered? She was the eldest, the shortest, the ugliest, the one whose heart had just been trampled upon and deformed. If she could not find happiness in this life, didn't she at least deserve to be remembered in the next one?

The outcome of that year was the opposite of what I would have expected. For all the passion and fire with which Anne had returned home from Thorp Green, the novel she wrote—*Agnes Grey*—was barf-worthy. Tame. Uninteresting. What of her venom? Surely this could not be the novel she'd set out to write. What had come of the hours pacing alone in her room? Why *Agnes Grey*?

I blamed Charlotte. During that year, she set herself up as the editor and collector of her sisters' work, a position she held until every last one of them was dead. She was the agent, the businesswoman, the entrepreneur. As she was the only sister who had been properly trained in writing by Monsieur Héger, I'm sure it was easy to convince the family that her knowledge of style and plot was far more developed than that of her sisters. It was only natural that she should read Anne's Top-Secret Manuscript and offer valuable feedback. Right?

I wished I could have been in the room when Anne showed Charlotte her first wild and unseemly manuscript, the one that documented all the gory details from Thorp Green. Had it been easy for Charlotte to convince God-fearing Anne that such vehement writing should be reserved for the home, not shared with the public? *Do you think it wise to expose such things?* Charlotte would have said. *Is it entirely proper for a Christian woman? Is it fair to your father? To us? To your dying brother? Think of our mother. What of our late mother?*

Anne would balk. She was a changed woman, but not as changed as one would have hoped. She would falter under her sister's moralistic outpouring, and become Annie again. Charlotte would win. As Anne abandoned her manuscript for the watered-down second draft—*Agnes Grey*—Charlotte would be quietly updating *The Professor*. This new draft, called *Jane Eyre*, would be filled with all the salacious details of Anne's own original and untold story. The central relationship between professor and student would remain the same, only now there was a new, sensational backdrop: Thorp Green, with its Gothic grandeur, its crusty staff, its pink-cheeked ward, and its mysterious servant, Ann Marshall. It was Anne's life, and Charlotte stole it. She sensationalized it, colonized it, chopped it up and sold it for parts.

Then, of course, came the Parsonage Fire. It was a veritable inferno, engulfing Branwell's bed, the curtains, the nightstand, and half of the wall. It took nearly an hour to extinguish and required the collective effort of all four siblings and the hastily awakened Patrick Brontë. Elizabeth Gaskell later reported that the fire began when Branwell drunkenly set fire to the curtains around his bed, and nearly killed himself. It was plausible, certainly, but I didn't believe it, not least because Gaskell had a habit of sugar-coating the truth. Branwell never seemed bothered by the fire afterward. He never wrote about it, nor did he seem to reference it at all. The only sibling who seemed traumatized was Charlotte. She experienced something akin to post-traumatic stress disorder, and eventually banned all curtains from the Brontë household for fear that the incident would repeat itself. It was she, not Branwell, who decided to incorporate a blazing bed into her first novel.

The fire in *Jane Eyre* occurs in a similar setting, past midnight on an otherwise calm and noiseless evening. Jane wakes up to a cruel laugh echoing through the hallway. Grace Poole, she assumes. The servant. She creeps out of bed to inspect, and finds Edward Rochester alone in his room, in a bed half-consumed by flames. She manages to extinguish the fire and save Rochester, but it is months before she knows the true culprit: Bertha, the madwoman. It was a woman she did not even know existed, but who had been lurking in the attic of her home for years.

Exactly how much of *Jane Eyre*'s fire scene was fact and how much was fiction was difficult to ascertain. This much I knew: the fire at the parsonage had most certainly *not* started in Branwell's room. Fire victims didn't generally walk away without emotional baggage, as Branwell had. (This I knew from personal experience.) No—the fire had occurred in Charlotte's room, and the only possible culprit was Anne Brontë.

Without a doubt, it was Anne. I could feel it in my bones, the way dogs sense earthquakes. I knew Anne Brontë like I knew myself. I could feel her burning rage inside of me—the horrible, wretched anger of a woman whose one story had been cruelly usurped by a jealous older sister. What else was there left for her? Few people would attribute attempted murder to a woman who made tea and wore a frock, but those, I knew, were the ones to look out for. I could almost feel Anne's bitterness welling up inside of her, taking her down the hall late in the night and into her sister's room.

I wished I knew the exact date the fire had happened. All anyone knew was that it occurred around the time *Jane Eyre* was written— either soon before it was published, or soon afterward. Each option presented a radically different version of the truth. Had Charlotte Brontë experienced a terrifying fire and decided to replicate the story in her novel? Or had someone read *Jane Eyre* after it was written, and tried to enact revenge upon the author in the most fitting way possible? Either Anne Brontë had been the inspiration for Bertha Mason, or Bertha Mason had inspired Anne Brontë. In one scenario, the madwoman inspires the book; in the other, the book inspires the madwoman.

In either case, I had an inkling that the madwoman in the attic was not quite as fictional as the world might have hoped.

<hr>

January was a black and silent month, dark and cold in ways I didn't know were possible. Orville saddled me with so much reading that I started taking meals alone in my tower. Over the next three weeks, we studied Edith Wharton, Samuel Baker, Ovid, John Davies, Dante, Rumi, Cicero, Henry James, and Confucius. Our syllabus was like a literary graveyard that had exploded. There was no chronology or thematic cohesion and it made me wish I had instead chosen to study engineering.

Near the end of the month, I descended upon the dining hall in search of lunch and signs of life. A freckled man served me cafeteria lettuce and a clump of something with Pommery mustard, and I entered the dining room with my tray. The former kings of England looked down from their portraits with characteristic disdain. Across the room, I spotted Hans, whose golden locks were shining in a way that defied science. When he saw me, he hailed me to come sit. I was surprised. I had not seen or spoken to him since the night *Jane Eyre* arrived, and I remembered the evening as one of the most awkward I'd ever spent.

"Samantha!" he said when I walked over to him. I had forgotten how clean and boyish his face was. He was classically attractive in a way that made Orville look like an oaf.

"It's been a while," he said, not introducing me to anyone.

I said, "Where have you been?"

"Fighting for truth, justice, and the American way."

I paused. "Benjamin Franklin?"

He said, "Superman."

"Ah," I said, feeling my cheeks growing red. "I think I had a dream about him last night."

"Who, Superman?"

"Benjamin Franklin."

Hans grinned. "Was I in the dream?"

I paused. "It took place at Oxford, so you were probably there, too, somewhere."

We started eating. Hans's friends all smelled of sweat. One was a beefy-necked rugby player with glassy eyes who was talking about vehicle repair. The friend next to him was French, and had a stricken look about him, as if he was secretly thinking: *A vehicle? Bah, she is a woman.*

Hans asked me what I was doing this weekend. I told him that I had decided to go to Paris.

He raised a brow. "What's in Paris?"

"My mother."

"Are you two close?"

"No, she's my mother."

"Sure."

I reached for the pepper even though I never used pepper. I needed something to do with my hands. I noticed that there were *Hornbeam*s fanned out all over the table.

"I really hate this paper," I said.

Hans didn't respond, only glanced at Beef-Neck and back at me.

"Why are there so many of them?" I snapped. "They look like multiplying bacteria."

"Noon is normally distribution time," said Hans.

I reached for one and took a cursory look at the new headlines, awaiting the usual burst of defamatory lies and slander. To my relief, I found nothing by Pierpont. The only thing on the front page was an allegation made by a student against her teaching assistant, who had supposedly propositioned her outside a sandwich shop. I flipped to page four, then page five. Nowhere was I mentioned. Page six, however, caught my attention. I squinted. On the lower right of the page was a very small article with a very small portrait of a very small woman. I let out a small gasp. No. Yes? No.

OLD COLLEGE FELLOW REBECCA DEFOE
RECEIVES AWARD FROM NATIONAL ACADEMY

I dropped my fork.

"What is it?" Hans asked.

"Rebecca," I said.

"Rebecca who?"

I blinked. I stared at the paper, struck by a confusion that verged on comical. The head shot next to the article was one of those blurry pictures from the eighties. The woman had beehive hair and the bleary look of someone who has just been kissed on the eyes. I knew this Rebecca. She was *my* Rebecca.

I looked between Hans and his friends as though we were back in middle school and someone had just played an insensitive practical joke. But Hans's face contorted in genuine confusion.

"Do you know who Rebecca Defoe is?" I asked.

Hans nodded. "The matriarch of the math department."

"Is she British? Did she write a textbook when she was twenty-five and does she wear multiple gold rings?"

"You know her?"

I blanched. My sanity was flapping wildly out of control. I held the limp newspaper in my hand. How could such small, two-dimensional words have the power to change entire worlds? Rebecca had died. *Died*, as in was no longer capable of accepting awards. And who was Rebecca Defoe? The woman pictured—the woman staring back at me from 1982—was Rebecca Smith.

Hans looked at me with his pair of peacock-blue eyes.

"Nothing," I said, answering a question he hadn't asked. "I just didn't know she was a professor here."

"She's quite well known."

"Is she? How convenient."

"Pardon?"

My cheeks were flushed. I racked my brain, trying to remember how my father had introduced us. He had called her a math teacher. Teacher. Not Oxford professor. A material omission, no? Regardless, the entire article was impossible—Rebecca had drowned. It was only a few months after my father had died. Her boat had crashed in the early hours of the morning, and she had sunk, along with her Greek lover, down to the bottom of the ocean. They found her days later, lying facedown on the floor of the cabin, like she had just popped down for a nap. I wasn't crazy—it had happened. And yet, according to this paper, she was alive and well and giving speeches at national conferences.

Hans said: "You don't look very good."

"I think it was the mustard stew."

"It was fish."

"Maybe that's it, then."

I looked back at his sun-streaked hair. How I wished the two of us could interact just once without another bit of my past resurrecting itself between us. We were doomed, he and I. I could never live a normal life, not when my life was overrun by ghosts.

Hans said: "I'll walk you back to your place, yeah? We can talk about it."

I didn't respond, and turned to look at the faculty table instead. For a moment, I thought I'd find Rebecca sitting in the front, grinning at me like a wolf.

"Where is she?" I asked. "Is she here?"

"She's not allowed to eat in hall."

"I thought you said she was the matriarch of the math department."

"That doesn't mean she hasn't been on probation."

"What did she do?" I asked. "Fake her own death?"

Hans said something but I wasn't listening. A small sound escaped my mouth that didn't seem to be coming from me. It was coming from the teenager who had awakened inside me, the one who had once been forced to learn trigonometry with an English woman's scented-toothpick collection. *What's twelve times seven, Sam, twelve times seven?* I pressed my palms into the cool wood of the table. It didn't seem right that cold, real objects existed in a world where Rebecca Smith might still be alive.

I stood and told Hans to stay where he was. I smiled at no one in particular and left the table. As I walked out, I had the feeling that someone in this room—a painting, a person, even a spirit—was watching me.

When I returned to my tower, I threw open the computer. I remember the exact morning when I had learned of Rebecca's death. I had been a fifteen-year-old in a robe, standing on our doormat with curlers in my hair. *Mystery at Sea*, shouted the headlines, over and over again. I remember feeling the strange, unconscionable excitement that only sudden tragedy can produce. The victim was London native Rebecca Smith. Age fifty-five. Teacher. Unmarried.

At the time, Dad was dead and my mother was living with me in Boston. I read and reread the headlines and paced back and forth on our patio, barefoot, clutching the paper in my hands and thinking how nice it was that at least Dad would never have to know. I never told my mother, since I knew it would upset her. She had never liked it when my father spoke of Rebecca. The knowledge of my former tutor's demise was my own burden.

Back in my tower, my fingers were numb and shaking and it took me three tries to type the right name into Google. *Rebecca Smith dies at sea, breaking news, lover, yacht*. I pressed enter. Immediately, several articles appeared. *Mystery at Sea, Mystery at Sea*. I felt vindicated, but only for a very short moment. A closer inspection and a more thorough reading told me that this was not, in fact, the woman I knew. This Rebecca Smith—the one who died—had been a grade-school teacher and romance novelist.

I sank back in my seat. My heart was no longer pounding; it was bleeding, spilling all over me. Whoever had invented this life for me had had a sick sense of humor. I was furious—not at myself but at the child version of myself, the one who had put curlers in her hair, read something in the paper, and wanted so badly to believe it that she must not have thought to finish the article. This, as my father used to say, was what happened when people didn't do close reading.

I thought of all the pity I had wasted over the years. In the days after Rebecca had "died," I dressed in black and refused to eat. I took a bath with all my clothes on, submerged my head, and waited in the dirty bubbles until I thought I would implode. I denied myself cheese and avocados, in a self-imposed mourning ritual whose genesis I can't actually remember. I pressed all ten fingers against my lips and blew a kiss to the sky, thinking, *God bless you, Rebecca,* even though I was not religious, and God probably didn't take requests from imposters. I did a lot of things out of guilt, because I had never had the courage to admit the truth: I hated Rebecca.

Really, very passionately—I hated her. It was a loathing so pure that in its absolute form, it might have passed for love. But it was the kind of hatred you could only admit to when someone has *not* died in unspeakable tragedy. Only after knowing she was alive was I able to acknowledge what I had been hiding for years. I was now, perhaps for the first time, a reliable narrator.

Memories came back to me in their uncorrupted, unfictionalized form: Rebecca sitting at the kitchen table, eating my mother's old Swiss chocolates; Rebecca by the paddling pool, taking my old spot next to my father; Rebecca using the master-bathroom shower, even on Monday mornings. She stayed over when our lessons went late into the evening and she didn't want to drive home—at least, that was what she said. As time went on, she started filling the master bathroom with things she would need for the night: toothpaste, floss, lipstick.

Sometimes, I would sneak in through the window and take things from the guest room where she slept. Yes, technically, I "stole." It was immoral, probably, but I saw it as just. I would nick her magazines, her scarves, her nail-polish remover—little things that at the time seemed like grand victories. Rebecca always made me return them to her, eventually, but I remained undeterred. I'm sure I made her life as miserable as she made mine. The only comment I remember her making on the subject of my thefts was also the only piece of advice she ever gave me: we were sitting down over linear equations one morning when she turned to me, coolly, and said, *The only thing you own in this world is your reputation, Samantha. Don't let it be tampered with.* I had never been able to decide whether she had been advising me or threatening me.

I paced the loose floorboards of my tower, refusing to look directly at the corner in which I had stacked *Jane Eyre*, *Wuthering Heights*, and *Agnes Grey*. I supposed I had found the woman who had delivered them. I felt cheated. If anyone were to come back to life, it should have been my father. I sat on the edge of my bed and methodically arranged the pillows around me. All I could think of were Rebecca's two blank eyes staring at me from the depths of a vast ocean. Quietly, I reached for my bedsheet and hung it back over *The Governess*.

That Thursday, I broke into Rebecca's office.

If that sounds drastic and illegal, it's because it was drastic and illegal. To be fair, I did not go to the Faculty Wing with the intention of breaking in. It was the day before my trip to Paris. My suitcase was waiting for me back in my tower. All I meant to do was pop by, politely request the rest of my books, and demand a thorough explanation of what the hell was going on.

Instead, it happened like this: I crept into the Faculty Wing at 4:55 p.m., and spent twenty minutes trying to locate Rebecca's office, which turned out to be in a vaulted corridor in the South Wing that reeked of rubber and shoe polish. I found the office easily enough—it was in the corner, with the same misleading last name that I had discovered in the paper. *Defoe*. Her office door was old. I noticed that the lock was on its last legs. I knocked once, then twice, then once more again, but there was no response. I knocked harder. I was angry. I had finally tracked her down—would she avoid me? I knocked again and again. I could feel the door rattling. I took the door handle in my hand and pushed on it, and then I pushed some more, and then, after one hard shove, there I was.

I had entered so easily that for a brief second I thought that it must have all been a trick: Rebecca would erupt out of the closet, ready to whack me with some partial differential equations. But there was no one inside. Her office was sunny and incalculably clean. The only thing that felt out of place was the wrappings of what must have been a meal once—tuna fish and cheddar, right on her desk. Hadn't she thought to throw away her lunch? What a pig.

My heart was pounding. I thought of the *Old College Book of Disciplinary Procedures*, and wondered if the punishment for stealing from a don's room would include the swift seizure of my lands and castles. I should have realized the gravity of my crime and left. I did not do that. Instead, I took a slow turn about the room. My lip curled in resentment. Rebecca has been alive this entire time, eating tuna fish. There was a refrigerator in the corner of the room—black, with a white rectangle in the middle. I thought of what I might find inside: a watermelon, jam, a bottle of white wine. Two Beefeater Gibsons. A human heart. On the desk was a pile of problem sets with some eigenvectors drawn in pencil. Nearby was a small sticky note attached to the lampshade, reading, *Thanks for the advice; I love you with all my heart, Rebecca*. I made a face, and looked around, as though the person who had written it was standing somewhere nearby, smoking something.

I set about searching for what I'd come for, except that I didn't know what I was looking for, exactly. Proof? Proof of what? Proof that the square root of any negative number was imaginary? Because in that case, there was ample evidence collected in a small avalanche of books on the desk: *Vector Calculus*, *Additive Problems in Combinatorial Number Theory*, *Graduate Texts in Mathematics*. They smelled like damp bread and deep June. They reminded me of algebra at eight in the morning, and the scent of freshly cut grass out the window.

One part of Rebecca's room demanded further inspection. On the wall behind her desk, she had hung dozens and dozens of framed documents. I peered closer so I could read them. I stopped. For a woman who had won a mountain of awards in her lifetime, the only documents on her walls were framed copies of what appeared to be exams that she had failed, letters of rejection from different universities, notes from various publishers who had spurned her first book. This office—this well-lit, corner office—was a symbol of her academic triumph, and yet she had decorated it with a lifetime of petty failures. I had seen only one other person do the same—my father.

Everything seemed wrong, all of a sudden. The seriousness of the situation piled on top of me. It occurred to me that in all the times I had stolen something from Rebecca's room in our own home, I had never gotten away with it.

Unease mounting, I searched through Rebecca's bookshelf quickly, with sloppy fingers. My heart was slamming against my chest. I scanned the books of matrices and linear equations and I panicked, because it occurred to me that Rebecca's sandwich might not be old at all. It was today's sandwich. *Stupid girl,* I told myself—*it was* today's. Rebecca would come back, and I would have to jump into the closet, which wasn't—

There. There it was. *The Tenant of Wildfell Hall.* It was wedged in between *Elementary Quantum Mechanics* and *Advanced Game Theory.* It was thick and swollen, like it had been fed and fattened for years and now couldn't fit comfortably into anything. I plucked it from its position on the shelf. There was no back cover. I recognized the spot on the front where it had been chewed on the corner—by what I had never exactly been sure. Yes, yes, it was my father's copy. It had been here the whole time.

I frowned. There was something new that I didn't remember from my childhood. A bookmark was sticking out of the middle like a grasping, empty hand. I flipped the book open to the marked page. There was Emily Dickinson's sneering face, peering out at me as if from behind bars. I didn't understand. My bookmark had been red. This one—this new, strange one—was yellow, and reeked of perfume. I had never seen a yellow Emily Dickinson bookmark in our house. I rubbed it between my thumb and forefinger. *Much Madness Is Divinest Sense.* I was short of breath. These were supposed to be father-daughter bookmarks. They were not supposed to be father-daughter-and-math-teacher bookmarks. I was supposed to be the sole benefactor of his strange little games. Had my father been splitting his affection in half?

I let out a small wheeze. I put both bookmark and book under my arm and headed for the door. I didn't bother looking back. I needed to leave. In a moment, I had ejected myself from Rebecca Smith's office. I slammed the door but the lock clanked and it refused to close entirely. It was broken.

Then, I did the same thing any criminal would do. I walked down the hall, quite calmly, and fled the country. I was under the English Channel before Oxford could even say, *Expelled.*

had begun a race against time. It was only a matter of days before Old College would discover that I had broken into a professor's office. I no longer belonged at Oxford. I had violated the implicit pact between teacher and student. The Serpent had sounded a gong, and there I fell, down from heaven. I would be ritually hanged and quartered, then retroactively denied dining hall privileges.

I spent Friday morning on the train to Paris, wallowing in guilt and visions of execution. There were two people seated next to me in the airline-blue, septic train booth: a man wearing an electric-green blazer and a mother wearing a squalling, fat-cheeked baby in a sack on her torso. Every few moments the kid would let rip its shrill harpy cry, and the man in green would look to the ceiling in response, as though he had taken up an argument with God.

"Don't worry," the mother said, sweating through a confident smile. She patted the baby on the back as it wailed. "I brought drugs."

The man said, "For us too?"

I had *The Tenant of Wildfell Hall* in front of me. I hadn't touched it since I removed it from my bag an hour earlier. The woman on the cover, a middle-aged brunette with a receding hairline, looked like someone who had gone through everything there was to go through in life—twice. Both she and I seemed to recognize the newfound responsibility that had befallen us. Mine was to understand her; hers was to make herself understood.

My ears popped and unpopped as we sped underneath the English

Channel, and the baby, on cue, released a blazing foghorn of a cry. His mother patted him on the back and started singing an original composition called "Wash my body, yeah, yeah, yeah." I realized that she was looking at *The Tenant of Wildfell Hall* with some curiosity, the way she would regard a sad Italian opera she couldn't quite understand: beautiful, but somehow useless.

Near the French border, I opened up the book. This novel was not a pleasure read. *The Tenant of Wildfell Hall* was a mess. Chaos. It was Anne's emotional vomit, masked in cool, reserved prose. She had written too many narrators, too many stories within stories, too many secrets that no one was allowed to share. It was what happened to an author when she was very, very angry, and trying to tell a complicated story far too quickly. *Tenant*—published after *Jane Eyre*, *Agnes Grey*, and *Wuthering Heights*—was the literary equivalent of a Russian doll: a diary inside a letter inside a book. This was not a story to get lost in. This was a story that reminded you, page after page, that it had been *written*. You could not help but be aware that there had been an author, that her name had been Anne Brontë, or that she had sat down one night at a lonely table, trying to figure out the best way to spill some secrets.

It was Anne's second novel. Her first book, *Agnes Grey*, had turned out to be boring and useless while its contemporary, *Jane Eyre*, had been dramatic and popular. Anne tried again, and this time, she was determined to not hold back. *Tenant* begins with a letter from a young man named Gilbert Markham, a badly disguised version of young Branwell Brontë. He is passionate, impulsive, and on the prowl. "I am about to give a sketch," he writes to a friend. "No, not a sketch—a full and faithful account of certain circumstances connected with the most important event of my life." The "most important event" of his life is, naturally, a woman. Her name is Helen Graham and she is a taciturn single mother who moves into a deserted old manor and paints morbid landscapes for a living.

The romance between the two does not end up being terribly romantic, since Gilbert expends most of his energy trying to figure out the secrets of Helen's sordid past. Why did she come to Wildfell Hall? Why does she have a son? Why are her morbid landscapes so morbid? Helen, in a moment of desperation, finally throws Gilbert her entire diary. It conveniently explains everything that has ever happened to her. Gilbert, naturally, transcribes all two hundred pages of this diary to his old friend, and the rest of the novel becomes the first-hand account of Helen's past.

Her past is suitably shocking. As an impressionable young woman, she suffered a misguided marriage with a fabulous rake and alcoholic-in-progress. After a few years, she couldn't take it anymore and decided to run away. In an act of defiance, she slammed her bedroom door in her husband's face. It was the door slam that rang around the world. This is the defining moment of *The Tenant of Wildfell Hall*, the instant in which Anne Brontë delivered to her readers all the empty promises of *Agnes Grey*. Helen Graham is the updated version of Anne's first protagonist. On the outside, she is shy and stern; on the inside, she is fiery, and as strong as a man.

The novel, not surprisingly, was panned. In the words of *Sharpe's London Magazine*, it was a series of "profane expressions, inconceivably coarse language, and revolting scenes and descriptions by which its pages are disfigured." But *The Tenant of Wildfell Hall* finally brought Anne the commercial success that was her due. Her novel outsold even *Wuthering Heights*, and went into its second printing after only six weeks.

My father and I both referred to this book as *Tenant*. Just *Tenant*. It was his tenant, our tenant, the creature who subleased our basement. Dad didn't love this book, but he respected it. This was the Hera of the Brontë literature—all-seeing and wise, yet lost in the wake of other, flashier gods. Dad and I never had the chance to explore the whole book together. The furthest we ever got, before he died, was the preface to the second edition. In the wake of her bad reviews, Anne wrote a small and biting essay defending both herself and her work. It was a bold move for a woman whose reputation was already at risk. Anne never once backed down or apologized. She fought back. Reading her preface to the second edition was the equivalent of watching someone you love very much begin to grow some balls. She wrote:

> . . . *When I feel it my duty to speak an unpalatable truth, with the help of God, I will speak it, though it be to the prejudice of my name and to the detriment of my reader's immediate pleasure as well as my own.*

Predictably, Charlotte did her best to crush *The Tenant of Wildfell Hall*. She reviewed her sister's book with even more contempt than Anne's numerous critics. "[*Tenant*] hardly appears to me desirable to preserve," she commented. "The choice of subject in that work is a mistake." After Anne died, Charlotte flatly refused the re-publication of her sister's novel. Perhaps she thought she was trying to preserve Anne's good name for posterity. But I wasn't sure Anne wanted to be saved. *The Tenant of Wildfell Hall* could have been as famous as *Jane Eyre*, had it only received proper marketing. The support of the Great Charlotte Brontë, if given, could have made Anne a star. Instead, Charlotte deliberately denied her sister the recognition she deserved. Anne died a social reformer who ended up reforming nothing.

The baby Martian across the train table gave a piercing war cry. With one solid right kick, the kid knocked the book out of my hands. Apparently even a baby could sense trouble when it was right in front of him. I glanced over at the man in the green suit, who had stopped arguing with the roof and was now watching me with the curious expression of someone who might be secretly cataloguing story material for one of his next books. I gave a small frown and pulled my hood over my head.

Paris was nice, I guess. The city reminded me of one of those people who didn't need to make an effort to impress you because you both knew you had to get along. My mother said she'd pick me up from the train station, so I waited in the main lobby, which echoed and glittered like a low-budget cathedral. Not too long after I arrived, I saw a familiar-looking woman wearing a fur coat and white-rimmed glasses waiting by the flower stand.

That wasn't my mother. Instead, my mother turned out to be the woman walking toward me in light jeans and a girlish multicolored top with puffy sleeves. I hadn't seen her in over two years, and she had dyed her hair a thick, bottomless brown. The old vision I had of her—the blurry blonde in my memory—seemed like a character in a book that had now been inched out of my imagination by the movie. The new face stopped in front of me with a smile I barely recognized. She was stately, with good stage presence, and her teeth sparkled like crystal.

"Let me give you a hug!" she boomed. She was massively tall. We hugged and pulled away, and I looked into her soft, young face. One thing about my mother—she was only forty-two.

"I'll get your bags," she said.

We walked outside and when a cab pulled over, Mom opened the door for me, blind-date style. She was more beautiful than I remembered, but maybe beauty came with age and confidence. We climbed inside. My bag rested between us like a small beached whale. She rattled off some directions to the taxi driver, then turned to me and said:

"You still remember your French, don't you, Samantha?"

"I spoke French?"

"Seat belt."

The car lurched forward. It was already late in the afternoon, and the day was dragging itself down behind the buildings. In its final moments, the wilting sun looked like a fist that had opened up to unleash five beams of pink and orange. To someone else, it was probably poetic. To me, everything looked like the inside of Rebecca's office. The break-in had swelled in size and magnitude in my mind over the last few hours. I felt ill. I was not a daughter visiting her mother; I was a fugitive here to be harbored by a familiar amazon.

Mom, however, seemed to be having a great time. The smile never left her face for the duration of the car ride. She patted my hand three or four times, and sometimes rubbed it. When she smiled, she looked very put-together, like a colleague, or a stylish aunt. If I were a kid and looking at her for the first time, I would have wished she were my mother. This, right here, was the prime of her life. It wasn't fair to resent her for how young she was, but I did. If she hadn't married so young, she would not have needed to run away.

Mom's new apartment was on the fashionable side of the rue de Magdebourg, on the seventh floor of a building that looked like a fancy chocolate. There were multiple locks on her front door, I noticed. A nice idea. Kept out criminals like myself. Inside, everything was squeaky clean and magazine-tidy. The furniture was shiny and angular. The centerpiece was a giant, glossy slice of sedimentary rock. It was very avant-garde. I guess it was supposed to represent the view of Earth as seen from a great distance.

Mom immediately disappeared into the kitchen. I dropped my bags and took a look around. There were no books. It made the space feel soulless. Or, maybe *soulless* was a term people used when everything was perfect and you just resented not being part of it. Mom had always wanted me to move to Paris. I chose Boston. At the time, I couldn't leave my father. I'd picked between my two parents, and my mother had lost. I didn't like to think about it.

"While you're here, I'd like to buy you something," Mom called from the next room.

"You don't have to buy me anything," I said.

"Do you know what you'd look great in?"

I said, "A Porsche?"

"Knee-length skirts."

"Hmm."

"The guest room is off to the right. I'll be there in a second."

I showed myself to my room. It was yellow and blue—clearly designed for a daughter. Ruffles. Curtains. A big orange bed. An artsy painting of a purple and green woman with six feet. Stacked on top of the nightstand were dozens of copies of French fashion magazines. Each one had a page whose corner was turned down, likely filled with shoes and knee-length skirts. It was as though some child had died in here and no one had touched the room since.

"Do you like it?" Mom asked.

I didn't realize she had returned, and I turned around to find her with a mug of hot chocolate in her hands. She handed it to me. Old-looking marshmallows bobbed on the surface.

"For you," she said with an expectant look on her face.

I paused. "Thank you."

It was the saddest moment we ever spent together.

I took a step back and accidentally knocked over my bag, out of which tumbled *The Tenant of Wildfell Hall*. I picked it up, as well as the dental floss that had also spilled out, and dropped them both on the bed. Mom's eyes rested on the book. She looked at it with alarm, like it was instead several thousand dollars' worth of cocaine.

She cleared her throat and said, innocently, "You've already read that, haven't you?"

I said, "Yes."

"More than once?"

"It's one of the books that arrived on my doorstep. Remember? I told you."

She paused. "And you carry him with you."

I didn't respond. Mom's smile fell, for the first time. There was a certain tragedy about her just then—one, ironically, that I knew my father would have found irresistible. Her gaze roved from my bangs to my neck to my ears to my nose and eyebrows and mouth and forehead. I had her cheekbones, her small rib cage, and her bone structure, but I knew she was looking for what else she could call her own. I was my father's daughter. She hadn't known what to do about it when I was a child, and she didn't know what to do about it now.

"Dinner is in thirty," she said. With a small smile, she left the room.

Dinner was actually in an hour and forty-five. I used the time to go through my e-mails. I came upon an announcement that had been penned at eight thirty-two that morning. My heart seemed to stop.

> *Dear Student,*
>
> *It has come to our attention that on the evening of Thursday, February 27, a room in the Faculty Wing was forcibly entered. We hardly need impress upon anyone the gravity of the crime. If you have any information regarding this matter, we urge you to reveal it to a college faculty member. Any person found to be withholding evidence will face severe punitive measures.*
>
> *Regards,*
> *Ellery Flannery*
> *Director of Student Affairs*

I was breathing heavily. Flannery might as well have taken dictation from my latest nightmare. Except that in my nightmare, it was Orville who had written the letter, and he looked like Rasputin. I tried to tell myself that no one had seen me, and therefore I could not be caught. Why, then, did I feel as though an invisible being were hovering over my shoulder, passing judgment? Surely, I would be found and expelled from Oxford. My lungs constricted. I was too young to have run out of time.

I whipped out my phone and carefully dialed.

"Hello?" came the voice on the other line.

"Is this James Orville the Third?"

A pause. "Samantha, how did you get this number?"

"You called me once, remember?"

My voice was breathless and urgent, and I imagined I sounded like a schoolgirl, with wide eyes the size of saucers. I couldn't quite believe my own nerve in calling him on a Friday night.

"So, are you busy?" I asked. There was noise in the background— he was at a party, at a bar, with a woman, maybe. Yes, he was busy. My heart pounded.

"Where are you?" Orville asked. "The connection is poor."

"I'm in Paris."

Something crashed in the background on his end, and there was a loud, cumulative roar of approval in the distance. I was jealous; I had hoped he spent his weekends reading books and being antisocial.

Orville said, "Listen, now is not a good time—is anything the matter?"

"No."

"Are you in some sort of trouble?"

"I—"

"Answer."

"No, I'm fine."

We waited. The concern in his disembodied voice was attractive.

I said, "I had a question about Anne Brontë."

Orville let out a breath. "It's a Friday night."

"I was homeschooled," I explained. "If you don't mind me asking—did Anne Brontë ever draft a third book?"

There was silence, which meant that it was either a ridiculous question or a brilliant one. He said, "How should I know?"

"It's just that *Tenant* still seems incomplete to me."

Another roar in the background.

Orville said, "Samantha, I'm busy at the moment."

"I received another book. *The Tenant of Wildfell Hall*."

A pause.

"Is everything all right?" he asked.

"Yes. But I have some questions about it."

Orville didn't answer for a moment. "Thursday next?" he said, eventually.

"Sure."

"You may write me an essay on it. Try to be creative."

"Like, I write you a poem?"

"I hope not. Good night, Samantha."

"That's it?"

"It's past your bedtime."

"It's eight thirty."

"I thought you were homeschooled."

I couldn't think of a quick response, which irritated me, and by the time I said, "Sir?" he had already hung up.

Dinner consisted of peas, mashed potatoes, and pinkish chicken. The meat was chewy and I supposed it was what salmonella tasted like. Mom seemed so pleased that I thought she might have shot and killed the bird herself. Conversation was slow and it felt like we were giving birth. I learned that Mom's interior decorating business was doing fantastically well; that her wedding dress firm had folded years ago; no, she was not dating anyone; and she did not actually feel a need to be married—after all, did I? I didn't tell her that Ellery Flannery had a warrant out for my arrest, because it wasn't the sort of thing you mention on a first date. There were long swaths of silence, which Mom and I weren't ready for at all. The two of us were the worst sort of acquaintances—people who only knew each other through one activity. Tennis friends.

"Tell me about your writing," she said. "I want to hear about your writing."

I said, "I stopped writing."

"That's a shame. Why?"

"I don't know, do you still paint?"

"I never painted."

"Exactly."

She took a slow swallow of cabernet sauvignon. Her eyes were two black bullets. "Samantha, are you all right?"

"What?"

"Happy. Are you happy?"

I looked up. "Not particularly."

Immediately, I wished I hadn't said anything. The words sounded angular and irreversible when spoken out loud—as though I were giving shape to something that could have otherwise disappeared.

"Tell me what's bothering you," she said.

I picked up my fork and pushed the peas from one side of my plate to another. "I figured out who left me that book on my doorstep. It's Rebecca Smith. That's who Dad entrusted to leave me his books. Only now she goes by Defoe."

Mom's eyes narrowed.

"Defoe," she said, picking up her wineglass again. Her voice had turned to tin. "Defoe was her middle name."

"You knew her?"

"Your father talked about her all the time."

We fell into a silence. She looked like she would like to be finished with this conversation so she could go to bed and wake up twenty years from now. I thought of the conspiratorial way my father had often looked at Rebecca from across the table. It was as if they were members of a secret, two-person club. Had my father ever looked at my mother like that? Surely I would have remembered.

Mom was staring me right between the eyes. The silence was killing me.

"I'm not in love with him anymore, if that's what you're about to ask," she said.

I looked away. "No, that's not what I was thinking."

"Well, I'm not. I'm the one who left *him*, remember?"

I said softly, "Was it because they were having an affair?"

I looked up to find her big black eyes still examining me. She didn't respond. She just picked up her glass again and took a large swallow. I felt a strange surge of affection for her.

"More chicken?" she asked.

"No thanks," I said. "She teaches at Oxford now, you know."

"Who? Rebecca?" Her voice was brittle. "She always taught at Oxford. Your father liked to visit her there when we were married."

I paused. "I see."

"I hear she came to Boston, after I left."

I could tell she was trying hard to act nonchalant. She looked away, then passed me the chicken even though I hadn't asked for any. The one trait she and I appeared to share was a tendency to squeeze our lips together when we were upset.

I said, softly, "Can I tell you something, and would you please not tell anyone?"

"Go for it."

I took a breath. "I broke into her office yesterday."

Mom squinted. "Whose office?"

"Rebecca's."

A pause. *"What?"*

Then, suddenly, I couldn't stop talking. I launched into an over-wrought explanation of the entire incident, from beginning to end, then back to the beginning. I told her it was inevitable, how I forced open Rebecca's door, then poked around, then snatched her book and left, how I didn't even seem to be myself, how I seemed to be listening to the angry bullied kid inside of me, though I actually was never bullied, was I? I kept talking and talking—about what, I'm not exactly sure—but by the time I was done, my mother was staring at me as though we had never met before, not even in our own dreams. The mother I had imagined and the daughter she had imagined still existed, somewhere, but not here.

At last, she said: "Goddammit, Samantha."

"I know, I know. I'll be kicked out if they find out."

She put her palm flat on the table. It made a swatting sound. "God*dammit*, Samantha."

I flinched. I wanted to be punished; yes, I needed to be punished. There was absolution in punishment. One zinging reprimand would welcome me into a world of normal mothers and normal, badly behaved teenage daughters.

Mom said: "The door? You used the *door*?"

I blinked. "Sorry?"

"Next time you use *the window*. Understand?"

My mouth closed. Mom stood up, and I heard the refrigerator door open and shut behind me. A pop and fizzle meant a can was opening. She returned and sat back down across from me. Then, at ten o'clock in the evening, on the fashionable side of the rue de Magdebourg, my mother handed me a beer.

We spent Saturday wandering around Paris. I learned a few things about my mother. She was from a hippie family in California—which I had always known, I suppose, but now I finally understood. She had worked as a bird researcher, and her first boyfriends included more than one member of an Irish punk band. We glossed over her life with my father, since it was irrelevant, and moved on to her life in Europe, where she had become fluent in Norwegian and blogged about wild dogs. She was now a CEO and had only four good friends because when you age, she said, you lose the energy to be fake.

In the early afternoon, we took a picture in front of Notre-Dame, strolled along the Seine, and bought my first eight-dollar hot chocolate. We went home and made angel-hair pasta for lunch, then watched a graphic French movie named after a Baudelaire poem. The day was aggressively European and felt like a small, absurd vacation. Mom had a laugh like a hyena. More than once, I found myself picturing how my life would have been as her daughter rather than my father's.

In the evening, she had to run to a client meeting but we agreed to meet up later at L'écume des Pages. I arrived early and set up shop at a back table so I could write Orville an essay. It's a curious crowd that lives in bookshop cafés on Saturday nights. The woman next to me was reading *Insects of the Rain Forests*. Nearby was a Frenchman who had come here, it seemed, to take off his shoes and release his foot odor. He wiggled his toes. I pulled out *The Tenant of Wildfell Hall* and began to draft my impromptu essay for Orville. I told myself I was writing this essay *for* him, but really, I was writing this essay *to* him. I couldn't help but write with the acute awareness that James Orville would be the one reading it, that maybe he'd scan the words on the page and hear my own voice whispering in his ear.

I sat back, my chair teetering on its two back legs, and tried to think of something intelligent to say. I had no thesis, no direction, and no ideas. It was nearly impossible to read my father's battered copy of this book, which is why I gave up halfway through and started skimming. He had underlined, starred, or scribbled next to almost every single line. There was one passage I knew he preferred above all others, and it was on page two of the preface, enthusiastically highlighted in red:

> *I wished to tell the truth, for truth always conveys its own moral to those who are able to receive it. But as the priceless treasure too frequently hides at the bottom of a well, it needs some courage to dive for it, especially as he that does so will be likely to incur more scorn and obloquy for the mud and water into which he has ventured to plunge, than thanks for the jewel he procures.*

It was, of course, the clue my father had given me for Christmas, the one that had once led me down a sanitary sewer. There was a "priceless treasure" in this book, too, much as in *Agnes Grey*.

I took out my pen. I decided to write about Helen Graham. The world knew her as a stable, reasonable, and pragmatic protagonist—*a tall, lady-like figure, clad in black*. And yet I was beginning to suspect that something was deeply off with her. Helen is shunned by society, not because of the existence of her bastard child and mysterious ex-husband but because of her peculiar behavior. She is described as a witch—pale, breathless, agitated. Upon meeting her, Gilbert comments that he would rather see her from a distance than be near her. There is an easy explanation for her unpopularity: Helen's independence is foreign and threatening to a remote nineteenth-century English village. Yet the depictions of Helen soon go a few steps beyond mere independence: *Lo! Mrs. Helen Graham darted upon me— her neck uncovered, her black locks streaming in the wind*. This is not necessarily how one would describe proto-feminism. It is, however, the way one might describe a madwoman.

I sat back in my seat. Yes, I quite liked that theory. I enjoyed the thought that Helen Graham may have been secretly off her rocker—that she was so wild and powerful as to be feared by everyone. It wasn't an altogether outlandish idea, either. The narrator, to use Orville's favorite expression, is unreliable. The man who tells the story is the man who eventually marries the protagonist. A besotted lover can never be objective. As the transcriber of Helen's secret diary, Gilbert becomes the editor in chief of her life, able to remove or twist anything that seems too shocking for his audience. Her character has been cleaned and beautified for the public. For all anyone knew, the real Helen could have been another Bertha, finally lashing out against her entrapment.

If Gilbert did, in fact, do some well-intentioned meddling with Helen's image, then I patted Anne Brontë on the back for her foresight. Anne's own biography had been written retroactively, her image shaped by an elder sister who might or might not have had her best interests at heart. Did Anne know this, and did she deliberately write it into her semi-autobiographical masterpiece, in an effort to publicize her own shackles? The real Anne and the real Helen were both trapped—under layers of narration.

"What are you reading?"

I gave a start. Mom had arrived early, and out of breath. The cold had left her cheeks mottled and red. She unwrapped the scarf from her neck like a bandage.

"Do you want a croissant?" she asked.

"No, thanks."

"I just ordered you one."

"Almond?"

"Almond."

She sat down. I could tell something was bothering her. There was a crease in her forehead in the shape of the San Andreas Fault. She glanced between *Tenant* and me, me and *Tenant*.

"I really hate that book," she said.

She sounded exactly like me.

"Your father made me read it when we were dating," she explained. "He told me that everything was right in front of my eyes, but that I would never be able to see a damn thing without being able to read more creatively. Does that sound like a nice thing to say to your future wife?"

"No."

Mom took a breath. Her weekend-long grin had settled into a deep frown. "I wanted to talk to you about something, Samantha, before you leave tomorrow. Do you know the Brontës?"

"Sorry, who?"

"Don't joke when I'm being serious. I want you to consider yourself cut off from them. From this moment on."

There was a small silence. Mom hadn't even taken off her coat, yet it seemed she had already spat out everything she wanted to tell me.

I waited, and when she didn't respond, I said: "I don't think you can do that?"

Mom pursed her lips. "Look at you," she said. "You're here, surrounded by Paris, and you are rereading that piece-of-shit book. Don't you find that sad?"

Because I could think of nothing else to say, I said: "*La merde.*"

"Your dad had a mistress long before Rebecca," she said. The word *mistress* was sharp and ugly, and yet she glossed over it as though she were describing a flat tire. "His obsession with the Brontës ruined every single relationship in his life—including, I'm afraid, his relationship with you."

I decided to ignore that. "You must have some idea of what he wanted me to find."

"Probably some old towels the Brontës used to clean themselves," she said.

"I'm being serious."

"Who says I wasn't being serious? You're complicating something that was never meant to be complicated."

"Learning how to complicate things is what makes you smarter."

"Only in a classroom."

I said, "Life is a classroom?"

"Christ, Samantha."

"Sorry," I said. "Sorry."

She gave me a fiery stare. "Your father may have been your idol, but I want you to remember that he was not always a good man," she said. "Have you ever met his doppelgänger, Sir John Booker? What a pair. A Cambridge professor, decorated like the pope, who wastes his talent hounding your father for years, following a mystery he invented. I want you to pay close attention to what happened to both of those men, Samantha. Your father died in his early forties. If the fire hadn't killed him, the booze would have done it not long after that. I'm sure he knew it. And Booker? Raving mad. A few years ago, he was found wading through the mud outside the parsonage in the middle of the night, looking for something, presumably. Read some articles on him, Samantha. It's pathetic. You'll notice that he is also divorced."

The croissant arrived in a paper bag. "*Chaud,*" said the girl in the green apron who brought it before disappearing. I took a bite but it didn't taste like much except salt. Mom stared at me for some time, then folded her hands in her lap in the shape of a small cradle.

"I worry about you," she said. "You've gotten so wrapped up with being alone that sometimes it feels as if you like it there."

My throat constricted. "It wasn't my choice."

She stared at me, solemn. "I never did a thing to you, Samantha. Don't create a delusional fiction and pretend I abandoned you. All I've been doing for the last seven years is trying to get you to move in with me. I know why you can't look at me, and it's because you see him every time you do. Well, you know what? I look at you and I see him too. He was a brilliant man and he was a scared man. He lived in the past because nothing was at stake there."

I didn't answer. She was much more confident than I remembered.

"I know you've suffered, sweetheart," she said. "You're determined to honor your pain because you think it defines you. I'm just worried that you've got a hell of a lot of things pent up in there, and someday that top's going to come blowing off and you're going to do something crazy and stupid that will get you in trouble."

"I already did something crazy and stupid."

"Breaking into Rebecca's office? It was illegal, maybe, but not crazy."

I ripped off a piece of croissant. I could feel the tears congeal behind my eyes. I knew they wouldn't spill; they never did.

"What's your point?" I said.

Mom's head tilted to the side and she pinned me with an empathy so ancient that I could easily have been looking at every mother who had ever lived.

"I love you," she said, matter-of-factly. "I'd rather not see you lose your mind."

I fell silent. I couldn't seem to look her straight in the eye anymore. I hadn't heard the word *love* in so long that I had almost forgotten what it could do to you. Even my dad never made wordy evidence of his affection for me; love was just another piece of subtext. I found my heart racing and for one brief, exhilarating moment, I wanted to forget my father entirely and come live in Paris with this strange, emotive woman in front of me. Why shouldn't I move on?

It was a pleasant thought, but it lasted only a few moments. Almost immediately, I was struck by a crushing grief. It was as if Dad's ghost was rearing out of its sleepy stupor and knocking me over the head with the punishing back of its hand. I looked down at my croissant and I remembered the soft weight of his bear hugs when I ran down for breakfast, and the way he'd scratch my head when I couldn't sleep. I remembered his perfect, worn, narrow face, irreverent and bespectacled and not of this world. I could still feel the warmth coiling right off him on those pancake mornings when it was just the two of us, alone against the world. I missed him to the point of physical pain.

Mom was wrong about one thing: I wasn't interested in some old books Dad left me. I wanted something bigger—a message, a lesson, anything—that was wrapped up in what might very well turn out to be a bunch of used towels. I wanted Dad's beautiful voice to speak up and tell me something profound and improbable—or at least to finish the conversation we had started long ago. I wanted, I suppose, what everyone wants: meaning. Happiness, in some sense, was irrelevant.

When I finally glanced back up, Mom looked lost. I didn't know what else to do, so I wrapped my hand over hers. Her fingers were cold. Eventually, I felt them returning my grasp, small and fragile.

CHAPTER 12

I returned to Oxford on Sunday evening to a stack of papers and pamphlets on my doorstep. The *Hornbeam* had milked the break-in story for everything it was worth. Pierpont's staff of vipers had published more than a few speculative pieces, many of which suggested that the culprit had broken in to change the mark given on an assignment. The articles were terribly written, but I was relieved to find that they did not mention me. One piece explained that the authorities were "close" to catching the "culprit" who was responsible for the "grand burglary" of the room. I didn't read past page two. I didn't know where they had found their "sources," but to me, it all seemed like a load of "shit."

That week, I finished my essay on *The Tenant of Wildfell Hall*. The complete product was less an essay and more of a story on the Brontës, which was reasonable, I thought, considering that Orville had asked me to be "creative." The final title was "A Very Sad and Pathetic Parable Indeed (Fable? Biography? Autobiography? You Pick)." By Samantha J. Whipple.

Now, here I was, walking to the Faculty Wing to turn it in before the midnight deadline. I would have gone earlier in the day, were it not for my all-consuming paranoia. I was sure that Ellery Flannery would pounce upon me and be able to read the crime all over my face. Since my return from Paris, I only left my tower in the wee hours of the morning or late at night, avoiding everyone I could.

The papers wanted a Strange Antisocial Brontë Heiress? Now they had one.

I hadn't been to the Faculty Wing since I had broken into Rebecca's office, and my heart was pounding. I was the mistress returning to the scene of the tryst. I took the back route. Halford's Well was blanketed in darkness, like a defunct German bunker. It didn't take long to reach the double doors in the front of the Faculty Wing. They were, as usual, locked. I pressed my palm against the frosty glass. How had I snuck in last time? Suddenly, I let out a small yelp. There, on the other side of the door, was a man's face, also pressed against the glass.

I clasped my hands to my chest. The door opened. It was only a college porter. He had wet eyes and reminded me of the Tin Man.

"Yes?" he said.

I said, "Hi."

"May I help you?"

"I have a paper to hand in?"

He didn't say anything. I held up my essay. It stood stiff for a moment, then flopped over my wrist.

"Name?" he said.

"Samantha Whipple."

He frowned and I winced. I needed to practice inventing fake names faster.

"The faculty is gone for the evening, miss," he said.

"I just need to slip it under my professor's door."

No response.

"May I?" I asked.

He regarded me for a moment—a long moment—then slowly stepped aside. Something creaked, either the door or his tin joints. I brushed past him and began walking through the foyer. I glanced behind me. The shadowy porter was watching me as I retreated, hands behind his back. Was I mistaken, or had the college hired sentries?

I kept going—past Geological Sciences, past Philosophy—until I made it to the English Department. The lights in the corridor were bright and sterile, and I squinted as I walked. Orville's door was closed, naturally. His brass knocker was bright and shiny, like a solitary, all-seeing eye. I bent down and slid the essay underneath his door. I meant to be quick about it, but I lingered, looking at the plaque in front of me. *James Timothy Orville III.* I wondered if my name elicited in him the same dull ache. I had thought about him dozens of times this week. Dozens? Hundreds. There seemed to be reincarnations of him everywhere I went, like he was a giant, exploded piñata whose bits and pieces had been showered indiscriminately over England.

To my great surprise, the door flew open. I jumped. There he was, in the darkness—Orville—wearing dark green boxers and a T-shirt with a werewolf on it.

"Oh," I said. "It's you."

His expression didn't change. "I thought I heard something."

"What are you doing here?"

"I work here."

For a moment, I thought he might be about to explain that he was with a student, and could I come back another time.

I said, "Do you live here or something?"

"Your essay is due tonight, did you remember?"

"And you were waiting for it?"

He glanced at the floor, where my essay lay at his bare feet, like an obedient, panting dog. He picked it up and tossed it somewhere into the room behind him. The chamber was dark, except for one square of uneven light.

"What are you watching?" I asked, nodding inside.

"*Jane Eyre,*" he said. "The new one."

I said, "I haven't watched a movie in years."

"Are you asking for an invitation?"

"No," I said. "No."

"Was that a no or a yes?"

"No. Yes."

"You'd like to watch it."

"I don't know," I said. "Maybe."

"Well, then, come in."

"What?"

"I said, come in."

"I—"

"Samantha."

I stepped inside. He was right; I had wanted an invitation. The room smelled like overheated electronics. Was I allowed to be here at this hour?

"Coat?" Orville said, holding out a hand.

I gave it to him.

"Sit," he said.

"Woof."

"Pardon?"

I sat. The movie was paused. There was a scene frozen on the screen. The woman must have been Jane. She was looking sultry and tanned, like she never had in the book. The camera seemed to have caught her mid-wander through an uncharacteristically wild English garden, which had been color-enhanced by one thousand different lighting engineers.

Orville walked to the corner of the room and deposited my coat on the chair by the deadened fireplace. Afterward, he opened the door of his mini refrigerator. A burst of canned light blasted against his face.

"Do you normally camp out in your office in boxers?" I asked.

"In England, we call them 'pants.' "

"My father called them 'hallelujahs.' "

He removed something from the refrigerator. "Did you say you like hot cocoa?"

"Do you have any beer?"

"How about some cereal?"

The door to the fridge closed, and I heard a cabinet door open. In a moment, something rattled and poured into a bowl. It sounded like kibble. Orville walked back to the couch and sat. He handed me a bowl of Bran Flakes. I was silent. The last time I had eaten cereal with my hands was when I was eight years old.

"Really, why aren't you at home?" I asked.

"Sometimes I find my flat lonely."

"As opposed to this office?"

"This is my true home. I've built my life here."

I nodded and glanced at the wolf on his torso. "Self-portrait?"

He shrugged. "You'll find out at the full moon."

I let out a laugh in spite of myself. That seemed to please him and he rested his heels on the table in front of us. In a moment, he had pressed play and the screen jumped back to life. I was right—Jane Eyre was wandering through an Edenic garden, looking innocent. It had always seemed ridiculous to me that she couldn't guess what was coming. Only an idiot could have missed the mood lighting, the eerie calm, the promise of torrential rain. Sure enough, the next image was of Mr. Rochester, who was not-so-subtly crouching in the bushes, waiting to strike. He was another overly tanned actor, with a strangely orange face and a strong, gladiator chin. I recognized him from the movie *Beast*. He was far too attractive to play Mr. Rochester. The man Jane Eyre loved was supposed to be older, gnarled, and knotted, with a face that made you believe in inner beauty. This Rochester—Beast—popped out from behind a gardenia and paused in front of the camera, mid-swagger, like he was waiting for the applause in his mind to die down. Jane didn't seem startled at all. She and Rochester faced off: employer and governess, in their perpetual dance.

I cleared my throat and asked Orville, "Any reason you picked this movie?"

"Do you always talk during films?"

I shut up. My posture was unnaturally erect, my arm hair static. Thinking about Orville sitting alone watching this movie was like imagining him arranging daisies in front of *You've Got Mail*. Had he been expecting me?

I waited patiently as Jane cried out the dialogue that I had committed to memory so long ago: *Do you think, because I am poor, obscure, plain, and little, I am soulless and heartless? You think wrong! I have as much soul as you, and full as much heart!* After which Rochester wrapped his arms around her nonexistent waist, yanked her toward him, and buried his face in hers. It was a cue for the rain, which fell thick around them. I expected the scene to end—this was where the scene always ended, right?—but this one kept going. The director must have forgotten to call "Cut!" Jane and Rochester kissed fervently, with disorganized passion. He began ripping off her coat—no, was this happening?—and she followed suit. No, no, no, this was not in the book. They were dropping to the dirt, they were covered in mud, and oh no, his shirt, there it went. My cheeks burned. I looked away from the screen, embarrassed not only for myself but for poor Charlotte Brontë, too, who had never written anything like this in her entire life, but probably wished she could have.

The scene ended.

"A wonderfully subtle moment," said Orville.

I said, "I'd like to see your idea of overt."

No response.

In the dark, I learned, silence has a way of killing you.

The movie kept going. I knew that it was nowhere near over, and that I would have to sit here the whole time, pretending to be comfortable. Whose stupid idea had this been, anyway? Jane still had to go through her internal battle, her external battle, her escape, her redemption, her resolution. Another one hundred and fifty pages at least.

Hours passed. Days passed. One thousand years passed. By the time the movie ended, I hadn't paid attention to the dialogue or the acting or the scenery. For all I knew, *Jane Eyre* had turned into a searing portrait of communist revolutionaries in Cuba. I had missed the madwoman altogether—had they even thought to include her, or was this just a sex movie? At last, the credits rolled. I didn't move. I was all too aware of Orville's body. It seemed to shift toward and away from mine as if we were two magnets. I stared at the screen with religious focus. The production designer was a man named Alpheus Thomas. How interesting it suddenly seemed. Orville and I waited throughout the entire sequence, until the production logo appeared. It lingered only briefly, then deserted us. At last, the screen went black.

"Well," Orville said, "what did you think?"

I glanced at the table in front of us with newfound determination and said, "Meh."

"What does that word mean?"

"I think Rochester is an ass."

He let out a half laugh, half grunt. "You dislike everything that threatens you."

"He's a forty-year-old married man who preys on a governess of eighteen."

"And?"

"We have a word for that in America."

"Which is?"

"Sketchy."

With the light from the television gone, Orville's features had decomposed into shadows. He was perfectly calm when he said, "Rochester is merely testing Jane, rousing passions that she would have otherwise never acknowledged."

I paused. "Jane could have come to know her passions independently."

"Not when she was raised to be sexually repressed."

"Maybe she was better off being sexually repressed."

"Pardon?"

"I should go."

I stood up so suddenly that the couch—and Orville—tipped slightly. I was very confused. For the first time, I had the inkling that my unrequited and entirely inappropriate infatuation with Orville was not entirely one-sided after all. The thought was so alarming that I wished I could jump behind the couch. I was comfortable being obsessed with James Orville III from a distance. I was quite good at that. But I didn't know what would happen if the two of us became any sort of reality, even in our own minds. Orville had it right the first time: I was scared shitless of him.

I searched for my coat. Orville walked with me to the door. I couldn't breathe. With one flick, he turned on the lights. The lights, by the way, should never go on. They were bright and hard, and I was painfully aware of the acne that I hadn't bothered to cover up. Orville and I were looking at each other as we actually were.

"How do we say goodbye?" he asked. "Shake hands?"

I said, "In America, we wave."

But we did neither. Instead, I nodded and almost wished him a merry Christmas. Before he could say another word, I opened the door and fled. Well—I didn't flee. After the door slammed, I stood on the other side of it for a long time, letting my back lean against the cool wood. I let out a long, slow breath. This was how it should always be. I would remain as close to him as I possibly could, as long as there was a solid barrier between us.

To: "Samantha J. Whipple" swhipple@old.ox.ac.uk

From: "Ellery Flannery" eflannery@old.ox.ac.uk

Subject: Inquiry

Dear Samantha,

    It has come to our attention you entered the Faculty Wing at 23:50 two nights ago, to drop off an essay for Dr. Orville. It was noted by the porter on duty that you did not leave until 3:15. I would appreciate it if you would please send me an e-mail explaining the reason for the delay at your earliest convenience.

Best,

E. Flannery

To: "Ellery Flannery" eflannery@old.ox.ac.uk

From: "Samantha J. Whipple" swhipple@old.ox.ac.uk

Subject: RE: Inquiry

Dear Dr. Flannery,

    I am having an affair with your colleague. Hope that clears things up.

Thanks,

Samantha

Delete, delete.

It was eight in the evening and I was sitting at my desk, hair unkempt, à la Beethoven. There was a half-empty bottle of wine next to me. I was tipsy. It was alternately pleasant and vile, depending on the way I thought about it. Drinking alone had a distinctly pathetic quality to it, but the idea that this was some poetic rite of passage made it wildly tolerable. For better or worse, I was becoming my father's daughter.

My phone rang. Orville? Orville? I snatched it from my desk. Open books and wilted papers were in disarray around me.

"Samantha," said the voice on the other line.

I squinted. "Professor?"

"John. Sir John."

"Booker?"

"Precisely."

I gave an audible groan. "I don't take calls over the telephone."

"I see," he said. "Can you make an exception?"

I thought about it. He misinterpreted my silence as a yes, and said, "Excellent. I was—"

"You know, I heard something about you the other day," I interrupted. "I heard that you were once found wading through the mud."

A pause.

"Are you crazy too?" I asked.

"Pardon?"

"I'm also wallowing."

He paused. "In the mud?"

I gave a small, soundless burp and sat upright. I said, "The proverbial mud."

"I'm afraid I don't understand."

"It's a metaphor, sir."

It wasn't a metaphor.

Sir John said, "I called to inquire after the state of your father's books. Have you received another?"

"You," I slurred, "are a sniveling worm by the name of Wackford Squeers."

"Are you throwing Dickens at me?"

"It was the only thing I had lying around."

He cleared his throat. "The books, Miss Whipple?"

"You have a one-track mind."

"You sound vague and unhappy, which I will interpret to mean that you need my help."

He was correct. "All right," I said. "Fine. *The Tenant of Wildfell Hall* arrived. A little gem. Eight pounds, three ounces. She's everything I thought she would be."

He ignored me. "Let us set up a time to discuss it, shall we?"

His voice was aggressive and unattractive. I imagined having a tutorial with him. I did not like the idea. Oxford had taught me that intelligence came with different personalities. Some were happy, some were pleasant, some were arrogant, some were hostile. Sir John's, I imagined, was the kind of intelligence that would sleep with you and never call you back.

"Fine," I said. "But only if we do this on my terms."

"Which are?"

"I'd like to see the parsonage."

A pause. "No, I'll come to you."

"Do you want to see the book or not?" I said. "You only see it if I can also get a personal tour."

"It is a long trip to the parsonage."

"I can handle it."

After another thoughtful pause, he said: "I will arrange a time."

"Groovy."

I had never used that word before, and I took a moment to recover from its unfortunate appearance in my vocabulary.

"Do not forget to bring the books if you come," he said.

"I'll have to ask first, but I think they will be up for the trip."

Another pause. I let out a slow peal of laughter, for no particular reason. We hung up. I let out a yawn. I could see my entourage of books—*Wuthering Heights*, *Jane Eyre*, *Agnes Grey*, and *Tenant*—stacked neatly in the corner to my left. They had won, it seemed. I had let go of myself and become one of them: strange, antisocial, obsessed, uncontrollable, artistic. I was not anticipating the inexplicable fondness that washed over me. I looked at those books and finally understood what it must feel like to be part of a loving, dysfunctional family, the kind everyone else seemed to have. Here was a group of people that I was beginning to love, if only because they were crazy, and mine.

To: "Ellery Flannery" eflannery@old.ox.ac.uk

From: "Samantha J. Whipple" swhipple@old.ox.ac.uk

Subject: RE: Inquiry

Dear Dr. Flannery,

    Thank you for your e-mail. My essay was due at midnight. Afterward, Dr. Orville and I spent some time analyzing allegory and sexual ethics. I'm sure he can explain it to you better than I can.

Best,

Samantha

CHAPTER 13

I didn't see Orville again until the following Thursday. When I arrived at his office, he was standing on a stool, back toward me, pulling books out of the top shelf. He had tossed his tie over his left shoulder. I tried, and failed, to think of something charming to say.

"You're late," he said to the shelves, then stepped down from the stool. He dropped a stack of books on the table. With his glasses pushed to the tip of his nose, he looked like he had just spent the morning contemplating the decline of capitalism. He stooped to pour two cups of tea. He didn't need to ask me which kind anymore. I glanced at my watch. I was forty-four seconds late.

Once I had my tea, he sat on the same couch where we had both been only a week before. His eyes were blacker than usual. I sat down across from him, tense. It seemed unnatural that we should go on naturally. I wanted to explain to him that things were uncomfortable and strained between us, in case he hadn't noticed.

I asked: "Did you like my story?"

His voice was flat. "Was it supposed to be a children's book?"

"It was a short story about the Brontës," I said. "A novella, if you will."

"Do you actually know what a novella is?"

"A novel for short people?"

"Very funny."

A hiccup of silence. He was acting unusually cold, as if the two of us didn't know each other at all. I tried to pick apart his expression, but anticipating the next move of a near stranger was exhausting. I was conscious of nothing except how singularly large his shoulders were, and how small his head seemed in comparison.

Orville said: "You've written me a history of the Brontë lives, but you haven't thought to include any facts."

"False," I said. "There are facts—you just have to look for them. Dig deep, or taste not the Pierian spring."

"I see," he said. His face was immobile, like that of a taxidermied goat. "Have you no respect?"

"Pardon?"

"You have written Charlotte as a monster."

My cheeks reddened, and I didn't answer. From the look on his face, I had just insulted his own sister. I suppose I had come across the genesis of his bad mood. We sat in suspended silence, as though we were playing roles in an agonizing postmodern play. Orville's eyes bored into mine.

"Exactly," I said.

The air was thick between us. He said, "Why don't you just come out and tell me what you wanted to say."

"'I wished to tell the truth, for truth always conveys its own moral to those who are able to receive it.'"

"This," he said, "is not the truth."

"Maybe not the literal truth," I said. "But you can understand the Brontës better through my story than through any history book. You see—it all *could* have happened this way."

"It could *not* have happened." His voice was sharp. My version of the Brontës must have collided with his, because his eyes had awakened. They were bright and cold. History, I had heard, was a deeply personal affair.

"Tell me one part that is implausible," I said.

He raised his voice. "Anne Brontë did not try to *murder* her sister."

"Ah. See, I've decided that Anne Brontë was a madwoman," I said.

"A madwoman," he repeated.

"Yes. *Jane Eyre*'s madwoman. Charlotte Brontë's madwoman. The real-life Bertha Mason. Of course she was a would-be murderer."

No response. I waited quietly for Orville to be impressed. I fancied that I had struck a gavel on an imaginary podium, and now I was waiting for the Earth to move. But Orville was not amused. His eyes seemed possessed with a self-generating blackness.

"That is catastrophically inaccurate," he said.

"It might be inaccurate, but it's still the truth. Do you think that Charlotte Brontë invented the madwoman in Rochester's tower? No—she saw what her sister had become after five years of being a governess. I think I've figured out the grand mystery of what happened to Anne at Thorp Green. She went crazy, just like many governesses did."

Orville was not amused. "The author of *Agnes Grey* was no madwoman."

"Yes, but the author of *The Tenant of Wildfell Hall* was. *Jane Eyre* and *Tenant* are the same story, just told in two different ways. One is narrated by a woman seeking to find a mysterious madwoman lurking in a manor; the other is narrated by the madwoman herself."

Silence. As a response, Orville ran his hands through his hair, like a man who understood life too well to be wasting his time with *Untermenschen*. I thought he would let me spout off about my thesis in more detail, but he said:

"The problem with you, Samantha, is that you are assuming that the madwoman is, in fact, mad."

I blinked. "Yes, a madwoman is mad. That's why she is called a madwoman."

"Do you remember our first tutorial? We had a conversation about a similar topic."

I said, "Yes, I remember."

I didn't remember.

He said, "Do you recall 'Porphyria's Lover'?"

I thought about it. "Yes. You said that the man who strangled his lover was not mad, that the murder was art and therefore we should forgive him for being an asshole."

Orville waited. He looked very tired, or very old, or maybe both. "Not exactly," he said eventually. "What I told you was that madness can be more rational than you assume. You have made the mistake of many inexperienced readers, which is to assume that literature's madwomen, like *Jane Eyre*'s Bertha Mason, for example, are unstable and violent. But I would like you to consider Bertha more closely, and then, if you must, Helen. Bertha Mason has been abandoned by her husband, locked in his attic, and forced to live in a virtual prison. These are actions that have been committed *against* her, rather than actions that she has taken herself. Consider the moments when Bertha Mason does act of her own volition. She behaves in a pragmatic and calculated way. Starting a fire in Rochester's bed is a premeditated act. I hardly need impress upon you the innuendo in this scene—or, judging from the vacant look in your face, perhaps I do. The fire occurs precisely as Rochester's feelings for Jane begin to manifest themselves. Bertha—rebellious, exotic, deeply sexual Bertha—'sets fire' both figuratively and literally to Rochester's bed. And in so doing, the neglected wife reminds her husband of where his true duty lies."

I made a face. "Can someone be 'deeply sexual'?"

Thwack.

I gave a small jump. Where had the meterstick come from? Orville was still seated on the couch, but the stick was now in his right hand. Perhaps he kept it behind the sofa, the way I imagined men used to store dueling pistols in their back pockets. He seemed to be attempting to restore a power balance that we had somehow lost in the last few weeks. I sat up straight.

"Next," he said, "when Jane is scheduled to marry Rochester, Bertha sneaks into Jane's room to rip apart her wedding veil. A coincidence?

Bertha attacks the very symbol of Jane's union to Rochester. This is not an act of insanity, Samantha; this is a careful warning to Jane issued by a woman who has already suffered the degradation of marriage herself. Bertha Mason is no more 'mad' than you or I. And as for Helen—if the community in which she lives treats her with contempt, it is only because she is a rational, single mother living at a time when rational, single women were condemnable. You view 'madness' as wild and violent; I view it as the logical reaction to wild and violent conditions."

A stifled *thwack* accompanied this last remark, but the meterstick hit a stack of newspapers and not the table. It seemed anticlimactic.

I said, "You are trying to destroy the most interesting character that Charlotte Brontë ever wrote. If you look at the madwoman as what she is—*mad*—then you admit that Charlotte produced a female character powerful enough to be locked away. If you look at the madwoman as *rational*, as you do, then you take away the most original character of the nineteenth century. Why write about a madwoman at all, if she's just a regular woman?"

"Because the madwoman is far more compelling if she *is* a 'regular' woman," said Orville. "No—don't interrupt. If she is a frothing lunatic, then she becomes the most unrealistic part of *Jane Eyre*, and the one character that transforms the novel into implausible Gothic fiction. If, however, we treat the madwoman as a sane woman who has been locked up, then we force ourselves to acknowledge what *did* exist in the Brontës' world: generations of women, who, silent and confined, reined in their passions and lived lives of seclusion. Consider the Brontës themselves. I find it best to respect their creativity rather than attribute their genius to insanity."

I didn't respond. A long silence ensued, the kind that follows the slamming of a door. Orville had won, and he knew it. Somewhere deep down, his version of reality was more real than mine. I felt a cold hostility. My work—my beautiful little novella—seemed empty and useless. Orville added:

"If you remember, I once told you to consider Grace Poole more carefully."

"Yes, I remember."

"If the madwoman in the attic is insane, as you say, then Jane would be frightened of her, no? But Jane does not fear the madwoman. She fears *Grace*. Grace is a minor character—a plain old invisible servant—who somehow occupies a disproportionately large amount of Jane's thoughts and fears. Jane compares herself to Grace Poole, hoping *not* to see any similarity between the two of them. Don't you see? If there's a danger in Thornfield Hall, it does *not* come from Bertha. Jane Eyre is not running the risk of madness. She is running the real risk of spending forty years as a lonely servant, like Grace. The physical madwoman, Samantha, is irrelevant."

A pause. My brain was spinning quickly, but I found that I could not answer. As if he sensed my internal struggle, Orville gave a maddeningly bright smile.

"You're itching to argue with me," he said.

"Except that I can't think of an argument."

"Is it because you've finally come around to thinking like an academic, and not a failed novelist?"

I bristled. He grinned. That smile—I wished he would just eat it. I stared at his coal-black eyes and fought desperately to win.

"Sir," I said.

"What."

"If I came to your room in the middle of the night and set fire to your bed while you were sleeping, I don't think you would compliment me on my logic."

"Don't get any ideas."

"Common sense dictates that there was some part of these women that was mad, even if they didn't thrash and froth at the mouth. Spend enough time locked away as a governess, and it's bound to happen to anyone. Maybe Bertha had well-articulated motives for trying to kill Rochester, but look at the state she's in by the time her brother finds her. Maybe they weren't born mad, sir, but at some point, these women were driven mad."

Orville raised his brow. "Well, for once, Samantha, perhaps we can find a compromise."

Then, as if a long, long torture session had ended, he leaned back in his chair and put down the meterstick. I waited.

"What? That's it?" I said.

Orville, to my surprise, just smiled. The clouds had lifted, it seemed. We had never had a meeting of the minds before. The room had changed. It was lighter, brighter. Everything felt inappropriately happy. My smile faded into a long, studious frown. What were we supposed to do now? Play cards?

Suddenly, the phone rang. I jumped. I hadn't heard a landline ring in so long that for a moment, I imagined we were back in the 1960s, in one of those old movies where all the men looked like news anchors. Orville said, "One moment," and walked to his desk. He picked up the receiver with his thumb and forefinger.

"Yes?" Orville said. "Oh, hello."

I listened to the faint voice on the other line. A woman? My interest was piqued in spite of myself.

"What do you want?" he asked. "Can this wait?"

Not a woman he liked, apparently.

"All right, go on," he said, glancing at his watch. "You mean now? Only if it's brief. I am with a student. What? Yes. Yes, fine. Very well— come up, I am here."

He hung up without saying goodbye. I wondered if I had just gotten a taste of what it would be like to be married to him.

"Who was that?" I asked.

"One of our dons would like to inspect my doorknob."

"That's nice."

"She is picking out a new one. A student broke into her room."

Just then, the world seemed to stop.

I stiffened. "Rebecca Defoe?"

"Yes, exactly. Now—where were we?"

Panic hit me in the upper throat, and I found it difficult to breathe. The room took on an out-of-focus quality. Was Rebecca coming here? I needed to leave.

Abruptly, I stood. "Well, this has been great. Anything else?"

Orville glanced at his watch. "It's been twenty minutes."

"Twenty really great minutes."

He narrowed his eyebrows. "You're pale. Is something the matter?"

"I'm always pale."

"Your eyes, too, they are very large."

"The better to eat you with."

He sat down and leaned back in his chair. He had a curious expression on his face and I looked away, certain that all my sins had become visible. My eyes blurred. He was different; I was different; this entire day was different. Already, our tutorial seemed to belong to the long-distant past. I was sweating. I needed to leave. All of a sudden, I was living in the present tense, moment by moment. *The clock ticks. The tutor's mouth moves. The girl standing slowly goes mad.*

I said, "I'd like to go home."

"I told you that we were not finished yet."

"I'd really like to go home."

"To your tower? Are you ill?"

"To Boston."

"Pardon?"

"Please, sir."

But he didn't let me leave, and I couldn't exactly refuse him, so I sat back down. The minutes oozed past. We tried to continue our conversation. If the madwoman were not, in fact, mad, then what were the implications for Jane? For Grace? For Gothic fiction? I asked to use the restroom and was flatly denied. Orville chatted on and on, and I sat where I was, waiting for the executioner.

Then, there it was—the knock on the door. My whole life, I knew, was about to end. There was a strange predetermination to the situation. I suppose the mistakes you make on page three always come back to bite you on page one hundred and eighty-three. Surprising, yet inevitable.

Orville, who had stood up to switch on the kettle, said: "Would you mind opening it, Samantha? This will only take a minute."

I stood. Somewhere inside, I was screaming. All the fragile little worlds I had meticulously created for myself were collapsing like paper lanterns.

I opened the door.

There she was—of all the horrors. Rebecca Smith. I recognized her immediately. She had long, dead-looking hair that wasn't quite gray and wasn't quite black, but was instead a shiny charcoal color, one that made her look like a statue that had been rained on for several years. Her eyes were bleak and watchful.

To her credit, her shock seemed almost equal to mine. Her eyes widened and narrowed in rapid succession. She looked at me with an icy expression hardened by sugarless tea and too many winters. There was no smile on her face, no glimmer of fondness in her eyes. She and I used to spend four hours every week together, as she taught me that triangles had three sides and that squares had four and that life was a logical, well-ordered phenomenon. Now here we were, looking at each other the way two Native American mannequins would stare at each other through the glass partition of a museum. It was the way, I feared, that Orville and I would look at each other someday.

My heart was beating furiously. Orville, who did not seem to realize something terrible was happening, came over to make pleasantries. My two tutors had a brief, cool conversation. I emptied my face of all expression and stared into the smeared gray ovals of Rebecca's eyes. She was talking to Orville but looking at me. She knew. I could see it on her face. She had just figured out that it was I who had broken into her room. I wondered why she hadn't guessed it long before now.

"Forgive me, I'm being rude," said Orville. "Rebecca, this is Samantha Whipple; Samantha, this is Dr. Defoe."

"Hello, Sam," Rebecca said. Her voice was terse and efficient; she could have been one of Hemingway's women. *Sam, Sam.* Memories poured into me like a painful injection. I remembered the bright purple shawl she used to wear, the pumpkin scones she brought in the morning, the smell of alcohol swipes in the air, the tea that spilled over my mother's tablecloths.

Orville looked between the two of us and paused. "Do you two know each other?"

Rebecca turned to him. Her lips were two raspberries on a cold, skull-white face. "This, James, is the student who broke into my room."

That's when my life officially stopped, as cleanly as if someone had snapped a book shut. Orville let out a half laugh and told Rebecca not to be ridiculous. In response, she cocked her head toward me and raised an eyebrow, the way she had when I was a child. She was attractive, in an evil sort of way. She told Orville to ask me himself. And then, my beautiful tutor's head turned in my direction.

He waited. "Samantha?" It was not an accusatory glance—just one of surprise.

I couldn't look directly at him. "Monsieur, I beg your pardon."

He paused. "Answer the question."

"It's not really a yes-or-no question."

His eyes were veiled. He and I could no longer be allies, not once he discovered that I had attacked his people. I had committed an academic offense. I might as well have murdered his cat.

"May I explain myself first, before I answer?" I said. "Perhaps in private?"

Orville took a sharp intake of breath. A look of horror crossed his face. "You *broke* into a *don's* room?"

I opened my mouth to answer, but no sound came out. Orville took a step back from me. Suddenly, I had the overwhelming conviction that I had never broken into Rebecca's office, that I was entirely innocent, that all of this antagonism was a boiling injustice committed against me by an unfeeling world. Didn't anyone remember my father was dead? Didn't that count for anything?

"You broke into a don's room," he repeated. I noticed that it was no longer a question.

I said, "I can explain."

"What were you thinking?" he said. "Are you mad? What is the matter with you?"

I flinched. "Which one of those questions do you want me to answer first?"

"This is insanity."

"I thought you appreciated insanity. I thought you said there was a lot of sanity in it."

Orville's eyebrows formed a solid, heavy line and his eyes glowed beneath them like smoking pistols. He was being unnecessarily cruel.

"It was an accident," I told him.

"How can it possibly be an accident?"

"Have you ever read *Rebecca*?"

"Focus, please."

"I'm just trying to explain this in a way you'd understand."

He didn't answer. The look on his face told me that he no longer knew who I was or what I was doing in his office. Rebecca stood in the doorway, smiling. She was enjoying herself very much. Her face sparked a chord of fury within me.

I turned back to Orville and snapped: "I was trying to find *The Tenant of Wildfell Hall*."

He said, "In the math department."

"Yes," I said.

"How—"

"Sir," I interrupted. I motioned to Rebecca. "This was my father's mistress."

A pause. I saw Rebecca's eyes flash, then cool. A strange silence ensued, the sort that tells you that the armies have shifted, and no one is quite sure which side is winning. Orville said nothing. He was a stranger to me.

"I can handle this, James," Rebecca said. Her voice was calm. "Why don't you give us a few minutes."

"Sir," I said suddenly, "please don't leave me alone with her."

"James, leave us alone," Rebecca repeated.

"I'm begging you, sir," I said. "You don't understand."

"James."

Orville did not seem to be adapting well to arguments between women. I watched his face wrestle with the decision of whose side to take. Student or teacher? Oppressed or oppressor? My confusion about our entire relationship seemed to rest upon this one response. Didn't men protect the things they cared about? I watched and waited.

Finally, Orville let out a breath. Without looking directly at me, he told Rebecca: "Please tell me what you decide to do with her. I will be in the lounge."

And without a single look over his shoulder, he quitted the room. The breath left my body in one tortured exhale. All I saw was a last glimpse of his face, perfectly framed by the door, before everything went bleak. I remembered something he had once told me, long ago. *And this? This never happened.*

I had died, apparently, and gone to hell. Orville was gone. Rebecca glanced at the closed door and then back at me. A thin little smile cracked the mask of her face. She and that smile sat down on the couch.

"Tea?" she asked sweetly. She was not a sweet person, and the sweetness fell flat on its face. She got up, walked to the kettle, and poured herself a cup.

"No," I said. "Thank you."

"Have a seat."

I noticed she no longer took cream. Was Orville really gone? I thought of all the little things I had worried about this year—what he thought of my essays, if he appreciated my punctuality, if he secretly liked the fact that I was so tall and didn't wear makeup. I should have instead wondered if he thought of me at all. He and I were not friends, nor had we ever been. He was just someone whom I was borrowing for the year. All I had was the illusion of intimacy.

I told Rebecca, "That was a very cruel thing to do."

"Was it? I could have just expelled you on the spot—would you have preferred that? That was not very clever of you, breaking into my room like that."

"I'm surprised you didn't notice the book was gone earlier."

"It's not something I check on a regular basis."

"*The Tenant of Wildfell Hall* is my property."

"No—it is *my* property. Your father gave it to me before he died." There was a note of possessiveness in her voice. "There was no need for burglary. I would have given it to you eventually."

"You mean in the middle of the night?" I said. "You have a funny way of delivering things."

She blinked. "I suppose I just never wanted to see you again."

My mouth opened slightly. She was much too old to be saying petty things, and I think the realization struck her as much as it did me, because she looked away. It had never occurred to me that teachers could loathe their students as much as their students loathed them.

"I seem to have interrupted an intimate moment just now," said Rebecca.

"We were having a tutorial, if you call that intimate."

She sat down and draped her arm over the couch. A small laugh accompanied the gesture. "Do you take me for a fool?"

"Pardon?"

"You're in love with him. It's as plain as the nose on your face."

I stiffened. "Who?"

"You're not the first one. Orville has been stealing the hearts of impressionable female students since he arrived. It is the most common citation other faculty members give when trying to steal his job. How can a man possibly teach in such a situation? It must be terribly inconvenient for him, having girls fawning over him when all he is trying to do is work."

"I don't much want to talk about it, if you don't mind," I said.

"Your cheeks are red, Sam."

"Why don't you tell me about you and my dad? You had a pretty close personal relationship, too, wouldn't you say?"

Her expression was lifeless. "I don't think you understand a single thing about your father's and my relationship."

"Then you won't mind telling me the whole story."

She waited a moment, then a thin smile crept up her face. "You're very much like him, you know."

"I know. We're exactly alike."

"He was not always a good man."

"That's the second time I've heard that."

She grazed her finger along the rim of the sofa. Her outfit was not quite right, I noticed. The blouse was not entirely tucked into her badly fitted brown trousers, and the wrinkled bits at the end stuck out on the sides. I had a fleeting image of her as a young girl—silent, smart, awkward. My father once told me that her parents had expected many great things from her, and she had systematically done all of them, as if by point-by-point recursive analysis. Top student, top professor, tenure. I wondered where seducing my father fit into that.

"He was brilliant at many things, you know," Rebecca said.

"Who, Dad?"

"What he could never handle was the strain of having two women in his life."

"Let's leave my mother out of this, please."

She shrugged as though I had said something irrelevant. "As you wish."

"You must have been very much in love with him, to ruin a marriage."

She let out a loud, hard laugh. "Look at your poor, inquisitive little face. You'd like to know everything, wouldn't you? What we did, where we sat, what we said. Admit it."

She had that rapid way of talking from black-and-white movies— the affected, clenched-jaw accent that makes you wonder, *Where's the audience?*

"Yes," I said. "I already admitted it. Where did you meet him?"

"Here, at Old College. I was teaching at the time."

I said, "You're lying."

"Goodness, already?"

"What was my dad doing here? He never lived in Oxford."

She paused and opened her mouth just slightly, as if I had either missed something terribly obvious or else didn't really know much about anything to begin with.

"How much did you and your father communicate?" she asked.

"In English?"

"I see he was selective with the stories he told you."

"Well, then, why don't you tell me the rest?" I asked coolly.

She paused, and for a brief moment I thought I saw a small note of triumph enter her expression. She stood and began to make a lap around Orville's perfectly kept room.

"What do you want to know about?" she said, hands behind her back. "Dates? Trysts? Scandals? I can see you love stories. Your father did too. It's why he died, probably. He visited me at Old College a month before it happened, did you know that? I hadn't seen him in quite some time. He looked very ill. Alcohol. Later, when I read of the fire, I knew he had won. He had turned his life into art. It was a well-crafted ending to an otherwise structureless life. A perfect, cata-strophic death."

I don't think I was imagining it—she sounded as though she was secretly enjoying herself. Her heels made bright popping sounds when she walked off the carpet.

"I remember the first day I met him," she said. "I was wearing a blue dress. He was wearing a gray jumper. He was young—imperti-nent. Nineteen? Twenty? I can't remember. We knew it would hap-pen. Our romance, I mean. It started with the occasional lunch. The occasional lunch turned into the occasional drink, which turned into the occasional weekend trip up north to obscure hotels. I was drunk on him—he was drunk on me."

If I wasn't mistaken, there was a touch of pride in her voice: yes, she had once experienced a grand passion, thank you very much. She reminded me of a shy teenager who finally has a boyfriend and hasn't yet discovered that the feeling of relief is sometimes stronger than love.

"One night, he came to visit me here and we were caught, just as I knew we would be, and long before I was anywhere near done with him," she said, speaking quickly. "We were found outside, on the lawns by the well. You've seen it, I imagine."

"What do you mean, 'found'?"

"A student stumbled upon us, and took a photograph."

I said, "I don't understand."

She glanced back at me. "What don't you understand?"

I paused. "Were you—not wearing clothes?"

An unexpected silence hit the room. I looked away, struck by a red-hot humiliation. I had an image that no daughter should ever have: her father, naked and vulgar and flawed and human. I could not escape the vision of him rolling around on the lawn with this strange, waxy woman. Rebecca's expression was direct and unemo-tional. She was watching my reaction closely, as though congratulat-ing herself on the impact she had administered.

I searched through my repertoire of retouched memories, questioning what I could have done to Rebecca to warrant such a strong dislike, other than stealing the occasional lip balm out of her room. She was staring at me the way a wronged wife would look at her husband's mistress. It was an expression that I had never seen on my mother's face, not once.

I cleared my throat. "Well, don't stop there. What happened next?"

She shrugged. "A few years ago, the university accepted my return. They watch me closely. Not as closely as they watch your tutor, perhaps, but close enough. This is why Orville will never look upon you, Sam. There is too much to lose."

Her voice was so calm and flat that I wondered if she had recited this story many times before, like it was *Tristan and Isolde*. So far she hadn't forgotten a single word.

"I don't understand," I said. "You were cast out?"

"Can't you imagine?" she said. "The story first appeared in the *Hornbeam*. Then the *Examiner*. The *Times*. Soon, there wasn't a person in England who hadn't seen it—an Oxford don, caught in a compromising position. I saw my reputation destroyed overnight. I resigned immediately. Years later, I was so desperate to escape England that I moved to Boston and tutored a spoiled teenage girl. Never underestimate the sacrifices you will make for love, Samantha."

I appraised her silently for a moment. Her cheeks were the color of sour cream. It seemed as though we were no longer in the twenty-first century but instead in a strange addendum to the nineteenth, where public shame was the inevitable response to a woman's freedom. One tryst did not seem like enough to warrant such a backlash; I wondered if Rebecca was leaving out a few key details.

"You know," I said, "you really don't sound as angry as you should about all of this."

She gave me a stony smile I was beginning to hate. "It was many years ago," she said. "I suppose I've learned to forget."

With that, she returned to the couch and took a seat. She was a terrible liar. She hadn't forgotten anything. This was the defining episode of her life, which she had crafted into a tidy story. I couldn't tell whether she was altogether here or I was talking to the mask of Rebecca—the version of herself she sent out as her PR person. There was a cold resentment lurking beneath her calm features that I found alarming. This story was not over for her—not at all. She reached for her creamless tea, which was the color of tar, and took a long sip.

"If my dad loved you so much," I ventured, "why did he ask you to leave Boston eventually?"

It was a terribly worded question—I had meant it to sound cordial. Rebecca's gray eyes flashed and she immediately put down the tea with a loud clank. Any expression she had dropped right off her face.

"All right, Sam," she snapped. "Let's get on with it. How would you like to be expelled? In public or in private?"

I blanched. "I don't think my father wanted you to expel me. I have a feeling you made him a promise that you'd take care of me here."

"A promise to a dead man is like sand in the wind. And I've done my duty already. I saved those infernal books for you, and I put you in that bloody tower."

My eyes widened. "*You* put me in the tower?"

"I had to pull several strings. It's a historical landmark."

"Well, thank you," I said. "It's quite the hellhole."

"Blame your father. He wanted you there."

"How did he even *know* about the tower?"

For the second time, a perplexed look came across Rebecca's face, as though she was unclear as to how, exactly, I had grown up to be so ignorant.

"Have you never listened to the tour that goes through your room?" she asked.

"No," I said. "But I notice you took advantage of it to leave me

Jane Eyre. Is there a reason you couldn't have just delivered the books all in one go, or in person—preferably both?"

"Your father had a very particular order he wanted you to read them in, and he wanted you to know they were important."

I didn't respond because I didn't believe her. She looked so borderline evil that I couldn't help but think that she had drawn out this entire process on purpose, to exact some sort of strange torture.

"So he comes to Old College before he dies, leaves you everything important, then takes an entire safe deposit box to leave me a lousy bookmark," I said.

To my surprise, a muscle in Rebecca's neck twitched. I had caught her attention.

"That's what he left you?" she said, her voice at a higher pitch. "A bookmark?" Her foot started tapping—soft and uneven.

"It was my Emily Dickinson bookmark," I clarified. "Red. Gold tassels. Looks a bit like yours?"

Rebecca was visibly uncomfortable. I don't know how, but I had struck a nerve. She stood, then walked toward me again, quickly this time. I thought she might be going for the jugular, but instead she stopped in front of me.

"I thought there were only two bookmarks," she said. "His and mine."

"He gave one to all his women, I guess."

Her poker face was even worse than mine. She took a few steps back, turned to face the fireplace, and stood there for a longer time than I thought she would.

"While you're ruminating over there, may I blackmail you?" I said. "I know several thousand people in the press who might like to give the story of you and my father a fresh go. Don't you think it will be a particularly interesting slant when this time, it's told by the wronged daughter, the Last Brontë? I'm very sorry to threaten you— really, I am—but I don't want to be expelled."

When Rebecca turned around, her eyes were steely. I had never blackmailed anyone before, and it didn't feel as great as it seemed to in films. Rebecca was expressionless. Her mind was somewhere else entirely. Had I won?

I didn't want to stick around long enough to find out. I said, "I'll go."

"Not so quickly," she snapped. Again, she walked toward me. She was not a young woman, and up close I could see how the years had carved wrinkles around her mouth.

"Yes?" I said.

Silently, she reached out to me with one hand. "My bookmark, please?"

I didn't know quite how to respond. I said: "I—that is—I don't carry it around."

Our eyes met. There was a cold malice in her face that told me how little I understood of her story—or anything, really. I took her silence as an opportunity to escape. Quietly, I opened the door and stepped into the hallway, leaving her in Orville's office.

With the door shut safely behind me, I ran down the hall and down the stairs and ejected myself from the building. I was gasping for air. I should have been relieved: I had avoided expulsion, for the time being. But as I walked into the cold, bright afternoon, I couldn't help but think that Rebecca's rancor was merely biding its time before it found me again. *So wise so young, they say, do never live long*.

***

At two fifteen that Saturday, there was a knock on my door. Three taps, followed by a loud bang. I leapt to the door to find Marvin, dressed in a scratchy black coat. Behind him was the usual pile of tourists—a smaller crowd, this time, perhaps owing to the arctic weather. Usually, Marvin apologized for taking me by surprise. This time, however, I'd been expecting him.

He frowned when he saw me. "Is everything all right?"

I realized that I was holding a broom and wearing a Sweeney Todd smile. I had been waiting for the tour all morning. My room was nearly sterile. The bed was made, the socks were gone, the bedsheet was no longer covering *The Governess*. Rebecca had suggested I pay attention to his tour, so here I was. It was possible—just possible—that Marvin was the answer to my problems.

I said, "Come in, please."

The tour group filtered inside. Marvin seemed to be debating whether he was entering some sort of trap. My cleaning spree had left the tower looking and smelling like a newly minted hotel room.

"Please, step inside, step inside," I said. "Come closer. That's right."

"Yes, yes," Marvin said. "Do come in." His voice was thin but loud, and he seemed to be grasping for authority. The last of the tour group squeezed inside.

"As I mentioned, this is the tower," Marvin said. "It was built in 1361 to quarantine victims of the bubonic plague. It is known by some as the Tower of Extinction."

I interjected: "They call it that because no one in here procreates."

Marvin looked at me in mild surprise.

I cleared my throat. "Is it all right if I take the tour too?"

He seemed surprised, then mumbled something I did not understand. It might have been "How delightful."

I heard a click. Someone had already snapped a photograph. It was the woman up front—baggy jeans, a pale rag of blonde hair—who was looking between me and Marvin as if waiting for the show. Marvin pointed the tour group in the direction of the back corner, and I took a seat on my bed, cross-legged.

"Some of the most famous and enigmatic inhabitants of Old College lived in this tower," he said. "If you look closely, you'll find that it became a tradition for each one to leave something behind for posterity, which is perhaps why the room holds so much interest for us today. Right over here—turn this way, please—you can see the exact location where Sir Michael Morehouse's cat was buried alive. Do you see the discoloration of the brick, right about here? That is exactly where the poor creature was buried. Not two centimeters away, right here, you can also see the claw marks left by the Beast of Bologne."

"Excuse me?"

Someone interrupted—I realized it was me. I was hugging my pillow, rocking back and forth slightly. The tour group turned to have a look in my direction.

Marvin looked back at me, eyebrow raised. "Yes, Miss Whipple?"

"Who was the very last inhabitant of this tower before me?" I asked.

Marvin looked ruffled. His mustache twitched. I wondered if I should tell him that it was slightly uneven.

He said: "I prefer to go chronologically."

I pressed, "Did anyone live here during the last century?"

"We are not quite there yet."

"Can we go in reverse order? I'm impatient."

Apparently, I had chosen to unleash my inner American at a very bad time. Marvin let out a shallow breath before saying, "Yes, yes—one inhabitant. You can glimpse his faded initials over that way—do you see?"

He pointed to three very faint, quiet letters etched into the wall, about a foot below *The Governess*.

J.H.E.

I paused. "I see."

"It—"

I interrupted him again. "The initials," I said. "What do they stand for?"

"Pardon?"

"The initials, the initials."

Marvin blinked. "Jack Halford, Esquire."

"Jack Halford."

"That's correct."

"Esquire?"

"Miss Whipple, are you quite all right?"

"I mean, shit."

Marvin's eyes flew open. "Pardon?"

"Shit."

Marvin looked around. Censors, censors?—where were the censors? I reached under my pillow and pulled out *The Tenant of Wildfell Hall*. Rebecca's bookmark poked out of it like a land mine. Marvin, now considerably miffed, continued talking. I stopped listening. It seemed as though I was standing on top of a tall building, seeing a city from a great distance. I flipped open the book. In enormous font at the top of page one were the words *To J. Halford, Esq.* J.H.E was Gilbert Markham's "very old friend." A fictional character, it seemed, had just popped up on my wall.

My chest rose and fell in quick succession. It was impossible, for a brief moment; then it was the most possible thing in the entire world. Tristan Whipple. Snodgrass Diddleworm. Jack Halford. My father's entourage of names. Dad was here—he had been here all this time, hiding in the corners of this room. I looked around in quiet disbelief. *J.H.E.* What had my father once said? *It's the only place you can read the writing on the wall.*

"Jack Halford lived here?" I interrupted. My mouth was dry. "He was a student? When?"

Marvin, who I realized had been midsentence, turned to face me. "The Thatcher years," he said, agitated. "Really, we'll get there in a moment, if you'll just wait—"

"Thirty years?" I said. "Goddammit, thirty years."

Marvin waffled, then turned to the tour group apologetically.

He explained, "Jack Halford was one of Old College's most famous eccentrics. His misadventures were legendary."

"Did he ever have an affair with a professor?" I asked.

Marvin snapped: "Let's not get off topic."

"Is that why they call it Halford's Well?" I asked him. "Because that's where they did it?"

"Would you kindly be quiet?" said Marvin.

The tour group stared at me blankly. Marvin cleared his throat to try to regain control of the situation. I leaned back on my bed. The room around me was fattening with significance, squeezing everyone else out. There seemed to be ghosts materializing all around me—applauding, applauding—welcoming me into the small world of people who had figured it out. Everything around me was suddenly different and precious. The boarded-up fireplace no longer seemed like a prison accessory; it was an intimate secret between friends and outcasts. All of this had once been my father's. He had been a student here, somehow. Every time I had paced or tripped over a loose floorboard or contemplated banging my head against the desk in frustration . . . my father had done the same, once upon a time. This room—this glorious, unruly room!—was designed for people who were hopelessly lost and trying to find each other.

I stuffed *The Tenant of Wildfell Hall* back underneath my pillow, wondering how my father had managed to pull off such an extensive disappearing act. Surely one could not invent a name so easily. And yet, my father always prided himself on his knack for invisibility when the time called for it. I suppose he and the Brontës had that in common.

All that I should have been doing, this entire year, was listen to Marvin. As he engaged the increasingly disengaged tour group, I made a slow sweep of the space with my eyes. That broom—had that been my father's? No, no. The desk? The bed? Were those his claw marks on the wall? Then, my eyes alighted on the painting on the back wall. It was half-visible from behind a bald man's shiny scalp. The Governess and I stared each other right in the eye. I breathed very steadily, in and out.

Sir Michael Morehouse had left behind his cat. The Beast of Bologne had left his claw marks. And Jack Halford? I kept staring at *The Governess*. Well—he had left behind his painting.

The next day, I made my way to the Plodge. I found Hans sitting there, looking like a shiny trophy. His computer monitor suggested he was working on a graph and a spreadsheet, but at the moment Hans had his feet up on the desk and was reading the *Hornbeam*. He was wearing a beaded bracelet, which I decided was not something I would remember in the story version of our relationship. When I walked in, he put down the paper in a hurry as if he had instead been watching porn.

"Hullo!" he said. I appreciated the way he acted as though nothing was ever wrong between us, even though nothing had ever been right.

"They make you work weekends?" I asked.

"Just catching up on some things," he said, moving a wad of papers off his desk. I was having a hard time remembering what his job actually was, but it was too far into our acquaintance to ask him now.

"You look out of breath," he said.

"It's cold out there."

"I'll make us something—hot cocoa?"

"Some water would be great, actually."

"No hot cocoa?"

"Water sounds easier."

He grinned. "So I want something hot, and you want something easy."

I blinked and didn't answer. I'm sure he interpreted my silence as disinterest. Really, I was just awkward. I didn't know what to say. I noticed he wasn't getting up to fetch a glass of water.

I sat down in the seat across from him and said, "Can I ask you for some help?"

"Always."

I let out a breath. "Your computer looks large and official. Does that mean you have the power to look up the records of old students?"

He laughed. "You have that power, too, through your student account."

"I see," I said. "Would you please look up a Mr. Jack Halford for me? I'd like to know how long he was a student here."

"Still thinking about that well?" he asked, smiling. But he turned to his computer and typed something on the keyboard. He was an aggressive typist and the sound brought to mind a horde of cockroaches.

"Jack Snodgrass Halford," he read, then looked back at me. "Looks as if he never graduated."

"Was he expelled?"

"It doesn't actually say, but that seems likely. It's fairly well known that he had an affair with his tutor."

"It was *his* tutor?"

"He was a student of math; she was his tutor."

I was silent for some time.

"Is anything the matter?" Hans asked finally.

"No. Yes. It's just very strange that he studied math, don't you think?"

He thought about it. "No, not really. Why should it be?"

I didn't respond. None of this made much sense. I could imagine why Dad chose a fake name—he always opted for invisibility in environments in which *Whipple* would draw too much attention. Yet I could not rationalize why he chose to study math—or, more important, why he never bothered mentioning it.

"Do we know anything about him?" I asked. "Where he came from? What he looks like?"

"I'm not sure," said Hans. "There was a picture taken the night—"

"Yes, I know."

"But his face isn't visible."

My cheeks grew red. How many people had seen a picture of my father's little tryst, I wondered? I studied my fingers and pretended to find something interesting under a nail. I suppose I now understand the high scandal Rebecca had spoken of; this was not an affair between two regular adults but an affair between a student and his teacher. Finally, I stood up.

"Thank you for your help," I said. "It was very kind."

"Wait a moment," said Hans. "Let's talk this out."

My breathing was shallow. "I can't. I have to call someone."

"Who?"

"I'm not sure yet," I said. "Maybe my mother."

"I thought the two of you didn't talk."

"It's my father who I'm not speaking to anymore."

I started walking to the door. I stopped, then turned around. "Hans?"

"Samantha?"

"Out of curiosity, have you ever seen anything perfectly ordinary lying around Old College that might be old and famous? Like a sketch? Or a rug? Or a really interesting doorknob?"

He frowned. "Pardon?"

"Never mind," I said. "Just curious."

I stepped outside, head pounding. I was pleased to confirm that Dad was once a student here. But I could not help but wonder whether he and I had been such good friends, after all. Friends confided in other friends; they told them all the lurid details about their pasts, even when those details were unflattering. It unnerved me to think that my father may have been closer to Rebecca than he had been to me. I thought back to the triumphant look I had seen on her face. They had a secret history, the two of them, and I would never be a part of it. I walked back to my lonely tower, with the sudden feeling that everything I'd ever known might vanish in front of my eyes.

To: "James Timothy Orville" jorville@old.ox.ac.uk
From: "Samantha J. Whipple" swhipple@old.ox.ac.uk
Subject: Request

Dear Dr. Orville,

Hello. This is difficult for me to write, as I would prefer never to see you again. But would you please drop by my Tower sometime tomorrow afternoon?
Cordially,
Samantha

To: "Samantha J. Whipple" swhipple@old.ox.ac.uk
From: "James Timothy Orville" jorville@old.ox.ac.uk
Subject: RE: Request

Dear Samantha,

No. I hope you understand.
Best,
O

To: "James Timothy Orville" jorville@old.ox.ac.uk
From: "Samantha J. Whipple" swhipple@old.ox.ac.uk
Subject: RE: RE: Request

You don't understand. I have a very old painting to show you. If you're worried that it will be a waste of your time, I'll make sure that we also do a dramatic reading of *Paradise Lost*.

To: "Samantha J. Whipple" swhipple@old.ox.ac.uk
From: "James Timothy Orville" jorville@old.ox.ac.uk
Subject: RE: RE: RE: Request

It will not work; I will be leaving town later tonight for a long weekend.

To: "James Timothy Orville" jorville@old.ox.ac.uk
From: "Samantha J. Whipple" swhipple@old.ox.ac.uk
Subject: RE: RE: RE: RE: Request

Then come this evening—early?

To: "James Timothy Orville" jorville@old.ox.ac.uk
From: "Samantha J. Whipple" swhipple@old.ox.ac.uk
Subject: RE: RE: RE: RE: RE: Request

Sir?

It grew late in the afternoon, and then early in the evening, and I still had not heard back from Orville. I began packing for my trip to the Brontë Parsonage. I did not appreciate that Orville was going out of town as well. Like an angry wife, I wanted to know where he would be and with whom he would be cavorting. It occurred to me that I didn't even know where his home was, let alone that he had one. Did he have siblings too? A closet stuffed with old shoes and a living room filled with crayon drawings? A Brazilian wife wearing black leggings and ballet flats? There was a huge storm forecast for this weekend; I wondered if he was about to escape to the tropics.

I sat down on my bed, staring at *The Governess*, which was hanging on the wall like an expensive Picasso. I had tried to find her in Sir John's book of missing artifacts, but she hadn't made it in. Sir John must have had no idea of this painting's existence. My father must have wanted it that way.

I looked my governess friend straight in the eye. Locked in her lonely frame, drowning in an indifferent black sea, she was a Brontë in her own right. Her formless body and blank eyes seemed to take up the whole room. It was a weekend of transformation, and the Governess, too, seemed different. Maybe she was just out for a nice swim with her favorite book. I sat down on my bed and stared at her wonderful, disturbed face. How had I not recognized her as a relative before? Perhaps my entire life was to be spent reevaluating all the people I thought I knew best.

"Is it always this cold in here?"

I jumped. The door must have been unlocked, because James Orville was standing in the doorway, holding his hat in his hands and looking irritable. He walked inside.

I said, "Come in."

There was an overnight bag slung over one shoulder, and he dropped it on the floor. I tried to seem as aloof as possible. I thought maybe he would detect my indifference and decide he was in love with me after all.

He took off his hat, then dropped a rusty nail on my desk. "I found this outside," he said. "Samantha, this room is a hazard. And don't you have heat in here?"

I glanced at the boarded-up relic that was decaying in the corner—a fireplace, in its first life. "Be my guest."

He paused. One of the lightbulbs was out in my desk lamp, and the room was bathed in a canary, infirmary yellow.

Orville said: "Surely, the college must know that this room is unin-habitable."

"It's all part of the tour."

He waited. "I see."

We stared at each other for so long that I wondered if he were test-ing out some new form of torture.

Finally, he said, "Well?"

"Well what?"

"What happened with Rebecca?"

"You left, that's what happened."

"I didn't realize that she knew your father."

"She did, in the biblical sense."

Another pause. "I see."

"She was his professor when he studied at Old College."

He shook his head. "Tristan Whipple never attended Oxford."

"Tristan Whipple didn't. But Jack Halford did."

Orville wore a deep frown. I turned away to tend to nothing in particular and gave him a moment to register the peculiarity of the revelation.

"You're angry with me," he said.

"I'm seething."

"I don't think you're joking," he said.

"Who said I was joking? You left me alone with her."

A silence. "I cannot treat you any differently than I would any other student."

I turned around to face him and I jumped—he was directly in front of me.

I swallowed. "Do you normally feed your students to the wolves?"

"Any other behavior from me would have been suspect."

I tried to decipher his expression. Was it one of guilt? Embarrass-ment? Compassion? Desperate, unrequited love? Apathy? He took a step closer. I panicked. I had never been this close to his face before and all I could feel was the difference in our levels of experience. In his past was an entire black book of ex-girlfriends; meanwhile, I could barely contemplate eye contact.

"Tell me what happened with Rebecca," he said. His voice was soft. "Quickly—I only have a few minutes."

"I'm fine."

I expected him to argue with me, but his eyes were big and concerned and I was finding it difficult to breathe. I wished I were ten years older. He was watching me carefully.

"Samantha—"

When he took a step even closer, I gave a small yelp and pushed myself past him to the other end of the room.

"If you only have a few minutes, I'd like to ask you something," I blurted, short of breath. "Do you see that painting over there?"

If Orville noticed my awkwardness, he didn't comment. He followed me to *The Governess*, as instructed. He stood staring at it for quite some time. I didn't know how to make a proper introduction. *Governess, this is James, James this is Governess. The Governess and I are fellow inmates; James and I are low-level friends. Have a scone.* But I realized an introduction was not exactly necessary. There was an odd expression on Orville's face. He moved closer to the painting. He did not seem pleased.

"She's still here," he said. He sounded as though he had run across a particularly vicious ex.

I said, "She? Do you two know each other?"

"It's foolish to leave valuable belongings around your apartment."

I waited. "I think this might be an original Brontë painting."

"Yes, I can see that," said Orville. "It's an Anne. I knew the first time I saw it."

"You *knew*?"

"Look at the brushstrokes."

I glanced back at the painting. "What?"

"And look at the date scribbled so hastily in the right-hand corner—there, see it? Look closer. Eighteen forty-three. Do you not recognize this scene?"

"No."

"I thought you'd read *Jane Eyre*."

"Pardon?"

He took off his gloves and threw them in the corner. "Book," he said. "Hand me the book." He was holding out his hand, as if to say, *Scalpel.*

When I didn't move fast enough, Orville strutted past me to my desk, where *Jane Eyre* was resting. He picked up the novel and flipped through its pages very quickly. I had a feeling he had done this many times before. It was like watching a master violinist perform scales.

"How many people know that this painting is in here, Samantha?" he asked, distracted.

"Just you, me, my father, Marvin, and some unsuspecting tourists."

"Your father?" His voice was sharp.

"Yes. He was the one who left it in this room."

"I was sure that you had put it here," he said. "I assumed that this was your inheritance, which you were trying to keep a secret from the world. I was trying to be polite and not mention it."

"You give me too much credit."

"Let's keep this matter between us, shall we?"

I looked around. "Who else am I going to tell?"

He didn't answer. He returned to the book. Focused men are painfully attractive. I asked him what he was looking for, but my voice seemed lost on him. He did not look up again until he had his finger on a specific page. Then he passed me the text.

"There," he said, urgently. "Read."

I took the book from him. My father had underlined and highlighted the entire page, as he had done with several other sections of this book. It was the moment when Jane shows Rochester three of her original watercolors. I read the description of the first, as I was told.

The first represented clouds low and livid . . . there was no land. One gleam of light lifted into relief a half-submerged mast, on which sat a cormorant, dark and large, with wings flecked with foam; its beak held a gold bracelet, set with gems . . . Sinking below the bird and the mast, a drowned corpse glanced through the green water; a fair arm was the only limb clearly visible, whence the bracelet had been washed or torn.

I glanced up at Orville, eyes wide.

"Do you see the problem now?" he asked.

I looked up at the painting, then back at the book, then back at the painting. "Problem?" I echoed. "This is great news."

I felt like a child in one of those implausible Christmas movies, when she wishes for something hard enough, and suddenly there it comes, barreling down the chimney. This was a literary magic trick. There they were, the book and the painting, connected by an invisible string. The words had materialized into a solid reality in front of us.

"Please remove that possessed expression from your face," said Orville.

I didn't respond. I was finding it difficult to concentrate. Fictional Jane Eyre had painted a painting, and there it was, in front of me. That *exact* painting. Immediately, I looked at the other books on the shelf. *Agnes Grey*. *Wuthering Heights*. *The Tenant of Wildfell Hall*. They were no longer books but eager soldiers who were waiting to be called to the front lines. They were looking at me with an expression that said, *What took you so long?*

Would all of Jane Eyre's watercolors erupt from the page? And Helen Graham's paintings, too—would they tumble out of the book, in one giant burst of smoke? Was I also to find the baby bird from *Agnes Grey*? Bertha's scarf from *Jane Eyre*? The tombstone from *Wuthering Heights*? The possibilities were endless. Somewhere in the distance, I could almost see my father clapping his hands.

"Tell me what you're thinking," Orville demanded.

"I'm thinking of what Anne's painting is doing in Charlotte's book."

"Pardon?"

"I was right. Charlotte was a thief."

"Don't jump to irrational conclusions," said Orville. "This is just a painting."

"Why aren't you more excited?" I said. "Do you think this is the Warnings of Experience?"

"I'd prefer it if you forgot all about this and went to bed."

"It's seven."

"I need to go out of town." Orville gathered his gloves and hat. He moved to the door.

"Why are you angry?" I asked.

"I would just prefer not to see you . . . in this way."

"What way is that?"

He lifted his overnight bag onto his shoulder. "Would you promise me not to do anything foolish? This is only a painting. Remember that. Say it to yourself over and over again. 'It's just a painting.'"

I raised my eyebrows. One of Orville's hands was on the doorknob; the other was dangling awkwardly by his side. He looked like a father whose child was about to enter the 1970s.

When I didn't respond, he said: "Well. I suppose I have said sufficient."

The door clicked shut on his way out.

CHAPTER 14

"A frankenstorm," as it was being called, hit England that weekend. The London *Times* called it the storm of the year, even more so than the storm of the year we had experienced earlier that year. Meteorologists from every major station were dishing out advice regarding flood safety; local stores ran out of flashlights; bottled water became more expensive than my college tuition.

I caught the last train north to Haworth, the hometown of the Brontës. It was a stupid idea, given the headlines, but I was desperate to escape. The last two days had not been kind to me. Old College had rapidly turned into my father's complicated tomb. After my chat with Orville, I'd spent the rest of the week scouring the campus for any other paintings, initials, or wall carvings I had missed in the past few months. I sought deserted corridors of the library; I rummaged through book collections in damp dormitory basements; I studied campus maps, monuments, mugs, drawings, doodles, scribbles, globes, ashtrays, chairs, tables, rugs, bathroom signs, carpet stains. Nothing seemed interesting, or even old, and certainly none of it screamed, "Warnings of Experience." In desperation, I called Hans, who was normally a wealth of useless college history, but this time, he asked too many questions in return. *I don't understand. Why are you doing this? What are you looking for? What is going on?* I didn't answer. As the days passed and it became clear that Oxford held no more clues for me, I found myself dwelling more and more on the Brontë

Parsonage. My father had once promised me that we would go there someday. Maybe he'd had a special reason in mind—like he had buried something in one of the old graves, or stashed something underneath a conveniently overlooked carpet. Both were equally unlikely, but I had run out of options. It was Haworth or Bust.

The thinning, bleak landscape suggested that we were approaching the north of England. I folded up the newspaper, which told tales of dying bookstores and accused war criminals. The train was not crowded, and at the other end of the car, a British woman was barking instructions to her son, demanding that he fill his bathtub with drinking water. *You remember what happened last year, right? Henry, are you even listening to me? Henry!*

The three-hour train ride to Leeds dropped me off in time to board the old and crumbling Keighley & Worth Valley Railway. The woman on the loudspeaker told us that we were riding on a historic, restored railway, which I might recognize had I ever seen *Sherlock Holmes*, *Sons and Lovers*, or *Poirot*. I wondered if the Keighley & Worth Valley Railway had also been the setting for *Dawn of the Dead, Daughters of Darkness*, or *The Omen*. Outside the windows, a skeletal forest stretched for miles, limbs entangled like some terrible battle had erupted but had been frozen in place. Eventually the forest thinned, and in its place appeared a vast, desolate countryside. The white sheets of land had a grasping enormity to them, the kind that had been killing people silently for centuries. We had, at last, arrived at the moors.

When the train stopped thirty minutes later, I followed the few lone passengers outside. Haworth was a dump. Old, lonely houses pressed against each other, shoulder to shoulder. In anticipation of the storm, shop windows were already bolted shut, and piles of sandbags had appeared on every sidewalk. There must have been no more flashlights for sale, because a stringy brunette walked past clutching a lantern.

My phone was dead, which meant my GPS was dead too. My hotel was to the east, I believed, but where were the taxis? Didn't train stations come with taxis? *Taxi? Taxi?* I walked along the silent streets, searching for a helpful local. I found a park, but no people. A closed coffee shop, but no people. The residents of Haworth must have already retreated into the safe havens of their tidy English homes. The only thing moving was a single page of a newspaper drifting past like a used tissue.

Were the Brontës shitting me? There was nothing charming or romantic about this prehistoric hellhole. I walked until I found myself on the top of a small hill overlooking the moors. The earth was blue and cold, the sky a suffocating gray. I looked out at the empty vastness. The rolling land stared back at me with cruel ambivalence.

Then, right there, when I turned around—a taxi. It was rolling down the street like an old cowboy. I raised a hand. When the car reached me, the window lowered to reveal a pirate-eyed man with a square jaw and an expression that seemed to say, *Laura? She's been dead for years.*

I said, "The Brontë Parsonage, please."

"Might be that the roads are closed, love."

Actually, I have no idea what he said. His accent was nearly impossible to understand. Northern.

I said: "How fast can you get there?"

He looked me over. "Get in."

I did as I was told. The cab grumbled into motion. I gave him the address and we crept down the old streets, passing the occasional loose-leaf advert for the Haworth West Lane Baptist Amateur Operatic Society. We passed small British houses, small British cars, and a bleak, gray park. A light snow had started to fall, which stuck to the ground and looked like the coarse, matted-down hair of a very sick dog. After only a few minutes, the car lurched to a halt, and the driver told me he could take me no farther due to flooding. We were close, he said. I paid the man his unreasonable sum and quitted the cab. My driver reversed down the old road until he was out of sight.

I wrapped my scarf tighter around myself. I didn't see anything but a decrepit cobblestone street spotted with puddles. I walked up the small path, past an old church whose low, broad tower was a gray beam against a grayer sky. It seemed familiar for reasons I could not place. I turned a corner, and there—suddenly, in front of me—was the Brontë Parsonage.

I would have recognized it anywhere: my ancestral home. Dad used to have a framed pen-and-ink sketch of it hanging above his bed, drawn by his great-grandfather Ernie. The building itself was gray and boxlike, with cookie-cutter, asylum windows. A gust hit me from the side, and a quiet female voice burst unannounced into my mind:

> *The house is old, the trees are bare,*
> *Moonless above bends twilight's dome;*
> *But what on earth is half so dear—*
> *So longed for—as the hearth of home?*

Up close, the house was strangely small and quiet, as though it had been biding its time for centuries. I walked up the old, forgotten path and tried to imagine the Brontës doing the same. *This* is what Emily did—and *this*, and *this*. Yet the effort of resuscitating my relatives was exhausting. I had a feeling that Emily did not want to be awakened. Somewhere, I just knew, she was giving me the finger.

I knocked on the front door. No response. The wind behind me was sharp and opinionated. I knocked again, and again. Would I have to break into another building? Twice more, and to my relief, the door flew open. On the other side was Sir John Booker. In a Quaker-ish black coat and a red scarf tied around his neck, he looked like he had walked here straight from *The Red Badge of Courage*.

"Are you out of your mind?" he snapped.

"I'm the new governess."

"There's a storm, Miss Whipple. I wasn't expecting you'd actually travel all this way."

"Well, I'm here."

"Have you ever experienced real weather?"

"You forget I was raised in Boston."

"This isn't Bermuda; this is the north of England."

"If you think Boston is Bermuda, you've clearly never been there."

"We are closing the parsonage shortly."

"I'll be quick."

I walked past him, into a small, clean lobby. I saw hardwood floors, newly painted walls, and a vase that could have come from IKEA. The house did not smell as old or stale as I would have hoped. In fact, it had been very well maintained. The floors were much too glossy. We might have been standing inside the fixer-upper of a young California golf couple.

I looked around. "Poignant."

Sir John glared at me. He had huge bat eyes. I had the feeling that he was not seeing a pale brunette with dripping boots—he was seeing a slightly balding man with glasses, an ill-fitting coat, and three fake names. I wondered when, exactly, Dad had visited.

Sir John forced a polite little expression onto his face. On the pop-up plastic table by the front door, I saw stacks of his new book. A few were upright and propped open, as if begging for money.

"Did you bring the novels, Samantha?" he asked.

"I brought *The Tenant of Wildfell Hall*."

"I'd like to see it."

"How about a tour first?"

His mouth twitched. His hands were spotted and gray, and they were shaking, ever so slightly. He looked older than when we'd last met, the kind of old that makes you unsure if the person can hear anything you say, so you want to say something outrageous just to find out.

"What is it that you're looking for here?" he asked.

"Whatever my dad found, when he visited."

Sir John gave a small tilt of his head but didn't say anything. Without another word, he turned to his right and opened the closed door. I dropped my bag and followed him, heart racing. We ducked inside a small, darkened parlor, decorated with a bloodred carpet and old-lady wallpaper. Lord, here it was! The gloomy, dramatic room where the three girls had written their novels. I had been in this room a thousand times in my own mind. It was a modest chamber that boasted a fireplace, three empty chairs, and a square card table. Emily had died on the black couch over by the back wall, right underneath the portrait of her brother, Branwell. I took a deep breath, as if I might be able to inhale all the fights and laughter and brilliance that had transpired in here. But this room was nothing like I'd imagined. It was much too quiet, and the smell of hand sanitizer caught me off guard. There was little to make me think we hadn't walked into an old mental institution.

I waited for grand and magical things to happen. Dad? Dad? Where was my dad? Had he left me any notes, riddles? *Come on, Dad—I'm here! Where are you?* I scanned the room for bits and pieces of him. Had he scratched something into the wall? Stashed something behind the couch? Sir John let me make a small sweep of the room. Everything was clean. Pristine. I felt a growing despair. Emily, Charlotte, and Anne had never seemed further away. I turned to Sir John, mouth slightly open. He stared at me coolly. I suppose I had discovered his secret. This house was dead.

Silently, I followed him out of the room. The tour of the upstairs was perfunctory and brief, like an irrelevant autopsy. Sir John let me pop my head into various bedrooms like a dog he was letting lead him to the scene of the crime (that is, before he shot the dog). Patrick

Brontë's room was small and tidy, featuring a handsome painting and a large, square window, out of which, I learned, he used to fire his guns every morning. The girls' old playroom was a dimly lit rectangle that did not receive much in the way of natural light. The window ledge housed a variety of mildewed books, whose varying states of dilapidation proved them to have been well used. Here were the authors and books that fashioned the Brontës' minds: Shelley. Byron. Sir Walter Scott. The Bible. To my displeasure, I did not find a single snoopworthy nook, cranny, attic, or secret passageway, or even one loose floorboard. All I found was one quill, which was arranged just so on Emily's old desk, as if someone were going to come back looking for it.

Charlotte's room was the dullest. Its only notable features were the bed in which she'd died, and a headless mannequin in the middle of the room, which was wearing an old, boxy dress, and lived in a thick, protective glass case. Nothing, it seemed, could be touched. Cases surrounded all of the notebooks on display. Sir John waited patiently as I made a thorough inspection of everything. I was hoping to find at least one piece of evidence that would point to the fire that had long ago ravaged this room—charring on the walls, perhaps, or a commemorative plaque. But I found nothing out of the ordinary. The walls must have been rebuilt in the last century, the scars washed away with time. Or, perhaps the fire I was so quick to associate with Charlotte had never had anything to do with her in the first place. What a thought.

Finally, I turned back to Sir John. "This is just terrible."

"What were you expecting?" he asked.

"Drama."

"You read too many novels."

"So did they."

I had always assumed that my relatives would be alive in this home, somehow, and that the job of a curator was to keep their ghosts as happy and well fed as possible. I was wrong. The parsonage was standing here only thanks to a century of life support. Sir John tended to it as he would a sick relative whose illness was worse than anyone knew. The excitement I'd felt earlier had melted off me. I was just a little girl in a big house, pretending that it was the other way around. I would not be finding the Warnings of Experience today. I would not even be finding the Brontë Parsonage.

I said, "You left Cambridge for *this?*"

It was the wrong thing to say, of course, but in my defense, it had sounded better in my head.

Sir John's eyes narrowed. "People do many things out of passion."

The word *passion* sounded foreign coming out of his graying mask of a face.

"I wonder what my father thought when he saw all of this," I said.

Sir John gave a bark of laughter. "Is that what he told you, that he came here?"

"Yes—why?"

"Your father never set foot in the parsonage. It was a matter of principle, he said."

I stopped. "But he told me I'd find him here."

"Your father said many things that were not true."

He leaned back against the doorframe. I fell silent. A familiar, exhausted anger welled up inside of me, directed at the invisible man with glasses and three fake names, and at his incurably gullible daughter. I tried to recall the exact conversations we'd had about this house, and found that the more I tried to remember, the fuzzier the memories became. Were they real at all, or had I just planted them there, years after the fact? It was becoming unclear to me which one of us had been the bigger liar. Who was the real fiction writer: Dad, or me?

Carefully, I reached into my purse and pulled out *The Tenant of Wildfell Hall*. I looked at it only a moment, then handed it to Sir John in an act of surrender.

It was over an hour before I could come downstairs again. I sat against Anne Brontë's old wall like a misbehaved child on time-out, who was waiting for her sisters to notice that she was pouting. I closed my eyes and strained to hear the conversations that had played out in this room one hundred and sixty-seven years earlier. But my imagination was not terribly advanced, and all I could hear was the soft whimpers from someplace deep inside my own torso. My body seemed to understand what my mind could not grasp yet: I was truly alone.

By the time I returned downstairs, it was almost dark. Sir John was sitting in the old chair by the front door. He was picking his fingernails. *Tenant* was resting on the table next to him like a sleeping tiger, next to dozens of wishful *Vast Brontë Estates*. I went to stand by a dirty glass window overlooking the graveyard. The storm had decided to get its act together. The beginnings of a white flurry swarmed around us like lost and frenzied shoppers.

"Well?" I said to the window. "What did you think of *Tenant*? Did it answer anything for you?"

"Your father's notes are incomprehensible," said Sir John, from behind me. He did not hide disappointment well; he sounded like a small boy who had just discovered he was not destined to be tall.

"I warned you about that," I said.

"The only note of his that I can even read is on the last page, where he wrote: *Econ 101*."

"Did he write that? I didn't make it to the end of the book this time."

"Does it mean anything to you?"

"To *me*, or to my father?"

"To your father, of course."

I turned around and pursed my lips. All I was, apparently, was a conduit of information between the living and the dead. No one had ever bothered to listen to my opinion—not Sir John, not Orville, and at times, not even Dad.

I said, "You should have talked to him yourself."

"I told you," he said. "He was impossible to get ahold of."

"You should have tried using smoke signals. He liked those."

Sir John glared at me. It was astonishing how sociable I felt in comparison with him. I understood his frustration, though. This copy of *Tenant* had solved no mysteries for him.

"Can I ask you something?" I said. Outside, the wind was howling at the house with extremely bad manners. "What ever happened to that Anne Brontë watercolor you discovered? Remember—the discovery that changed your life? You told me about it when we met. Is it here? I'd like to see it."

He pointed to the nearest copy of his magnum opus, *The Vast Brontë Estate*, which was resting with its fifty unloved brothers and sisters.

"Page two seventy-five," he said.

I walked to the table and picked up the nearest book. It was glossy and smelled of chemicals. I found the page and cracked open the spine.

"*Painting of Two Turtledoves?*" I said, looking up. "Is this it?"

Sir John nodded.

I inspected the page. Underneath the italicized title was a copy of a pretty little painting—a snapshot of two birds sitting on a branch above a young, blue-eyed girl. It was surprisingly upbeat for an original Anne. The birds were borderline cute. The girl was plump and vaguely sexual. One sleeve of her dress had fallen, exposing an ivory shoulder. I ran my finger along the shiny page. Midway through, I stopped. My eyes narrowed. The scene looked awfully familiar. I looked at Sir John, who was staring out at the storm, then back at the page. I was sure that I had seen this scene somewhere before—hadn't I? Maybe I had imagined it. Or had I perhaps *read* it?

Silently, without disturbing my surly companion, I put the book down and picked up *The Tenant of Wildfell Hall*. I flipped through the pages expertly, as Orville might have done. There, on page one hundred and twenty-one, I found a passage I recognized. I had read it only a few weeks ago, on the train to Paris. My father had highlighted the paragraph in pink.

> *I had ventured to give more of the bright verdure of spring or early sum-mer to the grass and foliage than is commonly attempted in painting. The scene represented was an open glade in a wood. . . . Upon this bough, that stood out in bold relief against the somber firs, was seated an amorous pair of turtledoves, whose soft sad-colored plumage afforded a contrast of another nature; and beneath it a young girl was kneeling on the daisy-spangled turf, with head thrown back and masses of fair hair falling on her shoulders. . . .*

I snapped the book shut.

Sir John glanced at me. "Is something the matter?"

"No," I squeaked.

He returned his gaze to the storm outside, which was slapping disorganized snow against the headstones. I waited, but nothing happened. Had Sir John, the Great Sir John, failed to see the resemblance between the passage and the sketch? Was it too simple, too obvious? It was right in front of his nose.

I reached for *The Vast Brontë Estate* and opened it back up discreetly. The two turtledoves stared innocently up at me. Anne must not have painted this with the intention of having anyone else see it. She had barely colored within the lines. There was a stray piece of green over here, a line of blue over there. The birds, too, looked fat and happy. Possibly drunk. Were they grinning? The more I stared at the girl, the more radiant she appeared. She might have just emerged from a Turkish bath. She and those birds looked like they were sharing a joke and couldn't quite contain themselves.

I would have to give Sir John a bit more credit—this painting was of no little significance. In *Tenant*, when Helen paints this picture, she is a love-addled teenager who is daydreaming of her (pre-alcoholic) dream man, Arthur Huntingdon. In a scene suspiciously similar to one of Jane Eyre's first encounters with Edward Rochester, Arthur walks in and stumbles upon Helen's secret stash of unfinished sketches. He begs to see them. "I never let anyone see them," Helen weakly responds before grudgingly showing him a self-portrait. Arthur is too intrigued for her comfort. Out of terror that he might show her work to other people, she snatches the drawing from him and tosses it into the fire. (Indisputably an Emily Brontë move.) There is only one explanation for Helen's behavior: her sketches are a reflection of her most private self, expressing sentiments that she would never expose to the world. Anne Brontë, the original artist of Helen's painting, must have felt the same way. Her sketches comprised a visual diary, one that would never have been sent to publishers around London. I closed the book.

"How did you recognize this as Anne's painting?" I asked. "It looks different from everything else she painted."

"Stylistically, it is the same."

I nodded. "Can I see it up close, please?"

"Pardon?"

"This watercolor. I'd love to see it."

"The parsonage is closing."

"It will only take a moment."

A pause. "It's not here."

"Where is it?"

"It's in its logical place."

"A more logical place than the Brontë museum?"

"You're very irritating, Miss Whipple."

He stood and turned to face the back window. His body was thin. With his sleeves rolled up, I could see every detail in his arms, which were covered with ropy veins and signs of decay. I walked around so that I was standing right in front of him.

"Well then—where is it?"

"Where is what?"

"The painting. Did you give it back to the man who owned it? What was his name—Elmes?"

"He asked me to see to it for him."

I paused. "Was there a knife at his throat when he said this?"

Sir John's eyes narrowed. "I beg your pardon?"

I swallowed. "Sorry."

"What are you insinuating?"

"Nothing."

We paused.

"Or—" I said.

"Out with it."

"Well—why would he give it to you if it's so valuable?"

"Not everyone is as selfish as your father was. He recognized that relics such as that painting should be in the hands of a qualified historian."

"So do *you* have it, then?"

"Why does it matter to you?"

"Because this is *my* family."

The words tumbled out of me with more verve than I'd anticipated. I had meant to put the emphasis on *family*, not *my*—but, well, there you had it. I had never been much for possessiveness, but I suddenly couldn't help but feel like these were *my* relatives, *my* story, and maybe even my house, too, that Sir John had rudely invaded, like it was the Ardennes.

Sir John's lip curled. "How similar you are to your father."

"What did you do with the painting, sir?" I pressed.

"I had to put it in the hands of someone who would appreciate and take care of it. Edward Elmes had no idea what this sketch was worth."

"And how much was it worth?"

"Nearly a million British pounds."

My eyes widened.

"There are people who would pay," he said.

"So that's what you did?" I asked. "You cashed in? You stripped it and sold it for parts?"

"I am an academic, not a pirate."

"Which means you probably needed the money."

His gaze turned brutish. "I will not be insulted like this. You may collect your belongings."

"I'm right, then?" I pestered. "No wonder my father didn't trust you. I bet you wanted to hunt down every single possession the Brontës ever owned, only to auction everything off. He was in the business of resurrecting his relatives; you were busy prostituting them."

"Don't be crude, Samantha, it's very unbecoming," Sir John said. "And to ease your overly inquisitive little mind, it was only the *one* painting, which would have been severely damaged had it been left above Edward's decrepit fireplace any longer. The man who now owns it is one of the premier art collectors in the country. It is in very, very safe hands. There. Has your curiosity been satisfied?"

"The man who bought it—is he a gravedigger, too?" I asked.

Sir John straightened his scarf. "The term you're looking for, Samantha," he said with a note of finality, "is *grave robber*."

I pressed my lips together. He walked straight past me, to the coat-rack. It bothered me that he wasn't more ashamed. Professors were supposed to be bastions of intellectual integrity, forces to be revered by friends and enemies alike. They weren't supposed to think of money, the same way they weren't supposed to think of women.

"Where will you stay tonight?" Sir John asked, changing the subject. He didn't seem to care what I thought of him at all—a talent I wished I could have stolen from him.

I crossed my arms. "I'm not sure. Some bed-and-breakfast."

To be honest, I had no idea where I was supposed to go. My phone was dead, and the storm was bellowing. I could hide away in this house, maybe, or else I could just wander out into the storm and die on the moors, like a true Romantic.

"You will never find a taxi," Sir John said.

"Don't be dramatic."

I brushed past him and opened the front door. A gust of frosty wind greeted me like a shock wave. I squinted. It was no longer light, but I still could make out the front yard, which was cupcaked in snow. He was right. I would never find a taxi. I shut the door.

We were silent. Sir John looked severely displeased, like a father whose duties disgusted him. He let out a breath. "I have guest quarters at my home, should you require them."

I paused. He paused. He seemed as unhappy with the prospect as I was. After all the insults I had just thrown at him, his magnanimity made me feel somewhat guilty.

I glanced behind me. "Maybe I should just stay here."

"You cannot stay here."

"I'll burrow under the carpet like Emily Brontë."

"Emily Brontë did not burrow under carpets."

"That's what you think."

He threw on his coat. "Make up your mind. Will you stay with me, or will you try your luck on the streets?"

I didn't answer.

He said, "Well?"

"I'm thinking it over."

He began fiddling with his keys. *No, no, no.* I did not want to spend an entire evening with Sir John. But when a blast of snow thumped against the door, I realized the decision was out of my hands.

I let out a breath. "How do we get there?"

He threw open the door. "We walk."

Sir John's home was close to the parsonage, yet it took us over thirty minutes to make it there, on account of how slowly he moved and how easily the storm confused him. Outside of a classroom, his disorientation was severe. More than once, he stopped where he was and sniffed the air like an old lion who knew he would one day collapse and be consumed by a rival pride. Cautiously, I offered him a steadying hand. He did not say anything, but his grip on my arm was tight.

His home was a squat, secluded house on top of a small lump of the moors. Next to nothing and no one, it was the sort of house you'd only buy if you were the curator of the Brontë Parsonage (and divorced). In the dim outside lights, the snow-covered shrubs looked like paws poking out of the padded white earth. We were thoroughly soaked.

The walk had not been kind to Sir John, who now looked a century and a half old. He took his time locating his keys. On his front stoop, I noticed a miniature Christmas village and several dead plants. When he shoved the door open, a shingle dropped off the wall.

"Leave it," he barked.

I left it. We stamped the snow off our boots and walked inside, where I immediately let out a small but healthy scream. There, pinned against the opposite wall of the narrow foyer, was a moose head. It stared at me with a quizzical expression that seemed to say, *I died disastrously in Alaska.*

I said, "Who shot this?"

"One of my sons."

"I didn't know people still hunted moose."

"They do."

"How many do you have?" I asked.

"Moose?"

"Sons."

"Seven."

Seven! I left my shoes where Sir John had put his, then shed my jacket and hung it on the wall. I found it difficult to imagine Sir John with an entire von Trapp family's worth of children. Where had they all come from? Certainly he wasn't the sort of man who thought about procreation. How savage.

I dropped my duffel bag and followed him into his living room. It was damp and smelled of tuna and old dog. The décor was less majestic than I would have anticipated. Half of me thought I would find an entire stash of stolen art, a bureau filled with awards and trophies, or at least a bust of his own head. But all I found in the center of the room was a dilapidated orange couch, awkwardly stationed there as though waiting for its final paycheck. There was a square card table and four old chairs. I recognized the novel on the table: *Peaches of Mirth*.

I looked up. "I didn't know you read my father's novels."

This one, I remembered, was Dad's sequel to *The Grapes of Wrath*. Sir John didn't respond. He just took a freshly poured drink to the couch, and wilted into his seat. He was panting in a series of short leaks. With each breath it looked like his long, lanky body might fold over like a piece of scrap paper. I sat on one of the chairs across from him. The fireplace was not lit, nor did Sir John seem to have any intention of putting it to use. Would there be a place to dry off? I thought I could feel the onset of pneumonia.

We waited in silence. All I could hear was the ticking of a clock that I couldn't see. I looked around the squalor of the little room and didn't tell Sir John what I was thinking, which was that he must have squandered all the dough he got from that original Anne Brontë painting. I bit my tongue.

There was a loud crashing noise upstairs. Someone said, "Is that you?" Sir John didn't react.

"Is someone else here?" I asked, motioning upstairs.

"My youngest."

"Is he the one who shot the moose?"

No answer. I wondered if he had even heard me. The stomping upstairs grew louder and louder, until suddenly I heard a series of bearlike footsteps pounding down the staircase. I turned around just in time to see a grown man barreling into the room. Six and a half feet tall, dark hair, heavy eyebrows. I gasped.

There—right there—was James Timothy Orville III.

No. And yet . . . ? No. My mouth fell open. My professor was wearing sweatpants and bright red socks, and his T-shirt—not quite long enough for his torso—exposed the bottom ribbon of a white, marbled stomach. I looked him over from head to toe, wondering if this could in fact be his impressive stunt double. But no—I saw the familiar scar on his right arm, the acne scars on his forehead, the scowl on his face. Right now that scowl lifted and in its place erupted openmouthed, wide-eyed shock. He might have just seen the bloody ghost of Achilles. We suffered a silence worthy of divorce.

Sir John looked at me. "Meet my son James."

There was no response from Orville and I gave a small curtsy to no one in particular. My cheeks burned. I found myself staring at him as I would an arresting seascape.

"James, James," I said. "What a familiar ring."

Orville recovered from his shock faster than I did. His face was impassive but his voice was pleasant.

"Hello, Samantha," he said.

His father—God, was he really?—frowned between us. "You two know each other?"

Orville seemed to be picking his words carefully. "This—that is—this is one of my students, Father."

One of his students. Was that all that I was? I wanted to be his best student, his only student, his wife-student. A look passed between father and son, and it was not a polite one. They seemed to be acknowledging a tapestry of unspoken emotions.

"I see," Sir John said briskly. "The daughter of Tristan Whipple? How strange that you neglected to mention her before, Jimmy."

Orville gave an innocent smile, but a look of hostility swept between them. He looked so much like his father just then that I wondered how I had never noticed the similarity before. Big forehead, big chin. Sir John straightened and turned to me not as an academic, but as a somewhat annoying parent.

"Jimmy is the youngest tenured faculty member in one hundred years," he said.

I nodded. "That must have been tough, going through puberty and a career at the same time."

Orville ignored me and turned to his father. "What kept you so long? You look terrible."

"I had to escort the lady home," said Sir John, with a cough.

"I told you I would come and get you."

"I am not quite so ancient yet, my boy."

"Let's get you changed."

"I can do it myself."

"Dad—"

"Enough."

The two of them fell silent. Orville moved to help his father to a standing position. The old man uttered a meek protestation but let his son lift him to his feet. He looked so very old. I turned away. I realized that Sir John had not invited me over because he had a spare guest room. He simply could not have made it home by himself.

I caught his eye. In that moment, as if he knew my heart was breaking, his expression changed. His near-black eyes, one of the last parts of his body to survive the onset of age, narrowed in resentment. He looked me over from navel to neck.

"You're nothing like Jimmy's last girl," he said.

I said, "Pardon?"

Orville urged his father toward the staircase. "Come, I'll help you."

"What was her name again?" asked Sir John, in a voice that let us know he remembered the name perfectly well. "Some rabbit-faced blonde. German."

I raised my eyebrows intentionally, hoping that Orville would see them and want to explain. But he looked at me and snapped: "Kitchen. Meet me there."

"Was it Abigail something?" Sir John said. But Orville was already helping his father mount the stairs. The conversation, for the time being, was over.

⁂

The kitchen was crowded and disorganized, with dark tiles and bright curtains. An old washing machine and dryer rattled fiercely in the corner like two enthusiastic marimbas. I tripped on a shoe on my way inside. Seven. Seven children. Family photos covered nearly every free inch of wall space, all featuring seven different versions of the same face. It was a strange place for photos. Sir John either wanted them where he could see them, or where he couldn't see them. In the largest photo—the one above the sink—all seven boys were together, wearing bow ties and school uniforms, and ordered by height and age. It looked like the entire crop of sons had been conceived in an Excel spreadsheet.

Orville returned fifteen minutes later. He was panting slightly.

I thought of the German girl. *Rabbit-faced.* What did that mean, exactly? I envisioned an orchard of freckles (the cute kind) and bright turquoise eyes. Orville must have hunted more than moose.

"Which one is you?" I asked, motioning to the family photo, even though he didn't need to answer. I already recognized him. He was the smallest one, with protruding ears, a crooked little-boy tie, and big fish lips that had apparently thinned with age and fatigue. He was shorter than the rest of his strapping brothers, and stood in the shade of six older men.

The new, thin-lipped Orville in front of me opened the refrigerator, revealing a half-empty shelf filled primarily with beer and baking soda.

"How do you like your eggs, Sam?"

"Over easy," I said. "Jimmy."

He took out a carton of eggs and smacked it on the counter. I'm sure several cracked. He pulled a pan out from the rack above him. The muscles underneath his T-shirt were thick and bloated, and I watched them in mild fascination. I wondered how Orville could walk around this house without a jacket. I was shivering.

"So," I said, wrapping my arms tightly around myself. "That's your dad."

"Yes, that is my father."

"You never told me he was my father's nemesis. Some people might find that suspiciously interesting."

"You never asked."

"He lives alone?"

"My parents split when I was eighteen."

"And you're closer to your mother than to your father?"

"I didn't say that."

He turned on the stove. Small purple flames licked the sides of the rusty old pan. Instinctively, I took a step back. In went a square of butter and then eight eggs, one after the other. Orville swirled them slightly with his index finger, then wiped his hands on his pants. I couldn't decide if he was angry or disinterested, and it concerned me that he could have the same expression for both.

"You will kindly remember that I asked you not to do anything foolish," he said. "Why did you come here?"

"What would you have me do, sit home and knit?"

The dryer, as if on cue, stopped. Orville crossed the room and yanked open its small, round door. He tossed me a gray V-neck and a pair of sweatpants.

"Take these," he said. "Stay warm."

The clothes smelled like him, but I couldn't make out exactly what that scent was. A meadow? Fresh parchment? Sweat? It was hard to say. I felt nostalgic, for reasons I didn't immediately understand.

"Thank you," I said. "Look west."

He turned away and I peeled off my sweater and shirt, which had been clinging to my body like leeches. I slipped on Orville's soft cotton T-shirt. I wondered what sort of man took care to buy such soft things, and if this really hadn't been purchased by a cotton-loving lady, and if so, I wondered which lady had bought it for him, and did that lady have a gaggle of freckles and turquoise eyes? I yanked off my jeans and kicked them into a corner.

"You're mumbling," Orville said with his back facing me. "What are you thinking of?"

"The green-eyed monster which mocks the meat it feeds on."

"Pardon?"

"I'm hungry. Is this dinner?"

Orville took out a spatula. Apparently "over easy" was too hard, because he started scrambling the eggs, carefully pulling them apart the way one might arrange toy battleships.

"I trust you've kept the matter of the painting in your room between us?" he said.

"Certainly."

"My father knows nothing?"

"Nothing."

The eggs smelled good. I pulled on the oversize sweatpants, which were worn in several places.

"There, I'm done," I said. "You can turn around now."

"Thank you."

"If you don't mind my asking, don't you find it cruel to keep your father from something he's probably wanted for the last twenty years?"

Orville turned to face me. "I do not believe in Pyrrhic victories."

"To be honest, sir, I've never known what that means."

He switched off the stove. "Ask your father."

Dinner was a quiet, desultory sort of affair. We sat at the card table and consumed Orville's varied culinary creations: eggs, tuna, olives, beer. I learned several things. Both father and son loved *The Philadelphia Story*; Sir John hated gum-chewers and used the word *tintinnabulation*; Orville was the fifth son to follow his parents into academia and the only one to willfully adopt his mother's surname. I noticed that Sir John had placed *The Tenant of Wildfell Hall* on the table. It rested between us like a small bomb.

Halfway through the meal, Sir John put down his fork. "Are you seeing anyone, Samantha?"

My eyes flew open. The eggs were all gone and I was working my way through Orville's *tuna impromptu*.

I said, "Sorry?"

"Are there any leading men in your life?"

"Several, but they're all fictional."

He wasn't smiling. "A girl as lovely as you? That surprises me."

I tried not to be insulted. When men said "lovely" in that tone of voice, it meant they didn't think you were lovely at all.

I said, "I suppose I don't understand men."

"Is that because you can't see how anything could possibly be so simple?"

He looked at me as though I was missing something obvious. Orville was eating and did not look up. My presence had caused a rift between my two dinner dates. They rarely looked each other in the eye, and when they did, it was to exchange a lingering, hardened expression. Were they allies, or at odds? It was very Greek.

Sir John pressed the subject. "Do you mean to tell me that in the most vibrant intellectual epicenter of the Western world, you haven't found one source of temptation?"

I said, "I have learned to fight against temptation, sir."

"James, did you hear that?" Sir John said to his son with a bemused smile. "Samantha fights against temptation."

"I heard that," said Orville.

"Tell me," Sir John said. "Do they allow you back in the dining hall these days?"

Orville slapped down his napkin. "Surely we can find something more interesting to discuss."

There was a moment's pause. Sir John's white hair looked static, like barbed wire.

"Very well," he said. His tone was unhurried, but there was an edge in it. He turned to me. "What are you fond of discussing, Samantha?"

I was sure that by *fond*, he meant *capable*.

Before I could answer, he said: "When Jimmy was young, we used to sit after dinner and discuss the invention of the paperback."

I said, "Until I was eight or nine, my father let me believe that the paperback was a type of whale."

There was no answer. Our forks screeched against the plates.

I motioned to the book on the table. "Perhaps we can discuss *The Tenant of Wildfell Hall*," I offered. "Sir John, you said months ago that you could help me understand it."

"No," Orville interjected. "It's impolite to discuss literature at the dinner table."

But Sir John looked pleased. He reached for the book.

"Jimmy used to *love* the Brontës, Samantha," he said. "I remember him sitting at our old dining room table in London, just like you are now, spouting a hundred misguided theories that we later had to correct. Remember, Jimmy, how you used to think Emily Brontë was bisexual? Do you remember?" He let out a crack of laughter. "Well, Jimmy, perhaps you'd like to be the first to offer your . . . shall we say . . . expertise."

"Jimmy" did not look amused. He shut his mouth like a small animal. For a moment, I didn't think either of them registered me at all. They looked like they might be about to snuff each other out.

"Samantha's father wrote in the margins, 'Econ 101,'" said Sir John.

"What of it?" said Orville.

"That's how Americans refer to elementary economics."

"I understand the reference, Dad."

Sir John tossed him the book like a final exam. "Why don't you give it your best go."

Orville's nostrils flared. I was terribly disoriented. I had never seen my professor as the student, with another man as his superior. I had an image of his sad little childhood: a big-eared boy cornered at a small table, bullied into reciting Proust. Orville did not pick up the book. Instead, he turned to me and released a long breath.

"Do you remember Elizabeth Langland, Samantha?"

I said, "No."

"We read her essays together."

"Did we? I can't remember."

Sir John was wearing an amused smile. He leaned back in his chair and crossed his arms. An unspoken question seemed to pass between him and his son: Was Orville a good teacher, or a bad one?

Orville cleared his throat. "What I think your father meant, Samantha, is that the book can be seen as a reflection of the emerging nineteenth-century economy. Helen has a trade; she is a professional artist. Gilbert is also a businessman, though his commodity is information. He defines the exchange of simple stories in economic terms. 'If the coin suits you, tell me so, and I'll send you the rest at my leisure. You would rather remain my creditor than stuff your purse with such ungainly, heavy pieces—tell me still, and I'll pardon your bad taste, and willingly keep the treasure to myself.' Don't bother looking it up, Father; the quote is correct. 'Treasure,' for the first time, can be someone's personal narrative. Helen herself is a 'treasure'—something to be bought, sold, or perhaps won."

He glanced back at his father—a student waiting for approval.

"Thank you, Jimmy," said Sir John. "That was quite good."

"Are we finished here?" Orville said.

"No," said his father. "The book, then, is a game of trade. As the puppet master behind these economic exchanges, Anne Brontë herself must have had a motive. She put her story on paper; now, what was she going to get in return?"

"Or maybe it was the opposite," I said. "Anne wanted her book read by as many people as possible. What did she plan on offering her readers in return for their close attention?"

Orville slapped his napkin down on the table. "Both of you, don't bring Anne Brontë into this," he said. "We're speaking of Helen."

"Of course we'll bring in Anne Brontë," said Sir John. "Anne Brontë set up her novel as one end of a bargain. What was her intention?"

Orville's eyes flashed in a way I now knew he had inherited from his father.

"Ah," said Sir John, smiling ever so slightly and turning to face me. "You see, Samantha, my son does not believe in authorial intent." He spoke as though his sad little heathen child did not believe in God.

The heat rose to my professor's cheeks. The two of them seemed poised to enter a dangerous but well-practiced intellectual sport. I had a feeling that this subject was one they had debated many times before—so often, in fact, that it had become something of a crusade.

"It is humiliating that every conversation we have about the Brontë novels ends with their *intention*," said Orville. "You cannot judge a work of art by the intentions of its creator. I will *not* allow you to fill an innocent mind with nonsense. This is my student."

I wasn't sure where he meant to place the emphasis—on *my* or on *student*—but I wished he had made it more obvious.

"Some books do not have the privilege of having 'produced' anything," said Sir John. "Some books have been overedited; they have been restrained by the author's concern over their reception. In these cases, you must look at external clues to piece together a text's original intention."

"If a novel did not produce anything of value, then I wonder why you find it necessary to study it at all."

"It is your responsibility as a reader, and as an empathetic human being, to unlock the author's true purpose."

Orville seemed very close to losing his temper, which fascinated me. "To reconstruct a dead person's intention is to create a piece of fiction yourself," he snapped. "*You* of all people should know this."

"Isn't there some truth in all fiction?"

"There's some fiction in all truth too."

There was a silence. Did they notice I was here at all? I glanced at Sir John, whose smile had frozen on his face. It was hard to tell whether he was proud that his son was an academic or embarrassed they had managed to end up on opposite sides. Orville, meanwhile, looked as hostile as I had ever seen him. Perhaps I had stumbled over the reason he had chosen his mother's name.

To my surprise, Orville turned to me. "What do *you* think, Samantha?"

The mention of my name made me jump. I wasn't keen to enter a family squabble, but it was nice to be asked for my opinion for a change.

"What do I think?" I repeated. "I think the interpretation of a novel depends on the reader far more than it does on the text or the author's intent."

Both Sir John and Orville scoffed at the same time. Orville rolled his eyes, and said under his breath, "The reader-response approach." Sir John gave a small chortle. I wondered if I had just been insulted, somehow.

"You're both wrong," I explained. "Ignoring the author's intention is just a way of not dealing with personal and emotional things. And yet, Sir John, you've twisted the notion of 'intention' in the exact wrong way. You assume that the Brontës' biographical objects— sketches, for example—attach new significance to Brontë novels. Have you ever considered that the Brontë novels allow us to attach new significance to simple objects?"

I was expecting some sort of response—a nod, a smile, even a grimace—but Sir John was silent. Was he listening to me at all? Perhaps not. He looked vaguely constipated.

I said, louder this time: "The books pointed us in the direction of possessions we might otherwise overlook, and gave those possessions meaning. And that, I believe, was by design. Intention, if you will."

"Who said that?" Sir John said, finally. "Your father?"

"No, sir," I said, and I could feel my cheeks redden. "I did."

Sir John stared back at me with the disinterest of someone who was too old to take a young person's ideas seriously. He wanted to talk to my father, and only my father. Instead, he was stuck with my dad's young, naïve public relations associate. Without saying another word, he clasped the edge of his seat and moved himself upward, slowly. He looked rumpled—damaged, even—the way you would after a failed marriage, or a wasted career. He took his empty glass in one hand and walked into the kitchen. A door closed behind him.

"Did I offend him?" I asked.

Orville was considering me gravely.

"What?" I said. "Are you going to tell me I'm ridiculous too?"

"No," he said. "For once, I'm not."

"Why not? Are you ill?"

He let out a breath. "What you propose is a risky way to analyze literature. But I do think it might be the only way to understand your father."

"I don't understand."

"Please pass me *The Tenant of Wildfell Hall*. I've been denying you something for quite some time now."

I passed him the thin volume. He took it from me and flipped halfway through. It took him several moments to land upon the right page, but when he reached it, he said, "You once asked me about the 'Warnings of Experience.'"

I stopped. "Yes?"

In response, he handed me the open book. I took it from him. Orville had opened it to page one hundred. It was the scene in which Helen throws Gilbert her entire diary. He takes it home with him, and says:

> *I have it now before me; and though you could not, of course, peruse it with half the interest that I did, I know you would not be satisfied with an abbreviation of its contents, and you shall have the whole, save, perhaps a few passages here and there of merely temporal interest to the writer, or such as would serve to encumber the story rather than eluci-*

date it. It begins somewhat abruptly, thus—but we will reserve its com-
mencement for another chapter, and call it—THE WARNINGS OF
EXPERIENCE.

Good God. I sat in an astonished silence. There it was, in—of
all things—capital letters. The Warnings of Experience. My inheritance. The heat rose to my cheeks. It was a cruel joke. The answer
had been in the book all along. The Warnings of Experience was the
title of Helen Graham's diary. It constituted a whopping two-thirds
of *The Tenant of Wildfell Hall.* I had been searching for something
that had been in plain view for one hundred and sixty-five years. My
father had dotted the boundary of the paragraph with small, friendly
smiley faces.

I looked at Orville, flushed. "Why didn't you tell me before?"

He ran his hands through his hair. "Because I thought you'd misun-
derstand it and assume the Warnings of Experience might be literal."

My breath was quick. "Of course it's literal. If a painting can
exist outside of a book, then what's to say a diary can't? Is this Anne
Brontë's personal journal?"

A look of pain crossed Orville's face, which now looked ravaged in
a way that I had not been expecting.

"No," he said. "Samantha—no. I knew about this passage—of
course I knew. But I also anticipated the way you'd react. Your ideas
about literature lead to a dangerous way of looking at life. You cannot
assume that if you believe hard enough, something will always physically materialize in front of you."

"Cathy Linton's ghost did, when Heathcliff called for it."

He looked at me with a gentleness that took me off guard. "I
know what you really want, Samantha, and I'm so very sorry, but I'm
afraid none of this will bring your father back to you."

My breath hitched in my throat. Instinctively, I looked away. My
enthusiasm for the Warnings of Experience momentarily waned.

Orville reached over and, to my great surprise, wrapped his entire palm over my hand. It was warm and smooth, and when he gave my hand a squeeze, I thought he really meant it.

There was a noise behind us. Immediately, Orville retracted his arm, like a child who has been caught cutting carpets with scissors. I swiveled around to find Sir John standing at the doorway to the kitchen, a fresh glass of water in his hand. I wondered how long he had been listening.

"You take an above-average interest in this young woman's education," he said to his son.

Orville didn't respond.

"What was her name, Jimmy?" asked his father. "The last student you dated?"

An ugly silence hit the room. My eyes widened. Sir John's nostrils flared as he breathed in and out, in and out. I turned to face my professor. I felt a strange new emotion, which was too unfamiliar to be properly articulated. It wasn't exactly terror—was it hope? James Orville had just become either heroic or evil.

His expression was immobile. He looked down and picked a fallen crumb from his sweater, only to pitch it to the floor. Then he stood, slowly.

"Abby," he said. "Her name was Abby."

And with that, he quitted the room.

Later in the evening, long after Sir John had gone to bed, and long after I had taken a shower and slipped back into Orville's oversize T-shirt, I descended upon the kitchen to find my professor sitting alone, on a rickety chair, hunched over *Far from the Madding Crowd*.

I sat down next to him. The oversize T-shirt, I knew, did not look good on me. It was too large, and drooped around the muscular shoulders that were not there. We didn't say anything. Slouching and despondent, the two of us could have been in an advertisement for the Great Depression.

I cleared my throat. "Are you going to tell me about it?"

He didn't look up. "No."

"Please? I like romantic comedies. Or maybe this one is a drama." I paused. "Film noir?"

"It was a very long time ago and I was very young."

"Was she younger than I am? Is that why your dad is mad? Because you're a felon?"

"She was older. A fourth-year."

"So she's a cougar? I guess here you call them 'sharks.'"

He put down the book and it landed on the table with a slap. "Nothing happened between the two of us, Samantha," he said. A pause. "At least not while she was my student."

"Then why can't you eat in hall?"

"Stop it."

"Please? I'd like to know."

He let out a breath. I knew he was angry, but I didn't much care.

"My colleagues didn't much fancy the idea of a recently graduated student dating a don," he said. "It was torturous, the interrogation they put me through." He reached for the table and took a swig of something—what was in his mug? Tea? Whiskey? "They were probably right," he said with a note of defeat. "I should have called it off long before I did."

I frowned. I had been wrestling with the idea of Abigail for the last hour. On one hand, I knew I should see his relationship with her as vile, immoral, one that violated its contractual and educational duty. On the other hand, I couldn't find the idea quite as revolting as I should have. A consensual relationship forged upon intellect and inquiry seemed immediately worthier than its more lustful counterpart. And it seemed somewhat contradictory that an institution dedicated to pushing the boundaries of human endeavor should be constricted by so many human rules. I found that I was bothered not by the fact that Orville had dated a student, but by the realization that he must have really cared for her. I had the dispiriting image of the two of them—Orville and his pale, articulate girlfriend—bicycling around some photogenic English town.

"Your father seems upset about it," I said.

"I believe it was very embarrassing for the family," he said shortly.

I tried to be comforting. "Your dad will get over it."

"My dad will 'get over' everything soon enough."

"Pardon?"

Orville glanced at me. "He is in a steep decline. Or haven't you noticed?"

I didn't respond.

"His physical strength is deserting him by the day," he said. "We can leave him alone in a classroom; we cannot leave him alone outside of one. The last time my brother and I visited, my father called to let me know he was on his way home from the parsonage. He never made it back. He got lost. I found him—my excellent father—up to his knees in mud."

I opened my mouth to speak, then closed it. I wished I knew how to be sweet with him. I wanted to put my arms around his elephantine shoulders and rub the pain out of him. But the only thing I seemed to know how to do was to brood and squabble. When Orville did look at me, it was with dead eyes.

"Listen to me—please, just listen to me," he said. "There is no artifact out there for you to find that will bring you anything resembling happiness. My father discovered a painting, once upon a time, just like you did. That painting was enough for him to abandon his career, his family, and the better part of his judgment, all so he could move north and pursue his one wild and fragile dream. Can you imagine?

A fellow at Cambridge, taking a position at an insignificant museum. My father's disillusionment has been great. He will not admit it to you, even now, but he has failed. That painting brought him nothing. The book he just wrote is useless, and he knows it. He did not find any Brontë artifacts. He did not become wealthy. He did not satiate his curiosity, or find inner peace. This is what happens, Samantha, when you believe in *things* and not in *ideas*. You disappoint yourself, and then you die."

I blinked. I had never seen Orville so dramatic.

"Maybe he's still more rational than you think," I said, trying to lift the mood. "Maybe he discovered plenty of worthwhile things and he just doesn't know what they mean. It wouldn't be fair, exactly, to burden his passion with charges of insanity—didn't you teach me that?"

A fist smacked the table with a booming crack. It was Orville's, and I flinched. For the first time, he raised his voice at me, cruelly.

"Why is this difficult for you to understand? Listen to me carefully. The Warnings of Experience is *not* a physical diary. It is the story of what happens to a promising young man who ruins himself with alcohol, and of what happens to a young woman when she chooses not to read the simple signs in front of her. I thought, on some level, that you'd understand this. No? For God's sake, Samantha. You are desperately alone and I'm afraid that this is what desperately alone people do—you attach significance to imaginary things to ease your sense of emptiness."

I blinked. Gone, it seemed, was the nice man who had taken my hand earlier. His voice was strident, and I found that he had managed to genuinely hurt me. I looked down, to the right, to the left. There were tears in my eyes. Curious, I thought, that they decided to show up now, years after they had begun to form. Orville was right. I made a quick mental tally of all the friends I knew in this world, and realized that the only one I had was sitting in front of me, and was this really the best I could do?

To my surprise, when I looked up, Orville wasn't making eye contact. He was massaging his palms, over and over again. It seemed as though an unexpected emotion had come into his repertoire and he didn't quite know what to do with it. He stood up and moved to the freezer. When he returned, it was with a bag full of frozen lemon bars. He set the plate on the table, and waited.

I said, "Those look terrible."

"I'll get you a fork."

"Americans eat with their hands."

Orville sat back down across from me. I didn't eat. I wondered if every dessert he had ever eaten had to come from a freezer.

He said, "I didn't mean to upset you."

"What did you mean to do?"

"I meant to be honest. I don't think many people are honest with you."

"I don't think many people are honest with anyone. That's why people have friends."

I could feel that Orville was staring at me but I refused to return his gaze. I was already retreating to a very dull, colorless place, one that did not accept visitors.

"Tell me what is upsetting you," he said.

"You, mostly. I am not '*desperately alone*.'" My words sounded pouty and childlike, even to me. "And I don't think you're allowed to blame me for attaching significance to imaginary things. Not when you teach literature."

"You have something under your eye," he said.

"Leave it. I like it there."

"Hold still."

"Stop."

But he leaned over the table anyway, his massive right arm extended like a tree trunk. In a different world, I might have thought he was leaning in to kiss me. But instead, he rubbed one thumb right underneath my eye, slowly. It was wet from the tear and a half I had managed to squeeze out, and I wondered if this was what he meant by "something under your eye." His skin was smooth and warm and my face felt small in his hands. I thought I might collapse right into him.

The moment didn't last long. In a flash he had returned his arm to his side of the table, then exited the room. I had the feeling that I had received the first apology he had ever given.

That night, I dream of going to the parsonage again.

The road is wet and the melting snow has left a muddy path. I am walking quickly because it is cold. The house looks quiet and cozy tonight. Circular puffs of smoke erupt from the chimney, as if a large man is lying on his back somewhere inside, smoking a cigar. There is a number of grotesque carvings lavished over the front entryway, among a wilderness of crumbling griffins.

Inside the front door, I see a long, clean corridor. It is warm and smells of lavender. I walk down the hall. To the left is a fine living room, whose palatial fireplace defies the skinny proportions of the house's exterior. It is a dimly lit chamber, filled with the echoes of recent laughter. The chairs are pulled away from the table, and one has tipped over. I spy fresh parchment, two quill pens, and a half-eaten chocolate chip cookie. The inhabitants must have fled, quite suddenly, without saying a word.

I look around, confused. Have my relatives abandoned me on the eve of my arrival? I know it's rude to break and enter, but then again, this is my dream, and doesn't that mean that I'm the narrator? I settle into the happy squalor of the room. It's large and pleasantly untidy. A vague smell of extinguished candle pervades the air. There is a cold draft piping through the chimney.

I take a seat by the fireplace and interlace my fingers, in the way of contemplative assistant professors. Rarely have I felt quite so at home. The last piece seems to have fallen into place, in a puzzle I didn't know I was a part of. I can't shake the feeling that my father has sat in this exact seat, doing the same thing.

I wait for something interesting to occur, but all I can hear is the clock ticking. If this is my dream, shouldn't fantastic things be happening? Gunfights, romances, premonitions? And should I feel this . . . awake? Maybe this is what a dream is supposed to be, and all of this time I've been doing it wrong.

Just then, I hear a rattling at the window. It sounds like a branch, rapping on the sill. Suddenly, a row of knuckles comes flying through the glass, and an arm comes right after it—I see the fingers of a little, ice-cold hand. A most melancholy voice sobs, "Let me in—let me in!"

I stand up straight, alert.

"I've come home," says the voice outside. "I've lost myself on the moors!"

The cold white fingers and cold white arm give way to a cold white body, which pulls itself through the window. It is a man, and he is wearing a bathrobe and holding a martini. It is, I realize, my father.

"Dad?" I say.

"Hi, kiddo," he says. "It's colder than a witch's ass out there."

I say, "What are you doing here?"

"I told you you'd find me here someday."

"Did I find you or did I conjure you?"

"Does it matter?"

I frown and take a step closer. Yes, it is most definitely my father. Those are his same weary, long-suffering eyes. I recognize his shock of black hair and his ski-slope forehead, and I congratulate my unconscious for creating such an exact image of him. He smells the same as he always has: warm, cozy, like an old, comfortable book.

"You're not real," I say. "I'm dreaming."

"If it looks like a duck and tastes like a duck, then it's a duck."

This, I remember, is one of his old battle cries. An ache wells up inside of my chest, one that seems to defy the parameters of a dream. Time has failed me, I realize. The Dad-shaped hole in my life has not, in fact, become any smaller. It has just grown less and less visible. I feel the slow panic that accompanies the onset of grief.

I clear my throat. "I don't totally respect you, you know."

"Oh?"

"You slept with a professor, you cheated on your wife, you drank yourself to death, and you abandoned me."

Dad gives his drink a swirl. "Nobody's perfect."

His voice—God, his voice. He takes a seat and I sit next to him. He hands me the martini.

"Try some," he says.

I refuse. Up close, Dad's face is strangely perforated, like a slab of cheese, or a thin cut of meat.

"Where is the book?" I ask.

"What book?"

"The one you left me. You left me a diary, yes?"

"You mean this?"

He reaches behind him and pulls out a small leather volume—barely the size of his palm. I can just make out the faint words on the cover: The Warnings of Experience.

I say: "Yes, I mean that."

"You've had it all along."

"That is clearly false."

"Tap your shoes together and say there's no place like home."

"Can you please be sober?"

He frowns. I know that he is angry. He chucks the book at the wall. It makes a wide hole and I see it land in the snow outside, in the church graveyard. It descends into the earth, hollowing out a large, black crater. The book sinks into the pit and disappears from sight. I turn to Dad for an explanation, but his face has gone blurry.

I say, "Are you going now?"

"I don't know—am I?"

"Please tell me what you'd like me to do. I'm too old to be doing this."

"You won't learn anything unless you discover it for yourself."

"Our lessons are over."

"If you think that, then I have failed you."

"Please tell me what you wanted me to know."

At this, he smiles, but only slightly. "'I wished to tell the truth, for truth always conveys its own moral to those who are able to receive it.'"

"Don't quote Anne Brontë. Not now."

" 'But as the priceless treasure too frequently hides at the bottom of a well, it needs some courage to dive for it.' "

I blink. I glance at the graveyard. The patch of snow where the book landed has formed a very deep and very dark pit—a tunnel to the center of the Earth. It looks like an old pothole in an old street in Boston.

"Shit," I conclude.

I stand up and stumble backward as I realize something of terrible importance. Suddenly, my father is gone; the house is gone; the world is gone. I am in a dark, cold place, goopy with black. Thunder shakes the house of James Timothy Orville III and I awake with a start.

"Orville."

   No response.

   "Orville."

   "Hrmm."

   Smack. *"Orville."*

   "What."

   "Wake up."

   "Amy?"

   "Who's Amy?"

The lights went on—well, one light went on. Orville had reached over and found the lamp beside the bed. He turned his eyes on me slowly. I was sitting on the edge of his bed, hovering over him, arms crossed. I wished that he had kept the lights off. He slept shirtless, and his white, white torso gleamed like the clean belly of a wet fish. Smooth and radioactively bright.

He blinked once, twice, three times. It had taken me four tries to find the right door, and now here I was, in Orville's bedchamber. With the light on, I could make out the dim outline of tangled phone chargers on the shelf above his head.

"Samantha—what is it?" he wanted to know. His eyes were puffy with sleep, and there was a pillow mark slashed across his cheek. "Is Paris burning?"

I couldn't seem to answer.

Orville sat up straighter. "You're trembling—what's wrong?"

"It's cold in here."

He paused. I secretly hoped he'd ask me to hop in, but he just said: "There's a blanket in the dresser."

I shook my head. "I just had a dream about my dad."

Orville didn't respond for a moment—then: "How was he?"

"Fine, thanks."

"Do you want to talk about it?"

"No," I said. "I want to talk about books."

He gave a sideways glance at the clock on the wall. "Four in the morning," he said. "It's four in the morning."

"You once asked me what reading meant to me. It was several months ago and we were at that pub. Do you remember? I have an answer for you now, if you'd like to hear it."

He lay back down and put his forearm over his eyes. "Now?"

I poked him in the chest with my index finger. It worked—he reopened his eyes. His skin was warm, almost baked. It was a bad time to emote, apparently. He looked tired and useless.

I said, "Courage."

"Pardon?"

"Reading teaches you courage. The author is trying to convince you something fake is real. It's a ridiculous request, and it questions the sanity of the reader. The extent to which you believe the author depends on how willing you are to jump in headfirst."

"Jump into what?"

"Can you please pay attention? Whatever the book has for you to jump on into."

"You ended that thought with two prepositions."

"Listen to me."

"Do you think we might be able to have this conversation in the morning?"

"You once asked me why I appreciated no authors," I said, ignoring him. "It's because I simply cannot feel things as a normal person does. No—don't look at me like that. It's true. I have never been able to properly invest myself in a book because books are lies, and I do not like being lied to. Reading well requires bravery, and it's something that I don't have. This is why I am neither a good writer nor a good reader."

Orville's eyes narrowed. "Courage is not a possession. It is a state of mind."

"Yes, one that requires a leap of faith. That's what my dad used to tell me. I always thought he meant a figurative leap of faith. But I think he meant a real leap of faith."

"I don't follow."

"As in, literal. Get it?" I made a leaping motion with two of my fingers, in case he needed the visual.

He squinted. "Are you planning on jumping off something?"

"What kind of wells are around here, if you had to guess?"

Orville exhaled and checked the clock again. "Go back to sleep, Samantha."

"No. I'm finally seeing things clearly."

"It doesn't sound like it." He rested his head on his pillow and closed his eyes. I poked him one more time but he didn't react. That's when I put my hand on his cheek.

Orville's eyes flew open. I blinked at my own nerve. My fingertips were cold and his face felt velvety. I had broken a barrier. I could almost hear the cymbals crashing; I could picture the portraits in the dining hall waking up with a start and screaming at each other to sound the alarm—*Be quick about it, man, awaken the troops!* But Orville did not move away. He just lay there with an immobile stare, a frown on his face. His chest rose and fell slowly. It grew very quiet. My life, I knew, was about to change.

Orville said, very clearly, "What are you doing."

But before he could say anything else, I pushed my face into his in a kiss that I hoped he would someday understand to be the surprising yet inevitable end to our torturous, imaginary courtship. I kissed him, and it was strong, and I wished I could say my blood was roaring, but really it was my ears that were roaring—maybe it was the voices of all those academics in their portraits screaming at me to knock it off, or debating all the heteronormative gender nonconformity issues that I was raising, and after all, had I thought this through? Or was I over-thinking this? Gosh, both seemed likely, didn't they? Time seemed to slow down, and what I felt was heat and sweat, but really they were both just coming from me, not him. In that moment, all I could think of was why the world's most basic task carried with it so many academic violations, and all the seriousness of a terrible crime.

I was about to call the whole thing off, when suddenly—and to my great surprise—Orville lurched forward. I squeaked, or was that the bed? His hand cupped the back of my neck—hard—and his face found mine, again and again. I felt a surge of helplessness, the kind I imagined people nearly died from. And yet I couldn't understand whether he was pulling me toward him or trying to thrust me off of him. I panicked with the weight of both options, and before either became clear to me, I did the only sensible thing I could: I threw his head back on the pillow—it landed with a thump—and I fled the room, like an airborne ballerina who's finally gone soaring wildly out of control.

CHAPTER 15

Dear Sir John,

This is Samantha. I snuck out of the house at 5:30 a.m. this morning, but I wanted to thank you for your hospitality, especially since you hated my father so much, and you dislike me too because I look so much like him and you think I am dating your son. (I am not dating your son; that would be gross.) I know you didn't know my father very well, but he was actually not a very bad man, and sometimes he could be a very good man. He did things that I don't understand, but if it makes you feel better, I don't think he did, either. I'm sorry if this handwriting is slanted and illegible; I have not slept in about a year. I am leaving my professor a note, too—would you see that he gets it?

All the best,

Samantha J. Whipple

It was almost eight thirty at night by the time I made it back to Oxford. The Haworth train was out of commission due to a broken rail, which meant the only option available to me was an obscure bus line. The storm had ended, but it was still an apocalyptic eighteen-hour ride, thanks to storm-chewed roads and piles of slush, which spat out from under our wheels like chopped salad. The time did not do good things to my mind. With horrific accuracy, I replayed the last twenty-four hours. I realized that my life of late had consisted of far too much dialogue and not enough exposition. I imagined an angry, bespectacled English teacher slashing his pen through the transcript of my life, wondering how someone could possibly say so much and think so little.

When I returned to campus, I dropped my bags in my room and then went straight to the Faculty Wing. Rebecca's door was slightly ajar, and so was her mouth. I must have looked like hell.

"Hello," I said.

She didn't answer immediately. Her expression told me that I better have a damn good reason for being here.

"That stench," she said. "It's primordial."

"Yes, I'm sorry. Never take the bus."

"Where are you coming from?"

"The First Circle of Hell."

She looked at me blankly.

I said, "That's the one filled with all the unbaptized pagans."

No response.

I clarified, "'Abandon hope, all ye who enter here'?"

Silence. We had nothing in common. I took a seat without being asked. The room was cold, and in the distance, I heard odd gurgling noises that sounded similar to several bodily functions. I tried to make myself comfortable, but I was wearing a scratchy wool coat and yoga pants that were too tight. I had only worn yoga pants once before, and it turned out the tabloids were wrong. They did not look good on everyone.

Rebecca looked suspicious, so I explained: "I was in Haworth."

"What were you doing in Haworth?"

"Visiting the Brontë Parsonage."

"I see," she said. Her voice was pinched. The only thing on her desk, I noticed, was a hammer. "James Orville was also there this weekend."

The mention of his name brought a blush to my cheeks. "Oh? Was he?"

"Did you know he would be there?" asked Rebecca.

"Pardon?"

"That is—were you there together?"

"Is that a pot of coffee?"

"You're blushing."

She didn't offer me any coffee. Instead, she took a seat behind her desk and smoothed her palms over her trousers. She seemed to be remembering something unpleasant. I recalled her telling me that she and my father used to take romantic trips up north for the weekend. It was all part of their tragic love story. An unfair twist of fate, perhaps, that my story did not seem to be playing out quite as tragically.

"I wanted to ask you something," I said. I tried to sound suave, but the effort of feigning comfort produced a larger discomfort than I was expecting. "Was Halford's Well named after my father?"

Her face barely moved. "I see you figured that out."

"Yes. He was your student."

"He was my student."

"Of mathematics."

"He knew how to read and write already. He believed education should be a challenge."

"I see. Someone once told me that people store their stuff in Halford's Well," I said. "Is that true?"

"It is Oxford's oldest wishing well," she said, impatient. "People have been throwing pennies in it for hundreds of years. Anything else you'd like to know?"

"Did people throw in anything besides pennies? Like, objects?"

"One throws one's wishes, not one's belongings."

I thought about it. "What if I wanted to go take a dip there tonight? Is it deep?"

Rebecca's "I'm not amused" stare was eerily like my mother's. Her expression told me that last night she had been dining with Keats and discussing poetry; now look what sort of uneducated ruffian she was with.

She repeated: "Take a dip?"

"Did my dad ever do that?"

"No sane person would swim in there."

"Exactly."

Rebecca did not want to pursue such a jejune conversation, it seemed, because she began packing up her things. A stack of ungraded papers from her drawer made it into her purse, and then came lipstick and earrings—things she carried around but apparently never used.

I walked to her desk, cautious. She looked tired. I thought about opening up to her completely, telling her what I felt and how I felt it, if not out of camaraderie, then because vulnerability was a currency and could be used the way some people used down payments. My breath quickened.

"I don't think you did anything wrong," I said. "With my father, that is. It was just unfortunate that people reacted the way they did."

She didn't respond.

"Love for a professor is not inherently pathological," I continued. "I think it has the right to be nurtured, just like anything else."

She gave me a cold, provisional smile. "And what, pray tell, has suddenly fashioned this new opinion?"

I took a breath. "You were right. I'm in love with James Orville."

The smile did not leave her face. She looked triumphant, for a brief moment.

"Then I hope you are prepared to ruin his life," she said.

"Pardon?"

"You think that you can eliminate the power differential between you two. You will not eliminate it. You will reinforce it. When a student loves a teacher, it is childish, natural, almost sweet. When a teacher loves a student, it is unnatural, a disease. He becomes a label. Predator. Manipulator. Monster."

"I am only trying to treat him as a human being."

"And by doing so, you will dehumanize him."

"Are you saying you regret being with my father, then? I thought you said you were over the whole thing."

She snapped her purse shut. "It's time for you to go, Samantha."

"No—please," I said, and my voice cracked in spite of me. I felt so lonesome, just then, that all I wanted was to be low-level friends, so we didn't have to keep staring at each other like this. Being vindictive took too much effort. Besides, the two of us should have been allies, not enemies—we were the only two people left who ever really understood my father. Rebecca must have noted the change in my voice, because her eyes narrowed.

I asked, again, "Do you regret it? Please tell me. I think you were treated very unfairly by the media."

She looked me over once, as if trying to decide if I was worth her time. "Have you ever been in love, Sam? Proper, reciprocated love?"

"No."

"It took me thirty-five years to find it," she said. "At that point, love is not love, but the end of isolation. You find that you do, in fact, belong—if not to a person, then to the rest of humanity, to silly novels and famous tunes. Tell me, if you can, that it's not part of the reason you love Orville."

I didn't respond. A slow, unfriendly smile came over her face.

"You and I are more alike than you think," she said. "On some level, you know this. I saw myself in you even when you were a spoiled child: alone and friendless, loved by only one person, but loved so strongly that it felt like the love of the entire world. My own father ran off with a family friend when I was young, and my mother moved to Guam. I found my therapy in math, just as you seem to have found yours in literature—two disciplines that help make sense of the world. I know what you want, Samantha, because it's the same thing I wanted. You want a reason to believe that there is something out there larger than yourself, something that makes all the petty things you've been through seem irrelevant. That's how love works. Do I regret falling in love with your father? Regret is made obsolete by the story you tell."

She leaned back in her seat. I wasn't expecting sentimentality, but there it was. She sounded strangely honest, like a real live human being. Her eyes were glassy and I wondered how many feelings she had bottled up behind them, and whether those feelings were organized in a Fibonacci sequence. It was my mistake, I suppose, to think that someone had to be all bad or not bad at all.

"Did you two stay together, even after you both left Old College?" I asked.

"Your father left England. For years we kept in touch through letters," she said. "They weren't beautiful or effusive, but you come to remember them as beautiful and effusive. Years went by, with him going and coming from England at will. At some point, he wrote me and let me know that a woman named Alice was pregnant, and he was going to marry her. Soon, I began hearing about you. You filled pages. You could have been your own epic. Every time he came to visit me, he would tell me how quickly you learned to read, how much you ate, how you jumped into the laundry hamper when you played hide-and-seek. *She'll be tall, Becky, she'll be a giant.* You were your father's best story."

She did not sound nostalgic, nor did she appear to be recalling a pleasant memory. Her face was sour, her eyes exacting. At the mention of "tall," my mother's face popped into my mind.

"You pursued an affair, knowing it would break up a family," I said.

"Your father did the same," she snapped. "Where is his blame?"

I said, "Did either of you ever think of my mom?"

To my surprise, Rebecca let out a cruel laugh. "Your mother didn't know your father, not the way I did. She married the father of her baby; he married the mother of his."

Rebecca's laugh was high-pitched. My mouth tensed into a small line.

I said, "And yet Dad broke up with you anyway."

I shouldn't have said it, of course, but the damage was done. Our temporary alliance was over. Rebecca gave me a good, long stare—the kind that could ruin you if you weren't careful. With one, deliberate motion, she took the square black glasses off her nose and placed them flat on her desk.

"I told you that he was unable to handle the competing demands of multiple women," she said. "In the end, I lost, and someone else won. After I left Boston, I didn't hear from him again until a month before he died, when he came back to Oxford. He visited his old tower, gave me all these damn books, and told me that when she was old enough, little Samantha was to read certain things and live in certain places, because he hadn't taught you everything he wanted. *Please, Rebs*, he begged me. *Please do this for me.* So here we are. Now, it is late and I want to leave. Do you have anything else to say?"

Her face went pale, her expression blank. *I lost, and someone else won.*

"Who was the woman who won out, in the end?" I asked.

Rebecca's lip curled. "Can't you guess?"

I didn't say anything. She was not looking at me as a student anymore. I was competition. I took a step away from my ex-tutor, feeling a surge of affection for my father. He'd picked me. He might have been a terrible husband, and a terrible boyfriend, and a terrible student, but he was, in the end, a great dad.

"I'll leave," I said. "Thank you for your time."

I wrapped my scarf around my neck. Rebecca, meanwhile, was

looking at me with a primal loathing I had seen only in movies and political debates. Here I was, inserting myself once again into the secret club she had built with my father and disturbing the tidy story she had invented for the two of them. It was a resentment I might have felt, too, had our situations been reversed. Maybe she had been right before—we were more similar than I thought.

To help ease the tension, I reached into my coat pocket and pulled out something I knew she would appreciate: her Emily Dickinson bookmark, the one I had found in *Tenant*. I had picked it up from my tower. I passed it to her like a white flag.

I thought she might be touched. But the bookmark accomplished quite the opposite effect of the one I had intended. She did not seem struck by a great wave of nostalgia. On her face was a look of spite, one so pure that I could not have replicated it if I tried. I had won—again. I was handing over her consolation prize.

"I'm sorry," I said. "I just—I thought you'd want it."

"Get out."

I blinked. "What?"

But she was already at the door, holding it open. I tried to say something, but her face had turned blank and hard. She didn't look at me when I walked past her. Once I was in the hallway, the door slammed behind me.

I waited, ear pressed to the closed door. For several minutes, all I heard was the sound of her pacing, back and forth, back and forth. Then, suddenly, there was a small knocking noise. If I was not mistaken, Rebecca was softly hammering the bookmark to her wall.

At three in the morning, I left my tower and walked to Halford's Well. Most of the lights had gone off in the Faculty Wing, and only scattered streetlamps illuminated the night. The majestic lawn was dark and empty. There were no porters wielding sticks, no reporters, no people. For the first time since arriving at Oxford, I was invisible. I felt an unexpected disappointment. I'd always thought that part of being brave was having an audience.

It was desperately cold. I had kept the yoga pants on but added a T-shirt, a thick running jacket, and an orange headband. Up close, Halford's Well was large and angular. It was old-fashioned, with a large triangular roof on top that was held together by decrepit slats and oversize nails. I walked to the cold rim and glanced inside. The stench was something medieval. It must have been the end of the world down there, and no one else had noticed. I looked around. There was no sound.

"All right, Dad," I muttered. "Your move."

I heard only the echo of my own voice. I was cold to the point of complete sensory deadness. The wind was aggressive, and it echoed in the long cylinder below. I spotted the vague outline of a rung in the well wall immediately to my right. It looked like a ladder, so I flung my leg over the side of the well to investigate. The ledge was thicker than I expected, and in a moment I found myself straddling the stone wall.

"Stop!"

My heart seemed to shrivel. I turned around and peered into the darkness. There—I would have known that voice anywhere—was Orville, marching toward me, coat billowing. A burning rage erupted inside me. How was it that the first time I did something truly outrageous, I was thwarted?

He stopped in front of me, panting. I wondered if he'd run here all the way from Haworth.

"What in God's name are you doing?" he asked.

"I'm trying to remember a time when I was doing anything, and you didn't show up."

His breath came out in a pearly white stream. It looked like a slow leak. "You left without saying a single word."

"Oops."

"There was a *storm*, Samantha."

"It was *over*, James."

At the mention of his first name, he fell silent.

I corrected myself: "I mean, Orville. Jimmy. Who are you, again?"

"You didn't answer your phone."

"How did you know where to find me?"

"Your note. It contained a line from *The Tenant of Wildfell Hall*. Were you aware? Yes, I'm sure you were. The priceless treasure remains at the bottom of the well, and it takes courage to dive for it, et cetera. At first I thought you were trying to be ironic. Then I discovered that you were gone, and I remembered our conversation. I thought that you just might, in fact, be unstable enough to come find a well."

"It took you ten minutes to figure out what that sentence meant? It took me ten years."

"I thought no one could be so idiotic as to take such a ridiculous statement literally. Then I realized it was you. I waited for you at the well in Haworth this morning. I figured that it was the obvious choice."

I blinked. "There's a well in Haworth?"

He didn't answer, because he seemed distracted by my positioning on the ledge. I was straddling the rim of the well like I would a horse—awkwardly.

"Let me see if I understand this correctly," he breathed, as if wrestling with a new concept. His white, white breath seemed to form arrows in the air. "You are actually proposing to jump inside? Have you completely lost your mind?"

"Possibly."

"You are not about to lower yourself into this—this—"

"What."

"Pit of excrement."

I blinked. "Aren't you being a bit dramatic?"

He took a step forward, and it seemed as though all the times he and I had sparred, or fought, or anything, were nothing but a rehearsal for a drama of this caliber. His voice was brittle.

"Samantha, listen to me, and listen to me carefully. The Brontës did not leave you anything at the bottom of this well."

I said, very evenly, "The *Brontës* didn't. But my father did."

"Why would he leave your inheritance here?"

"Why not?"

"Do you know what sorts of things people throw down here?"

I decided I didn't want to know, so I flung my second foot over the ledge. I felt around on the inside of the wall until my foot landed upon the first step of the ladder. I didn't get very far—Orville immediately grasped my shoulders from behind. I struggled with him, but he hooked his arms underneath mine and pulled me out of the well, and then several steps out onto the lawn. When I gave a kick and tried to shove him off me, he wrapped his arms around my waist and yanked me back with such force that I thought I might lose my dinner.

"I will fight you," I warned.

"As you wish," he said.

I struggled in vain; the moment I pushed myself against him was the moment he twisted me around and pinned my back to him. There he held me, very tight.

"Shall we do this for two more hours, to see if it's possible?" he breathed. His grip tightened and I let out a squawk.

I said, "You're hurting me."

He relaxed his grip. We squared off. All of a sudden, it didn't seem to matter what I would find at the bottom of the well. I just wanted to jump in. I had rarely been able to call myself stupid and impulsive, and didn't everyone deserve to?

"If you stop me, I will just come back later," I said. "You can't patrol the area forever."

He swore beneath his breath. "Then I'll go in. You stay here."

"You don't know what to look for."

"Do *you*?"

I didn't answer. Orville seemed to know that he was going to lose—at least, he stopped arguing with me, and ran his fingers through his hair. I took off my shoes, which I hadn't thought to do earlier. I didn't see why he thought he had to stay and watch; deep-sea well diving was a solitary sort of activity.

"You'll want to take off your pullover first," Orville said.

"Pardon?"

"You'll catch a chill if you have nothing warm to wear after."

I nodded and attempted to lift my running jacket over my body without undoing the zip. I say "attempted" because my fingers were fat and useless in the cold. I struggled until Orville told me to stop. He took a step forward and his fingers found the edge of my jacket for me. After a clumsy moment with the layers, he tried to lift it over my torso. It would have been a seamless operation, but the neckline got stuck around my nose and I floundered, arms raised in the air. I could feel my cheeks redden, but fortunately, no one could see them. Orville wrestled with my jacket until he removed the entire thing. I thanked him but couldn't seem to look at him. Instead, I turned back to the well, lowered my legs over the side, and stepped back onto the ladder.

Before Orville disappeared from view, I saw him wagging a finger at me. "One word, and I will come after you."

I nodded and began to descend. The night sky faded until the only thing in front of my face was the stone wall.

"Well?" Orville called.

"It's really nice down here," I said. "We should do this more often."

"Just be quick about it."

"How many diseases are down here, if you had to estimate?"

He didn't respond, which was worrisome. The pit was deeper than I'd anticipated. I peered into it, envisioning the monster that was lurking in those unholy depths.

Quite suddenly, my bare toes hit water. I forgot about Orville; I forgot about my father. It was a humorless cold. The water hit my shins, and after that it moved up my shins to my knees, and then to my thighs and waist, and as I lowered myself I let out a small scream because it was so very cold, and my body was so very bony and out of shape. I was breathing heavily, and the noise filled the air around me. The water was midway up my body, and once it was there, my lungs constricted painfully. Everything around me seemed to be a long way away. I heard something from a distance—it was Orville, calling my name. I strained to catch his words, which were either echoing around the dark cave, or just in my mind—was he saying that a light had gone on somewhere?

I tried to respond, but the belt of water had tightened around my lungs like a noose. The water reached my torso, my shoulders, my neck. One more step, and it was at my chin. The last bit of humor dissipated from the situation. I took a gulp of icy air and plunged into the filthy water. I screamed small, wet screams and felt a wild rush of water by my ears. I flailed for the bottom of the well.

My foot struck something solid—which then moved. I had landed upon a bed of pennies. I felt around with my toes and my foot hit something sharp—a syringe? I kept sweeping my toes from left to right but there was nothing there but bottles and pennies and hundreds of old dreams and wishes and petty disappointments. I was wrong, and Orville was right. I would find no boxes, no books, no gold, no answers, not here. I screamed at nothing and no one, and my voice was lost in the ancient water, which seemed to have heard it all before. I had been wrong. Good God—I had been wrong?

I pushed myself up, up, until I broke the surface and gasped for air. I couldn't breathe. Somewhere above me, a man was yelling. *Do you hear me, Samantha? I'm coming down there—do you hear me!* I stopped listening, and not by choice. My entire body was shaking. Dead? Was this what being dead felt like? I couldn't pull myself upward. Breathing was a luxury, and I was suddenly too weak for it. I steadied myself on the ladder until my lungs slowly began to fill again, gulping the cold, frosted night air. I heard nothing. There was nothing in this world but my shallow breathing, my fat fingers, my small, small lungs. My hair was as heavy as a rug. I ordered my fingers to move and to my surprise, they did as they were told. They grasped the ledge—but I still couldn't pull, could I? Then how was it that I was moving? I must have been climbing, because the waterline was no longer at my waist. My breath was rapid and—*aha!*—the water was back around my shins. This was curious—I seemed to be being yanked up by a crane—was it a crane, or a human? Orville, I realized, had leaned over and grabbed me underneath the arms and then around the waist, and then was pulling that waist upward—up, up. I tumbled over the ledge and away from the well. I made it to my feet and there was Orville, above me, pulling me further upright and rubbing my arms at a frantic pace, cursing at himself, and cursing at the cold. His coat was gone and instead I realized that it was what was now wrapped around me. He was running his hands through my hair, over my back, calling me *mad, dammit, mad*—stroking my back with the wide palms of his hands. *Stupid girl . . . silly . . . stupid . . .* But his voice was mellow, and somewhat sweet, and after a moment, he wrapped both arms around me and held me very still.

"Orville," I muttered.

"We need to get you inside," he said.

"I d-didn't find anything."

"Of course you didn't. This was an imbecilic project."

I didn't move. I was clinging to him. He tried to pull me off but I didn't let go.

"I didn't find anything," I gulped.

"Yes, you said that."

"I really thought it'd be there."

Orville fell silent. The wind came over the lawn. "We need to go. This is not a good place to be found."

"No, it's here. It has to be here. Just help me find it. Please. Please help me find it."

My lips were thick and heavy. I looked up at my professor and he looked back at me with an expression he might reserve for a sick child.

"Your father would never have left you a book in *water*. It would be destroyed. Didn't you think of that?"

I muttered, "Not if he put it in a waterproof box."

We didn't say anything, and the absurdity of the statement lingered in the air. He tried to steer me away from the well, but I stayed where I was. Courage. I had finally found courage, and where had it brought me?

Orville shook his head. "Look at you. You look like that infernal woman on your wall."

I frowned. "Pardon?"

"Come. We're leaving."

"Oh, God," I said.

"What is it?" Orville snapped.

I thought of that old friend, the Governess, in her wild-eyed, drowning disappointment. I said, "You're right. I picked the wrong well."

"I can see that."

"No," I said. "I did. I picked the wrong well. There's another woman who fell into the water, and she had a book in her hands. Remember?"

"If you don't get a move on I will carry you."

I was shaking. Orville's coat, which had been wrapped loosely around me, slid cleanly off my back and landed on the grass. I tried to bend and reach for it, but my fingers felt as though they might crumple into frozen ash. I swayed and almost fell. Orville put a steadying hand on my waist.

"We need to get you inside, Samantha," he breathed.

"Where do insane people go at Oxford?"

"They jump into a well," he said. "Come. Walk." Once again, he tried to urge me forward, but I leaned against him and pushed back. The wind came down at us, sharp and senseless.

"No," I said. "Insane people go to my tower. They always have."

"Move, or I will carry you."

"Much madness is divinest sense. . . . Assent—and you are sane. Demur—you're straightway dangerous—and handled with a Chain."

"You're babbling."

"Don't you see? The book has been home all this time and I haven't seen it. It's just like Dorothy."

"Dorothy who?"

A blinding flash of light brought me back to reality. Was it lightning? Eternity? Orville and I turned around in time to see that it was neither—it was the flash of a camera. There it went again, another burst of light.

"Who's there?"

I thought I had said it—at least, my mouth was open, ready to speak, but it was Orville who had shouted. Ahead of us, not ten feet away, was a shadow. The figure stepped into the light, and I gave a small start.

"Hans?"

Yes, I do believe it was Hans, standing there like a pale fish. There was a fancy camera draped around his neck and he was looking between Orville and me as though he couldn't believe his good fortune. He looked so blond and Nordic that I almost saluted.

"Why are you here?" I asked.

"Why are you wet?" he replied.

Orville said, "There is no story here."

Story? I glanced at Hans's perfect face. I was trembling. I glanced from my professor to my so-called friend, and at the professional-looking camera draped so comfortably around the latter's neck. A truth dawned on me, the sort of truth that later gets written in capital letters on tombstones.

"*You're* H. *fucking* Pierpont?" I said. "You're the one who's been writing about me all *fucking* year?"

"Samantha," Orville warned.

I lurched, but Orville caught me around the waist and pulled me back. I shouted to Hans: "Go away. I'm just on a walk."

Another photo. Snap, snap.

Hans grinned. "Dressed like that?"

"We can continue this conversation inside," Orville said. "She's not well."

I knew it then: Orville and I would both die here, by this old well, and in front of the entire world. Die, or else be disgraced. The pictures would be all over the news, with incriminating head-lines. I saw the rumors multiplying; I saw my mother reading about it secondhand in a salon. Hans started firing pointed questions at Orville, but Orville just stared silently back at him, which meant Hans Fucking Pierpont was getting a better story than he could have possibly expected. Why wasn't Orville saying anything? It was highly uncharacteristic. But I realized that he was not looking at Hans at all. He was looking directly past Hans.

My eyes adjusted. We were not, in fact, as alone as I thought. There were two more people behind H. Pierpont. One, I realized, was Ellery Flannery. Another was Rebecca Smith. The light from the faculty offices gave the contours of her waistless body a precise definition.

"Are we interrupting something important?" my old math tutor said, coming forward. I hoped she looked at me and saw a face filled with disappointment, the kind that haunts people forever. She was a small, small woman. She had picked the ending to her story: revenge. I remembered something she had said about my father's death. *It was a well-crafted ending to an otherwise structureless life.*

My glance darted back to Hans. What would I say—was I out for a romantic walk with my professor, or was I out to dig for Brontë gold? Would I choose to be Samantha the Strumpet, or Samantha the Last Living Brontë? Judging from the look on her face, Rebecca already knew which one I would pick. She was doing to me what my father had done to her. She was bequeathing me her story.

There was some commotion on the path, and two more specta-tors approached. Students? Didn't this university have a curfew? One student was whispering to the other. No one, I realized, was look-ing at me. They were instead gawking at Orville, who looked like a wounded leopard cornered by a pack of hyenas. My heart thudded. Flannery came to stand in front of him, kicking aside the coat at his feet. Orville did not look at me, he just began spinning his glorious British sentences. Yes, Samantha had wanted to take a swim, what of it? He did not mention my midnight project or the Brontës. He just kept talking and talking, and I'm afraid I stopped listening. There were hooded figures coming out of the Faculty Wing. Were they hooded, or were my eyes simply closing? Golden bubbles appeared in the distance—flashlights?

All of a sudden, I was swaying, or was everyone else swaying? No, no, something was very wrong. I was neither as young nor as invinci-ble as I thought. My body was trembling. All I could think of was sud-den fainting syndrome and how Victorians had used it to great effect. I was only vaguely conscious of falling. Before I knew it, I had col-lapsed to the muddy lawn and Orville's body was looming over mine as a small crowd gathered, and someone was asking someone to fetch something, or do something, or get someone. *Samantha? Samantha!*

CHAPTER 16

Anne Brontë died on May 28, 1849, at the age of twenty-nine. It was pulmonary tuberculosis that killed her, after a sudden and hopeless illness. Hers was an unfair departure, and she seemed to know it. "I wish it would please God to spare me, not only for papa's and Charlotte's sakes, but because I long to do some good in the world before I leave it," she commented. "I have many schemes in my head for future practice—humble and limited indeed—but still I should not like them all to come to nothing, and myself to have lived to so little purpose. But God's will be done."

God's will was indeed done. Anne left this world peacefully, at 2 p.m. in the afternoon, somewhere in Scarborough. Only Charlotte was by her side, a grieving eldest sister splayed out next to her youngest until the end. Emily and Branwell were both dead, and now it was just Charlotte, alone against the world. For all of the pair's rivalries and petty competitions, this was surely not the ending Charlotte had in mind. What was her writing, without its inspiration? What was fame, without her family?

To this day, no one knows the words that were spoken between Charlotte and Anne, or the sentiments that were exchanged. It was a distraught Charlotte Brontë, to be sure, whose later lines of poetry spoke for themselves: *There's little joy in life for me / And little terror in the grave; / I've lived the parting hour to see / Of one I would have died to save.*

It seemed like an appropriately sad little ditty, but I had to wonder what Charlotte meant by "save." Was she referring to Anne's life, or Anne's soul? I sincerely hoped it was the latter. I hoped that Anne's spirit was so wild that it would severely complicate her afterlife, and I hoped that everyone who had ever been close to her knew it. It was my one great hope that after her death, little Anne Brontë took wing and blossomed in a way she didn't while alive. I wished this to be true so fervently, and with so much of myself, that I think I put a bit of myself into Anne, or maybe it was the other way around. My youngest cousin was suddenly very much alive to me. Imagination can be a terrifying and precise thing, when you want it to be.

Anne's final words to her sister were brief and resolute:

"Take courage, Charlotte," she said. *"Take courage."*

"What I don't understand," said my mother, days later, "is why you felt the need to take off your clothes."

It was a very warm day outside, or so I was told. I was in bed in my tower. Several bandages enclosed my right foot and the whole thing stuck out of the covers like a seal surfacing for air. My room smelled of fever and salt.

"I told you," I said. "To avoid getting sick."

"Right," she said. "Well, you *are* sick, so I see that it didn't help."

"I took off my jacket because I wanted to wear it afterward."

"Oh?"

I gave her a look. She had obviously been reading the papers. I said, "Who are you going to believe—me, or H. Fucking Pierpont?"

"Don't swear. It's very American."

Mom had arrived from Paris only an hour before, and was now

sitting at the foot of my bed, stroking my leg. She insisted that there was nowhere else in the world she would rather be. The *Hornbeam* rested on her lap, her daughter's frozen face plastered over the front page. I looked like a wet-T-shirt-contest winner standing next to her Smoking Hot Professor. The latter was staring into the camera with such broiling rage that it seemed uncontainable by any two-dimensional news form. *Rendezvous at Well Reignites Old Tradition.* Mom had read the article twice already. Once out loud. "I told you you'd crack one day," she said the moment she arrived.

I recalled little about the rest of that damp and frosty evening except coming to full consciousness in the blasting heat of a taxicab, which was rushing a professor I didn't recognize to the hospital. Why was this professor going to the hospital? Then I realized—it was I who was going, and this was my escort. Where was Orville?

As it turned out, there was nothing wrong with me except for a mild case of hypothermia and a badly scraped foot. As soon as I was released, at 7:17 the next morning, I returned to campus. It was a cold, crisp morning. I bought a ham and cheese sandwich (with sprouts) and went straight to my tower, after which I helped myself to a glass of water, got dressed, and then found my inheritance.

It was a smooth and easy discovery, as easy as if I had been taking dictation. When I removed *The Governess* from its perch on the wall, I found *The Warnings of Experience* casually strapped to the back of the canvas. It was a worn, thin, insignificant book, the width of my thumb. It had been here all along. And there, between the last page and the back cover, was Emily Dickinson. My father's bookmark. I had held the book in my hands for several moments, feeling the soft old leather and the flimsy, battered pages. I opened it up to find faded black ink sinking into every page in small, slanted, intimate hand-writing. Here, in the palm of my hand, was Anne Brontë. The real Anne Brontë.

Something else slipped out of the book, as well—a ripped scrap of printer paper, where my father had scrawled his own note in bright red ink.

> Men have called me mad, but the question is not yet settled, whether madness is or is not the loftiest intelligence—whether much that is glorious—whether all that is profound—does not spring from disease of thought—from moods of mind exalted at the expense of the general intellect.
>
> All my love, Dad

It was Edgar Allan Poe. One of Dad's favorites. I was overcome by an incurable sadness. Dad used to tell me that the journey was the important part of anything. He also knew that you only realized you'd had one when it was over. I had called my mother right away, for no reason except that I was crying and I never cried. I didn't explain what had happened. It didn't matter. She sounded as though I had just given her the greatest gift in the world. She boarded the train a day later, and now here she was, sitting on my bed and patting my scraped foot among the mess of newspapers.

I scanned the fragment of the article on my stomach. *Did Tristan Whipple Secretly Attend Oxford?* I pushed that one aside and reached for another that I had already read once, twice, three times.

> *. . . It is not the first time that he has faced questioning of this sort; Dr. Orville drew sharp criticism from the Old College staff several years ago after a close relationship with student Abigail Baasch. Both were cleared of charges on the grounds that no one could prove Baasch was a student during any of the assignations. Others, however, still contest that the affair remains a violation of Oxford's very foundation: the sanctity of the relationship between the educator and the educated.*
>
> *"Dr. Orville has brought this upon himself," Dr. Ellery Flannery told the* Hornbeam *on Sunday evening. "I will always maintain that an education is useless if corrupted of its objectivity."*
>
> *Others, however, insist that the fault lies not with Dr. Orville, but with*

"immature and reckless" undergraduates, and that the ability to induce infatuation in a young student is not an intrinsic flaw, but rather, as one anonymous academic commented, "a regrettable occupational hazard."

In response to recent developments, Dr. Orville has taken an indefinite leave of absence. Neither Abigail Baasch nor Samantha Whipple could be reached for comment.

Carefully, I folded the sheet of newspaper into an airplane and tossed it into the corner of the room, where *The Warnings of Experience* was now resting, serving a lengthy time-out. I hadn't touched it since I had discovered it. Yes, I had found my inheritance, and yes, the thought was somewhat satisfying, but everything was tainted now. What did it matter if I had the book, when Orville was lost to me? Who would I show it to now? I wasn't sure what a "leave of absence" meant, exactly, and if that weren't just another phrase for "solitary confinement." Oxford was Orville's life, and I had destroyed it. In the process, I had also truncated the best education I had ever received.

Mom, to my left, cleared her throat.

"I didn't realize that Halford's Well was also the scene of a similar assignation twenty-five years ago," she said. She had moved away from the *Hornbeam* in favor of the *New York Post*, which she had brought with her as a present for me. I had made page six. *Jane Eyre Rises from the Grave.* I refused to look.

I said, "Yes, it was."

"How strange." She made a face. "I mean, what kind of person fornicates in public?"

A small silence. I didn't answer because I didn't want to say *Your ex-husband,* and she didn't continue because I think she was afraid I would say *Me.* I sneezed violently, and the conversation ended.

Mom took off her glasses. "Well, are you ever going to tell me the truth? Why were you at that well?"

I blinked. "To commune."

"With?"

"Dad."

Her expression fell. She looked disappointed, then angry. "Don't tell me he was the one who put you up to this."

I pointed at *The Warnings of Experience* at the other end of the room. "That's my inheritance."

Mom looked over. "I see an old book."

"Correct."

She frowned and stood up so she could walk over and pick up the small, ragged volume. She brought it back to the bed. I couldn't look directly at it.

"This is what he left you?" Mom said. The book was dangling between her index finger and thumb as if she had encountered an unsavory piece of raw meat.

"It's a diary," I said.

The longer Mom stared at it, the more triumphantly sympathetic her expression became. If this was my inheritance, then she had won. This was nothing but an old, dirty, disgusting, rotten old wad of paper with some illegible print inside. As usual, Dad had screwed up. He had tried his best to do something epic, but he had failed.

Mom must have sensed my mood, because she checked her cheerfulness and gave me a "you're right, this isn't funny" frown.

She turned the book over in her hands, reading the cover. *"The Warnings of Experience."*

"Yes."

"What will you do with it?"

"I don't know."

"Have you read it?"

"Not yet."

Mom put down the book and cleared her throat. "I want you to come live in Paris with me," she said. The way she said "Paris," it sounded like "mental hospital."

"I'm happy here."

"You are miserable here."

"I'd still like to stay."

"I can see no reason for that."

"I'm learning."

"About?"

"Myself?"

"Don't bullshit me."

"Don't swear. It's very American."

We fell into silence. Absently, I took the *Hornbeam* in my lap and looked at the photograph. Orville's fingers were clutching my waist as if in a death grip. Had I enjoyed it, being so close to him? I had forgotten to appreciate the moment. The two people in that grainy black-and-white photo were wrapped around each other like they were in love. The image sent an ache through me, in a way I hadn't experienced during the moment itself. The girl in the newspaper was just another woman I envied. Orville—the real-life Orville—had not responded to my e-mails or messages.

I took Mom's hand in mine. "Thanks for coming."

She seemed momentarily taken aback. "Well, of course I came. I can't have my girl sick and alone, can I?"

I let out a gulp.

"What is it?" Mom said. "Have I upset you?"

"Can I tell you what bothers me the most about all of this?"

"Sweetheart. Tell me."

"He's gone."

"He's always been gone."

"No—but now he's really gone," I said. "I found what he wanted me to find."

"That's a good thing."

"No," I said. "Now he and I have nothing left to talk about."

I looked down and away. I was crying openly—again. It was very embarrassing, and I had a terrible feeling that at any minute Hans would enter with his camera.

Mom's voice softened. "Samantha, the man left you a diary before he died. You say he also left you a painting. God knows how many other things are out there, waiting for you to pretend they're important."

I didn't respond, and wiped my nose on my sleeve. Mom paused, as if uncertain of whether or not she should express her next thought out loud. Finally, she took a breath and said: "It doesn't sound like you're ending a conversation with him. It sounds like you're just beginning one."

I looked up. Her chest rose and fell. I reached for her warm, compact hand and held it very close.

⸙

My last tutorial took place on a Thursday afternoon.

We had reached the final week of Hilary term. In two days, faculty and students would enter a four-week holiday before Trinity term. To celebrate, small white flowers recklessly crept out of the ground; leaves blushed with faint color. The sun ended its retirement, and so did a population of pale students, who emerged from their dormitories like wide-eyed shock victims. All around was a delicate beauty that you couldn't help but resent for having been gone for so long.

In anticipation of this meeting, my professor—ex-professor, I suppose—had his office door open and his curtains pulled back. The room looked like an opera house during the daytime—tranquil, somewhat nostalgic. The windows were open and a light, apologetic breeze came inside, perhaps repenting for an entire season of bad behavior.

I had not seen Orville since Halford's Well, and our only communication had been to set a time for this meeting. Today, he was clad in jeans and an Oxford sweatshirt, with a red rag draped across his shoulder. He was pulling out books from his shelves and stacking them around the room in teetering, uneven cliffs. I noticed empty boxes and packing tape. On my way inside, I passed over several piles of Molière, Twain, and Dumas, which were bathing in columns of daylight on the floor. There was little organization, and I doubted he knew what he was doing.

He must have heard me walk in. He said, "Hello, Samantha."

I blurted: "Are you really moving to Ireland?"

"Who told you?"

"About fourteen people, all separately."

The wind ruffled the curtains. Orville and I didn't say anything else for several minutes. We seemed to be approaching the strange and inevitable end to our contractual relationship. I would leave this room and his life would go on. The memory of me would be wiped clean; the entire last two terms would simply vanish. I would become nothing but another data point in his growing list of would-be lawsuits. I would graduate, grow old, and die, and James Orville III would politely disappear from my life, as swiftly as a boat drifting out of a harbor.

"Well," he said at last, from across the room. His voice was low, and it seemed to echo among the empty shelves. "You found it?"

"Hmm?"

I realized that he was motioning toward the book in my hands. I had almost forgotten that I had brought *The Warnings of Experience* with me. I was holding it to my chest the way some people clutch their cats. Compared to the beautifully bound, engraved editions all around us, my book looked like a discarded human organ.

"Yes, I found it," I said, taking a seat on the couch. On the way there, I bumped into a pile of Hemingways, which toppled over like vaudeville props.

"Where was it?" he asked.

"Behind the painting, *The Governess*, in my room. It was tucked in the back."

"In the back."

"Of the frame."

"This whole time?"

"This whole time."

He opened his mouth as if to ask a question, or offer congratulations, but the thought must have only lasted a moment, because he turned back to the shelf. We lingered in silence. I couldn't look directly at him, not when he was stuffing his boxes with such indignity. I was sweating profusely.

Finally, when I couldn't take it any longer, I let out one, perfect sob. "God, I've ruined your life, haven't I?"

"Please," he said. "Have a seat."

I was sitting already. I put the book on the table.

"Are you furious with me?" I said. "Let me fix this for you. I will do anything to get you your job back. Please. *Please*."

He looked back at me, surprised. "I am not at all angry," he said. "Why would you say that?"

"You're quitting the career you've spent your entire life building. Let me come out to the press and show them this book. I'll explain what I was really doing there, and you'll be off the hook."

"I'm afraid that will be seen as an even more outlandish and desperate excuse. And can you imagine the hysteria that will ensue if you reveal this book? I'm trying to protect you."

I leaned back in my seat, hands to my head, wanting to writhe, or bellow, or implode—anything but watch Orville pack his books. I moved my hands so they covered my ears, in the style of *The Scream*.

I said, "What did your father say about the newspapers?"

"Don't worry about him," Orville said.

"Then I suppose it was awful. I don't even have the vocabulary to express how sorry I am. I wish I could jump into a hole."

Something must have struck him as funny because when I removed my hands from my head and looked over at him, his lips had curved into a half smile.

"I'm proud of you," he said.

"Don't make me feel worse."

"You dreamt all of this up, and now that book is in front of you. How does that feel?"

I looked at *The Warnings of Experience*. "It feels okay."

"Just okay?"

I turned the book over in my hands, then back again. "I never realized how much effort my dad went through to make sure I'd read *The Tenant of Wildfell Hall* before finding this diary."

"What do you mean?"

I glanced up at him. "What if I'd mistakenly found the diary first, and didn't think anything of it? Or, worse, what if I thought the diary was just a tool to understand the novel, when really it was the other way around? He was trying to teach me the right way to read."

Orville didn't seem to be listening. He was very intent on unloading all his copies of *The Epic of Gilgamesh* from his shelf.

I held up *The Warnings of Experience*. "Here," I said.

He turned back around. "Pardon?"

"This is for you. A gift."

Orville just smiled and returned to his work.

I said, "Don't you want to read it?"

He took the red rag from his shoulder and began wiping down the now-empty shelf in front of him. I didn't understand his disinterest. This was a literary treasure.

I pressed, "I brought this for *you*. As a present? I thought you'd want to see it. Is this the diary of Anne Brontë or Bertha Mason? Or Helen Graham? I promise you that this diary will change the entire meaning of Anne Brontë's novels."

Silence. Orville had the otherworldly look of someone who was contemplating his next meal.

I breathed out once, sharp. "Forgive me, sir, but *don't you care*?"

When he looked back at me, there was a serene smile on his face. He said, "No. I appreciate that there is a physical book in your hands, and that perhaps it once belonged to someone famous. But this makes no difference to me. I will continue to honor Anne Brontë's novels as they are, not as she might have intended them to be. Tampering with a finished novel now will only lead to the inevitable destruction of what you seek to protect."

"Are you telling me that you are not even slightly curious?" I asked, waving the book at him like I might a long salami sandwich.

"A diary is worthless on its own," he said. "It's like that painting of yours. It is meaningless, is it not, without the story behind it? *Jane Eyre* can survive without the painting in your room, and yet the painting is nothing without *Jane Eyre*. You know which one I would prefer."

He must have sensed the epic frown growing on my face, because he added: "I am impressed—truly—that you found this. But people write diaries and unpublished novels all the time. I myself have written a few."

"But this is a *historical artifact*."

He gave a sad smile. "No, this is a family heirloom. Think of how many fathers and grandfathers that book went through to get into your hands. This is—shall we say—a personal matter? If your father thought Anne Brontë wanted her confessions released to the world, I doubt he would have kept this to himself."

At that, I leaned back in my seat, deflated. It was not the response I'd been expecting, nor was it the answer I wanted to hear. I was hoping he might kindly explain the diary's significance to me, in clear and irrefutable terms. I put the book back on the table. To be perfectly honest, I didn't want to read it, either. Several nights ago, I'd read a few passages, but quickly grew so upset that I had to put the whole thing down. The diary wasn't exactly dull, but it also wasn't what I'd call exciting. It wasn't really anything at all. The author was not an Anne Brontë I recognized; she was just another person who decided to chronicle all the things she had done during the day. It was difficult to decide whether she was happy, or bored, or livid. The answer would have been obvious, I'm sure, to someone who knew her well. What I *did* discover was that a large number of pages had been entirely ripped out. By whom, I suppose I would never know. What I had in my possession was the skeleton of something that may have once been great.

I hadn't opened the book since, and my vexation had only worsened. *The Warnings of Experience,* I realized, had the power to disrupt all the careful, meticulous little worlds I had built for myself, and for the Brontës. Here, in my hands, could be the spoiler for every story I had ever invented; it was the movie that made you forever un-see the book. If I read Anne Brontë's diary, then I ran the risk losing an old friend who I was only just beginning to regain. The Brontë sisters *I* knew would disappear in a poof, and then where would I be?

I let out a huff of air. "I didn't read it."

"I figured that might be the case."

"Oh?"

"Your father's purpose may not have been to leave you an outrageous diary, but to show you that an outrageous diary could exist— and out of fiction," he said. "What did you call it before? Literal truth."

I shook my head. "No. No. That's what I thought earlier too. But then I realized that Dad must have had this diary his entire life. And what did he do with it? He just sat in his study, reading and rereading the novels. If he were concerned with discovering 'literal' truth, shouldn't the novels be useless once he had the diary? The diary is like reading a map with no legend."

"Yes? What are you saying?" Orville asked.

I slunk into my seat. "I think I've been focused on the wrong thing this entire time. This diary is not terribly valuable unless we understand Helen Graham, and the reason she wrote the diary in the first place. Nor is the diary terribly interesting unless we understand

Bertha Mason, and all the potential inside a repressed female brain. Anne Brontë's life doesn't give meaning to this diary; the Brontë novels give meaning to this diary. The fiction is more real than the reality."

For the first time since I knew him, Orville beamed. He positively beamed. He put down his books and stood up straight.

"Very good, Samantha," he said. "That was very good."

I looked up. "You're not going to argue with me?"

"No. I quite like that theory."

I blinked. "So this is V-E day?"

"Pardon?"

"Victory in Europe."

"I'm aware of the term."

"That's what my dad called it whenever he won arguments over-seas."

"Ah," said Orville, with a nod and the ghost of a smile. He added, "Ergo."

And with that, he turned his back toward me and returned to his shelves. I saw a fresh copy of *Pamela* drop into the box beneath him. He turned and began to unload the next shelf. Was that it? A fresh wave of sadness hit me. We would be departing soon—I to my tower, Orville to the leprechauns. I had never had to say goodbye forever to someone who was not dead.

"Tell me," he said over his shoulder, "do you know who your new tutor will be?" If I was not mistaken, a note of protectiveness had crept into his voice.

I said, "Not you."

"I am aware of that."

"I suppose I will now have to become an uneducated heathen."

"Don't be dramatic."

"My life is over."

I didn't mean to sound as apocalyptic as I did, but there it was. He was leaving the country—was I supposed to be happy? I had injected more of myself than I had ever intended into our nonexistent relationship. Now I would have to relocate the bits and pieces of myself that I had lost, and put myself back together, like a waterlogged puzzle whose pieces didn't quite fit anymore.

I kept my eyes down. "Ireland is a long way away, sir."

"Not really."

"It is a long way away from *you*."

"Pardon?"

I rested *The Warnings of Experience* on the table and stood up. I took a few steps toward him. When he sensed me coming, Orville put down his books. I looked him straight in the eye. The devastation on my face was entirely out of my control.

I said, "What would you like to do about us, sir?"

He said, "Us?"

"Brother Heathcliff and Sister Cathy."

There—right there. The Subtext collapsed like the backdrop of a busy theater, exposing all the intricate workings behind the set. Orville frowned. At last, he knew. He knew that I loved him. Perhaps he had always known, and the game that I'd thought I was playing so subtly was in fact anything but. He was looking me straight in the eye. He knew.

He didn't respond right away. It was a fragile moment. We seemed to be in Act V of a Shakespearean play that could end either in marriage or in premature death. I was breathing heavily.

"We've been good friends, have we not?" he said.

I felt robbed. "That's it? That's all you're going to say?"

"You must understand that anything between us is impossible."

"Does that mean you at least acknowledge that there is something between us?"

He paused. "I forget how young you are sometimes."

"That seems somewhat irrelevant."

"When you are older, you will realize that the things you feel to be true don't require verbal confirmation."

I let out a breath. "Fine. I'm still young. Give me verbal confirmation, please."

Orville looked toward the windows and began scratching the back of his neck. He opened his mouth, then closed it, then opened it again.

"I care for you a great deal," he said.

"Fantastic," I said. "What happens now?"

"We say goodbye."

"You are rejecting me?"

"It is not rejection when nothing has been offered."

"I offer you my heart, my hand, and everything I have."

He looked back at me. "Then yes, I reject you. Please don't take it the wrong way."

I swallowed. Somewhere inside, I began screaming, quietly at first, and then louder and louder, like a kettle reaching the height of its temper. I tried to read Orville's impassive face, but he looked like a mannequin.

"I don't understand why this is a problem," I said.

"I have an uncomplicated loyalty to duty."

"But you're no longer my professor."

"What difference does that make?"

"You have no more duties anymore. You can go back to being a libertine."

He sounded strained, like he was giving birth. "I will be someone *else's* tutor, and someone else's tutor after that. Do you not see the problem? I am an *educator*. Propriety mandates that you and I will stay friends, Miss Whipple—if that."

"'Miss Whipple'? Let's not get carried away."

"I cannot continue this conversation."

"You're just afraid."

I was speaking with more confidence than I felt, only because inside, I was dying, and very slowly. I could feel emptiness widening like a balloon inside my torso, replacing what had once been Orville with more and more empty space. Years from now, maybe the balloon would shrink, but it would never disappear. It would just become a small satellite, orbiting my heart.

Orville took a step closer and we stood face-to-face.

"Think of it," he said slowly, in a way that suggested he had already thought about it several times. "Think of what you are asking me to do. Teaching, academia—it is my life. It is not a hobby, nor is it a game. I *cannot* be with you, Samantha. You believe that our stations have changed. They have not changed. As long as you are a student, we will never be equals. I am in a position of authority. I will always be right, and you will always be less right. Is that what you want out of a relationship?"

"What I hear you saying is that you want to wait to be together until I am independently intelligent," I said. "But don't you think there's more to a relationship than just intellect? Aren't you being a little superficial?"

He looked irritated. "Do you think this is easy for me?" he said. "I am leaving for Ireland so I can *escape* you. Don't look at me like that—I'm sure you know it's true. I refuse to be tempted against my better judgment, and it is not right for you to believe that as a student you are a source of temptation. You are an exceptionally bright and rare creature and you deserve an education. This is my final word. You can argue, but I am too fond of you to have it any other way. Understood?"

I didn't say anything. Orville must have spent himself on his verdict because he wiped his forehead with the back of his hand and turned back to his packing. I stood silently as he presented me with the unyielding line of his back. We didn't say anything for several minutes. I had nothing to do but glance down at the great authors at my feet. Try as I might, I found that I could no longer hate them.

I felt at home, suddenly, standing among the Hemingways and the Nabokovs and the Tolstoys and the Porters. Here was a cushion of the world's most famous broken hearts, alcoholics, and lunatics. They were here, in this room, right now—I could almost feel them breathing on me, offering their support. Austen, Fitzgerald, Burney, Dostoyevsky. Out of all their collective misery came a tapestry of hope, one so real that it seemed almost fictional in its convenience.

I turned back to the sofa and reached for my coat, which I had left slung over the armrest. I picked up *The Warnings of Experience*. What a cruel, cruel trick that the book should exist, when the only fiction I had ever wanted to become real was James Orville III.

And yet . . . ? I turned around, heart slamming into my chest.

"I hope you know that you've left me no other choice but to become a writer," I said.

"I beg your pardon?"

"Me. Writer. I will have to invent an alternate ending to this. I see no other solution."

"Are you leaving already?"

"I'm leaving."

"You're crying."

"Am I?"

A strange thing happened just then. Orville looked at me with a pain so deep that for a moment, I wondered if I had conjured it on his face out of sheer will. He seemed different somehow, like a portrait I had painted that was now stepping out of the canvas to show me my work. I'd thought our conversation was over, but in the span of a few seconds, he had closed the distance between us and was kissing me—so forcefully, and with so much confused passion, that I don't remember much else, which meant that it was either a very good kiss or a very poor one. I assumed it must be the former, because I forgot myself entirely, lost in something more powerful than I had anticipated. As he tightened his arms around me, I felt bound to him by a strange, externally mandated and crushing inevitability. He broke away only to whisper something so soft and sweet that I thought perhaps I was narrating the scene myself.

Suddenly, it didn't seem as if we were leaving each other at all— no, quite the opposite. I recall a sense of belonging unlike anything I had ever experienced, and a feeling of freedom in which anything seemed possible. When we emerged on the other side of the room, his arms were wound so tightly around me that his hands were my hands, his chest was my chest. Then and only then did the two of us say goodbye. I walked past him and to the door.

When I turned around one last time, I saw that all the Wordsworth books behind us had spilled over the floor like confetti.

Reader, I married him.

Not that day, and not that year, and not even in five years. But we did marry and it was a beautiful, small wedding in the north of England. James Timothy Orville III proposed at Oscar Wilde's tomb, as he ought to have done. There were birds and dresses. I ended up writing two long-form memoirs, which Orville complained lacked style and artistry and any semblance of a realistic ending but whose numerous drafts he kept on his nightstand in small stacks and which he loyally read over and over, until they were eventually published. It was a life I could have created almost entirely out of thin air.

But on this point, I think I have said sufficient.

ACKNOWLEDGMENTS

First, to the magnificent Jennifer DuBois, one of the best writers and teachers I know, and to the inimitable Elizabeth Tallent, who made me want to be a writer in the first place. Thank you to Charles Baxter, one of the finest teachers I ever had, and to the entire faculty and staff of Stanford's English Department, especially Adam Johnson, Tobias Wolff, Tom Kealey, and Shimon Tanaka. None of this would have been possible without the guidance of Linda Paulson, whose seminar first inspired the novel, and the brilliant classes of Emma Plaskitt, one of the most engaging lecturers out there. Thank you to some very special mentors and teachers—Phil Gutierrez, Jeff Symonds, and Carrie Waldron-Brown—whose insights and advice have stayed with me for over a decade.

This book would have been impossible without the endless enthusiasm of my dear friend Kate O'Connor and her homemade Heathcliff-inspired Brooding Hunk manual. An enormous hug goes to Michelle Gumport for her unconditional support and to the lovely Patrick Hanlon for his hours of proofreading. A big thank-you goes to my wonderful agent, Chelsea Lindman, to my sage editor, Sally Kim, and to the entire team at Touchstone for their great energy and ideas.

Mostly, thank you to my patient parents for kindly reading the few hundred first drafts, and to my lovely big sister, one of the best people I know.

ABOUT THE AUTHOR

Catherine Lowell received her BA in Creative Writing from Stanford University, where she was awarded the Mary Steinbeck Dekker Award for Fiction. She currently lives in New York City. *The Madwoman Upstairs* is her first novel.

THE MADWOMAN UPSTAIRS

CATHERINE LOWELL

FOR DISCUSSION

1. "He was great in the way that only dead fathers could be great." Describe Samantha's relationship with her father, both in life and in death. In what ways does Samantha idealize her father? How does her perception of him change as she learns more and more about his life and his past through the course of the novel? How does Samantha's unresolved grief impact her relationships and actions during her time at Oxford?

2. How do Samantha's memories of her father differ from her mother's and Rebecca's recollections of his life and character? Which woman's depiction do you think is closest to reality, and why?

3. "Questioning the reliability of the narrator was an attempt to prove that every novel written—every verb, every comma—existed solely for the sake of subversion." Although Samantha hates the question of whether or not a narrator is unreliable, when we read fiction, it is a question that often deepens our understanding as readers and forces us to ask critical questions about memory and truth in the narrative. In your reading of the novel, did you find Samantha to be a reliable narrator? Discuss key moments when you trusted her account, and key moments when you suspected that the real story diverged from her telling.

4. "My lack of literary talent was more a tragedy than a disappointment. The real problem was: my father was in the grave, and I could do nothing to write him out of it." How does Samantha's failure as a writer impact her feelings toward women writers, particularly the Brontës? Do you think that Samantha would have gone to Oxford and felt the drive to search for her inheritance in her father's posthumous scavenger hunt if she had been able to reach a sense of closure about him through her writing?

5. How does Samantha's father leave clues for her about his true identity and her inheritance even while he is alive? Why is it so important for Samantha's father to reveal his inheritance to her in the cryptic way that he does?

6. Samantha and Orville differ in their fundamental approach to interpreting fiction. Orville believes that the text represents an emotional truth—that the inspiration for events depicted in a novel come from the author's imagination and feelings—while Samantha believes that the text represents a literal truth—that the inspiration for events depicted in a novel come from the author's actual experiences. Whose perspective do you agree with, and why?

7. Speaking about the character of Bertha in Charlotte Bronte's novel *Jane Eyre*, Orville tells Samantha, "You view 'madness' as wild and violent; I view it as the logical reaction to wild and violent conditions." Based on this conversation and your interpretation, what does "madness" mean in the purview of the novel? Do you believe that the so-called "madwoman" in *Jane Eyre* is truly insane when she sets fire to the curtains, or do you believe that, as Samantha and her father's bookmarks read, in the words of Emily Dickinson, "much madness is divinest sense"?

8. How does her time at Oxford change Samantha? Do you think that Samantha becomes "the madwoman upstairs" of the book's title?

9. Sir John Booker bases his writings and career around the idea that by examining the objects of the Brontës' everyday life and creations in other media, the reader can "find a true portrait of three of our most enigmatic authors, one that helps unlock the riches inside their most cryptic novels." What value do you see in this argument? Have you ever tried to analyze the work of an author, musician, or filmmaker in this way? Do you think we should judge a piece of writing by an author's life or motives, or do you think that a novel should be a self-contained piece of art that gets diminished when considering too many extraneous facts and biographical information?

10. How and why do Samantha's feelings toward the Brontës shift throughout the course of the novel? ("I looked at those books and finally understood what it must feel like to be part of a loving, dysfunctional family, the kind everyone else seemed to have," she says.) How much of this change is due to Samantha's relationship with Orville? Why isn't Samantha able to have this sort of relationship with the Brontës while her father is still alive?

11. Were you surprised when the true nature of Samantha's inheritance revealed itself? How does the search for her inheritance change Samantha?

12. By the end of the novel, do you think Samantha has reached a sense of peace about her father's death?

A CONVERSATION
WITH CATHERINE LOWELL

Where did you come up with the idea to write a contemporary novel based on the mystery of the rumored Brontë estate?

There's a great quote by Ralph Waldo Emerson that I really love—he said, "There is creative reading as well as creative writing." The possibilities of creative reading have always intrigued me, particularly when it comes to old, famous, and heavily analyzed texts. I was especially curious to see what new discoveries could emerge from an unorthodox reading of the Brontë novels. Where is the line between reading creatively and just being ridiculous? Or is there still a grain of truth even in the most ridiculous ideas? I became very interested in the idea of a lost Brontë estate—did the Brontës just leave us with their novels, or is there something else hidden within those books that is only available to an experimental reader?

Which Brontë novel is your favorite? Which novel influenced this book the most?

The Tenant of Wildfell Hall, though not my favorite, was a big influence on the book. The narration is confusing (the entire book, for one thing, is a letter), to the point where it's unclear whether Helen's voice is actually Helen's—Gilbert is the one who transcribes her diary and tells her story. In that sense, Helen reminded me of Anne Brontë, another woman whose voice we rarely hear directly. This book, more than any other, made me wonder what Anne Brontë was really like—and what was really going on behind the scenes at the Parsonage!

How did your time at Oxford influence the writing of this novel? Does a tower like the one Samantha lives in actually exist (and if so, did you ever live there)?

My time at Oxford did influence the novel—but not for the obvious reasons! I was having an awful bout of insomnia at the time, and the initial jet lag upon arriving in England didn't help. I remember one freezing evening, I had been awake for nearly forty-six hours. I still couldn't fall asleep, so I figured I might as well just get up and write something.

At the beginning of the novel, Samantha states that she despises women writers—do you feel the same way? If not, which female writers do you most admire and why?

I love early women writers! They were incredibly brave. Since many of them saw enormous success in their lifetimes, it's easy to forget that women like Charlotte Brontë, George Eliot, Frances Burney, and George Sand made huge sacrifices to practice their craft. Remaining true to yourself despite enormous pressure is a skill that will never go out of style, regardless of when you live.

That said, it was much more interesting to explore the psyche of someone who resents her ancestry rather than someone who adores it. What sort of duty do we owe to the people who gave us independence? Is Samantha wasting the freedom her ancestors fought for? Like many forms of hatred, Samantha's resentment stems from her own insecurity.

As far as my favorite woman writer goes—I would really love to grab a beer with Aphra Behn.

Do you have a favorite Brontë sibling? Do you hope that your book will bring some new attention to Anne and her work?

I love Emily. She seemed so delightfully odd. If we put her in one of those standardized test questions—"which one of these is not like the others?"—I think she'd win each time, regardless of the topic. What I admire most about her is that despite having very limited worldly experiences, her one novel showed the depth and breadth of someone who has seen everything. It's encouraging to think that you that you don't necessarily need wildly exciting life experiences to arrive at some universal truth—the greatest insights can often come from carefully observing mundane things.

I really do hope people start paying more attention to Anne! Her two novels are so different—in *Agnes Grey,* you get the sense that Anne is deliberately holding herself back, perhaps out of concern over her novel's reception. But in *The Tenant of Wildfell Hall,* she's somehow developed into a fiery activist. You can really get a sense of her development between those two books. It's easy to think of the Brontë sisters as indomitable pillars of strength, and forget that they were also human beings, fraught with the same insecurities that everyone has felt at some point. Anne is the sister who always made me remember that the Brontës were relatable people—sometimes underdogs, sometimes heroes.

Where do you stand on the argument between Samantha and Orville over how a text should be interpreted?

Regarding the debate between "literal truth" and "emotional truth," I think the most interesting part of the relationship is the uncanny way in which the latter can lead to the former. The empathy we feel for make-believe characters feels real in our bodies, as if those characters were in fact long-lost friends. Fiction remains one of the only ways we can viscerally experience things that never happened to us.

If I were to weigh in on the debate over authorial intent, I'd have to give the somewhat dissatisfying "find a happy middle ground!" answer. Too much concern with external information runs the risk of limiting a book's scope, but books are so inextricably linked to history that to disregard the context in which they were written is often to waste an opportunity to better understand both the text and the era. *The Odyssey* is a great book regardless of any outside knowledge of Ancient Greece—but to understand its impact on Greece is to also understand how one story helped shape an entire civilization.

What about the Brontës do you think has helped their work to stand the test of time?

Most of the Brontë protagonists aged extremely well. They are still the kind of people we all want to be: confident, whip-smart, self-reliant, and able to be happy despite all the odds. The plots themselves have taken a page from Cinderella—almost all of them tell the story of underdogs, and everyone loves an underdog. Then, of course, there's the picturesque drama of the Brontë's lives, and the courage with which they lived—both of which still inspire readers today.

What are you working on next? Do you think you'll ever return to Oxford as a setting, or the Brontës as a topic?

The next book tackles one of my other favorite subjects, World War II. Stay tuned!

ENHANCE YOUR READING GROUP

1. Read another Brontë novel of your book club's choice—select from *Jane Eyre*, *Wuthering Heights*, or *The Tenant of Wildfell Hall*. What similarities and differences do you find between the novel and *The Madwoman Upstairs*? If you decide to read *Jane Eyre*, discuss Samantha's theory that Charlotte essentially stole Anne's experiences and turned them into her most famous work.

2. Watch a *Jane Eyre* movie adaptation of your book club's choice. See if you agree with Samantha's negative assessment of Hollywood reenactments of Bronte novels: "An unknown actress would play Jane, and she was usually prettier than she should have been. A very handsome, very brooding, very 'ooh-la-la' man would play Mr. Rochester, and Judi Dench would play everyone else."